HIS CONVENIENT NEW YORK BRIDE

ANDREA BOLTER

COOKING UP ROMANCE

LYNNE MARSHALL

This book is produced from independently certified FSC™
paper to ensure responsible forest management.

For more information visit: www.harpercollins.co.uk/green

Printed and bound in Spain
by CPI Antony Rowe

MILLS & BOON

First Published in Great Britain 2020
by Mills & Boon, an imprint of HarperCollinsPublishers,
1 London Bridge Street, London, SE1 9GF

His Convenient New York Bride © 2019 Andrea Bolter
Cooking Up Romance © 2019 Janet Maarschalk

ISBN: 978-0-263-27865-1

0120

HIS CONVENIENT
NEW YORK BRIDE

ANDREA BOLTER

For Marci

CHAPTER ONE 張

"WOULD YOU HAVE expected any less from a bully like him?" Jin asked as he stirred milk into the mug of coffee in front of him. "I could have guessed he'd find a way to try to hurt my mom and I from his grave."

"Tell me again what the will stipulates," his friend Aaron asked, following suit by splashing milk into his own cup before the two friends left the kitchen to sit down on the sofa in the living room. As they had a thousand times before, they both put their long legs up on the coffee table and crossed them at the ankle. The only real difference was that their seventeen-year-old selves would have held game consoles instead of java.

"Wei Zhang bequeaths to his only child, Jin Zhang, full ownership of the LilyZ fashion corporation and all of its interests with the following condition," Jin said, quoting the document his father's attorney had read to him an hour earlier. He had a printed copy in his briefcase and one on his phone but this section was already committed to memory. "Jin Zhang must be entered into a legal and lawful marriage before ownership is transferred."

Jin tried to mentally control the irritating vein that was throbbing at his temple. Death hadn't stopped his father from continuing to create chaos.

"That's just bizarre. Did your father really care if you remarried or not?"

"Oh, he cares...cared, plenty. After I left Helene, he knew I would never marry again, no matter what."

"Understandable after what she did to you."

"That's why he had the stipulation written into his will. Because he knew it was something I would never do."

"What happens if you don't follow the condition?"

"The business gets dissolved."

"You either get married or lose the fashion label? Who does something like that to his son?" Aaron shook his head in disgust.

"Wei, of course." Jin's temple continued to pulse as he tried to process the information he'd learned that afternoon. "Destroying the company was what he wanted to do. He mismanaged just about everything he could while he was alive. And then thought of a way to ensure LilyZ's demise even after his death."

After Jin had met with Wei's attorney he'd come straight over to his best friend Aaron Stewart's apartment, as he'd been doing for years. Not far from the Chinatown building that housed LilyZ's studio and Jin's living quarters, Aaron's place was a sanctuary for him.

The two men sipped their coffee in silence, their brains turning over the information as dusk became night.

"Your father was so vindictive he wanted to take

down the business his own father worked so hard to build into a respected name in fashion?"

"He hated me. And my mother."

To Aaron, and to Aaron's younger sister Mimi, Jin could say anything. The three had been hanging out together for more than thirteen years, had seen each other through a lot of life changes already. Aaron and Mimi's mother dying. Their father dying a year later. Jin's parents' divorce. Jin's divorce from Helene. Now his father, Wei, dying with this, his last act.

"Maybe you never saw it," Jin continued.

"I don't think I ever really knew him," Aaron said. "I do remember the way his nose would wrinkle in a grimace though whenever your mother was mentioned after they split up."

"Because she dared divorce an alcoholic, cheating, mean-spirited spouse."

"He never wanted the business in the first place, did he?"

"No. He resented inheriting LilyZ from my grandfather Shun from the beginning. My grandfather worked eighteen hours a day for decades to create and sustain a legacy brand that would continue past his death but my father felt it interfered with his drinking and womanizing."

"Then he should have been happy to leave it to you. You've been mostly running things, anyway."

"I'm telling you, he despised me and wished for me to fail because of my relationship with my grandfather. Shun and I were the same. We loved LilyZ and took pride in it. My father was always the odd man out, because he never cared about anything but himself."

"And it was clear you took your mother's side in the divorce."

"So for his final act, he did what he could to leave us penniless and humiliated."

Jin could hardly compute all of this. For the past few years, he had taken unofficial control of LilyZ, their high-end, ready-to-wear fashion label. He'd had to. Wei hadn't even shown up to the studio every day. And when he did stumble through, he was often rude to the staff or disruptive of operations. His only son had been forced to take charge.

In addition to the will, the attorney had also shown Jin his father's many financial misrepresentations.

"On top of it, I've only just found out that our books are in shambles. My father withheld information and made one bad decision after the next. If the company were to be broken up, at this point every penny would go to creditors."

"The will says you have to get married." Aaron pondered the situation. "Are there any other specifications?"

Jin exhaled with a whoosh of exasperation. "I don't take possession or have any power over the financials until I prove that I'm legally married. I must remain married for a one-year probationary period during which I'm officially CEO but not yet the company's owner."

"Wait, that means that you only have to be married for one year?"

"Theoretically. But he knew I would never get married again so he did this to set me up to fail."

"What are our options?" Aaron wondered aloud.

Jin's best friend was always thoughtful and contemplative. With his deep-set eyes and curly hair, Aaron looked like a philosopher whose likeness might be rendered in marble outside of a great library.

Aaron and Jin always worked through things together, considering each other's problems their own. Even though two heads were better than one, Jin had his doubts that they were going to be able to solve the problem this time. Because not only was Jin never going to marry again, he wasn't even going to enter into a serious relationship. Never ever. Not after what he had gotten in return for his devotion to Helene. Jin had been married to her for three years, and she had cheated on him the entire time. A selfish liar, she was. Just like his father. It was he and his mother who were left to pick up the pieces after their spouses took a wrecking ball to everything they'd held true.

Jin flexed his hands. After six months, those hands finally looked normal to him without the wedding band that had once sat on his finger. The ring that had symbolized fidelity and partnership and loyalty. What a joke that was.

The dead bolt turned on the front door with a clack and Jin's eyes shot to it. With a crank on the handle, Aaron's sister Mimi walked in. She dropped her bag on the side table, not noticing Jin and Aaron were there at first. Suited up for the late winter cold, Mimi removed her beanie hat, her auburn hair cascading past her shoulders in loose waves. Having been friends for so long Jin knew that Mimi's radiant hair color didn't come naturally, but that her curls were her own.

Yanking off one glove then the other, Mimi tossed them next to her bag. Her pale hands set free, she next unwound the gray scarf that was wrapped twice around her throat and had played nicely against the navy color of her coat. A small, and wholly inappropriate, twitch surprised Jin's shoulder blades when the last of the scarf revealed some more of that creamy skin, this time her neck.

Buttons undone, she removed her coat and hung it on the stand by the door. She wore a terrific pink dress, with a belt of the same fabric that hugged her lavish curves. Mimi was the best dresser he knew and, being in the fashion business, that was saying something.

"Aaron?" she called out before turning around to find her brother and Jin sitting on the couch in the very same room. "Oh. Hey, bro."

"Sis."

"Hey, Jin, I didn't know you were here. Have you guys eaten? I'm starved."

"How did the interview go?" Aaron asked her.

"Lousy. Just like yesterday's."

Mimi was a junior fashion designer. Jin had always felt a little bit of personal pride that she had gone into the business herself, having spent many teenage years around LilyZ and learning about the industry. Aaron had chosen the world of stocks and bonds but with Mimi's innate fashion sense, it was meant to be.

It irked Jin that she was having employment problems after she'd quit her job because working with her ex-boyfriend was unbearable. All she kept hearing was *no*, and she'd been forced to move in with her brother to cut expenses.

Aaron was stable but Jin and Mimi were both going through an awful time, made worse by the fact that Jin had recently found out that the last affair Helene had had while they were married had been with LilyZ's lead designer. Who he'd promptly fired.

It was piled up.

Mimi needed a job.

He had to find a new designer for LilyZ. And now, apparently, a wife.

The events for New York Fashion Week Spring were starting up and LilyZ was not presenting anything because, before he'd died, Wei had blocked Jin from finishing the collection on time. Jin would now need to soothe the ruffled feathers of retailers who counted on his inventory. He had to make excuses. Pretend like everything was under control.

Jin's headache tightened. What an inconceivable mess!

"Order some food in," Aaron told his sister when she reemerged from his bedroom. Having taken off the pink dress she'd designed and sewn herself, Mimi had slipped on comfy black leggings, thick white socks and a red pullover.

"That could be considered sexist, you know," Mimi teased him, "making the woman take care of the meal."

"When said woman is living in her brother's apartment for free it could be called singing for your supper."

"All right, you've got me there."

She glanced over to Jin on the couch, who had changed positions while she was in the bedroom. No longer with his feet up on the coffee table, he sat in his black slacks with one long leg crossed ankle to knee in a posture Mimi found so decidedly masculine it gave her a flutter.

What was more, it occurred to her that Jin was sitting where she slept, as Aaron's sofa opened to become the convertible bed she'd been unfolding every night. Jin had been over and sat on the sofa before, but for some reason the thought that it was her bed hadn't dawned on her. She took a mental snapshot and filed it away in her brain. And then moved on, or tried to, from that picture.

"Jin, are you staying for dinner?"

"I want ramen. I need a huge steaming bowl of noodles."

"Sounds good to me," Aaron voted in. "From that place."

"Yeah," Jin agreed, "get the kind we liked that one time."

"Okay." Mimi knew exactly what they meant and placed the order online.

Afterward, Jin explained to her about the stipulation in his father's will.

"Does your mom know?" Mimi asked. "I talked to her on the phone yesterday and she didn't say anything." The Zhangs and the Stewarts had a long history together and she knew Jin loved it that Mimi was close to his mom.

"No," Jin stated firmly. "As his ex-wife she wasn't

included in the meeting with the attorney. I don't want her to ever find out about it."

"What is it that happens if you don't get married? Do either of you want more coffee?"

Aaron shook his head no but Jin thrust out his large, square hand and Mimi moved toward him to grab the mug he held. While doing so, her fingertips brushed against his and she registered the signature heat that always emanated from his hands.

It was as if fiery little sparks that only she could see ignited every time his hands made contact with her skin. Which, during exchanges like this, or during a hug goodbye, or a hand up an unsteady surface, had happened about a million times in the thirteen years she'd known Jin.

Jin's sparks were Mimi's deepest secret.

As she went about making more coffee, Jin explained about the will.

Mimi looked from the coffeepot to the blank wall above it.

"It's so unjust that your father is still in control," Aaron piped in. "Even though you've been effectively helming the business for years."

Mimi kept her eyes focused on the wall. Aaron was right. Jin had completely taken over everything regarding the clothing label as Wei's drinking and carousing got worse. It infuriated Mimi to hear that Wei had invented this disruptive will instead of simply bequeathing the company to Jin as was his due.

And Jin marrying again? The mere thought of that was upsetting.

"You didn't know anything about the finances?" Aaron asked.

"I didn't have the information on how bad it was. We all know the last two collections didn't fly. My father wasn't on top of trends or fabrics or colors or much of anything, and still wouldn't relinquish any final decisions to me. Even when he was only attending meetings via telecom he'd always shoot down my ideas."

"You were captaining a sinking ship," Mimi said.

"What did I go to business school for if he wouldn't let me implement changes?"

"You wanted to grow and modernize." Mimi acknowledged the thoughts he'd shared with her many times before. She knew he wanted to go from retailing in twenty stores worldwide up to fifty. "But you were too busy mopping up his messes."

"My grandfather would be ashamed."

Descended from a long line of clothing manufacturers, brave Shun Zhang had come to the United States from Hong Kong with little more than a dream to start a label here. With his own two hands, he'd built LilyZ into a multimillion-dollar company that had once had an impeccable reputation.

Jin's voice rose to a volume Mimi knew conveyed just how upset he was. "My father hid the debts. He withdrew funds to supposedly pay bills but instead spent the money on himself and his latest arm candy. And instructed his accountant to keep it confidential, even from me."

"So you were *blindly* captaining that ship," Mimi restated. She brought Jin his mug but this time set it down on the coffee table so as not to have physical contact with him again so soon. That was a little game she'd played with herself before. Unfortunately, the hitch of a smile he gave her in receipt of the coffee pinged right into her chest, defeating her strategy.

The upturn of his straight-set lips had the same effect on her as it had when she was fifteen and had first met Jin Zhang. Utter fascination. The same with the high cheekbones that defined the shape of his face. At seventeen, his cheeks were fuller than their sharp angles of adulthood now. The dense slashes of his eyebrows were the same. As were his luminous dark, dark brown eyes. They had held less stress in them then, although the toll of living with an alcoholic and unkind father had always been visible on him.

He regrouped in a more even-keeled voice. "I'm sure that I can turn the company around. I love LilyZ just as my grandfather did."

Mimi knew that before his grandfather died, Shun had told a teenaged Jin that he didn't trust his own son. That he'd known the responsibility for the label would rest on Jin's broad shoulders when he came of age.

Which Jin had regarded as an honor rather than a burden.

Because that's who he was.

Oh, Jin, with the one button undone on his crisp dress shirt—never more, just enough to call her attention to the length of his throat. Lean and six feet tall, he was effortlessly sophisticated in his tailored shirt and trousers. For a man in the fashion trade, his own look was always understated and polished.

Mimi was sorry for all his turmoil. He didn't deserve it.

"Plus," Jin continued, "I have to consider my mom."

"Does Mamabai know anything about the state of the company?" Aaron asked, using the nickname that he and Mimi used for Jin's mother, Bai, who had been like a surrogate mother to them both after their own mother had died. While Wei barely acknowledged their existence, Bai had always made sure they knew how much she cared about them.

Bai and their mother, Delia, had been close friends. Mimi couldn't confirm it, but she wouldn't have been surprised if on her mother's deathbed the two women had had conversations about Bai providing support after the inevitable.

"She doesn't know a thing," Jin said. "Since her divorce settlement ran out I've been giving her money out of my own pocket from what I draw as salary."

"If the label folds…" Mimi began.

"Not only will I have to worry about how to support her, it will be a public embarrassment to her on top of all the humiliation my father caused with his behavior."

Mimi hated to think of Mamabai enduring any more pain. Even after the divorce, Wei had been indiscriminate with his carousing. Showing up all over New York, and within the industry, with other women.

Bai had had to see her son's marriage fail as well, with Helene unfaithful just as Jin's father had been.

When the food arrived, Jin, Aaron and Mimi used chopsticks to dig into their piping hot containers of Japanese soup. As they slurped and chewed, the conversation turned to her interview.

"It seems as if Gunnar has informed the entire industry that I'm talentless and worthless."

"I never liked Gunnar," Jin said. "You were way too good for him."

Mimi chomped noodles so that her reaction wouldn't be transparent on her face. Why did Jin always have to say things like that? Things that made a girl, day after day, year after year, question if impossible things might be possible.

Mimi had recently broken up with her boyfriend of two years, well-known designer Gunnar Nilsson. He had also been her boss and, incensed that she had been the one to call things off, he'd made the work environment terrible for her with his constant badgering and criticisms until she couldn't bear the antagonism any longer.

Yet making Mimi's life miserable wasn't enough for Gunnar. He'd gone on to find out what other companies she was applying to work for and then bad-mouthed her to them before she even interviewed.

"I think Francois Boucher met with me as a courtesy to you," Mimi told Jin. "He told me he was sorry but that because Gunnar wasn't *able* to give me a good recommendation he had stronger candidates to consider."

Jin had been calling in favors all over the New York fashion world to try to help Mimi get a new job. But, so far, Gunnar had undercut every attempt. Apparently he was as ruthless in life as Wei was from his grave, simply wanting to control and ruin things out of spite.

"Did you meet with Kiki and Pietro?"

"Yup. Same thing. No one I've met with knows Gunnar and I dated so they assume his negative review of me is based on my work."

"Did you show them your portfolio? They weren't impressed?"

Mimi slowed a minute, appreciating that Jin never failed to tell her how talented she was.

He had become something of a professional mentor to her. Letting her use his tools and equipment anytime she wanted. Giving her important feedback on her own designs. Helping her find opportunities to further her career. Cheering her on. Out of the corner of her eye she watched him eat, stopping to rub his temples, which she knew was a sign of his stress.

She could never repay Jin for all he'd given her. Yet every night for the past thirteen years she went to sleep longing for what he hadn't.

"What are you actually going to do?" Aaron asked Jin two days later as they went one-on-one at the public basketball court near his apartment. "Is there a way to contest Wei's will?"

Jin swooped around Aaron's left side as he tried to steal the ball. Aaron pivoted away to keep his dribble going. "I spoke with my lawyer about it. I would have to establish that he wasn't of sound mind when he wrote it and that's almost impossible to do after the fact."

"You'd have some witnesses."

"Being an infidel and a drunk doesn't mean you can't make decisions. My lawyer said I didn't stand a chance."

"So, what then?"

"I'm wracking my brain trying to figure it out."

Aaron took a shot from midcourt and missed, Jin grabbing the ball on the rebound. He swerved left and right to avoid his friend's vigorous attempts to get it back.

"Consider this for a minute," Aaron said with a lunge. "Is there any way you could work something out with Helene to make it seem on paper like you were back together?"

"You've got to be kidding." Jin dodged Aaron's attempt to steal the ball.

"Desperate measures."

Helene was out of his life forever. He'd never speak to her again. Let alone involve her in something as important as his inheritance of LilyZ. To think, there was a time when he thought he'd always be with her.

When he'd first met Helene Carlson, she was working for an advertising agency with several clients in fashion. She introduced Jin to a New York party world he had never been a part of, preferring to keep his nose down and his mind on work and graduate school. Ironically, the same qualities she said she had liked about him.

With her swinging blond ponytail that was always in motion, Helene was fun and Jin got temporarily swept into her orbit of nightclubs and red carpets. Until the late-night revelries got to be all the same, and not worth the tired mornings. By then they were already married. Busy with the constant job of cleaning up the disasters his father had created, Jin couldn't keep up with his wife's social life. However, Helene wasn't done with that lifestyle, and continued to stay out until all hours most nights of the week.

Word trickled back to Jin that Helene wasn't spending her time away from him alone. When confronted, she claimed innocence but when photos of Helene with other men appeared on fashion gossip sites, Jin had had to face the truth. That time, she hadn't denied the accusations. He'd ended their marriage certain he'd never trust anyone ever again.

Jin had had two people in his life show him how easy it was to betray marriage vows. His father and his wife. And both had managed to put a cherry on top. Wei with his will and Helene by having an affair with LilyZ's lead designer, Javier Ferrer.

Aaron hustled Jin's attempt at a basket. The ball tipped the rim but didn't go through the net. Aaron was able to retrieve it on the bounce and regain possession.

It was a fair question Aaron had asked, but Jin couldn't bear the idea of even calling Helene again, so that was out.

What did make sense was the idea of marrying someone in name only. He knew he'd never marry again for love and he also knew he wouldn't lose LilyZ. Something had to give.

What would *in name only* actually look like? Some sort of marriage arranged for mutual benefit.

Jin took a shot at the basket and made it. "He shoots. He scores."

It wasn't that weird. People got married left and right for all sorts of reasons.

Aaron overtook the ball and dribbled away from him. "Show-off."

Jin stole it from him and did a quick-footed spin away.

If Jin was really going to consider this, he could call his cousin Ling in Hong Kong. He and his uncle Fu owned the manufacturing end of LilyZ. Perhaps they employed a young woman who might want to have a career in the States.

In the distance, Jin saw Mimi among the throngs climbing up the steps from the subway station by the basketball court. Aaron must have texted her that they were here.

He had no trouble picking out her face in the crowd with the alabaster skin and plump lips that he'd seen develop from those of an awkward teenager into a full-blooded woman. She and Aaron both had the same light brown eyes as their mother. Mimi's hair was tousled and tumbled down her shoulders. She spotted him and lifted her fingers to give him a gentle wave.

Once he saw Mimi coming toward them, he realized he'd never be able to go through with an *in name only* situation with a stranger. It had just been hypothetical thinking. Because if he was ever to do something like that he'd be sharing his life, his mother's life, and the life of LilyZ. He surely wasn't going to do that with someone he didn't know.

Perhaps that's why, as soon as he'd conjured the idea, he wanted to be sure Mimi never knew about it. It was too preposterous, too dishonest. Despite what he'd gone through with his father and with Helene, he wouldn't destroy the sanctity of real love for people who still believed in it. People like Mimi. She'd missed the mark completely with that idiot Gunnar. But he knew that she and Aaron thought in terms of the happiness their parents had shared before death took them too young. Mimi and Aaron hadn't grown up like Jin had, witnessing how little the marriage contract meant to some people.

"Hey, you guys," Mimi called out as she approached the court. Her hips swung side to side in that *va-va-voom* way as she walked, her sloping curves sashaying. Jin liked that she always wore fitted outfits and never hid her hills and valleys under sloppy clothes.

"Hey, Mimi."

"Sis." Aaron got control of the ball while Jin focused his eyes on Mimi. Was there something different about her lately, or something he hadn't noticed before?

He wished that she was more successful in love than he had been. She was the total package. Men should be lined up around the block.

"Are you done, do you want to walk home together?" Mimi asked as she reached the chain-link fence separating the court from the New York sidewalk.

Jin and Aaron moved to the bench where they had their bags. Each located their water bottle and took in big gulps. Then found their towels and wiped the sweat dripping down their faces. Jin mopped up his hair as well and when he pulled the towel off noticed the side-eyed way Mimi had watched the whole maneuver.

"I'll walk part of the way with you but I've got a cocktail reception thing tonight at Boutique Charli." New York Fashion Week Spring was upon them, when the international fashion industry converged on the city. Buyers, media, VIPs, celebrities and invited members of the public gathered for event after event that showcased the latest creations.

The major design houses mounted elaborate runway shows and extravagant parties. Exclusive ready-to-wear labels like LilyZ tended toward private showings. Boutique Charli was an influential shop in Chelsea and Jin had to make everyone he encountered believe it was business as usual for LilyZ. That while they didn't have a collection to show this season, which he could blame on Wei's death, they were still on track.

To redeem the lies he'd be telling, Jin needed a new designer. Immediately. Of course, it couldn't be just anyone. He'd interviewed five people in the past two days and none of them were right.

Even though shooting hoops with Aaron had helped clear his mind, his to-do list came flooding back into the stress points of his temples.

After he bid farewell to Mimi and Aaron, he went home to shower and dress. When he arrived at the Boutique Charli party he was distracted, and it wasn't as easy schmoozing with the crowd as he'd hoped. He accepted the cocktail a waiter offered and struggled with the chitchat he needed to do.

A runway model trotted toward him. He couldn't remember her name. With a kiss on each cheek she almost choked him with her flowery perfume.

"Hi Ji-in." She somehow made his name stretch out to two syllables. "You remember me from the De La Costa show."

He didn't, but smiled politely. Looking ready to swallow him whole like a snake would, she had no reason to know that women were off-limits in Jin's life. That he'd never put himself out there and chance getting burned again.

A typical rail-thin, six-foot-tall fashionista, the model wore a blouse made of peach-colored rayon. Styled after a man's shirt, it had buttons down the front. On one side the shoulder was cut out completely, revealing the wearer's bony clavicle and her bare arm down to the elbow. The other side of the blouse was a regular cut with silver trinkets shaped like bunnies sewn down the line of the sleeve. Jin knew that rabbits were part of Milan label Fortnight's theme this year so guessed it was theirs.

Fashion was so subjective. That blouse could look ridiculous to one person and be the height of couture to the next. When Shun Zhang started LilyZ, he'd never had aspirations to see his clothes on the catwalks of Paris or in wild editorial spreads of fashion magazines. His intention was to create expertly made clothes that a woman could wear for decades so Jin's grandfather chose the finest fabrics and used time-consuming craftsmanship.

Shun had an innate sense of how to foreshadow or interpret a trend but work it subtly into his collections, so that his clothes never went out of style when the fashion winds blew in a different direction. Customers responded and LilyZ became a multimillion-dollar enterprise.

To uphold those traditions, Jin needed a designer. While he himself occasionally generated ideas that ultimately became finished pieces, he was not a designer and couldn't develop a sketch into a pattern and then into a sample and finally to perfection. What he needed was somebody talented and trustworthy to come into his troubled company and turn it around. Somebody like... Mimi!

Looking at the model's rabbit trinket shirt, Jin thought of that smashing pink dress Mimi was in the other day. She had a real knack for sensing what would look good on someone. It wasn't just that she was a woman with hips and an ample bosom, a shape that was still outside the norm for the industry. No, what Mimi had was real artistry in merging a classic look with a mood, creating something that made a statement with delicacy and grace.

If only everything was happening a few years from now. If Mimi had more experience, he could hire her as his designer. She was part of the family already and, as a unit, they could take LilyZ as far as it could go. He could count on her.

But a company of LilyZ's standing couldn't name a junior designer to lead. He, and she, would be the town's laughingstock.

Unless? An idea popped into Jin's mind.

It was too crazy.

But what if it wasn't?

CHAPTER TWO

"CAN I TAKE a shower, please?" Mimi poked her head into her brother's bedroom. It was inconvenient that she had to go past his bed in order to get to the bathroom but that was the price paid for camping out on his sofa bed while she was unemployed.

"Gaaaaah…" was Aaron's half-awake reply as he rolled over and pulled the blankets over his head. "Get. A. Job."

"Working on it, bro."

As she showered and dressed, she knew she was at the point of overstaying her welcome. Aaron's place was, plain and simple, a compact New York apartment meant only for one person or a couple at most. Minimalist and sleek with black furniture, it was perfectly detailed for the up-and-coming lords of Wall Street such as her brother.

Aaron had offered to lend her money to get her own place when she broke up with Gunnar and moved out from the apartment she shared with him. But a junior designer didn't command a very big salary and she didn't know how she'd pay her brother back. She knew he'd absorb the cost if he had to, but she also knew that he was saving money to buy an apartment rather than continuing to lease, and she didn't want to derail his plans.

After showering, she made breakfast.

"You interviewing again today?" Aaron asked when he emerged clean and suited up for his workday.

"Yep."

"Maybe you'll get this one."

"We'll see if Gunnar has managed to ace me out of yet another job." Mimi shrugged as she portioned out the eggs she'd just scrambled, handing one plate to Aaron.

He went to sit down at the table but there was no-where to put his dish. The surface was piled high with everything from Mimi's sketch pads to her electronics to her sewing machine. She rushed over to make room, stacking things on one of the chairs and the sofa bed. "Sorry."

The coffee table had been moved aside in order to open the sofa bed, which was not yet folded up for the day. Mimi's clothes and shoes and whatnot were also spilling out of two suitcases in the middle of the floor. There were fabric swatches and sewing tools every-where, and even a pair of slippers on the end table. In short, Mimi's life lay in front of them.

"Honestly, Mimi, I don't know how much longer I can live like this. You know, Jin asked me again if you'd want to stay with him. He's got the huge flat all to him-self now and there's plenty of room."

"No, I, no…" Mimi tripped over her words.

It was true that the whole third floor of Jin's China-town building was living space. The showroom was at street level and the second floor was the studio. Shun had bought the building when he'd started to make some money with LilyZ and it had never been occupied by anyone other than the Zhang family ever since.

When Bai finally couldn't stand Wei's disrespectful ways one minute longer and divorced him, she moved to the Upper East Side to be near her sister. No one knew where Wei had stayed before he died. Jin had lived in the Chinatown flat by himself until Helene moved in, and was now alone there again.

However, Mimi staying with Jin would be intoler-able. How could she ever tell him or her brother that just the proximity she typically had with Jin was, and always had been, enough of a struggle? Seeing him sev-eral times a week, sharing meals, hovering together over a garment, confiding their joys and sorrows.

Feeling his sparks.

It was all already too much.

If Jin was behind her in a room, even if she didn't see him she'd know he was there. She could recognize the sound of his breathing. Knew what size shirt he wore. His favorite movie. Song. Flavor of ice cream.

But while they'd shared cottages in the woods and summer beach shacks, moving into his flat would be another matter entirely. Going to sleep under the same roof, waking up to each other day after day, night after night.

That would be skidding too close to thoughts that were only allowed out in the wee hours.

Aaron and Mimi finally sat down at the cleared table with their breakfast. Changing the subject, she reminisced, "Remember how Dad used to snip fresh chives onto eggs?"

"I like that you always put cheese in them. But yeah, he'd bring the little potted plant from the windowsill over to the table."

The siblings had grown up in a happy home full of warmth. Delia and Benjamin Stewart walked arm in arm together down the street just as they did through everything in their lives.

Until the death do us part bit came too soon.

"Mom and Dad had something very special." Which is what Mimi longed for. That kind of union, a friendship and a romance all mixed into one.

"Unlike Wei with Bai."

"It must have been so hard for Shun, to have an alcoholic son he didn't know how to help."

The siblings forked up their eggs.

Shun had only recently died when Aaron first met Jin. The two teenaged boys played together on the high school basketball team. Their moms got to know each other while cheering on their sons during games.

Mimi was two years younger, fifteen at the time, and not that involved in her brother's life. When she'd come home from her after-school babysitting job, her pulse would pound to see dark, handsome Jin sitting at their kitchen table eating her mother's food.

Little did she know at the time that the Stewarts' apartment had become a refuge for Jin, a place to escape the negativity of the Zhang home. Nor did young

Mimi understand how to interpret the intense stares Jin always gave her. Over the years, she'd come to learn that the look in his teenaged expressive eyes was pain and emotional fatigue.

Aaron put his fork down. "I wish there was a way we could help Jin."

"That's what I keep thinking."

"Can I show you something?" Jin asked Mimi while she was sitting at a sewing machine in his studio a little later. "Just a couple of new things I was playing around with."

"Sure, just let me finish up this seam," Mimi said as she turned her head toward him and then back to the dress she was doing in muslin as a prototype. She'd come in after her interview to use one of Jin's industrial machines, as she had been doing for years.

He kept a few machines near his office in the back, along with a cutting table, tools and shelves with fabric set aside for special projects. Now with his grandfather and father gone, nobody but Jin used the office.

Employees busied about in front creating virtual models on the computers, fulfilling back orders and doing alterations for the customers who had bought pieces from the showroom downstairs. While the major manufacturing was handled by his uncle Fu in Hong Kong, there was always plenty of activity at Jin's building.

He pulled out some drawings he'd done.

"I was toying with this," he explained as she got up from the machine to join him. Pointing to details on the sketch he explained, "Wouldn't this be kind of a practical look? Comfortable separates but with fine tailoring so that a woman can wear them anywhere? Business casual. With this maybe," he said as he pulled over some fabric swatches.

He handed Mimi a twill he was considering. Their fingers brushed in the process. The Jin sizzles that were as familiar to her as her own heartbeat crackled up her spine.

A smirk she fought to hide reminded her of Aaron's suggestion of her moving in with Jin. Living with this man, who occupied her dreams day and night, was out of the question.

Although, really, she'd have nothing to worry about because in all the years she'd known him, he'd never done anything to encourage her secret feelings. There was no reason to think he ever would. The big brotherly hugs, chaste kisses on the cheek and the professional cheering on was the way they were with each other. For so long now it was set in stone.

She rubbed the fabric between her fingers. "This would be wrinkly by the end of the day. Can you go with something stiffer?"

"Will you work it through with me? I can't meet my retailers with nothing to show."

"And you have no designer."

"I haven't found anyone suitable to hire."

"You're thinking of doing your own collection?"

Jin slowly nodded as he looked over his drawings.

"Was I wrong to fire Javier so hastily? Right before Fashion Week?"

"Once you found out about him and Helene, how could you be expected to work with him every day?"

"I don't know what I'm going to do."

Mimi lifted one sketch off Jin's desk and inspected it carefully. Then she reviewed another. She trailed her finger along the drawing of a blazer jacket, commenting, "You could run a curved seam here, and here, and give it a little flare at the hem."

Maybe this was how she might help Jin. Offer what assistance she could in pulling together some pieces without a designer.

"I like that," he said, understanding her concept.

"Kind of a nineteen-seventies vibe."

"Hmm. You're good."

"I know! If I could ever get a job."

"How did it go today?"

"Thanks, but no thanks."

Mimi had always wanted to be a fashion designer, even before she met the Zhangs. Whereas others loved music or books, she loved clothes. The artistry of fashion. The details. The variety. The act of personal expression that had to be combined with an almost science-like approach to construction. She'd taught herself to sew as a young girl and sitting in front of the hum of a machine was her happy place. For birthdays or holidays, she'd ask for gifts of fabric and supplies. Her parents encouraged her to chase her ambition so she'd gone to design school.

Now here she was, unemployed.

"Gunnar Nilsson is not going to bring me down." Mimi grabbed a pencil from the holder on Jin's desk and was quickly drawing a revised idea for his casual suits. "Didn't your grandfather do a collection like this way back when? I feel like I've seen some photos."

"Yeah, it was a big hit in the eighties. With exaggerated shoulders and peg-leg pants but the same theory. I've heard that half of New York produced imitations after that."

"It will be a tribute to him, then."

Mimi continued making adjustments to the sketch. "See, I'm saying do a subtle pouf at the shoulder. A little all-business and a little rock star."

"That is fabulous, Miss Stewart."

Jin moved toward her for a hug that included three friendly pats on the back, like someone might give their long-lost uncle. Never did he give her the kind of embraces that Mimi fantasized about. "You're a pal."

A pal to Jin, she was. Always would be.

She pointed to her sketches. "Can I apply for the designer job?" she kidded. Was she really kidding, though?

"Good night, Cynthia," Jin called out to the last employee to leave the studio. He leaned back in his desk chair and clasped his hands behind his head. Closing his eyes for a moment, he listened to the unusual din of nothingness. With equipment running, and people collaborating and coming in and out, the LilyZ headquarters was never a quiet place.

As his staff walked or took buses, subways and trains back to their homes for the night, Jin experienced urban solitude. Something he might have enjoyed after the chaos of his marriage. Right now, though, he had too much on his mind to relax.

His eyes sprang open again.

The drawings he and Mimi had been working on earlier were scattered at the side of the desk while Wei's will sat front and center. Jin read the words *legal and lawful marriage* a couple of times, as if he'd find something different in the words than he had before. A new solution.

He was still musing on that marrying *in name only* concept. He'd ruled out any strangers because he couldn't take any chances with LilyZ. Whoever he chose, that was *if* he chose, would have to be someone he already knew well.

The prospect seemed impossible.

Jin glanced over to Mimi's drawings. She was really so bright and intuitive. Like today when she'd made such fabulous improvements on what he was imagining, the two of them talking in the shorthand of two people who had known each other for a very long time.

Known each other for a very long time.

Mimi had asked him straight out if he could hire her as his designer. The weird thought that had been nagging at him for days surfaced again. His brain focused on it, on seeing it all the way through.

What if? How desperate was everybody at this point? No! It would never work. A nice fantasy, though.

A new notion popped into his head out of nowhere. If there was any hope of him finding some kind of pretend wife that was someone he already knew, what about an ex-girlfriend? He'd dated women before he married Helene.

How about Leslie Wang, his college sweetheart?

Leslie was a nice enough girl. They'd broken up on friendly terms, after which she'd left New York.

So, what, Jin was going to abruptly call her out of the blue and ask her to be his phony wife? Even if he did, what would she gain from the deal? Was she a person who needed money? What if she was unattached and wanted children? Would Jin be willing to give *that* to someone in return for LilyZ?

Of course not, the voice in his head shouted with certainty. The ruse was to stay married for a year after which time Leslie, or whomever, would carry on with the rest of their lives. He couldn't father a child and then not be part of his or her life.

Pondering how he would even get in touch with Leslie, he grabbed his laptop.

He'd search for her on social media.

With Wang being a fairly common surname, he located an unruly amount of possibilities. Fortunately most people had a profile photo so that he could eliminate the majority of them. When he found her photo, Jin knew he wouldn't be reuniting with Leslie Wang, who also used the name Leslie Franklin. No, she clearly had her hands full in the photo, surrounded by three young kids who resembled her. Behind them stood a proud-looking man, his thick arms encircling his brood with a hug.

All Jin could do was laugh out loud, the sound ricocheting around his empty studio. Whatever would have made him think someone from his past was available and waiting for his call?

Mimi's drawings next to the will caught his eye again and that crazy inkling, and it was definitely *crazy*, picked at him.

He scanned a panorama of the studio, all the machinery dormant and only the night-lights illuminating the cavernous space. The tall windows up front facing out to the Manhattan night. This company meant the world to him.

Desperate times called for desperate measures, didn't they? Aaron had said those exact words himself on the basketball court the other day.

Maybe it wouldn't hurt to talk it through.

He called Aaron's cell phone.

"What are you doing?"

"Tripping over Mimi's stuff that's all over my apartment."

Mutually beneficial agreement?

"Can I buy you a beer?"

"You bet."

"The place on that corner."

"Fifteen minutes."

Jin reached for one of his favorite possessions—one of his grandfather's thimbles. While Jin had kept many of Shun's tools, this was the most special to him. Made of heavy bone china, it had an intricately painted scene on it. A Chinese Junk boat sailed in blue ocean waves at sunset. The sky above was purple then red then orange. As a young boy Jin had thought it was nothing short of a miracle that someone could have done a painting on an object so small.

That thimble was a sort of talisman for Jin. Shun did not travel to the United States on a boat. He'd arrived on a plane to a New York airport. But the thimble's depiction of a lone vessel under the sunset always filled Jin with respect for perseverance and risk.

He placed it back in the caddy on his desk that held loose items—a button here, a spool of thread there. After he collected his phone and wallet to go meet Aaron, Jin changed his mind and grabbed the thimble again, slipping it into his pocket.

At the crowded bar, the two friends stood close in order to hear each other. They each nursed a long-necked bottle of beer. Aaron looked Jin in the eye after he'd laid out his plan. "So you're asking me a question?"

"I suppose I am." He'd never go forward if Aaron objected.

"How *old school* of you."

"With your father long gone."

"Have you actually talked to my sister about this?"

"I wanted to discuss it with you first."

Aaron snickered. "It would solve my housing problem. Although there must be a simpler way."

"Consider that a bonus."

"You're sure this would be a good business move for her?"

"I'd be giving her an opportunity she could never get elsewhere at this point in her career."

"We go back a long way," Aaron said, tapping his

bottle on the bar. "But I've got to say it out loud. I think she might be in…"

"She might be in what?" Jin tried to coax him into finishing.

"Are you sure you and she could pull this off without anything…you know…physical happening between you?"

A fair question. One Jin was ninety-nine percent sure he had the answer to. He was only human. Mimi was very beautiful. And they'd be saying good-night to each other under the same roof, night after night.

With everything that was at stake, though, Jin would never do anything that would risk harming her. "I could only do this with someone I trusted."

"Right?"

"It would be all business. Wouldn't change anything between us."

"I'm not sure it's that easy. But talk to her about it. I'll support you both either way." Jin tipped his bottle toward Aaron's and they clinked. Although Aaron finished the toast with, "You might be my best friend. But she's my blood. You do know that if you hurt her I would have to tear off every limb of your body piece by piece?"

Jin chuckled. "Understood."

When they got to Aaron's apartment, Mimi was in pajamas, hand stitching a pair of pants. She looked sweet and pretty in her baby-pink T-shirt and matching leggings. Aaron excused himself to take a shower.

"Mimi." Jin inhaled deeply to muster up his courage as he moved toward her. He pointed to her sewing. "Would you mind putting that down for a second?"

She placed it beside her on the sofa and gave him her full attention. "What's wrong, Jin?"

Even though she didn't find it with Gunnar, he knew Mimi believed in love—she'd grown up surrounded by it—but what Jin was offering was something quite different.

Just talk to her about it, he coached himself. *She can say no if she wants to. Do it. Now.*

He dropped to one knee in front of her. Then reached in his pocket for his grandfather's thimble. Picking up her hand, he placed the thimble on the top of her ring finger.

She shot him a baffled look.

"Mimi, would you marry me?"

"Would I *what*?" Mimi's heart thundered against her chest. Jin was in front of her on bent knee, having just asked her to marry him!

Was this actually happening? She may have dreamed of this happening before, albeit in softer focus. But she definitely wasn't asleep now. If it was a dream she'd be dressed better.

"You know I've been trying to figure out how to satisfy the condition of the will," Jin began, still on one knee in front of her with a wrenching look of vulnerability on his strong face that was so unlike his usual sureness. "Which led me to think about motives for why people get married. That it isn't always for love. How

nobody but me would know if I got married to someone for a different reason."

Mimi deflated.

This wasn't the moment she'd been holding out hope
for all these years. Just the opposite. He was making it
clear that he wasn't in love with her. Stating up front
what she already knew to be true.

Which made perfect sense. Jin never had an inkling
of what she held inside, so he wouldn't know to be sen-
sitive with his choice of words. It was his business that
he was concerned about.

Rightly so.

"I see," was all she could scratch out. Still, the hairs
on her arms stood at attention.

She indulged a quick fantasy. Her Jin had finally
come to claim her. To begin their life together, at last.
Children. A home filled with joy. Like her parents had
had. She'd show him the meaning of loyalty, and the
wounds cut into him by his father and his ex-wife would
heal. He'd learn to love again.

Reality check.

That wasn't the proposal being offered.

"You know I'll never marry again in earnest. So I
got to wondering," Jin continued as he rose up from
one knee and gestured for Mimi to make room for him
on the sofa.

Suddenly self-conscious about the skimpy jersey fabric of her pajamas she scooted across the cushions, as
far as she could, as a matter of fact. She folded her arms
across her chest in modesty. Jin had seen just about

every inch of her body over the years, but not while he was proposing marriage.

"Wondering?"

The thimble was still fitted over the top of her finger as it pressed against her other arm.

"What if I married someone for practical purposes and then divorced a year later after I fulfilled the requirements of the will?"

"Uh-huh." So that was his scheme. Disappointment rang through her.

"Then I thought about *that* from a realistic standpoint and realized it couldn't be just anyone."

Mimi's breath sputtered at the acknowledgment that she wasn't *just anyone* to him. There was a bit of satisfaction in that.

His eyes seemed to be pleading for her to connect the dots so that he didn't have to lay it all out for her.

They might be friends but there was no way she was going to make this easy for him. Not after all she'd had to swallow for the past thirteen years. She'd hear out his proposition before issuing a resounding no. After all, she might as well stretch the moment out. It was the only time she'd ever hear those words coming out of his mouth.

What a thought. Fake married to Jin. To live as man and wife except for the love part.

A fate worse than death.

"I see."

"We're practically family already, Special Agent Mimi," he said, referring to a silly taunt he and Aaron had used as teenagers when she would disclose to them school gossip they knew nothing of. "Would you consider this ultimate con to help me save LilyZ? If not for me, could you do it for Mamabai?"

She scrunched up her face at him. If he was trying to draw on the loyalty they had for each other, he was doing a pretty good job. It was just this morning that she and Aaron had been talking about finding a way to help Jin out of his predicament. But marriage! That was beyond a line she could cross in the name of duty or anything else.

"There must be another solution."

An image passed across her brain. She was in an elaborate lace wedding gown with a long train, the type she wouldn't wear in real life, walking down an aisle toward Jin in a tuxedo. She strode in rhythmic paces, each one taking her closer and closer to her beloved.

Wait. It wasn't her in that mental picture. It was Helene. The woman Jin had actually married. In reality, on that fateful day Mimi was cast off to the side with two other women, the three of them in pewter-colored bridesmaids' dresses. Later, when her brother, who had acted as best man, asked Mimi why she had dabbed streaming tears from her eyes during the ceremony, she'd told him it was because she was so happy for Jin.

It had been one of the hardest days of her life.

"I've considered it left, right and center, and I can't come up with any other way," Jin said, bringing her attention back to the here and now. "Hear me out. I'm trying to think logically about a way this could be a good step for you, too. You could come stay with me.

You could have the master bedroom and bathroom all to yourself. I'll take the guest room."

The master suite. Where he slept. Again he was making crystal-clear that his proposal had nothing romantic attached to it. He wanted to be sure she received that message loud and clear. Separate bedrooms.

"You've already offered to let me stay with you," she quipped, perturbed by this whole suggestion.

"Why haven't you said yes?"

She uncrossed her arms and twisted the thimble on her finger, studying its painted details. Unable to answer Jin's question.

To tell him anything would be to tell him everything. Which she never had and never would. She'd decided years ago to settle for the friendship, the concern, the trust and the fun.

It had never been easy but it had always been worth it.

"We could make it quite simple," he insisted. For him maybe. "No one would know that we were living apart under one roof."

"I'd like to help but…"

"Please—" he glanced at the thimble then back to her eyes "—let me finish. As I said, I know this is a huge thing to ask of someone. I'd want it to be worth your while. What if we got married and I named you as LilyZ's new designer?"

"What?" Lead designer for his prestigious label? Otherwise known as an ultimate career goal? Her eyes bugged at the suggestion.

"You could do it. I know you have the talent. I'll teach you everything else you need to know."

Like thousands of others who go through design school, Mimi's goal was to have her own fashions manufactured, sold and actually worn. It was the carrot every young designer was chasing. Not to merely assist a company with their ideas, but instead to be the one creating the vision. Only a few made it that far. Others adjusted their expectations into other occupations in the industry. Some left it altogether.

Be careful what you ask for, the saying went. *Because you just might get it.*

Life had a sense of humor, though. Offering Mimi what she'd always wanted.

In more ways than one.

Except the most important.

"Look, if I could, I would hire you as my designer with no strings attached. But the industry would crucify me for appointing an apprentice as my lead. And I've got employees with far more experience than you. They would feel betrayed and overlooked. I could never do that to them."

"And this way?" Mimi was still trying to process Jin's idea.

"We'd be a team. I'm mentoring my wife and we're designing together. It may not be fair but at least it's understandable to people."

"So everybody would think I got where I was simply because I was your wife?"

"I'd make sure you got credit for all of the designs." Unlike Gunnar.

"I'm sorry, Jin, but I have to say no." Could he let her leave it at that?

"Aaron said that…"

"You talked to Aaron before you…" Comprehension stopped her. "You asked my brother for his permission? For my hand in marriage?"

"So to speak."

She wished it didn't, but Jin's old-fashioned chivalry tugged at her heartstrings. With her father long dead, Jin went to Aaron. Even though the discussion was about a charade of a marriage, Jin had thought to discuss it with her brother.

Mimi's lungs ached. The hour was late, the proposition enormous. Yet she knew that pretending to be Jin's wife would be the end of her. She'd just endured a horrible disappointment in Gunnar. Which left her much too raw for something as emotionally risky as a fake marriage to Jin.

Of all people. The man against whom she measured all others. The only man she ever truly…

"You know I'd like to help you. But I can't."

She recalled dancing with her brother at Jin's wedding. The newlyweds were on the dance floor as well. Jin had spun his bride under his arm until she circled back into his hold. Despite the well-wishers and the photographer, their smiles were only for each other. Mimi had watched them for as long as she could stand it and then had to look away. Peered again out of the corner of her eye. Gulped back her emotions. Until the wee hours when she had cried herself to sleep.

Her fingers stiffened with tension as she absentmindedly stroked the side of her face with the bone china thimble.

"Think about it, Mimi. Please."

For reasons beyond his control, Jin had set out to marry. If it wasn't to her, it would be to someone else. One way or another, Mimi would have to dance at another one of Jin's weddings.

CHAPTER THREE

"YOU LOOK AMAZING," Jin told Mimi after the taxi he'd
hailed pulled up to the curb. Wearing another dress he'd
seen her put together at his studio, she was celestial in
pale lavender. The dress had an organza overlay that
shimmered with hand-sewn crystals.

"Thanks. Do you think this ruching at the center
here works?" She pointed to the gathering of fabric at
the décolleté.

"I'm not sure if I love it."

"I can rip it out and then it'll just be a straight hori-
zontal portrait collar."

"Let me think it through. The whole effect is phe-
nomenal." His jaw ticked at the snug fit across Mimi's
hips. She'd finished her outfit with beige leather pumps.
"Really great."

Figuring she was probably cold in only a caramel-
colored wool cape against the winter chill, he ushered
her into the cab.

"Isn't Mamabai coming?"

His mom was attending the Leo Berringer show,
as well.

"She'll meet us there."

Last night, Mimi had refused Jin's marriage proposal. He glanced over to her and a snicker crossed his mouth at how silly that sounded. Of course, it was an offer of a business arrangement and not a declaration of eternal bonding. Nonetheless, she'd said no and he actually felt a little bit rejected.

It was a lot to ask. He knew that Mimi took marriage seriously. After the disappointment with Gunnar, he was sure she wouldn't be rushing into any relationship anytime soon. In the meantime, he reasoned that his one-year ruse could give her a boost to her career that couldn't happen any other way.

Plus, he surely wasn't suddenly going to marry into a real union himself, so his old friend had nothing to worry about in that area if that was on her mind. He was quite done with romantic relationships.

Been there, done that.

Something in him once thought that if he had a legitimate marriage it might erase the wrongs of the fractured home he'd grown up in. However, he'd made a colossal mistake in choosing Helene, who was actually just like his father with her cheating party-girl ways.

Lesson learned the hard way. Over and done. He'd never have such naïve fantasies again.

Which was all the more reason he wasn't ready to give up on the Mimi prospect. Especially since it was the only one he had. Maybe she just needed to get used to the idea. He felt a tiny bit guilty in insisting she come to the Leo Berringer show with him today partially so she'd be reminded of what he was offering her.

Leo had a label about the size of LilyZ's. While the smaller labels didn't always do runway shows like this was to be, there was always a glamorous party or gathering in their studios during Fashion Week. Didn't Mimi ultimately want that? A collection of her designs being presented to retailers?

Maybe today would show her what she could have.

The Berringer event was being held in a small art museum near Gramercy Park. As Jin and Mimi exited the taxi, photographers snapped guests while they made their way in. Jin had worn a finely cut gray suit and white shirt, choosing a silver tie. In his opinion, the press should be taking notice of Mimi's dress so he did his best to position her in their direction.

Onlookers behind velvet ropes called out the names of a few recognizable faces from the entertainment industry who were in attendance.

As was always the case during Fashion Week, venues were chosen for dramatic effect. The Gothic architecture of the museum gave an interesting backdrop against the moody music that spilled out from the entrance doors.

Once inside, Jin spotted his mother and waved. Bai Zhang was a chic woman with short dark hair who never let the shame and heartbreak she'd endured show. Jin took Mimi's hand and navigated his way through the crowd.

"Mom," he greeted Bai with a kiss on each cheek.

"Mamabai," Mimi said, and followed suit.

"Nice dress."

"Do you like the ruching?" Mimi repeated the question she'd asked Jin before they got in the taxi.

Jin needed to remember that she was still only an apprentice. It took years, if not decades, to hone talent and craft. He had a moment's consideration that if, in fact, he could convince Mimi to take him up on his proposal, he'd need to bring in some reliable colleagues to be sure her designs were really worthy of his label. After all, he owed that much to his grandfather, to make sure that every LilyZ garment lived up to Shun's promise of quality style and quiet elegance. That decision shouldn't be his alone.

"No," his mother said decisively about the ruching.

"Help me fix it," Mimi said to Jin as she shouldered herself toward him and away from anyone else's view. She pulled a seam ripper out of her small purse and handed it to Jin. Last-minute modifications were something everyone in the industry was used to, so her actions came as no surprise to him.

He reached to her décolleté to swiftly sever a couple of threads that allowed him to undo the stitching, which changed the dress's neckline completely. In doing so, his fingers grazed against the milky skin on that delicate area of her body. An unexpected bristle ran through him.

Mimi adjusted the new neckline to her satisfaction. Jin nodded once in approval.

Several rows of chairs were set up on both sides of a runway that was positioned in between marble statues of longhaired nudes on pedestals. Some guests were already sitting, and the space was resonant with piereing laughs. A few pairs of eyes turned to watch when the three of them entered the seating area.

As they stood near their seats, Bai struck up a conversation with someone. Jin noticed Mimi watching Bai.

"She's never lost her brave face," Mimi leaned over to whisper in his ear.

"No one should have to go through what my father did to her, especially in the end. Attending parties with gaudy gold diggers on his arm. Drunk and stupid enough to think that whoever it was would give him a second glance if she wasn't trying to get something out of it."

"No respect for his wife at all."

Jin winced when he thought about how Helene had disrespected him the same way.

Wei's marriage to Bai was arranged. Shun had hoped a proper girl from a respectable family would straighten out his wayward son and Bai's parents had also come to New York from Hong Kong. They'd opened a restaurant in Chinatown, which grew to seven throughout Manhattan.

However, a happy marriage wasn't in Bai's destiny. Just as it hadn't been for Jin.

"I have to save LilyZ," he reconfirmed to Mimi. And gestured toward his mother. "For her sake if nothing else. I'm not going to let my father destroy her."

Mimi blew some air out of her cheeks.

"I…"

"I didn't mean to make you feel guilty." Jin guessed what she might have been thinking. "You have to do what's right for yourself."

"Believe me, it does burn me up inside that Wei wished her ill. After she had to witness your marriage falling apart, too. It's a lot for someone to take."

"That's why it can't end the way my father wanted it to. Punishing both her and I."

"If you were going to up and marry someone, how would you even present that to Mamabai if she doesn't know about the will?"

They both studied his mother as she listened with sincere interest to the people she was standing with.

"I haven't figured it all out yet. If you had agreed, I was going to tell her that after your breakup and mine, we decided that as old friends we'd partner up. Don't people always say that if they're not married by thirty they'll marry a friend? To form a partnership based on camaraderie and history. I'm thirty, you're twenty-eight."

Mimi was silent.

He pivoted his head to look at her.

All at once, her cheeks had gone ashen and her eyes were watery. "Mimi," he said, and gripped his hand around her upper arm, "are you okay?"

She didn't turn to face him, instead swallowing a couple of times. Her prolonged intakes of oxygen suggested that she was in turmoil.

Mimi uttered slowly, almost under her breath, "Mamabai…has…always been so good to Aaron and I."

"She loves you like her own. Wasn't that the promise she made to your mom before she died?"

A wry smile crossed Mimi's lips.

Then she returned to herself a bit. "You'll make your

mother so proud when you grow the company in the ways you have planned."

"If I ever figure out how to actually inherit it."

"You will."

He nudged her with his elbow. "Hey, you don't happen to have any girlfriends who might need a husband, do you?"

Mimi glared through him like he was from Mars.

Lights began highlighting one nude statue and then the next, creating shadows on the stone walls. Bai excused herself from the people she was talking to and the three of them sat down.

The music got louder as the first model strode out from the staging area. Before the show was fully underway, Mimi kissed his mother on the cheek. "I love you so much, Mamabai."

As Mimi watched the runway show with Jin on her right and Bai on her left, thoughts paraded across her mind as swiftly as the models on the catwalk.

She was haunted by what Jin had said to her about how they'd present it to his mother if they really were to marry. *Old friends...a union based on history.* His words lodged in her throat.

Firstly, because they were true. With Jin betrayed by Helene, and Gunnar turning out to be hardly what Mimi had hoped for, it made sense even to her that marrying a longtime friend, with whom you knew what you were getting, didn't sound half bad.

Although, the words were agony in what they didn't say. Time and again, Jin took pains to make it clear that he didn't share the yearnings Mimi had been harboring all these years. She knew he didn't, but hearing the constant confirmation in the midst of marriage proposals was a lot to take.

The final dagger to her heart was when he asked if she had any girlfriends who might want to get married. Unimaginable, him with one of her friends, even if it meant a way for him to save the label and Bai's dignity. As excruciating as it was to watch Jin with Helene during the years they were together, at least Mimi hadn't previously known his bride. Which had given her a certain distance that helped her keep her emotions under wrap.

Even though she'd said no, Jin's proposal was out there in the ether. Regardless of the outcome, it had happened and she couldn't stop mulling it over. Marrying him might be the worst decision of her life. Not marrying him might be the worst decision of her life. What if marrying him was a way into her secret wishes? What if his platonic feelings changed? That happened all the time. People moved toward each other in marriage. Grew to lo—

"This should be you, Mimi," Jin said, gesturing with his head as a line of models strode the catwalk for the finale. Leo Berringer, flanked by two models in the star pieces of his military vibe collection, closed the show. "This *will* be you." If she was being honest, Mimi *could* see herself in the designer's shoes. She knew she had talent and was a tireless worker.

She whispered into his ear, "Yes. This is what I want."

Although she hated the bargain he was suggesting rather than just hiring her as his designer, she understood his reasoning. Presenting a twenty-eight-year-old junior designer as his wife would be easier for the public and the industry to comprehend. It made perfect sense.

For him. He didn't have the emotional issues that complicated the proposition.

After the show, they went back to the Chinatown flat and Jin ordered food. Bai commented, "It still smells like Helene in here."

"What did Helene smell like?" Jin asked in earnest, surprised by his mother's comment.

"Lies. Same as your father."

How painful it had been for Bai to see Jin's marriage fail. Her only son, a man filled with innate decency, disgraced by a woman who didn't see how precious he was. How he deserved to be valued like the finest jewel.

If Mimi were ever lucky enough to be with someone like Jin, she'd guard and keep him as if her life depended on it. Because it would.

It could surely help avenge the hurt Helene had left behind if Jin was to marry someone worthy of him. Someone Bai liked.

"What a lot we are," Bai said, looking to Jin and then to Mimi, "three broken hearts. And Aaron still single." Little did Bai know who really had the ability to shatter Mimi's heart.

"What's wrong?" Bai asked Jin as they sat down at the table to eat. Her son massaged his temples, distraught.

"Just tired," he clipped. Maybe going to the Leo Berringer show today had taken its toll on him, exacerbated his worries. And protecting his mother by keeping mum about the will must be so difficult for him.

Mimi knew firsthand what a burden secrets were to carry.

She recognized frustration on Jin's face. His dark eyes spearing through everything they surveyed and the tight set of his straight lips. Breathtakingly handsome as always, but the weight of the world was bearing down on his strong shoulders. How much more could he handle?

He might lose everything.

During late nights over cocktails or coffees, Jin had told Aaron and Mimi about his plans for LilyZ. He looked forward to returning to the practical yet refined clothes that Shun had founded the company on.

Comfortable and tailored clothes with a bit of retro thrown in was exactly what Mimi longed to create. Pieces that would look great on every woman, that she could wear to work, on a date night, or out to dinner with the kids, as well. Couture, but that made sense in a wardrobe.

Jin offered her a chance to do just that.

In return, all he asked for was a year of pretending when they were in public. Twelve months that would transform her life. Couldn't she put her personal cautions aside to let her professional instincts soar? To design for a label she'd always had a connection to. Where she knew that in Jin she'd have a fair boss who wasn't threatened by other people's talent.

Okay, she wouldn't have come by her title on a conventional track but what difference did that make? She'd prove any naysayers wrong with her dedication and work.

If her parents were alive, they'd tell her to embrace her good fortune and make the most of it.

And what about Bai? A woman who had looked after Mimi and her brother when they needed someone the most? At eighteen and twenty respectively, she and Aaron really had no one after their parents died and Bai made sure to either see or talk to them every single day.

Shouldn't Mimi do this for her? To ease the pain of Wei's mistreatment? To balm the sting of Jin's divorce? To protect her from the embarrassment of LilyZ's demise?

If not for her own career, and if not for Bai, shouldn't Mimi do this for Jin? Even as a teenager he'd been a spokesman for the label and the legacy his grandfather had left. Jin never once said a bad word publicly about his father. Even though he grew up in unstable chaos, Jin had always held his head high.

How many times had he had to go to the studio to make peace when Wei had upset a valuable employee? How often had a shipment been late due to Wei's indecisiveness? Or when Jin didn't even know that a vendor's bill hadn't been paid and he'd have to come good even if it meant taking money from one account to pay another?

"Aren't you hungry?" Mimi blurted to Jin, who hadn't touched his food.

"Sure. I'll eat in a bit." His voice sounded distant.

Hadn't this amazing man suffered enough? Wouldn't she do anything for him? Isn't that what her heart told her? Even though she'd never have what she wished for with him, wouldn't it be enough knowing how much she could help him by accepting his request?

Could Mimi be willing, and able, to make this dangerous move? It might destroy her. It meant a year of salt applied directly to open wounds every single day. Every night. Was she tough enough? Would it be worth it?

With one *yes* she could secure for him the thing he cared about the most. She looked at him again, chin in his hand, staring off into space. The bond they'd create by doing this together would transcend romance.

Or would she really always be hoping against hope that something more would blossom?

That would be her personal battle to fight. A measure of her devotion to him.

She reached across the table for Jin's hand. He took hers, absentmindedly, while still lost in thought. The shiver went through her, as it always did when she had any physical contact with him. But touching could be kept to a minimum, and only for show.

She was going to do this.

For the people she cared about.

For the only man who ever mattered to her.

"Mamabai," Mimi began, unsure of the words to use but propelled forward by an unseen force. "We have something to tell you."

His eyes opened in surprise.

"Yes?" Bai signaled her attention.

"Jin and I have decided to get married."

Jin's mother looked to him in shock. "You and Mimi? Married?" A wise grin came across Bai's pale lips.

Eyes darting back and forth across the room, Jin knew he needed to respond. After Mimi had initially refused his proposal, it seemed she'd changed her mind. She had, however, neglected to inform him of the news.

He turned to her with a squint. She had taken his hand when she made her announcement. There they were still, linked at his kitchen table.

Ready. Set. Go. He began the hoax by stroking the top of Mimi's hand with his thumb. Even though he'd held her hand a hundred times before, he was surprised again by its remarkable suppleness.

"Yes, Mom, we wanted to tell you when we were home alone, that's why we didn't say anything earlier today." Jin's mind suddenly whirled with all the truth-bending and excuses this arrangement was going to necessitate.

Mimi concurred with a lilt to her head that was almost a parody of a blushing bride. She released his hand. Strangely, Jin instantly missed her touch.

Tears pooled in Bai's eyes.

"Mom."

On one hand, he'd like nothing better than to make his mother happy. On the other, he and Mimi were now out-and-out lying to her, and he didn't anticipate how uncomfortable that was going to make him feel. All in all, though, Jin believed this masquerade was for the best so he bowed his head to Mimi with a silent gratitude he hoped she'd register.

"I have to confess," Bai said as she placed her hand at her neck, demurely composed. "I've always wished for this. In my heart, I've long thought you two belonged together."

"You did?" Mimi asked.

"Look how you've stayed the best of friends all through the years. You've supported each other through thick and thin. You laugh together. You've cared for each other. Haven't we seen that's what matters?"

"That's the conclusion we came to," Mimi piped up. "After Helene and after Gunnar, Jin and I realized that what matters is our friendship. That we could grow a life together out of that. We decided to make a practical decision and partner up."

How was Mimi saying all of that so calmly? She was a brilliant actress.

Right before his very eyes and ears, Mimi was solving his first set of problems. He'd inherit LilyZ as was his due. He wanted to grab her and hug her and thank her a million times over for that alone.

He vowed to himself he'd make this worth her while. He wouldn't ruin anything for her. She'd have her big and true love later in life. This was just for a year.

"Jin has been so good to Aaron and I." Mimi smiled sweetly to her future mother-in-law. The thought of which again caused Jin to flinch a bit at the lie they were espousing.

"You two have meant just as much to me," Jin chimed in. "Mimi will also sign on as our new designer."

Bai's eyes danced with her continued delight. "Yes. As it should be."

"We figured it would make more sense outwardly if we got married at the same time. So that people will understand us as a design team and not focus on Mimi's lack of experience."

"It will be my honor, Mamabai, to help grow LilyZ to where Jin wants to take it."

In that moment, Jin wanted to take Mimi in his arms and give her a kiss, as a soon-to-be groom would. He wasn't sure if the impulse was to put on a convincing show for Bai, or simply out of appreciation. In any case, he held himself back.

"Have you thought about your wedding?" Bai asked excitedly.

Jin most certainly hadn't, as this was all happening so fast. With Helene, he'd had a traditional wedding. They'd walked down an aisle, him in a tuxedo and Helene in, now that he thought about it, an awful puffball of a wedding dress.

As a matter of fact, Mimi had been one of the brides-maids, looking better than the bride in a simple pewter-colored gown. They'd had a reception with a deejay and food he couldn't remember before departing on their honeymoon to Bermuda where Helene ordered cocktails with breakfast every day.

"I think under the circumstances, given that Jin and I are old friends, and that it will be a second marriage for him, we should just have a courthouse ceremony with you and Aaron in attendance," Mimi answered Bai.

"I thought you always wanted a traditional wedding," Bai said. "Wasn't it a tasteful gown with forest green velvet trim and a pearl headband rather than a veil?"

Mimi mulled that over, a troubled expression coloring her pretty face. She said finally, "I was a lot younger then."

Jin and Mimi needed to talk about this in private. He did not want her disappointed.

Bai gushed. "I'd like to do something for you kids."

"We're not exactly kids," Jin protested.

"Let's have some friends join us for a nice dinner somewhere. Mimi, can I buy you a dress?" Bai still didn't know that every dime she spent came out of Jin's personal pocket, that in reality LilyZ was on the brink of ruin. He and Mimi would need to turn that around.

Strangely, Jin suddenly thought that with Mimi by his side anything was possible.

CHAPTER FOUR

"WHY DID YOU shock the heck out of me by announc-
ing to my mom you'd agreed to marry me without first
letting me know?"

After they'd put Bai in a taxi, Jin walked Mimi home
to Aaron's. The cold night sky didn't empty the New
York streets as neon lights still blinked in storefront
windows, horns honked, pedestrians boldly jaywalked
and dog walkers did their diligence.

"It just slipped out."

"Slipped out? After you had given me a firm no?"

"You're angry. I'm sorry."

"I'm not angry but it might have been nice to know
I was engaged before my mother found out."

"I know. But isn't that why you insisted I come to the
Leo Berringer show? So I'd see what I could be doing
and change my mind? And that's why you invited your
mom. To tug at my loyalties."

He laid his palm flat over his chest in mock indigna-
tion. "Special Agent Mimi on the job again. You saw
through my master plan."

"It worked." Mimi hadn't actually meant to blurt

her acceptance to Bai without talking to Jin about it first. However, thinking about the career opportunity combined with her devotion to the Zhangs brought it swirling together in her brain all at once. She'd decided to leap before she changed her mind. "I hope fooling Mamabai is the right thing to do, Jin. I can't say I like it."

"Thank you for caring that much."

Later that night, she tossed and turned in Aaron's sofa bed, unable to get the day's proceedings off of her mind. She was second-guessing her decision to help Jin in a way that might cost her too much.

Reaching over to the side table, she grabbed the thimble Jin had given her as a stand-in for an engagement ring. Fitting it over each of her ten, she found it was most comfortable on her ring finger.

Twirling it around and around, she convinced herself that she could see this deal with Jin through. Although during the night, she woke experiencing a translucent hallucination of children's laughter filling Jin's apartment.

In the morning she went straight to the studio. Although it was early, Jin was already there at work and let her in.

"Good morning, fiancée," he greeted her with a friendly uptick.

"To you, too, dearest husband-to-be." If he was going to play, so was she. "Can I ask you something? It was nice of your mom to offer to buy me a dress. But do you agree that we're not going to go the formal gown route?"

"Whatever you want." He sat down at his desk then

glanced up at her. "I know you and my mom always talked about all of that wedding floof. You should have it. Someday. Wait until you fall in love and I'll throw you a huge wedding with every little detail."

Oh, that was rich! Jin was going to pay for her *real* wedding somewhere down the road. Mimi didn't know whether to laugh or cry. She stared at him, into those deep, dark orbs of his. The knife's-edge cheekbones that gave his face its exquisite angles.

He didn't have the slightest idea what he was talking about when he spoke of her finding love from which a genuine marriage grew. She did give second best a try with Gunnar, but there would be only one love for her. Always had been and always would be.

"What I was saying—" she gamely tried to regroup, her voice a bit wobbly "—is that I'd like to make a dress to wear to the courthouse, if that's okay with you."

"Of course. What are you thinking?"

"Off-white?"

"I'm sure we have some silk dupioni you can use."

"That would be great."

"And didn't my mom say you were talking about forest green velvet trim? I'm sure we have some of that somewhere, too. From the winter collection three years ago."

"That was if it was to be a gown. Let me just start a dress."

"Yeah, you might want to save that for your honest-to-goodness wedding later. Why waste it on this?"

Waste. He was referring to this wedding as a waste of good materials. She knew what he meant, that the ceremony was just a formality to put their charade in motion. Nonetheless, the words burned.

"You never know, Jin. This may be the only wedding I ever have."

"I doubt that, Mimi. Someday, a very lucky man is going to see how incredible you are. He's going to grab on to you and never let go."

The day before the wedding, Mimi was at the studio again putting the finishing touches on the dress she'd made for the occasion. After the decision to have a courthouse civil ceremony with only Aaron and Bai in attendance, Mimi could have worn something from her closet or just bought a simple suit. Instead she decided to use a modern, practical wedding between friends as an inspirational concept.

"That dupioni worked out nicely," Jin commented as he walked by. "Or is the groom not supposed to see the bride's dress?"

"I think when the groom provides the fabric and the equipment, he can do whatever he wants."

"Whatever I want." He lifted one eyebrow. "That's a bit racy, future Mrs. Zhang."

Mrs. Zhang? Flirty talk? There went another rocket launch through her body. "Jin, you hadn't mentioned me taking your name. Is that a condition of the will?"

"Certainly not," he snickered. "I'm sorry, I was just using it as a figure of speech."

Good, Mimi thought with a flashback to the kind of doodles teenage girls like her made in the margins of their school notebooks. Trying on a surname with her own first name. Or as Mr. and Mrs. So-and-So. Drawing initials inside of a heart, linking her name with a pop star's.

Or, in her case, something like that.

"Let me try it on and get your opinion?" Mimi held up the dress.

"Of course."

She got up and pulled one of the privacy curtains near the mirrors that were used for fittings. She knew she didn't have to, that she and Jin had seen almost all of each other's bodies over the years. In a funny way, though, she felt more modest around him now that they were to be married. *They were to be married.* Was she going crazy or was this really happening, albeit in its own twisted way?

She rolled off the loose black sweater and slacks she'd thrown on with a coat to brave the morning. Then shimmied into the clean-lined sheath-style dress with a wide boatneck collar and three-quarter-length sleeves. Slipping off her boots, she stepped into the sling-back heels she planned to wear with the dress.

"Can you get this?" Unable to reach it herself, she moved to Jin's desk and turned her back to give him access to the zipper.

The feel of his hands on the cloth sent tingles up her vertebrae. The exquisite torture of Jin's touch. It had been known to linger in her mind for hours, days even. As a married couple, there might be more of it than ever before. Still, Mimi remained convinced that she could endure it. As she had for so long already.

What she wasn't expecting was the way, standing so

very close behind her, he tugged the fabric down at her hips. "I don't like how this is laying."

"It's a little too loose?"

He reached to his desk caddy to grab a few pins and returned to her right hip, his hands grazing her backside as he pulled the fabric in order to pin it. Her eyelids fluttered but she sprung them open.

"Yeah, take it in this much. Turn around."

She obeyed and he carefully scanned every inch of the dress. His gaze brought a tingle to her skin. Once again, nothing new. She'd had to contend with her physical response to him for so many years now. Hoping he wouldn't notice her blush, she touched her cheek to take its temperature. Hot.

"It's another good dress. I could see us working on this for a collection. With a matching overcoat?"

"I was thinking the same thing. I don't have time to do it for the wedding, but it's not like it matters for that."

Those words hung in the air for a minute.

It was to be a weekday afternoon wedding with two witnesses. If they so desired, they could wear tracksuits. With fashion in their blood they wouldn't, but they could.

"Well," Jin reasoned, "I suppose we should take a few photos to send to industry press. So it isn't like our union dropped out of the sky."

"Okay."

Mimi knew she'd want to look her best simply because for the rest of her life she'd remember the day. As bizarre as it was, tomorrow she'd marry Jin.

Really, life could hardly get any weirder.

* * *

Mimi, Jin, Bai and Aaron met on the courthouse steps the next day at four o'clock. Mamabai looked distinguished in her red coat. An acknowledging smile overtook Mimi's mouth at the sight of her, knowing that she'd chosen it because the color symbolized good luck in Chinese culture.

Mimi was pleased with how her own dress had finished up. Jin insisted on expertly tailored clothing and had been right to push her for those final alterations. Looking at him now, her tall and distinguished groom in his perfect black suit and red tie, shimmers went through her anew at yesterday's feel of him adjusting her dress this way and that, as if the fabric could absorb his touch so it didn't affect her.

Her brother, who had kindly left work early, stood handsome himself in a pinstriped suit.

Bai presented Mimi with a bouquet of pale pink roses.

"You remembered."

"I'm proud of you, son," Bai said as she pinned a single rose onto Jin's lapel. He kissed his mother's cheek.

Jin held out his elbow for Mimi to slip her arm through. Aaron took Bai's hand. Together, they ascended the courthouse stairs.

Even though this was to be a fake marriage, it seemed wrong to Mimi that her parents weren't there to witness it.

The short ceremony felt as if Mimi was playing a role in someone else's drama. She'd reminded herself enough times that this wasn't for real. So much so that the masquerade came naturally. Aaron knew the truth. It was a show really only for Bai's benefit.

After the officiant pronounced them husband and wife, Mimi turned to Jin to give him the cursory kiss their charade dictated.

What happened next left her so dizzy she had to reach for a chair-back in the courtroom to steady herself.

Because when Jin's lips touched hers, the ground beneath her crumbled.

His mouth took possession of hers, claiming it, giving her no option. It was a captivating kiss that offered no escape. His parted lips were insistent, passionate even. They conveyed merging and synthesis, joining and amalgamating into one entity.

The kiss was far too intense and went on for far too long.

It was a kiss between two people who had just consecrated their love.

"From this coupling may great things grow." Bai led the champagne toast at the austere hotel restaurant. "To happiness. To prosperity. To children."

Children? Jin hadn't thought to consider that in marrying Mimi, his mother might assume that they were not only planning to expand LilyZ but the Zhang family as well. He knew that ultimately an heir was expected of him.

It's what his family had been doing for over a century in the fashion business. One generation passing skills and knowhow down to the next. Helene hadn't wanted children, so Jin had pushed the issue away.

If he was being honest, Jin would have certainly wanted them had his marriage worked out. He'd adore showering his kids with love and praise and attention. To give them the father he never had. It was too late now, though. He'd never have the perfect family he might have imagined.

In a year, he'd set Mimi free to have all her wishes come true with someone else. Whereas Jin was resigned to spending his life alone, plain and simple. The damage from his past was unfixable.

"To Jin and Mimi." Aaron gamely echoed Bai's toast and lifted his champagne glass as the four of them clinked.

With big brother protectiveness, Aaron had made Jin promise not to hurt Mimi or violate this unusual arrangement. Something Jin worried he might have already done, and they'd only been married for a couple of hours.

"Send another bottle of champagne to room—" Bai turned away from the waiter she'd flagged "—what is your suite number?"

"Penthouse Four." Jin's mother had insisted in booking them into what was sure to be a lavish hotel suite for their *wedding night*.

"Send them chocolate-covered strawberries. And a fruit and cheese plate."

The waiter nodded and left the table.

"I'd still like to treat you to a honeymoon," Bai continued. "How about a couple of nights in Miami or Las Vegas?"

"Oh, Mamabai, thank you," Mimi piped in to cover for them, for which Jin was grateful. "But Jin and I want to get right to work. Everyone is in town for Fashion Week and we want to have something to show them."

"Maybe afterward?" Bai took another sip of her champagne. "In any case, I hope you'll enjoy your evening together tonight."

Jin's mind spun like a top. First of all, when he thought about this marriage ruse he hadn't yet envisioned a wedding night for him and his pretend wife. With Mimi, or with anyone else for that matter. Once they were away from Bai, he'd need to put Mimi at ease.

Secondly, something strange had happened at the courthouse and Jin was sure he was going to have to do some backtracking. He'd promised Mimi, as he would have anyone who agreed to the setup, that nothing of a romantic nature would be demanded of her other than superficial displays of togetherness when they were in public.

Somehow, though, after the officiant pronounced them husband and wife, Jin had ignored what was going on and gave Mimi a kiss that went past the harmless affection they'd always had for each other.

Was it the actual wedding vows spoken that made time freeze for a moment? To where his mind was wiped clean of the memory that he had once been married, a grave error in judgment that left him with enough scars to last a lifetime? And void of the thirteen years he and Mimi had known each other in friendship?

Jin peered over at Aaron and admonished himself for already breaking his promise to his friend.

Because once his lips made contact with the velvet that was Mimi's mouth, he'd cushioned into the kiss as if they were floating on a cloud. For a minute, he was immersed in the pleasure of connection that he'd been so sure he'd never have in his life. For a second, he'd enjoyed his own desire and optimism. For a moment, he'd been a blissful groom. And Mimi his gorgeous bride.

So smooth and warm were Mimi's lips that he let the joining linger longer than he should have although, if he was being honest, not as long as he would have liked. His core fought to shut out his mind. It almost won, as his reaction to her jarred through him like electricity. It almost angered him, his body's reaction to her.

After the aura had swirled around them, encircling him and Mimi in an embrace that felt too real, he snapped back to his senses and pulled away. He saw that the expression on her face was shock, and maybe upset.

Jin swore to himself that he would never, ever, let that happen again. He owed his old friend Mimi that much. In fact, he'd have to choose his words and actions with the utmost care from here on in. Absolutely no more accidental kisses or touching. It was up to him to set parameters for anything physical between them, be it to fool Bai or anyone else they wanted to convince of their marriage. He needed to take the lead on that.

As they said good-night to Bai and Aaron, Jin had some trepidation that there was now nothing left to do but go up to the suite and *not* behave like newlyweds.

When he opened the door into the posh penthouse

forty-three floors above the Manhattan streets, Jin noted to himself that he would not be lifting his bride over the threshold as was a custom. He stepped in and held the door wide for Mimi. As soon as she entered, she kicked off her shoes.

"This is spectacular," Mimi said, walking over to the glass wall to take in its view of the city and of Central Park. Manhattan was magnificent from this elevated view, with the grid of the park surrounded by the majestic buildings that lined it.

Jin joined her to survey the vista. As they pointed to a few recognizable landmarks, he pushed out of his consciousness the blossoming sadness that reminded him that this was not an authentic wedding night.

That he wasn't in love.

Nor loved in return.

Between his father and Helene, he'd thought any longings he might have once had were thoroughly squashed into the ground. It was disturbing to realize they weren't. Even though Mimi was beside him, loneliness tore him up inside.

At the moment, though, her comfort was all that mattered.

"Would you like to get changed?" he asked.

Their bags had been sent up, and Mimi quickly retrieved what she needed and slipped into the bathroom.

Jin took off his jacket and hung it over one of the chairs at the table. Shoes off, his feet took note of the plushy carpet, as he was used to wood floors. The large space had two couches upholstered in slate gray facing each other with a stone coffee table in between.

Farther into the suite was a bedroom. Jin noticed the one king-sized bed, opulently appointed with a striped duvet that echoed the white and gray of the furniture fabrics.

Jin had already decided that since it was Mimi he was embarking on this phony wedding night with, they could probably share the bed when it was time to sleep. They'd slept together plenty of times before, on vacations or long weekends over the years.

If he'd married a stranger, he might offer to sleep on one of the couches, and he'd be happy to if Mimi preferred.

Even though it was his pal Mimi, in actuality his plan felt more awkward than it had in his mind. That kiss at the courthouse had really thrown him for a loop. What was happening to him?

"So, this is weird," Mimi said as she exited the bathroom.

"I know. I'm sorry. My mom planned it before I had a chance to say no." He pointed to the room service items that Bai had ordered.

"She's really happy. I hope we don't break her heart when we call this off after a year."

"We'll take it one step at a time."

Mimi busied herself laying out her *wedding* dress. They'd already discussed how that dress done in a bold color, but keeping its slim fit and midi length, might make its way into a collection, so they'd be sure to carefully return it to the studio as a prototype.

When Mimi was in the bathroom, Jin had to admit to himself he'd had a minute's dread as to what she was going to appear wearing. He'd hoped it was nothing provocative as might befit a bride on her matrimonial night. Mimi had looked good in the clingy pajamas she'd had on at Aaron's apartment the night Jin proposed to her. She was sexy in just about anything. That was torment he didn't need. He was still a breathing, responsive man, after all.

For her wedding night, she'd chosen a soft cotton nightgown with spaghetti straps and a matching robe, both in a sweet sky blue. Yes, her voluptuous body was on full display with the fitted design and the low cut at the bosom. And yes, Jin's hips made an uncontrollable sway forward, which he quickly took control of and stood straight.

After this year was up, he reasoned, he might need to start having sex with some regularity. Nothing serious ever again, but his body ached for release.

Needing an activity, he uncorked the champagne and poured two flutes.

"To you, Mimi." He lifted his glass to clink hers. "I will never be able to thank you enough for this. You are a hero."

"We're all lucky to have each other."

Mimi sat down on one of the couches and Jin joined her.

"You know what those remind me of?" He pointed to the copper lampstands on the side tables with a recollection from years ago.

"That cabin in the Adirondack mountains."

"The wattage was so low we could barely see our way around."

"Your arms got ravaged by mosquitos."

"You were kind enough to put ointment on them but we had to hold candles up close to my arms to even see the bites."

They both laughed. Many adventures had already been shared by them.

"Why wasn't Aaron there? I can't remember."

"He got sick at the last minute."

"Oh, right. The owner wouldn't cancel the reservation. So just you and I went."

Mimi turned away from him as she stared at an abstract painting on the wall.

Funny that tonight he would recall that trip. He'd often thought that if anything romantic was ever going to happen between him and Mimi, it would have been that night. He had been twenty-two and she twenty. Unexpectedly alone once Aaron wasn't able to come.

They'd decided to use the fireplace and the cabin was toasty with the smell and crackle of the fire. Like a couple, they'd lain in front of the crackling logs on a thick rug while sipping hot chocolate from oversized mugs.

The way her body had sprawled on the rug that night, looking like a row of sand dunes with her perfectly rounded hills and valleys, had sent his hormones into high gear and he hadn't been able to take his eyes off her.

Aaron and some of the other guys they knew used to tease Jin that he had an enviable fantasy come to life with his family being in the clothing business and him, therefore, getting to be around fashion models all the time. It was true that during fittings at the studio there was never much in the way of modesty and from a young age Jin had seen pretty models, often in their underwear.

His grandfather Shun had spoken to him about it early on. How they were in an unusual business that Jin needed to understand. He wasn't to stare at the women's bodies. They were only doing their job. Certainly, Shun's resolve was easier said than done and there were plenty of times Jin had had to avert his eyes or, at least, tell himself not let his gaze linger too long.

But he'd learned. And perhaps from the overexposure, it came to be that he found he was not attracted to a female's body parts like some men might be. He discovered that he only liked a woman if he liked her essence, something about the whole of her. If he felt good around her.

He thought he'd felt that way about Helene but it turned out to be only an illusion.

That night snuggled up with Mimi at the cabin in front of a roaring fire gave him an awareness he'd never forgotten. In addition to allowing himself to appreciate her shape, he was so at ease with her. They'd lain there for hours, listening to music and shifting positions every now and then. He recalled lying on his back and she'd put her head on his stomach. From the angle she placed herself at he could smell her freshly washed hair and he'd actually had to instruct himself not to touch it.

If he was ever going to instigate anything romantic or sexual between them, it would have been then. But he'd held himself in check. Besides, he had no idea what she would have thought of any advance he might make.

There was something young and innocent about her that signaled to him she was off-limits.

They'd never talked about it. He remembered chanting to himself *she's your best friend's little sister.* That's what she'd always be. Nothing more.

"That ended up being a fun night," Mimi wistfully reminisced as well. "You were able to start a fire. I was impressed since we were such city kids."

"I was hoping you would be."

"We didn't have these," Mimi said as she got up from the couch and retrieved the tray of chocolate-covered strawberries. Sitting back down, she held one by the stem and brought it to Jin's lips. He bit into it, the hard crack of the chocolate coating filling his mouth with sweet tastes and the juiciness of the fruit underneath.

As he watched Mimi eat one, fitting the strawberry between her full lips, desire washed over him. For her? For a woman's touch? For a true wedding night? He didn't know which. All he did know was that the evening was becoming a punishment. Would it never end?

Because starting the next day, the Zhangs would set off on a partnership Jin needed to be a step forward in all of their lives.

CHAPTER FIVE

MIMI WOKE UP in the hotel suite to watch through the floor-to-ceiling windows as a heavy downpour of snow blanketed the city. While the beautiful sight was comfy viewed from under the thick duvet in the luxurious bed, the empty cool space her hand reached for let her know that she was in the bed alone. Her husband, and what a shock it was to think those words, was no longer creating the body heat that had kept this bed warm all night long.

"Do you want coffee?" Jin's voice came through the doorway before he did. Bearing a cup and saucer of the hotel's signature dishware, he rounded the side of the bed and laid it down on the nightstand. It needed no confirmation, one look told her that the cup had just the right amount of milk, as they'd certainly learned over the years something so basic as how one another liked their drinks.

"Thanks." She sat up and wiped sleep from her eyes.

What Mimi might not have learned yet was how to sleep in the same bed as her husband without experiencing a warm flush pulsing through her body all night long. Yes, she'd shared a bed with Jin before. If she was being honest, it had never been easy to sleep next to the man who inhabited her dreams. But nothing was like being with him in a hotel suite on her wedding night.

Wedding night! With memories of the kiss he gave her at the courthouse that went beyond the conduct this little masquerade they were enacting required.

"Did you sleep well?"

In reality, she was bleary from the long night during which she thought dawn would never come. She didn't say anything in the dark hours because she didn't want him to know that she wasn't able to sleep.

"Maverick Choi is having a party at his showroom tonight. I think Amanda Boswell will be there. I'd like to talk to her."

Mimi knew Amanda Boswell was one of Jin's retailers that he needed to keep in good contact with as he wasn't delivering a collection for this season.

There was Jin, always thinking practically. In a little while, they'd take showers, check out of the hotel and go downtown to the studio to work. He'd sent a memo to LilyZ employees and a simple notice to the press about their marriage and naming Mimi as his designer. Neither of them knew how the news would be perceived. And no one would ever find out what had happened, or hadn't, in this hotel room on their wedding night.

Jin sat at the side of the bed while she sipped her coffee, perhaps both of them not ready to face the world or its expectations. Inspecting the most handsome profile in all of creation, a gush of sadness washed over Mimi about what her marriage didn't mean.

When Mamabai had toasted them at the hotel restaurant, she'd spoken of children and Mimi had had to
hold her breath not to let any emotion show. Children
were always in the future she'd imagined for herself.
Although she'd be lying if she said she'd fantasized
about the father of those offspring being anyone other
than the man beside her now.

Jin reached over to take her cup so that he could
have a sip.

Mimi was mesmerized as the swallow produced a
bob in the Adam's apple of his long elegant neck.

Last night, after they'd had champagne and nibbles,
there was eventually nothing left to do but go to bed.
Jin had offered to sleep on one of the suite's couches,
as they'd agreed it would be most appropriate for the
two old friends who had just made a deal to serve everyone's interest.

They'd said their good-nights and Mimi had gone to
bed, although she hadn't closed the door separating the
living area from the bedroom. She'd seen no reason to.

As soon as she'd lain down on the bed anguish came
over her and the brave face she'd worn all day crumbled.
Would she ever have a real wedding night? Fall into the
arms of the man who would be her cohort in triumph
and in struggle? A partner to satisfy the passion that
she kept bottled up inside? With whom she might fulfill
her wish of having children? Who she'd have to lie to
and never tell him about the man downtown who held
her heart in his large hands?

She wasn't sure exactly why last night Jin had
brought up that cabin in the Adirondacks from oh, so

long ago. Maybe he'd remembered that weekend as she did, as the one time something physical beyond friendship almost transpired between them.

Throughout the years, Mimi had wondered about that night, lying by the fireplace with her head on Jin's toned stomach. If she had wiggled up to his face and given him a kiss would she have been refused? She could have never withstood the embarrassment of the rejection if it had come.

There was something in the air that evening, but she'd never know if he felt it, too.

Either way, it would have changed the dynamic between them forever. Thank heavens she hadn't acted on the impulse, to bring her parted lips to his for a kiss. She'd pictured him taking her into his strong embrace, within the wingspan of his broad shoulders. Maybe rolling her over to lie on her back where he'd get on top of her, as they learned the few things left that they didn't already know about each other.

Wisely, she had done nothing of the sort that night. She knew it was too great a chance to take. That while she and Jin might have succumbed to the moment, there was too much potential for agony in the morning. Yet that night after he'd fallen asleep, in the cabin's rustic bathroom mirror, she'd watched as the tears streamed down her face.

She needed to remember that pain. As this year passed, Mimi had to make sure she had some of herself still left at the end, that her feelings for the man she couldn't have didn't eat her alive. Because she had to believe that someday she'd meet a different man, who might want to be with her forever. For her, not just for a business agreement.

Last night, just after she'd had those thoughts during the twenty minutes or so of silence in the large suite, Jin had padded into the bedroom. "Are you still awake?"

"Yeah."

"The sofas are too soft. Can I sleep with you?"

"Of course."

Mimi had moved sideways from the center of the bed, leaving Jin half of the pile of overstuffed pillows. The room was pitch-black but as he slid under the covers, she'd felt that signature Jin heat that she'd recognize anywhere.

They'd rested quietly beside each other on the bed. Finally, Jin had reached for her and they'd hugged. As honorary brother and sister. As two old pals.

"If we're going to be convincing as a married couple," Jin had said while she was still within the envelope of his arms, "we should learn everything about each other and not have any secrets. Tell me something about you that I don't already know."

Mimi froze.

Should she tell him who she'd voted for in the last political election? No, he already knew.

About how scared she was when during college she'd fallen forward on a crack in the sidewalk and hurt her wrist? Nope, because Jin was the one who took her to get an X-ray and talk to a doctor.

Something deeper? An honest discussion about their beliefs and values? No. They already knew how the other felt.

As far as Mimi was concerned, there was only one fact about her that Jin didn't know. The thing she could never tell. Because it was about him.

Was there ever a bigger irony than that he had asked that question on their wedding night?

"My shoes were killing me at the courthouse today." That was all she was going to give him.

"Thank you again for doing this," he'd said after several quiet beats during which he'd probably intuited that she didn't want to be grilled at that moment. They really did understand each other in a lot of ways. "And thank you for caring about my mom so much."

"What you went through with Helene was such a disappointment for her."

"I feel like I let her down."

"You met Helene. You fell in love. The way she treated you wasn't your fault."

"I shouldn't have married her." His fingertips had caressed Mimi's shoulder as his voice dropped even lower than usual. "I'm going to tell you something I never have. Looking back, I wasn't in love with Helene. I've never been in love."

The words tolled in Mimi's head as she'd lain silent, buying extra time to process the information.

Jin hadn't been in love with his wife.

He'd never been in love.

That cold fact had rushed through Mimi's veins like ice water.

"Why…" she'd stammered, so grateful they were lying in the dark so he couldn't see the shock that no doubt blanketed her face, not wanting to miss her chance to get him to answer. "Why did you marry her?"

The hand that had been on her shoulder made one long sweep down her back and pulled away, leaving her starving for its return. "She was a high-energy girl. Kinetic. There was a vortex around her. I got swept up in the excitement for a New York minute. You know there wasn't much fun going on in my house."

"Did you *think* that you loved her?" Mimi couldn't help asking. He'd never mentioned this before. Was he telling her because she was his wife and somehow entitled to know?

No. That he hadn't loved Helene had no connection to the current situation. No impact on the decisions that had just been made. Didn't change anything about Jin.

Yet the news had enthralled her.

She'd cautioned herself not to think anything foolish, like his admission might make him receptive to a genuine love if he fell into it. Even if that was the case, it still had no bearing on Mimi's life. She was just his best friend's sister. His friendly caresses would always be pulled away before they could be misconstrued.

"Love is not in my cards," Jin had said, not directly answering her question. "Look what it got my mother. Nothing but heartache. And your father? Having to watch the love of his life die. It killed him in less than a year."

That was the truth. Benjamin couldn't live without his Delia. After she had died, he'd stopped eating. Sleeping. Smiling. He suffered a massive stroke ten months after she passed away and died within days. In losing their mother, Mimi and Aaron lost both of their parents. That was everlasting love at its most brutal.

Jin had moved on the bed after his admission, farther away from her so they were not touching at any point.

He'd reiterated, "I never want to be in love." Mimi hoped Jin would remind her of that frequently. It would hurt less every time.

Fortunately it was still early when Jin and Mimi arrived at the studio, so there wasn't a full staff of employees that they were going to have to do their fake marriage dog and pony show for. The staff who were there worked quietly at the machines in the front of the studio, nodding their respect to Jin's authority. Several of them offered quiet congratulations to him and his new wife. Then went right back to their tasks.

The Zhangs went back to Jin's office area to see if they could make a little professional magic as they surely weren't making any personally.

Jin sorted through anything urgent that had come in the day before, after he'd left work early to get married.

He then pulled out a photo album from a drawer in a cabinet. He glided a hand across the cover as if to give it love.

"Here's what we reference," Jin said as he opened the album and looked at the first page. "Shun's collection thirty years ago. Office attire reimagined."

They had spoken of updating this particular theme that Shun himself had revisited over the years. Creating a uniform for a woman that was appropriate for any occasion while still being polished and comfortable. With the careful manufacturing and impeccable tailoring Shun insisted on, women had found LilyZ and stuck with it for decades. Customers said that they wore LilyZ for their entire lives, even passing on treasured pieces to their daughters and granddaughters. Nothing made Jin happier than hearing that.

"I want to do one jacket, two types of pants and two skirts." Jin confirmed what he and Mimi had already talked about and done some preliminary sketching on.

"Six blouses, but just to show the retailers we can probably get by with three for now," she added.

"I like this twill I showed you the other day," he said as he pulled one of the fabric bolts over. The other day. Before they were married. Married!

Mimi took hold of it and gave it a long rub between her fingers. "It won't look fresh all day."

"It's durable."

Mimi insisted, "Jin, I don't like it. Plain and simple."

"Listen to you, boss lady."

She chuckled. "What else have you got?"

They looked at some swatches that Jin had ordered.

"Now this I like. Stretch corduroy, cotton with a bit of spandex."

"Black? Gray?"

"That's ordinary. How about maroon?"

Jin blew out some air. "Maroon. That's radical."

"It's a new neutral. Makes a statement. Looks good on everyone."

"This." Jin called her attention to some of the photos in the album. "We have these pieces in storage."

"Okay, but details like here—" she pointed to the

waistband and pockets on one of the skirts "—are too fussy."

"Show me what you want to do."

Mimi grabbed the drawings they'd started and made refinements.

"I hate it."

"Why?"

They hovered over the drawings, their bodies grazing along one side. Mimi knew this feeling well, collaborating with Jin when they got so involved in what they were doing the world melted away. They were on a creative high. It was exhilarating. Was she imagining it or was he leaning into her even more than he usually did?

"When you take that leather pocket detail away, you're left without interest around the hips."

"Leather makes no sense," she argued.

"It needs something," he barked.

"A woman's body fills out the *interest*, as you call it."

Jin turned his head to glare into Mimi's eyes, as if he was suddenly angry. He moved the slightest bit away from her, enough for her to notice the air between them.

The dynamic had changed. It was no longer Jin with all of the expertise and Mimi looking up to every word he uttered. If she was LilyZ's designer now, she'd have to fight for what she thought was right, even if he disagreed. Which he clearly had. Why else would he have stepped away from her? Or was something else at play?

In a flash, he moved very far away, busying himself at his desk.

Things had gotten awkward, quickly.

"Jin?" After all, this was Mimi here. His friend. Who he could talk to.

Finally, his stare returned to her eyes again.

He considered his words. "I did something wrong and I want to be absolutely clear with you."

Did he think she was upset because they'd argued about the design detail?

"Uh-huh?"

"After the wedding ceremony, with my mom so delighted and the whole mood of everything…"

"Uh-huh?"

"I know that I kissed you in a way that was inappropriate. I got caught up in the moment and lost control. I owe you better than that. I'll watch myself more carefully. You have my promise nothing like that will ever happen again."

"Of course," she replied in the tiny voice, calling on the composure it had taken her thirteen years to achieve. That she finally believed was convincing. The blank wash to her face that had to wait, just like that cabin mirror so many years ago, for her to get to a place where she could let her heartache pour out.

A runway model stretched out her arms to show off her diaphanous oversized white mini dress. It hung off her slim shoulders and was as short in length as it could be while still legal. "Jin, I heard you got married. I thought you were saving yourself for *me*."

"Sorry, Girara." Jin stepped back from her, turning to Mimi who was on the other side of him. "Please meet my wife, Mimi Stewart."

"Didn't you get a catch?" the model said after blowing an air kiss to each of Mimi's cheeks.

"Indeed I did." Mimi made a big gesture of slipping her arm through Jin's. She was used to seeing Jin being flirted with, hunted even, by beautiful women. No one could blame any of them for taking their shot. He was an incredibly good-looking man with scruples and business smarts. Why wouldn't they want to be with him?

"Congratulations!" Amanda Boswell approached the circle as Girara blew away. She was a LilyZ retailer and the main reason Jin had wanted to come to Maverick Choi's showing. Probably a former model herself, Amanda stood about six feet tall and was about eighty years old. She wore a white fedora hat, a colorful kimono covering a black turtleneck, and black pants with bright blue patent leather loafers. Fashion run riot, Mimi thought while smiling gamely.

"I'm delighted to meet you." Mimi jumped in. Jin had briefed her on who was going to be in attendance.

Mimi looked past Amanda to survey the scene. Rather than a runway, designer Maverick Choi had his models walking around the showroom parading his latest looks, even inviting guests to touch the clothing if they so desired. Green-haired Choi, working a schoolboy nerd outfit with plaid pants, stood in a corner holding court.

There was some kind of cotton candy theme to the event. Pastel-colored balloons that floated all over the floor were clumsy, forcing people to kick them out of the way to get where they were going. Columns of other balloons hung from ribbons attached to the ceiling.

Waiters dressed in orange tuxedos passed around

pink cocktails, each with a rainbow-hued candy stick in them as a straw. It was a mostly well-executed concept that fit with the angelic clothes.

With Mimi's arm still through Jin's she mentally flashed on how they appeared to other party guests, who would have no reason to guess that the newlyweds were not really together. The media had reported impartially on Jin's news that he had recently married and named his wife as his new designer. Things were proceeding according to plan.

As they worked their way around the room with hellos and introductions, Mimi never let go of Jin's bicep, hard and solid under his suit jacket. She let her eyes travel sideways and upward to his straight lips. Those same lips that had kissed her for too long at the courthouse after they were pronounced man and wife. Mimi would never find out if any of the imaginings she'd had about what those lips could do were accurate. Jin had made that explicitly clear earlier today by calling his matrimonial kiss a mistake.

"You're doing great. What's the matter?" Jin bent down to whisper in her ear, sensing her unease. "Everyone has been wishing us well. Even if they're surprised I got married, they're never going to know why I did."

She couldn't tell him that it wasn't the party guests that were causing her discomfort. No, as her rib cage expanded more than it should with each breath, it was that she was doubting her ability to pretend at something she'd spent thirteen years reminding herself that she could never have.

"I'm fine," she said, covering. "Just getting used to it all."

Mimi needed to focus on company business. Even before this phony marriage, she and Aaron had been a sounding board for Jin. She knew a lot about LilyZ's history and exactly what should, and shouldn't, be discussed in a professional setting. She handled herself competently.

As a matter of fact, while Jin was called away by Amanda Boswell, Mimi entered into a conversation with a flashy French photographer clad head to toe in denim, probably twenty years older than her. He had a sarcastic take on the industry that made Mimi laugh.

Like laser beams shooting through her, she suddenly sensed Jin's eyes from across the room. He removed himself from the conversation he was having and made a straight line toward her, kicking away the balloons on the floor with annoyance.

"Jin, do you know Marc-Claude Robar?" she asked by way of introduction. "This is my…husband, Jin Zhang."

"Ah! You charlatan! You've entranced me only to tell me that you won't be mine," Marc-Claude said, pretending insult at Mimi. He turned to Jin and gave him an exaggerated handshake. "You are a very lucky man, monsieur."

"I know," Jin replied, grabbing Mimi by the arm and leading her away. "If you'll excuse us."

Jin was clearly upset. Could he have been angry that she was talking to Marc-Claude? Why would he care who she did, and didn't, chat with? Although the older man was flirting with her, Mimi was not returning the advance. She'd merely been schmoozing. It wasn't as if Jin could be thinking she was acting improperly in her role as wife. And he couldn't have been genuinely jealous, because why would he care one way or another who she spoke with?

"What's wrong?" she asked after Jin ushered her into a taxi.

"Nothing," he clipped out unconvincingly, and peered out the cab window the entire ride home. Mimi leaned her head back on the seat. As well as she knew Jin, she didn't know his every trigger, wasn't familiar with every single thing that would please or displease him. They had some learning to do. She'd let this one go.

When they got home, Jin undid the knot in his tie. With a yank, he pulled it out from under his shirt collar. A motion millions of men made all of the time. But when Jin did it, Mimi's knees bobbled.

"You'll take my room," he said as he peeled off his jacket and slung it over one of the dining table chairs. What he meant by *my* room was the master bedroom that his parents used when he was growing up, that he later shared with Helene during their marriage and where he had been sleeping alone after his divorce.

"You're going to use your old bedroom?" Mimi gestured her head in the direction of the two other bedrooms in the large apartment. One had been a guest room and the other was Jin's as a boy.

"I sent a courier to Aaron's to get your things." Jin pointed to the suitcases in the hallway. Grabbing several of them, he left only the lighter items for Mimi. With her following him, they entered the master suite.

Mimi eyeballed the bed. When Jin had ended things with Helene, Mimi remembered him talking about going from sleeping on one side of the bed to the middle like he did when he was single. How awful that had felt to him. Like a defeat, he'd said.

Mimi had experienced something similar going from Gunnar's ultraexpensive bed to Aaron's lumpy sofa.

She had expected to wear a big fat diamond ring courtesy of Gunnar Nilsson. Raised in Stockholm, the wiry blond never ceased to remind Mimi how lucky she was that he chose her to be a junior designer for his label. That should have been a warning sign right away that he was self-centered and controlling.

Their work together had included long hours at his studio that, when they were alone, had turned into middle-of-the-night erotic encounters with the famous and commanding man. Mimi had begun envisioning a future with him, full of success. Through him, she'd hoped to leave behind the shackles she wore for Jin that served her no purpose. Especially after Jin married Helene.

Swept into the domestic and professional bliss she'd thought she was living in, it took Mimi a while to realize that she wasn't happy. Gunnar had a huge ego that needed constant feeding. He was moody, turning from seemingly content to snappy and critical.

At his shop, he'd referred to Mimi's designs as *their babies*, even ones he'd had no part in. When he'd begun to take full credit for her work, reality had sunk in. Gunnar didn't care about her. Nor did she for him. She'd been trying to invent something with Gunnar to quell the constant longing for Jin that had defined her. She wanted a happy marriage like her parents had had and because she couldn't have it with Jin, she'd tried to find it elsewhere.

But no one broke up with Gunnar Nilsson! Civility at work was out of the question. He'd ridiculed Mimi until she was in tears every morning, dreading having to see him. Finally, unable to handle it, she'd quit. With no money in the bank, she'd landed on her brother's sofa. Until now. Now she faced Jin's king-sized bed.

"I bought all new bedding for you," Jin said as he put her suitcases down. "If you don't like it, I'll have my housekeeper change it."

"No, that's very nice," Mimi said as she took note of the sheets and blankets in what Jin knew was her favorite color, purple.

"You can do whatever you want with the room. Are you cooking with my mom on Saturday for Lunar New Year?" Chinese New Year celebrations were an annual tradition for them.

"Of course."

"When she comes over, we'll have to make it look like we're both living in the same room or she might get suspicious."

Right. Mimi nodded. Outside of this apartment, the world was supposed to think that Jin and Mimi were a typical married couple. Who would, naturally, share a bed. It was only behind closed doors that she and Jin would know what was to really go on here at night.

Nothing.

CHAPTER SIX

JIN WOKE CONFUSED, because in his sleep he'd forgotten he was in his boyhood room. The last few years had been spent in the master, with Helene and then without. His second wife now occupied the suite. Jin vigorously scrubbed his face with his hands as it still seemed unreal to fathom that he was married to Mimi.

The wood desk he'd used for schoolwork as a child now served as nothing more than a surface to display his old basketball trophies. On the wall were his framed diplomas from both undergraduate and business school. There wasn't much else that was personalized in the room anymore, as it had been purposed and repurposed several times over the years. Save for one photo on the nightstand of him with Mimi and Aaron smiling at the beach, not long after they first became friends.

"Good morning. Can I come in?" Mimi poked her head into the doorway.

"Uh, yeah," Jin answered, yanking up his blanket to cover more of his naked body.

"I remember that day," she said, pointing to the snapshot from Coney Island. "I didn't want you and Aaron to know how nauseous I got on the Ferris wheel. I was sick in the ladies' room so you wouldn't find out."

Jin shrugged his bare shoulders with a snicker. "Look closely at me in the picture. Can you see what a mess I was? I'd been awake the entire night before."

"Why?" Mimi sat down on the side of the bed. Jin slid over to make room for her. He wasn't certain having her on his bed when he was naked was a good idea, especially after that courthouse kiss. He reasoned that she was *on* his bed, not *in* his bed, hopefully an important distinction.

With her auburn curls tousled this way and that, and that thin, sky-blue bathrobe she favored, in his still hazy state Jin thought she looked like something out of a naughty dream. Mimi was all grown up.

"Why were you up that night?" She pressed the question.

"It wasn't long after my grandfather had died. I think I'd just wanted to talk to my dad about something, but he couldn't be bothered with me. By the time I was a teenager I was used to it, although for some reason that night really hurt."

"Oh, Jin, I had no idea that day," she said, leaning toward him to squeeze his arm. Her touch was so utterly lovely it was almost agonizing. "Shun accomplished a lot in his life but he was never able to help his son. Wei was born mean and selfish, and that's all there was to it."

Toward the end of his life—his wife Meiling having died when Jin was a young boy—Shun would have quiet Sunday afternoon conversations with his grandson. Preparing him to take over the business when the time came. "If I've learned anything about how to move through life, I learned it from Shun. How to be fair and just. How to be a leader."

"Because he always knew in his heart that Wei wouldn't be able to properly run LilyZ?"

"More than that. He felt it was his duty to teach me how to be a man because he knew my father wouldn't. But it's true that my father never wanted the company nor was he apt at running it. Fashion is what my family has done for over a hundred years, one generation to the next. He wasn't given the decision."

There was much unspoken amongst the Zhangs. Things that were simply not to be dignified with words, though they stood as elephants in every room. Addiction could be a great shame in any family. To a Chinese family, it was unthinkable. That's what it all came down to. As a young man, Wei had discovered alcohol and drugs. He'd never found a path away from them. "He made a haphazard effort to run the business, but his heart wasn't into it. My father wasn't granted choice in his personal life, either. It didn't matter that the wife chosen for him was a fine woman who might have turned his life around. His shadow was too dark to allow someone to stand near him."

Mimi glanced down.

What Jin had just said, about Wei being chased by his own shadow, had come to describe him as well. Unless he decided to change that. Which Mimi was forcing him to question. An unexpected development.

"Your mom once told me she was glad you were a boy," Mimi said, setting her eyes back on the photo at the beach.

"Because the men in your family were traditional enough to insist on siring a male heir to carry on the Zhang name. She considered it just as well that she didn't bring more than one child into a less than harmonious home."

"Hmm." Bai had never said that directly to Jin but he'd sensed it.

He remembered a father who was distant and uninterested in him. Wei demanded all of Bai's attention, although not that of a loving husband as he was more like a child himself. Jin felt shut out of the dynamic, as Bai was helpless, constantly trying to pacify her husband.

Jin had spent a lot of evenings in this room. It was often a matter of staying out of his father's way until he drank enough to fall asleep. As long as Wei didn't become upset about something, the night would pass. While, fortunately, he was never physically violent, Wei in a bad mood would blow throughout the apartment like a cold wind. Tirades, rants and condemnations were followed by sloppy apologies and promises to do better.

By his teenage years, Jin would hardly glance up from his video game during Wei's histrionics. Although, in truth, they did penetrate into his subconscious mind where they still lay unresolved.

Other evenings Wei would decide to go out, leaving Bai and Jin at home. In the wee hours of those nights, Jin would wake to hear his father stumbling in, never knowing where he'd been. Or he'd hear his mother crying alone in the kitchen. The night before that beach day, Wei hadn't come home at all.

Jin couldn't have put it into words at the time, but it was a lonely childhood.

When he was grown and Bai simply couldn't take

it anymore, she'd finally divorced Wei. He could tell his mother had experienced a quiet relief after that, although they hadn't talked frankly about it until Jin's own divorce created an unfortunate empathy.

"This wasn't a house based on kinship or loyalty." Mimi returned her gaze to him. "I'm so sorry you had to grow up in that. You didn't tell Aaron and I much about it then."

"I saw how your family was so different. I think I was embarrassed." He found himself gravitating toward the Stewart household. Appreciating the tranquility, not to mention Delia's blueberry muffins that she would make especially for him.

That same sense of serenity had been settling into *this* apartment since Mimi moved in. It was nicer than Jin could have ever imagined, having her to talk to and share meals and spend evenings with. Secure. Not a word Jin would use to describe the first thirty years of his life.

Maybe now the warm winds were blowing in the Zhang family's direction.

"None of that was your fault, you know," Mimi added as the moment came to a natural close.

"Yeah, I know," he said with an elbow nudge. "Okay, get off the bed and go get dressed. You're my employee and I need you to report to work."

As soon as they entered the studio, Jin fired up his computer to many emails and messages. Fortunately, his lawyer was able to get the legalities of his and Mimi's marriage processed quickly so that Jin could see all of the financial disclosures on matters pertaining to LilyZ.

And plenty of matters they were. Unpaid debts, unresolved disputes over shipments, and unfulfilled orders, to name a few. The only way out was through sales, so he was pleased another workday toward the new pieces could begin.

"Oh, great, the maroon stretch corduroy came in," Mimi said, noticing a bolt on the counter. She called over, "Do you like it?"

"Let's cut a skirt so we can see how it drapes and moves. I saw your muslin mock-up but go ahead and use the fabric."

They'd spent the past few days fine-tuning the ideas for the comfortable work wear set, debating over every last detail. Which Jin appreciated. It was going to take more than one opinion to turn the label back to the elite and profitable company it was in years past.

Mimi kept track of trends so she knew what was current. Something Wei hadn't stressed, adding to the reasons why the business had faltered from its prior glory. Shun had an unspoken promise to his discriminating customers that he'd keep them up to date without being faddish. In his heyday, loyal customers often wore nothing but LilyZ. Jin hoped he could someday experience that same pride as his grandfather.

Mimi set to work and very quickly manufactured a skirt that she held up for Jin's perusal.

"What size did you cut that?" he inquired, as obviously it was not in the usual industry standard.

"Not a sample size," she called over her shoulder as she stepped behind a privacy curtain to slip her pants off and put the skirt on. "One that fits me."

"We are really going to pull this off in a full range of sizes?"

"We'll do it in the sizes that fit our customer. She's not runway."

"Agreed." Another aspect of the business Jin's father Wei had ignored was producing a size range that fit all women. Many potential customers were excluded because of that.

"I've been concentrating on how this would look on every body type." Skirt on, she strode over to Jin's desk with a slightly exaggerated sashay to get some swish out of the fabric. "From an average size, to a larger girl like me to someone petite."

Watching Mimi's hips swing from side to side, Jin was almost distracted from the skirt's design. Her femininity was so overt.

Honing his attention on the garment, he got up to circle Mimi as she modeled. He did like the drape of the full skirt, the length falling just above her knees.

"What do you think? The bit of spandex makes all the difference."

"We won't get the stretched-out look as the day wears on that I was worried about."

"Corduroy is perfect for that nineteen-seventies vibe you like."

"The jacket is the trickiest."

Jin knelt down to inspect the skirt's hem.

"I don't like that geometric pattern," he said, "on the swatch for one of the blouses."

"It's better than the one with roses."

"That sort of rose collage? I like that."

"No. That screams too sweet."

"It's kind of retro."

"No."

"Okay, boss," he said, glancing upward while still crouched on his haunches in front of her.

From his vantage point looking up, she was nothing less than a goddess. Despite a lifetime in the often cruel preconceptions of fashion and beauty, Jin was always attracted to womanly figures, not the ultrathin bodies the industry had chosen to carry the clothes.

While he had tried not to think about it too much in the past thirteen years, he'd always found Mimi to be the sexiest woman he'd ever known. A fact that had been cropping up unanticipated as they settled into their life behind closed doors.

It's just Mimi who you've known for years, he'd been telling himself.

Nonetheless, feelings of attraction to her were growing harder to ignore with so much time spent together. Earlier this morning when he'd confided some things about his childhood he'd never said before, he had to rein himself in from hugging her on his bed while naked, which would have been highly inappropriate.

Last night he had done his best to avert his eyes when they were watching television and that maddening blue robe of hers edged open, giving him a glance of bare leg that stretched almost up to her waist. Or, the other morning when, after her shower, she'd breezed past him in the kitchen and the whiff of her light perfume produced a shocking clench in his core. Never considering that living with her was going to be a challenge to his manhood, he needed to gain control of those responses.

They had so much to accomplish together. He couldn't afford to mess anything up.

Jin had surprised himself at the Maverick Choi show, seething with jealousy when he saw that creep Marc-Claude Robar taking up too much of Mimi's time. He was almost mad at Mimi for it, which was unfair.

It was no responsibility of hers that Marc-Claude appreciated Mimi's charms. Yet all Jin could think about was splitting the two of them up, which he did by impulsively taking Mimi home.

His ex, and his father, had turned Jin into a jealous beast. He'd never put his faith in a woman's promises of fidelity again. After all, Helene had stood up in a white gown in front of a hundred people and lied through her teeth. She hadn't been faithful to him for one minute of their relationship, despite her wedding vows.

Not that he thought Mimi would ever deceive him.

What about him? What if he followed in his father's footsteps, if there was some kind of genetic code that led him to become a cheater? Just like children who were abused sometimes grew up to be abusers.

No, Jin was most definitely done with relationships.

Which is how this phony marriage to Mimi came about. No love, no promises, no romance, no disappointment.

Yet it was he who began with a rocky start right off the bat. Because the judge hadn't pronounced Jin and Mimi husband and wife but one minute before he gave his bride a kiss that neither of them would ever forget.

He couldn't stop ruminating over it.

It wasn't planned. It had come out of nowhere. He'd regretted it the moment he'd done it. Then, worried that he might have confused Mimi by saying one thing and doing another, he apologized and promised her it would never happen again.

Furthermore, her reaction had confused him. He'd hoped that she'd be relieved by his apology because he'd assured her that nothing physical was going to be required of her in this marriage contract.

Instead of reassured, she'd seemed disappointed.

Just as it had been the first time around for Jin, marriage was complicated.

"Mamabai, mine always come out lumpy," Mimi said in a singsong voice although she was only half joking.

"No, they're wonderful," came Bai's encouragement. The two women stood side by side at work in the Zhangs' kitchen. "How many years have we been making dumplings to commemorate Lunar New Year?"

"This is our fourteenth. You taught my mom and me how to make them not long after we met you."

Once the boys became friends, Bai had invited Delia over to enjoy some of the festivities of the Lunar New Year, the most observed holiday in Chinese culture. Mimi's mother had dragged her along.

Mimi was, of course, reluctant at the time. The last thing she'd wanted to do was go to Jin's house. She'd felt nervous and clumsy around her brother's extraordinarily handsome friend with the low speaking voice.

At fifteen years old, Jin was the first boy that she'd ever been physically attracted to.

Not quite understanding her feelings in the beginning, all Mimi knew was that her body overheated when Jin was in the room. Her breath labored. When he looked at her, she could actually sense her face reddening and she'd leave the room mortified. It took her at least a year until she could share a meal at the same table with intense Jin Zhang.

"I remember, Mimi," Bai replied. "Your mother said she used to take you and Aaron to the annual New Year's parade when you were young children but had fallen out of the habit. Let's switch to the vegetable filling."

Bai and Mimi had already made a tray full of dumplings with the minced chicken stuffing. They went through the same preparations as they did every year. A constant that meant so much to Mimi, especially after her mother had passed away. It was lovely that Bai included Mimi and Aaron in her family's New Year's celebrations.

Mimi came to later understand that it meant a lot to Bai as well. Wei was often not around, out drinking or with his latest conquest, having no regard for family traditions. Rather than have the occasion marked by her and her only son being abandoned on a holiday meant for family togetherness, Bai brought the Stewarts into their fold. Something which gave her great pleasure.

For the dumplings they made a dough, rolled it out thin and cut it into round discs. Then they made the fillings. One with chicken and onion. The second, a mix of vegetables with beautiful flecks of orange carrots and green cabbage, were particular favorites at the Zhang house.

A small spoonful of the filling went onto the dough and then it was pinched together to form a packet symbolizing prosperity and letting go of the old to bring in the new. They would then be steamed and devoured.

"Thank you for always letting me cook for New Year with you, Mamabai."

"This is *your* kitchen now, Mimi. Someday I hope you'll do this with your own children."

Mimi bit her lip and continued her task with her head down. As far as Bai was concerned, Mimi and her son Jin were two dear friends who had decided to make a life together. Bai was never to know that wasn't the case, that the motivation was something different entirely. The business agreement would be over in a year.

There would certainly be no children born of their deal. Although they'd go along and let Bai think otherwise. Goodness knew the woman deserved any happiness they could give her. She'd been through so much already.

Mimi wouldn't personalize the kitchen, this flat, in any way even though she was theoretically the *woman of the house*. Giving herself any visual indications that she was living here as Jin's wife was a bad idea. She should leave everything as it was so that she wouldn't forget the temporary nature of their arrangement.

In anticipation of Bai's arrival today, Jin had lugged all the belongings that he had brought into his boyhood room back into the master bedroom so that Bai would assume they shared a bed as husband and wife. It was an exercise that Jin felt he had to perform.

Ironically, it was in his childhood room a couple of days ago that Jin had divulged to Mimi some of the hidden scars he wore that were born under this roof.

How diametrically opposite Mimi's childhood had been to his. While she knew nothing was as perfect as it seemed, her parents' marriage had appeared idyllic. A home filled with compassion and work they cared about—Benjamin was a college professor and Delia had a small accounting business—and the knowing gazes they had only for each other were seared forever into Mimi's mind.

They would go out for their date nights two Saturdays a month, Delia telling Mimi that it was important for a married couple to make time just for themselves away from their kids. Benjamin would pretend he was interested in the romantic movie that Delia wanted to see, even when the new action film he'd been looking forward to had just opened.

Benjamin had also been to every doctor's appointment with Delia as cancer had slowly claimed the love of his life.

"You know," Bai said, turning Mimi's attention back to forming dumplings into parcels of savory deliciousness, "I grew up just like Jin did, a Chinese American New Yorker. But once I had him, I decided that I wanted to create some Chinese traditions for him so we started acknowledging the New Year beyond simply going to the parade."

Mimi had heard all of this before but listened to the familiarity of Bai's voice. One thing she didn't know anything about was Bai's relationship with Jin's ex-wife

Helene. With this fake marriage clout, she felt emboldened to ask Bai whether or not she truly liked and approved of her first daughter-in-law.

"Mamabai, did you ever cook with Helene?"

If she had, it wasn't during Lunar New Year. The Stewarts were always invited to the Zhangs' house for the occasion. Mimi had done her best to have a cordial relationship with Helene even though the thought of her with Jin was like a sore picked to bleeding point. But Mimi couldn't think of a time when she'd seen Bai and Helene in the kitchen together. In fact, she'd never seen any real closeness between the two of them. Perhaps they had moments, but Mimi had never witnessed any.

"Cook with Helene? What do you think?" Bai snickered with a quirk to the corner of her mouth.

Mimi's impression of Helene was that of a superficial social butterfly. Always a kiss on both cheeks to everyone. Then she'd launch into a dishy recap of the last fabulous party she'd been to. She was the kind of person who never once asked how someone was doing.

"Helene was not the right woman for Jin," Bai continued. "I knew it in my heart, but what could I do? It was not my decision to make. For whatever reasons he chose Helene, it was not for me to stop."

"I was sad when the marriage didn't work out for him." Mimi stuttered the half-truth. She did want Jin to be happy. And always tried to convince herself that since he would never feel for her what she wanted him to, he should find contentment with someone else. Although she wasn't sure if she ever really believed that.

Nonetheless, seeing the misery Jin went through with

Helene and the aftermath of his divorce hurt Mimi. Because for Jin to feel pain was for her to bleed, as well.

"Jin belongs with you," Bai stated plainly. "He always has."

"What?"

Bai's words gushed through Mimi like a raging river. Nobody had ever given voice to the very thoughts Mimi had never dared to utter.

"Come with me." Bai finished the dumpling she was crimping, placed it onto the tray and moved over to the kitchen sink, gesturing for Mimi to join her. Together, they washed their hands and dried them on opposite ends of the same towel.

Bai led Mimi to a closet in the hallway between the living room and the master bedroom. She opened its door.

"Did I ever tell you about the New Year's tradition of *huìqì*?"

"No."

"During the New Year period, some people thoroughly clean out their houses to rid it of any *huìqì*, or bad spirits."

The closet held a rack with coats and jackets. Folded clothes filled the top shelves and a few small boxes were stacked on the floor. Bai bent down, pulled out one of the boxes and opened it. Inside was a pair of women's shoes and a scarf.

"What are those, Mamabai?"

"Helene's. She left them behind."

"Jin kept them?"

"Not intentionally. He never noticed them. I was the one who put them in this box."

"Why?"

"For this very moment. So that when Jin was ready for love in his life again, I'd have something to throw out to make room for it."

"Jin doesn't know about this?"

"No. And if he had gotten involved with another woman who was wrong for him, I would never have shared this with her. But I'm sharing it with you, Mimi. Do you understand?"

Only too well. When Mimi told Bai that she and Jin were going to get married, Bai had said something about knowing this day would someday come. Mimi suddenly suspected that Bai knew her secret even though she had never told it to her.

Feeling exposed, whether it was warranted or not, all Mimi could do was alternate her stare between the box with Helene's things and Bai's face. Didn't Mamabai understand that Jin wouldn't love her that way? He had never considered Mimi a possible mate. Never would. It was not their destiny.

This year would pass and the two friends would amicably divorce. Maybe in time Jin would be able to open his heart to another woman after the betrayal of his first wife and the mistake of his second.

Perhaps someday Mimi would meet someone who would give her the camaraderie and pleasantry that she ached for. Someone she cared about, although never as much as the person who owned her love. Who could never be hers.

She wanted children. Maybe children would compensate for a future marriage that was likely to be more of a partnership than a romance.

The front door opening yanked her from her thoughts.

"Hello? *Gung hay fat choy*." Jin called out the New Year greeting.

"We're in here," Mimi yelled out as Bai shut the closet door and they came forth to greet him.

A pleased grin came across Jin's face at the sight of Mimi and Bai. When Jin wore a happy expression it was the most glorious sight the world could ever see. It was as if he was bathed in light.

Jin Zhang, with all of his magnetism, his penetrating eyes and the smile that only broke out when it was sincere, could turn a gray sky blue. All of this discussion about finding the right person was quite simple. Because Mimi knew there was no one on the planet who compared to Jin.

He kissed his mother on the cheek. Mimi steeled herself in preparation for his kiss onto hers. She'd gotten pretty good at anticipating his kisses and cautioning herself not to read anything into them. They were only evidence of how well Jin and Mimi were performing the masquerade they were starring in.

"I have something for you and Mimi," Bai said to Jin.

"You do?"

Bai went to her coat and pulled from the pocket a red paper envelope. "Do you remember when I would give you kids eight dollars in red packets for New Year's?"

Bai always thoughtfully prepared three envelopes so that Mimi and Aaron would have a present alongside her own son. It was custom to give a gift of money for New Year's. Eight was thought to be a lucky number so presents might be amounts that were multiples of that. And red was considered lucky as well, hence the color of the envelope. Bai's gesture was always appreciated. The three friends would go off and spend it on a treat of fancy coffee or pizza eaten on the street, which never tasted better.

Today when Bai handed her the envelope, Mimi's eyes squinted at the contents. Not wanting to be tactless and count it out, she estimated Bai's gift this year was eight one-hundred-dollar bills.

"I want you to buy something for this apartment, Mimi," Bai said, and squeezed her hand. "To start making it yours."

Mimi glanced up to Jin. Both knew that they had to keep the truth from showing, had to continue this lie to Bai that they had begun.

In an instant, Mimi was holding back tears. Because this house would never be hers. Perhaps pretending otherwise in front of Bai might be more than she could manage.

Next year she and Bai would make dumplings again. Shortly after that, Jin would tell his mother that he and Mimi had decided to split up. Mimi would remember to leave some *huìqì* things behind when she moved out so that Bai could find them and throw them away if Jin was ever to find his true love.

Mimi offered, barely above a whisper, *"Gung hay fat choy."*

CHAPTER SEVEN

"Jin, come look at Mimi," Bai called out. Jin dutifully crossed the apartment to the master suite. Mimi and his mother had finished preparing the food for the New Year's feast and had busied themselves with something in the bedroom. He got quite an eyeful when he saw what.

"I haven't seen you in a *cheongsam* in years," Jin exclaimed from the doorway.

"Mamabai brought this for me. I was going to wear it to dinner tonight if you think it's okay."

The traditional Chinese dress was made of silk brocade in a bold and bright red. Gold metallic threads intricately embroidered into a leaf and flower detail decorated the entire dress, giving it specialness perfect for the New Year holiday. While the style of dress was sold inexpensively at souvenir shops throughout Chinatown, the one his mom had bought was expertly handcrafted with fine materials.

It was closely fitted, which on Mimi meant it hugged arcs and planes from every angle. The round, stand-up Mandarin collar led to the knotted cloth buttons fastened diagonally across the right side from clavicle to shoulder and Mimi's natural posture made the customary slit at the thigh look provocative.

Jin remembered the last time he'd seen Mimi in a *cheongsam*. It was before he'd met Helene. They were going with Aaron to a Lunar New Year's party at a club and Mimi's dress had been a yellow brocade with tiny pink flowers. Mimi had looked pretty that night, but he hadn't given it any further thought. Unlike the thoughts that had been cropping up since he'd made his good friend his wife.

He rubbed his chin as he watched Mimi slip on a pair of gold pumps that accentuated the embroidery in the dress. As the images and flickers that had been dancing around in his mind coalesced into a clear thought he realized that during this little playacting gig they were performing in, Jin had become attracted to Mimi. In *that way*. The way he'd promised both of them wasn't going to happen.

It had started with that kiss at the courthouse. Then solidified when they were at Maverick Choi's showing and Jin had almost blown up with jealousy when that creep Marc-Claude was making advances toward her.

Leave my woman alone and other macho combative words he couldn't articulate had shouted from his brain, and from his loins. He'd felt a primal possessiveness of Mimi that was a side of himself he'd never seen before. He had been sure he'd wrestle Marc-Claude to the ground if he got any closer.

Jin needed to separate the long-standing platonic love Mimi and he had for each other from the new and disturbing emotions he couldn't shut down. These two women in front of him, his mother and his friend, meant the world to him and he'd protect them from any possible threat. Including himself.

Jealousy. His bane. Once a man is cheated on by his wife, it's hard not to have jealousy appear as a monster gaining strength until it is set free from its own chains to run riot and destroy everything in its wake. Jin couldn't withstand any more of it. Jealousy could be the end of him. Which is why he'd vowed to guard himself, to never put himself in a position where that demon could get at him again.

For that and every other reason, he needed to shut down these unexpected desires he'd started to have for Mimi. He sincerely hoped that later in life Mimi would meet the man who would love and treat her right for all of eternity. He would be no part of denying or sullying that for her. She deserved as much.

For now, the two friends had made a business pact, and Jin needed to uphold his end of the bargain. Rebuild the label, make sure that Bai was taken care of, and help Mimi's career ascend while he was at it.

That was enough.

That was plenty.

So when Mimi turned around to get his approval on the back of the dress, her shiny, wavy hair billowing over her shoulders, he fought the surge in his body as he contemplated her lush beauty.

"We should go," Jin said slowly after a too-leisurely gander.

"Thank you for the beautiful dress and for the money," Mimi said as she and Bai hugged.

Jin liked the two of them together, always had. As an only child, Jin was glad that his mom had Aaron to fuss over and, in Mimi, the daughter she'd never had. His mother looked contented today, something he hadn't seen much of over the years. All the more reason Jin had to execute everything according to plans. No one was to get hurt.

"Let me get my coat and I'll leave with you," Bai said.

They bundled up to go out.

"Mamabai, we'll see you tomorrow. We'll go to the parade and then come back here to eat. Aaron is leaving work early."

Outside of the building they kissed one another on the cheek. Jin helped his mother into a taxi headed uptown. He and Mimi walked the couple of blocks toward the restaurant where they were meeting Dickson Wells, an A-list retailer who oversaw several of LilyZ's European outlets.

They strode arm in arm in the cold. There were lots of people going this way and that on the streets and energy filled the air. The storefronts in Chinatown were decorated for the holiday with bright banners and flags. Fashion Week often coincided with Lunar New Year, making it a busy and exciting time for the Zhangs.

At the restaurant that specialized in haute cuisine renditions of classic Chinese dishes, Jin gave his old acquaintance Dickson a hug.

"This is my wife and new designer, Mimi Stewart."

"A pleasure," the short, curly-haired man replied.

The restaurant hostess showed them to their table, where Jin ordered a variety of dishes intended for sharing.

When Dickson excused himself to take a phone call Mimi said, "Let me throw an idea at you."

"Yeah."

She leaned toward him, soft curls brushing against the side of his face. Pinching the fabric of her *cheongsam* she asked, "What if we did the blouses for the collection like this? We could do three different blouses in brocades, each of them with some traditional Chinese detailing. Wouldn't that be great as something kind of global and fresh?"

"My grandfather did some collections with Chinese styling. We could go back and find the pieces."

"It would be another nice way to pay tribute to Shun. As his grandson takes over the company."

"Hmm," Jin affirmed the idea. "I like your thinking, Mrs. Zhang."

"Why thank you, Mr. Zhang."

When he returned to the table, they tossed out the concept to Dickson, who loved it.

As Jin and Mimi trekked up the stairs to the flat after dinner, he found himself looking forward to the New Year's celebrations more than he had in ages. Maybe it was that with Mimi's never-ending stream of good instincts for the business, he had renewed hope that he'd be able to lift LilyZ back to its heights. Or it could be that his optimistic attitude was because he was finally getting over Helene, the hurt and betrayal she'd dealt him now blessedly receding a little into memory. Whatever the cause, he was grateful.

In the apartment, Jin and Mimi had gotten into a comfortable habit of giving each other a hug good-night in the hallway. One direction led to Mimi's master suite and the other to Jin's boyhood room. Their hug spot was a kind of halfway point.

A few mornings ago, Mimi had come into his room, symbolically crossing the border into what was to be only *his* space. Rather than oppose it, he'd welcomed her intrusion. He hadn't understood that he still had so much inside of him to release, and felt his burden lightened after talking to her. Maybe that was a matter of course in real marriages where people trusted each other. He wouldn't know. But found himself strangely curious.

"It was a nice day, cooking with Mamabai and then meeting Dickson."

"I'm looking forward to eating what you and my mom prepared."

"We go back a long way, don't we? A lot of celebrations."

"And bad times endured. I hope our future brings only good."

Jin reached over and ran his hand down the length of Mimi's hair, which had been bewitching him all evening. He twirled one of her curls around his fingers. An impulse so strong it overcame him insisted on three wispy kisses to her cheek. He was about to make a move he'd said he wouldn't. But as that warning flitted across his mind, he took her face in his hands and touched his lips to hers.

"I don't know what I'm doing," he confessed and kissed her mouth again. Grasping a handful of her hair, he gently pulled away so that he could look at her face. It was almost as if tears were filling her eyes. "What's wrong?"

"Nothing, Jin. Nothing is wrong."

She reached her arms up and wrapped them around his neck. His hands slid slowly from her face to her arms and down to her waist, bringing her tightly to him. Locking her against him. Experiencing her body's pliancy. Hearing the sound of her breath stutter as he explored her back, her sides, everywhere his hands roamed.

He found her lips again and delivered the kind of deep lover's kiss that he'd never shared with her. The far recesses of his brain yelled at him to stop but he was unable to. His need for Mimi had been growing. It had now become an entity unto itself that demanded liberation.

His hands hardly knew where to go next, so eager was his body to explore hers. Many more kisses told her of his need. Hers answered back, with each kiss becoming more urgent than the next. The sweet song of her sighs drove him to a near frenzy.

He lifted her into his arms, right there in the hallway. Where their separate bedrooms beckoned.

Not tonight.

They'd deal with the fallout tomorrow. It would all work out. He couldn't convince himself to heed any further warning. Tonight they would lie together in the master bedroom. Man and wife.

With her arms around his neck, he carried her toward the threshold. "Is this okay, Mimi?"

"Yes, Jin. Oh, yes."

Sounds were coming from every direction. They fueled the buzz that was already shooting through every fiber of Mimi's being. People lined the sidewalks, cheering and waving flags. The annual Lunar New Year Parade was well underway.

As always, the dragon and lion dances commanded Mimi's attention. Human participants held the long colorful costumes above them with poles, sometimes as many as a dozen just to hold up one dragon. After no doubt rehearsing for months to synchronize their movements they zigzagged and circled, making the dragons come to life. The lion dancers used martial arts movements as they charged forward along the parade route.

Every cymbal crash, gong and drum beat vibrated through Mimi. As was the intention, the loud percussion and the faces of the dragons and their aggressive dancing were thought to drive away evil. It was a spectacle of great power, one that Mimi always looked forward to.

From their perch in front of a friend's shop that afforded a perfect view, Mimi, Jin, Bai and Aaron took in the sights and sounds as they had for years. It was another constant in their lives together as two families.

In the beginning, Mimi's mother, and sometimes father, came along. If it was a year that Wei was making more of an effort to be a family man he'd be here, too. And, for a few of the years, Jin had brought along Helene. This time it was just the four of them. Time had marched on.

But there was nothing ordinary about this year.

Certainly not after last night.

The memory of which was another thing coursing through Mimi.

She darted her eyes to Jin standing next to her, bundled against the cold weather in his navy blue pea coat, scarf and beanie.

Last night.

A gong echoed through her.

After thirteen years, last night Mimi experienced what she'd tried to imagine thousands of times. When they'd finished dinner with Dickson Wells and returned to the home that kept them as a married couple, they went to bed together as husband and wife.

They made love.

And everything about it was beyond Mimi's wildest dreams.

She felt her cheeks flush, the crowd cheering around her as parade cymbals crashed while she recalled the evening. They'd been in such sync at dinner with Dickson, completing each other's sentences and anticipating the other's moves. Both sipping from the same cocktail glass not because there was a shortage of drinks but because there was something natural about it.

When they got back home, Jin punched in the entry code to the door and then Mimi switched on the front hall light as had become their pattern. After hanging up their coats, Mimi kicked off the gold heels that she'd worn with the *cheongsam* Bai had given her.

Almost to the inch, they stood facing each other at the exact spot where they'd been saying good-night to each other every evening. Where the charade of them as a married couple fell away and the two longtime friends returned to their true selves, making do in the apartment that implied truth to their lie. Where, figuratively, they patted each other on the back nightly for a con well played. With a pact to do it again the next day.

Last night, though, that wasn't what happened. When they'd reached to each other for a hug, their bodies instinctively melded into each other's in a way Mimi had believed was eternally forbidden. Up until that moment, when the barricades were blown open. For as much as Mimi had been in contact with almost every bit of Jin's body over the years, last night's touch was instantly different.

He had squeezed her to him, her flesh malleable putty in his commanding hands. He'd pressed all of his maleness, his hard angles, into her, making her feel a more feminine earthiness than she ever had before.

His mouth on hers was both familiar and brand new at the same time. While those lips and big hands had touched her before, it was in another way, with another intention. Last evening, each brush, each caress, each push forced arousal to grow in both of them. Until it couldn't be contained.

Mimi had thought to protest. To share that final intimacy with him, at last, was to fly too close to the sun. Because Jin wouldn't love her like that. What if she burnt into a million ashes when he came to his senses? Yet she'd wanted him too much for too long. She couldn't say no, she'd take her chances. There was no way for logic to prevail.

"Look," Jin said into her ear, the timbre of his voice coating over her like a blanket, as he pointed to a parade float coming into view. She instinctively leaned her face up toward his, drawn to him like a magnet. As always.

"Remember that year with those dogs dressed in red-sequined sweaters?" Mimi reminisced about a pet groomer's float that they had found hilariously funny and talked about for months after. "With the country music?"

Jin's huge smile sent Mimi's head spinning.

Like last night.

After Jin lifted her into his arms he'd carried her to the bedroom. He'd laid her down on the purple bedding he had picked out for her to sleep on alone. With tiny, slow-moving kisses from her jaw down the side of her neck, his lips had traveled as far as they could within the confines of her *cheongsam*. Confidently, he undid the buttons and slid the dress up and off her.

When she was eighteen, twenty-one, twenty-four and so on, she'd lie in bed and wonder what it would be like to make love with Jin. To taste his kisses. To feel his strength possessing her. His weight on her. His whispers in her ear.

Fantasies were one thing, but to know him in the flesh was quite another. It was infinitely more magnificent than anything she could have ever conjured in her mind. The passion gave urgency to their coupling. Yet they were able to take their time, to explore the bodies they'd never shared with each other in quite that way.

They taught each other touches both unspeakably tender and savagely intense. His every stroke, every sound, every move filling her to the brim with the life force that only he could. It was what she'd been waiting for, for as long as she could remember.

Jin brought her to the brink of ecstasy then pulled back, over and over again until she was desperate to cross over. When they had let go together, it was with an otherworldly white heat that carried them through the galaxies in each other's arms.

Standing beside him now, Mimi was half on the ground and half still soaring, untethered, in that other solar system he'd shown her.

Later, after the parade had passed by, the foursome returned to the apartment for the feast they'd planned.

"Here, Aaron." Mamabai handed him a red envelope.

"We're grown up now, you don't have to do this anymore," he replied and gave her a sweet hug.

Mimi glanced over to Jin who was reaching the top shelf of the cabinet for the gold-rimmed dishes the Zhangs used on special occasions.

What was going through his mind, Mimi wondered? Was he daring to have the same thoughts that she was? That them, together, for real, at last, felt so right? As if the moment in time was there just waiting for them to arrive at it. It was a slow journey but they'd finally made their way through the darkness to the end.

Mimi had lived for thirteen years in doubt that it would ever happen. She had had to watch her parents die, she had had to be hurt by Gunnar, she had had to see Jin marry and then suffer the agony of divorce. Had all roads led to this crossing, one they were finally ready for?

Could that be what he was thinking, too?

When the food was ready, Jin carried a steaming soup bowl to the table. Mimi dished up the long-life noodles, a customary New Year's food so named because they were said to symbolize longevity.

"These noodles really are so long," Aaron joked as he worked to capture them in his soup.

"You mustn't cut them," Bai reminded them, even though they already knew. "That would be to cut your life short."

"To long life." Jin toasted with his tea, tipping his cup toward Mimi and winking at her. Her stomach fluttered at the way he looked at her. Like they were together.

Together together.

"This year we celebrate Mimi and Jin. To a healthy and blessed life." Bai raised her cup to the middle of the table.

The other three brought their cups to meet Bai's toast but then retreated, each experiencing a moment of caution at the toast that was, in reality, a falsehood.

"Let me have another dumpling." Jin pointed with his chopsticks toward the serving plate next to Mimi.

Bai portioned the whole fish they'd cooked as an emblem of abundance.

As they finished stuffing themselves, the meal concluded with the tangerines served on New Year's to symbolize good fortune. When the evening ended,

Aaron escorted Bai downstairs to help her into a taxi before he walked the short distance to his apartment.

After Mimi and Jin straightened up the kitchen, they gazed at each other. Throughout the noise and activity of the day, they hadn't acknowledged what had happened the night before.

"Gung hay fat choy," Jin said to his wife.

"Gung hay fat choy," Mimi repeated.

From outside they could hear the revelry of the fireworks ceremony, another traditional event to ward off evil spirits.

Mimi drew Jin into an embrace that set them both aflame as they made their way again to the matrimonial bed.

"I've got to go to a fund-raiser for Dressworks. Do you want to come?" Jin asked Mimi as they walked home from the grocery store. From their haul he fished out a paper bag that held a Danish pastry.

The Zhangs had been affiliated with the charity for many years. Dressworks supplied women in need with business and formal wear to help them reenter the workforce after circumstances had left them unemployed. The organization held their primary fund-raiser of the year during Fashion Week because with so many people in the industry in town, it was an optimal time to receive the most donations.

"You go to that every year, don't you?"

"They raise a lot of money at the dinner. We've also been able to furnish some clothes."

"I can look around the showroom and back in your storage closets."

"Do you want to go to the dinner with me? It's kind of stodgy, black-tie affair uptown."

Was Jin kidding, Mimi thought to herself? Would she like to go to a black-tie fund-raiser with him? A charitable New York evening with her handsome husband. *Uh, yes.* Funny that he'd even wonder if she'd go. She supposed he was being polite in letting her know that she wasn't obligated to attend every event he went to just because she was his wife.

"Do you have something to wear?"

Mimi had been to some formal evenings with Gunnar and had a couple of gowns that he'd made for her. She wrinkled her nose at the mere thought of those. She'd rather not be reminded of anything to do with him anymore.

"Hey, would Dressworks want a couple of old gowns I have?" They were her personal *huìqì*, which she'd be glad to get rid of.

"I'm sure they would, but do you have one to wear yourself?" Jin took a bite of his Danish from its paper bag. He sensed her hesitation. "Oh, they're Gunnar's?"

"I don't mean to sound wasteful but I don't want to wear them ever again."

"I can understand. If you did and then somebody asked who you were wearing, we wouldn't want to have to say Gunnar Nilsson."

"Right."

He brought the pastry to Mimi's mouth and she took

a bite of it. Just like married couples did on the street, sharing a snack as they rushed about their days.

After all the years of picturing herself doing those little day-to-day things with Jin, it was actually happening. Her eyes took a moment to shift from left to right, to preserve in her mind the simple freeze frame of being fed a pastry from a paper bag on the block where she lived by the man who mattered to her most.

"We don't have time to make you a gown," he said, reaching over to brush flaky crumbs from her mouth. His fingertips on her lips instantly made her the thirstiest person in New York so she nicked a sip of coffee from the paper cup she was holding, and handed it to Jin who drank some and handed it back.

"LilyZ never did evening wear, did you?"

"Not that I can recall."

They resumed their walk, side by side.

"Should we call another label we like for a dress?"

"We'd have to think of who we'd want to give the free advertising. Because whatever you wear, you will be asked."

They continued in silence, both thinking.

"What about something vintage?" she asked.

"Now you're talking. You look great in those older styles. Do you know where we should go to get something?"

"I sure do," she answered, remembering some shops in Chelsea that were known for vintage formal. "All those years of charity store shopping."

"I used to love that, you know, those dresses you used to wear."

Before she started making and wearing her own clothes, Mimi would slip into any secondhand shop she encountered. Sometimes she found nothing, as was the way with vintage shopping, but on other outings she was victorious, leaving the stores with treasures folded into recycled paper bags with handles.

"You were really always into a retro look. Borrowing from the past informs all of your work."

Mimi could hardly believe her ears. While Jin had always respected her ambitions in fashion and been complimentary about her work, no one had ever so seriously analyzed her style and put it into words. It made her feel like she had a mark to make, hungry and ambitious and proud.

"What's that smile about?"

"We'll go to the vintage shop at the end of the day. I have to get some work done first. I have a very demanding boss."

After they closed up the studio for the night, Mimi and Jin headed to Once Again in Chelsea. Mimi had called the owner, who she'd met before, and asked her to put aside some dresses she thought Mimi might like.

"Hi, Mimi." Bette looked to the shop door as soon as they came in. With her black-framed glasses and a floral dress that would be described as farm chic, Bette was a retro hipster who was the perfect emissary for her store.

"Do you know Jin Zhang?" Mimi asked by way of introduction. Jin held out his hand as they approached the display case that held jewelry and purses, some looking to be a hundred years old.

"No, we've never met. I've always been a fan of LilyZ." Bette grasped Jin's hand for a shake. "Look what I just bought at an estate sale."

She reached from a rack to show them a midnight-blue blazer with black lapels.

"1984. Fall." Jin identified the jacket immediately. "Shun said his customers loved that blue."

The garment was a fine example of how Shun took a trend such as the exaggerated shoulders of the nineteen eighties but incorporated it subtly. While that was not a current fashion, a woman could still wear the jacket and look stylish and timeless.

"I can't keep LilyZ in the shop," Bette added. "As soon as I put something out, it sells."

"As I told you on the phone we need something black-tie worthy," Mimi said.

"Come in the back, let me show you what I pulled for you. Nineteen twenties to nineteen fifties."

Bette escorted them to a private area where three full-length mirrors were set up to present a three-hundred-and-sixty-degree view. Off to the side was a rack with some dresses.

They all heard the chimes of the front door opening.

"Have at it," Bette offered. "Let me know if you need any help."

"Thank you," Mimi called out as Bette left to attend to the shop floor.

"What do we have?" Jin asked as he leaned against the wall and let Mimi inspect the rack.

Bette had put the dresses in a sort of chronological order. Mimi picked up a dress from the nineteen twenties made of silvery beaded chiffon atop a gray under slip. "It's amazing how heavy this dress is," she said as she balanced its weight between both hands.

"Try it on," Jin encouraged. With the utmost care, he helped her into the delicate, well-preserved dress. After surveying he decreed, "Hello, Miss Flapper. You need one of those long cigarette holders."

Although she stood barefoot and without a hairstyle that would befit the dress, she shook her head no right away. The dress hung straight down to her calves with no shape whatsoever, as was the style then. "Look how boxy and almost boyish this is."

Jin nodded in agreement. "Does not do a curvy girl any favors."

"This beadwork is unbelievable, though." She lifted a section up from the bottom to show Jin the detail.

"Next."

"Okay, Bette left me one from the nineteen thirties." Mimi didn't need any help sliding the cream-colored satin over her head. With the bias cut and body-grazing design, it was a prime example of the era's style.

"My, my, my." Jin mimed fanning himself as he made an ultraslow study of her from top to bottom. "That's too sexy on you. It looks like a nightgown. Your husband simply will not permit it."

Mimi laughed outwardly. Inside, she was screaming. Jin was her husband at last. Who she'd made ravenous love with. Who had just referred to her as sexy.

Don't get too secure. This is make-believe, Mimi cautioned herself.

Although she didn't want to heed her own words.

Can I play for just a little while longer? she begged the universe. Heaven knew she'd been waiting long enough.

She checked herself out in the mirrors. With its halter top and low-cut back, the gown did look ready for the boudoir.

"Thank you, Bette—" Mimi gestured toward the sales floor "—for taking us on a trip through the decades."

"What do you have for the nineteen forties?" Jin crossed his arms across his chest, clearly enjoying the moment, as well. They were entitled to relax a little, with all the pressure they'd been under.

"Zip me in." Mimi had to carefully navigate into the next one, a mint-green gown with long sleeves. It had an elaborate sequinned appliqué of a butterfly at the waist. "I'm so unused to long sleeves on evening wear. That was the look then."

Jin scrutinized with a bit of a frown. "I'm not sure that suits you, either."

"It's too matronly on me." She rose up onto her tiptoes. "Though imagine it with heels."

"The shoulders are broad and the neckline is high with your..." He hesitated.

"Big boobs, Jin." Ever the gentleman, he had been looking for loftier phrasing.

They both giggled.

"Moving on."

"Now, the era made for my shape. The nineteen fifties."

Mimi hardly needed to take the next selection off the rack to know that it was the one for her. A strapless dress with a full skirt in black, it had white lace detailing at the sweetheart neckline and along the scalloped hem. As she unzipped it off the hanger, Jin took hold of a section because he wanted to examine the construction.

"Wow," he said softly, appreciating the workmanship. "Boning."

Indeed, on the inside of the bodice were rows of channels that allowed thin plastic strips to be sewn into the garment. "That's what you'd call structure and foundation."

"Everything stays where it should in a dress like this. Even your…big boobs," he joked with a nudge to her side. "Put it on."

"All the women will be in long gowns," Mimi said as Jin helped her into the dress. "It'll be radical if I'm in ballerina length."

"Hot young designer wearing vintage."

Mimi stretched her arms out to her sides and twirled around in the dress, still barefoot. "I love it."

Jin smiled.

After a minute of watching, he moved toward her and encircled her waist with one arm. He bolstered her against him, asking, "May I have this dance?"

Not waiting for an answer, he took one of her hands in his and began waltzing her around the dressing area, to the music of her giggles. Round and round he spun her, until she was sure she was actually at a formal ball dancing with her dashing prince.

When she stole a glance of the two of them in the

mirrors, her spirits soared higher than any time she could ever recall.

With the perfect dress purchased and being sent to the studio, Mimi and Jin left the shop. Walking down the street, she slowed in front of the window display at a home furnishings store. There was an armchair she really liked, one she thought would look good in their living room.

Theirs. Her and Jin's living room.

Maybe she'd personalize the apartment a little bit, after all.

CHAPTER EIGHT

"HOLY COW." JIN was literally stunned when Mimi modeled her complete outfit for the Dressworks fund-raiser.

"Thanks for thinking to send the hair and makeup people. They surely know what they're doing."

The strapless black dress with the white lace edging she'd picked out from Once Again was perfect, one of a kind and a real statement of fashion. Adding in the red lipstick and whatever that seductive updo of her hair was called, she looked like a movie star ready for a Hollywood premiere.

"Can you do my bow tie?" Jin asked as he crossed the apartment, needing to know which of her perfumes that exposed neck would bear the scent of. His nose was rewarded with what smelled like honey as it grazed the silky skin of her throat. His lips traveled upward for a kiss on the cheek.

"Give it to me." Mimi took the tie from him and worked it around his neck under the stiff collar of his tuxedo shirt.

"What is that hairdo called?" He had to know more about the elegant upsweep.

"A French twist."

"Oui. C'est magnifique."

She tied the bow tie and tweaked it for perfection. "Am I going to know people at this event tonight?"

"Probably not. It's more mass market garment manufacturers than small labels like ours. We just happened to get involved with this charity when someone asked my mom for a donation of clothes."

"Thanks for inviting me. I don't go to many black-tie events."

"Thanks for agreeing to come. I bought you something." He dashed into the kitchen and returned with a clear plastic box, which he handed her.

"A corsage!" she exclaimed as she opened the lid to find the three mini lilies wrapped in silk ribbon along with a pearl-tipped pin.

"I know, old school. It just seemed to go with your dress. May I?" He removed it from the box.

"That's so thoughtful of you. How adorable."

"No, it's you who is adorable. The flowers are just decoration."

She pointed to where on the dress she wanted him to pin the corsage.

Afterward she asked, "Should we leave?"

Jin removed his tuxedo jacket from the hanger that was hooked over a chair, grabbed his wallet and phone, and they headed out the door.

"Thank you. Jin bought them for me," Mimi acknowledged a gala guest's compliment on her corsage. "LilyZ was named for our founder Shun Zhang's favorite flower plus the first initial of his last name. When you think about it, isn't it rather amazing how Shun came to the States all alone and made an enduring name for himself in ready-to-wear?"

As Jin sipped his glass of champagne, he couldn't believe what was coming out of Mimi's mouth. She knew LilyZ's history almost as well as he did and had apparently appointed herself their goodwill ambassador with all the friendly introductions she was making.

"No, I never had the honor of meeting Shun."

The moneyed crowd was older and sedate. Mimi was the liveliest person there to be sure.

"We're thinking of eventually getting into accessories. Purses and sunglasses and items like that are not only good for our business, but a way for women who might not be able to afford our clothes to have a luxury piece they can cherish."

The Dressworks fund-raiser was held in an old uptown ballroom, an event space that had probably seen a thousand weddings and other social functions. Huge crystal chandeliers hung from the ceiling, overseeing the formally set tables with their white floral centerpieces, black tablecloths and too many forks at each place setting to understand. On one side of the ballroom, racks held the donations of many clothes including the surplus LilyZ items Mimi was able to find in their storage.

Jin watched a couple on the dance floor. They'd obviously learned to partner dance, the white-haired gentleman confidently leading his silver-haired lady with precise steps. Had they taken formal dancing lessons, or did they learn to waltz and fox-trot at high school dances or in ballrooms like this one? They looked like they'd been dancing with each other for a long time as the woman's tiny shoes anticipated her man's next move.

Partnering up. It was what humans did. Even some animals. Mating for life.

How jaded Jin had become. During long nights spent alone in the apartment after he'd asked Helene to leave, he'd developed a bitter and warped view. He'd come to think that most people were solitary even if they were in a relationship. That each person trudged their own path, had only him or herself to count on. That Valentine's Day and corsages and anniversaries were just advertising, and behind closed doors most people were as painfully alone as he was.

For the first time, he questioned those beliefs.

A sea change was occurring. Precisely because of their long history, Mimi was able to reach into him in a way that no one else could. She was showing him an alternative he didn't know if he was ready for. He was straddling somewhere between terrified and elated.

"May I have this dance?" he asked, hoping to get out of his own head. With an exaggerated flourish that made Mimi giggle, he sloped his arm around her waist and led them off. His hands took notice of the intricate structure of her vintage dress, throwing him back in time, like they were really at a ball.

The moment mixed in his mind with dancing with her at Once Again. Watching her at the shop, arms outstretched, spinning barefoot and uninhibited, had poured into him a dangerous sort of euphoria. One a person could become addicted to. That could make a believer out of the most jaded soul.

Except...

It was as if Cinderella's clock abruptly struck midnight. As he swept Mimi across the ballroom floor he noticed the older couple that had been dancing were sitting at their table. All at once, the woman slapped the man across the face, fury in her eyes.

Jin's head snapped back as if he had been the one to receive the smack.

The woman grabbed the beaded evening purse beside her and stood up. The man rose as well and, as they left the table, he tried to take her elbow in his hand. With a jerk, she shooed him away.

Jin's heart pounded, still experiencing what he witnessed as if it was happening to him personally.

"What's wrong, Jin?" Mimi sensed his upset.

Yes, the ballroom was disintegrating into a rotting pumpkin all around him. Jin was turning into a dirty sewer mouse.

Heaven only knew what had transpired between those two people to make the woman so angry. They could have just met, not had the decades as a couple Jin had decided to imagine. In any case, he was reminded about deception and appearances. His parents had probably attended a formal event like this, and to onlookers seemed to be a long-married couple committed to walking forward as one in life. Same with Jin and his ex-wife.

"Did Helene and I look happy together?" he whispered as they continued to dance, his voice sounding tinny and faraway. He pressed impatiently. "Did we?"

"No, Jin," Mimi answered, breaking their dance hold to caress his cheek with her cool palm. "You didn't."

"Good morning." Jin rolled over with his eyes still closed as his hands sought the source of warmth that was making this bed the most comfortable place on earth. It didn't take him long to find Mimi's soft skin only a few inches from him. As his eyelids finally unstuck, the first thing he saw was a crazy tangle of her satiny hair strewn across her bare, alabaster shoulders.

Running his hands through her strands prompted her to roll over as well, where they took each other into a still-sleepy embrace. Jin kissed the top of her head as his hands wove through her locks.

He held her in silence for a few moments before confirming the decision he had been making. They had to talk about the fact that they'd been making love, which was a most unexpected turn of events.

"Mimi, my friend." He exhaled, not even knowing what it was he wanted to say. His thumb began to trace a slow line from her wrist to the crook of her neck, which was counterproductive to the conversation they needed to have. "You know that when I asked you to do this pretend marriage with me, there was no expectation of…this."

A hint of a chuckle escaped her lips. "Why are we doing it then?"

"I don't know. The playacting took on a real quality that I have to admit felt good to me."

"Me, too," she squeezed out, her voice apprehensive.

"But, of course, this has never been part of our relationship." His thumb pad continued its leisurely journey. Clouding his concentration.

"Uh-huh."

Mimi's head was bent with her face against his shoulder. Jin was grateful to not have to look her in the eye.

"Maybe it's natural that we had some curiosity. Living as husband and wife."

Over the years he'd had, on occasion, carnal feelings toward Mimi. They saw so much of each other. As a teen he'd reacted to her sensual body—after all, he was only a mortal. Pressed close side by side on a subway seat, wet from swimming at the beach, curled up on a picnic blanket, their physical proximity had seen thirteen years together.

Although through the years, Jin always knew that he would never act on any of the sensations or desires he might have had. There was a list of reasons why. Mimi was his best friend's little sister, who always seemed much younger than him even though there were only two years between them. And Bai loved her like a daughter, just to name a few.

They'd both had some casual relationships before he married Helene and Mimi got serious about Gunnar. So, in their adult life, there had never been a right time for something to develop romantically. Plus, they valued their lifelong friendship. This charade to save LilyZ and help Mimi's career shouldn't have changed anything.

It wasn't supposed to.

That wasn't the plan.

"I love you like a sister," he continued, still fumbling for the words. "In a million years I could never repay you for what you're doing for me."

"But?" Mimi finally raised her head and looked at his face, making his task more difficult. Why did she have to have such a luscious mouth?

Oh, how he enjoyed claiming her lush lips, melding his into them until they were joined as one being.

Making love to her was to visit with the divine, as their essences merged along with their flesh and blood. Even though so much about her was familiar, their couplings were voyages to discover everything he didn't know. How she moved her fluid body during their lovemaking, yielding to him, welcoming his rhythms. Until she taught him some of her own. He had never experienced passion like he had with her, surging up in him as he grabbed her for dear life, making the world around them disappear.

"But…" He tried to summon what he needed to say. He knew he should tell her that having sex had been a mistake. That they needed to remember they were only pretending to be together and that the very reason they thought this arrangement would work was because there was no fear that either of them would start to believe the illusion.

As a matter of fact, he chastised himself for letting them take these lovemaking risks that could lead to disaster. It was his sole responsibility to be sure not to jeopardize the relationships, not his nor hers or Aaron's or his mother's.

Further still, he was not open to a lasting relationship. With anyone. He would not have his hope betrayed again. Was never going to subject himself to the certain jealousy and pain that loving someone would entail. Look at how he'd almost lost his mind when that weasel photographer Marc-Claude Robar merely flirted with Mimi.

At the Dressworks dinner, he'd gotten irrationally bothered when he saw that older couple in conflict. Reminding him that things weren't always what they seemed.

Coupling was no longer for Jin. He couldn't take it. Which was why this ruse with Mimi had made sense. They'd swerved in the wrong direction by making love but he'd correct the mistake right now and they'd proceed forward, back on track.

That's what they'd do.

His brain was forming the sentences. Really, it was.

Then Mimi reached to pull the warm blankets over them, rendering him unable to utter words as his best intentions faded into the morning air.

A bit later while Jin and his wife had their breakfast, he checked messages on his phone. His brow scrunched at one from his attorney marked as urgent.

The set of financial numbers caused his temples to throb as he read them a second time.

"What are you reading?" Mimi immediately noticed the tension that came over him.

"My father had rung up thousands upon thousands of dollars on a personal account."

"That you didn't know about?"

Jin covered his mouth with his hand as he went through the figures a third time. "Credit card purchases. Travel. Gourmet food shops. Top-label clothes. What was the man thinking?"

"If we can get a small collection produced sooner

rather than later, we'll know that income will be flowing back in soon."

Mimi's brain went right toward solutions.

"I've got a make-nice dinner with Thandy Luard in a few days." Their uptown retailer. "If we've got something, I'll invite her to the studio instead. She can feel like we're doing a private showing for her."

"Well then, what are we waiting for?" Mimi said, standing to collect her breakfast dishes. "Let's rock some clothes."

Jin shook his head back and forth. If he didn't watch himself, all his plans about this being a fake marriage were going to swirl down the drain.

His best friend's sister. Who he'd bedded after promising Aaron he wouldn't do anything to risk Mimi's feelings. Worse still, he wanted to do it again. And again. And again.

But he couldn't. Seduced by her lovely body in the shelter of the bed earlier, he wasn't able to get said what he needed to. He would, though.

No more marital relations.

He needed to put a stop to it. To protect them both.

When they went down to the studio, Mimi set right to task. She'd already completed the details for the two skirts. Together, they worked and reworked the wide-leg pants for hours, getting that nineteen-seventies flair she wanted while still being current and appealing.

"How fast can you get me the *cheongsam*-inspired swatches for the blouses?"

"On it," he replied, sending an email to a fabric house where he knew he could get them.

They reviewed the drawings for the three tops. One was to be a menswear style button-down that would be a revelation done in the traditional Chinese brocade with flower embroidery. What Mimi needed, though, was a wearable and durable fabric.

"I'm hoping for something with green and black in the pattern and the maroon. Too much to ask for?"

"Let's see what they can do for us."

The next top was a simple shell that would look good under a blazer.

"So what, a single button at the back of the neck?"

"How low a scoop are we doing in front?"

"Let me show you what I'm thinking. And for the third I want to do a tunic."

"To go with the slim pant. But make sure it looks good with the pencil skirt. We need that mix-and-match option."

"Okay."

Hours later, they'd created samples of the blouses and ordered sandwiches. Day had turned to night and the staff had come and gone. Jin had fielded a thousand questions, as he always did, but he and Mimi had diligently stuck to their work. Jin felt comfortable asking Thandy Luard to come to the studio, sure they could complete the pieces in time.

"I have a new thought," Mimi announced. "Let's invite some other retailers. Not just Thandy. How about a few you've never worked with before?"

"This late in the game? I like your aspirations but I don't want any embarrassments. It's bad enough how many missteps my dad made. We'll be lucky if anyone wants to work with us again."

"I'll have them done."

"If you're really ready to show these, I'll call some people I know at the magazines tomorrow. We need to have some fashion editors take a look." Massaging his forehead, Jin was tired and ready to turn off the lights and go upstairs to bed. He squeezed Mimi's shoulder as she finished up a seam on the machine. "Enough, my hardworking partner. We'll rest now."

Leaning her head back into him standing behind her, her hair brushed against his waist. "You're right."

She stood, arched her back and then followed him upstairs.

In the morning, Jin called upon some magazine editors he was friendly with and they were able to come by to look at the samples for Mimi's mini collection. They suggested some very helpful changes with regard to balance and proportions. Uri Azoulai, a tall older man who carried himself like royalty, was effusive in his praise for Mimi's designs. He asked her a dozen questions about her background and point of view on what women wanted to wear.

It was a professional high for her, one of the best days of her life.

They worked until the middle of the night again before heading upstairs, incorporating the comments they'd received from the editors. Still brainstorming, they both flopped down on the bed in the master bedroom.

"Let me just try a slightly slimmer leg and a shorter hemline."

"What, to graze the ankle?"

They fell asleep discussing her suggestions. In the morning, they were eating apples in bed with their sketchbooks when they heard the click of the front door.

"Hello?" came the sound of Aaron's voice, Mimi's brother using the spare key he had to let himself in.

Mimi and Jin snapped their heads to look at each other. Aaron wasn't aware that the game had changed between his sister and his best friend. They were supposed to be living out the fake marriage they had agreed upon, complete with separate bedrooms.

"Just a second," Mimi quickly called out. "I'm not dressed."

She bolted out of bed and gathered up the clothes that had been tossed on the floor in their tiredness. Hastily pulling hers on, she gestured for Jin to do the same, tossing him the pants that were on the floor at her feet. She felt like a misbehaving teenager who was going to have to suffer the consequences of her actions.

But their haste wasn't enough as Aaron, with the comfort around each other they had always taken for granted, stepped into the hallway. Where he could see into the bedroom as Mimi and Jin scrambled to get dressed. Aaron's eyes focused not on his sister but on Jin, as his best friend met his glare.

The two locked into a stare-down so intense Mimi's jaw began to pulse.

CHAPTER NINE

IF JIN NEEDED any reminding, the look on Aaron's face confirmed that what he and Mimi had morphed into was wrong. As Jin finally slid his eyes away from Aaron's disapproving gape, he watched numbly as Mimi tugged on her boots.

"It appears the Zhang marriage is quite a success," Aaron spat from the hallway. Jin knew his best friend to think before he spoke, and he could only stand in waiting as Aaron mentally put the pieces together. "You made some promises to me, Jin. It doesn't look like you kept them."

Jin's temple twitched. Yes, the game had changed. Truth be told, he'd gotten lost in a soft-focus domesticity living with Mimi, in a way he hadn't expected. Which led to the celestial passion they'd discovered. A pull toward each other that he couldn't stop thinking about and one he had never imagined feeling with anyone. Certainly not with her.

He surely hadn't been thinking about violating his words to Aaron when he first took Mimi into his arms.

Guilt stabbed at him, as well it should. It didn't occur

to him that this exact moment might come, when the only person besides he and Mimi who knew their marriage was a ruse would learn that the con wasn't being played by the rules.

Jin had asked Aaron for his sister's hand in marriage, with assurances about the nature of their agreement. He gave his friend his word that Mimi would be helped, and in no way harmed, by the deal. Could he still make that commitment to her brother?

If Jin was being honest, he knew that embarking on a physical relationship with Mimi would be risky. He, Aaron and Mimi had always spoken of their value to each other and had vowed never to put their familial bond in jeopardy. Which romantic liaisons always seemed to do.

The three of them were supposed to be all for one and one for all. Except now they weren't. They'd hurt Aaron by going beyond the terms they had agreed on. Jin questioned if everything that had transpired, even the idea for the phony marriage, had been a mistake.

Posing as a couple had become as natural as brushing their teeth. They moved as one now, a sum greater than their parts. Mimi spoke of LilyZ as if she'd been part of the company for her whole life. With her, Jin didn't need to sensor himself and was the freest he'd ever felt.

Yet the *behind closed doors* part wasn't going according to plan. A reversal that Aaron had known nothing of.

Until now.

"I can't say anything to defend myself." Jin shrugged as he walked through the bedroom doorway and closer to his friend. "Under the unusual circumstances, Mimi and I found we had feelings for each other that went beyond our platonic history."

"What happens if that doesn't work out between you? What if this newfound romance blows up in your face?"

"Then I will have made the biggest misstep of my life."

Jin meant that. If he wronged Mimi, or Aaron for that matter, he would carry that with him until his dying day. To lose either of them would be worse than his divorce, so important were these people to him.

"Let's say your little honeymoon doesn't last," Aaron continued, anger flickering in his subdued voice. "How are you going to work together?"

It's not that Jin hadn't had those cautions crop up. But he'd been keeping them at arm's length with so much else on his mind. Trying to quickly rebuild the label and take care of his mother. To prevent his father's double cross and to protect his grandfather's legacy. That was as much as he'd been able to manage.

It fulfilled him to hold Mimi, to stroke her smooth skin, to give his manhood license to explore. Surely he should be allowed some comfort through all of this.

Jin didn't even know how Mimi really felt about this new development between them. She'd bent just as easily toward him as he did to her. Although with thirteen years of friendship behind them, they should have at least talked it through.

What if she fell in love with him? After all these years. He was determined not to get close to anyone. After Helene's betrayal and his father's, he knew he'd be a suspicious and jealous partner who would make happiness impossible for his mate. The *real deal* wasn't for him. The outcome could only lead to Mimi being hurt.

Jin already had examples of how unfit a partner he was. His blood had boiled when that photographer Marc-Claude Robar was monopolizing Mimi's time at Maverick Choi's party. Which was nothing compared to when they had the editors in and she chatted with *Fashion Forward Magazine's* Uri Azoulai. At the quickest whiff of what looked like him flirting with Mimi, Jin was ready to abandon his gentlemanly decorum and claim his woman, even if he had to take Uri out to a back alley. Which was, of course, ridiculous as Jin did not settle disputes in back alleys. He was already in too deep with Mimi if he was having those animal instincts. Those were the thoughts of a man in love.

"What are you doing, Jin?" Aaron's judgment threw everything into a different light. Jin's chest seized with regret.

Mimi stomped out of the bedroom. "Hey, it wasn't like Jin forced me to do something I didn't want to do. Believe me, it was consensual."

Jin appreciated her trying to defend him, but she lowered her eyes immediately afterward, perhaps embarrassed to be having this conversation with her brother.

Aaron kept his eyes on Jin, demanding more explanation than he was able to provide. "You promised me you were going to protect her."

"I didn't intend for this to happen," Jin quickly retorted. "Things changed between us." He turned his head to Mimi, whose eyes were wet and glistening.

"You're playing with fire. Don't you know that she's in lo—" Aaron halted himself as his sister's eyes implored him.

Mimi finished pinning an alteration on the sleeve of the tunic. This morning's words ricocheted front to back and left to right in her brain. With the wisdom of a third party looking in on the scene, Aaron had admonished them for taking unnecessary risks with their longtime friendship.

Aaron was right, of course. Mimi had been lying in the hushes that night had brought, Jin's long arms wrapping her up like a package. After their moans and utterances of each other's names had filled the room like music, it had been easy to shove away the obvious reality.

For a brief interlude, she'd been living out her secret dream, the one that Aaron had almost blurted out loud. How was it that he even knew? She'd never told a living soul what had been on her mind for thirteen years. Was it obvious to her brother? Had he known all along?

After Aaron had caught on to what was going on in the Zhang household, he, Mimi and Jin were all annoyed with each other. Finally Jin and Mimi had apologized for hiding what had been developing. No one was quite sure what was going to happen next.

As Mimi ironed a portion of the tunic she'd just finished, she glanced over to Jin on the phone at his desk. While he concentrated on his call, he used his fingers to rake back his thick hair. The gesture made her gasp. As it had hundreds of times before, but even more so now.

Fear pummeled through her as she thought about what the future held. So swept away was she by the desire between them that had finally been given flight, she had neglected to shield her emotions in any way. Jin had made it clear he would never love again, never marry again in earnest.

What would happen in a year's time, when they would announce their amicable split? Would she crumble like her father had after he'd lost her mother, unable to exist without her?

Would the divorce be *amicable*? Was this physical relationship they were exploring going to run its course and then they would settle back into the comfortable friendship they'd always known? She realized it was quite possible that they'd wrecked their friendship by making love. Now that she'd had a taste of what romantic love with him could be, her mind might not be able to turn back to simply appreciating him as her loyal pal.

Worse still, she was sure that she would never feel about anyone the way she did about Jin. That in the end, she'd have no one. In not settling for less, she'd instead end up with nothing.

Mimi didn't know how she was going to survive any of the possible endgames.

She was packing up a portfolio for her meeting when Jin approached after his call. "Do you have a minute?" he asked, indicating for her to come into his office.

Her stomach tightened with worry. Was this going to be the moment when he told her that he'd come to his senses? Would this be his declaration that they'd never share each other's bodies again? That he was sorry for what had happened?

Even if it was, she was already running late for her appointment and had to leave. "Can we talk a little later?" she eked out.

"Oh," he answered, not expecting her to be unavailable. "Sure."

In a blur, Mimi grabbed her things and her coat, and flew down the studio steps.

Half a block away, she spotted Uri Azoulai at the café where they had agreed to meet.

"Nice to see you again," he greeted her with a polite kiss to both cheeks.

She hadn't asked him up to the studio for their meeting because she wanted to surprise Jin. When they'd invited some media influencers in to see the new pieces, Uri had asked her if he could do an article on her for the next edition of *Fashion Forward*. An interview in a major fashion magazine, read throughout the world, was a recognition that could be very important for LilyZ. She hoped Jin would be thrilled. Uri said they'd send a camera crew on another day to do some shots of her at work.

After they ordered hot drinks and took a window seat, Uri explained that he was doing a series of pieces on young designers who were shaking up the high-end ready-to-wear market and that he'd like to feature her.

"I'm so flattered," Mimi replied. "This is a great time for our company. We're coming into our next phase and hope to honor our founder Shun Zhang's vision for generations to come."

"What has been the response to your sizing concept?"

"Positive, so far. Our promise at LilyZ is to create a wardrobe for every woman that's realistic to her life. We all want to look put together while being comfortable at the same time. No more marginalizing a woman based on her size. From petite to plus-sized, we're all leading the same lives and need our clothes to work for us."

"You'll produce your collections in a range of sizes that's wider than what we typically see in quality fashion?"

"Yes, it's…" Mimi's mind drained blank when she glanced out the café window. Pedestrians hurried past, darting this way and that in the endless bustle that was New York City. But amongst the movement, one stationary figure caught her eye.

It was Jin. Wearing his heavy black overcoat, he stood still, glaring at Mimi through the glass window, where she huddled inside at the small table with Uri.

Jin's lips were slightly parted. Eyes wide open. Brows raised. Shoulders so tense they almost lifted to his ears. She'd never seen a more pained expression on his face.

Mimi gestured for him to come inside and join them. Instead, after a final piercing look into her eyes, he disappeared in the moving crowd.

She needed to concentrate on this important conversation with Uri. So she allowed her mind only one question before she wrangled her attention back to business. Could Jin have seen her with Uri and been thinking something personal was going on between them?

After the meeting with Uri, Mimi returned to the

studio. Unbuttoning her coat, she snuck a glance to see that Jin was at his desk, head bent down at some work he was attending to.

She entered his office and he looked up, expression bleary in contrast to his dress shirt, which was crisp as always.

"We need to talk," he said.

"Okay," Mimi replied and took the chair opposite him.

"I assumed it would be obvious, I didn't think that I was going to need to tell you this. Kindly don't make me the laughingstock of the industry yet again. Helene was enough. During this year that we are posing as husband and wife, should you decide to date someone, please don't be seen with them in public."

"Jin, I'm not dating Uri."

"It was my mistake not to clarify that to you in the beginning," he continued without taking in what she'd said. "I thought after Gunnar that you were on a romantic hiatus, and that this timing would work out for you."

"It is, Jin, it is. I'm surely not doing anything personal with Uri. Do you want to know why I was having coffee with him? I planned to surprise you." She proceeded to explain about the interview opportunity. What incredible exposure it was going to give to LilyZ. How much it meant to her that Uri took her seriously. For someone her age, to appear in *Fashion Forward* magazine was a huge career leap.

She might as well have been speaking a foreign language that Jin was unable to understand.

"I step out to get some fresh air and a cappuccino, and I find…"

Mentally, he stopped to regroup, seeming to acknowledge that his triggered fears about her dating someone were unfounded. "I think Aaron discovering that we'd let our relationship move away from our original intention was probably a good wake-up call. We've been friends forever. That's what we were meant to be."

"I see." Tears welled up behind Mimi's eyes as she concentrated on not letting any spill out. She'd predicted she would hear those words from him, yet they branded into her with a flesh-searing iron nonetheless.

Of course Jin was going to break up with her, for lack of a better expression. The cloud she'd been floating on was too plush to last, she'd known that in the center of her being all the way back to the kiss he gave her at the courthouse after they'd married.

"Mimi, I can't be *that guy*, the one who becomes almost murderous with jealousy when I see you with another man. I watched my father betray my mother. Then Helene. Once you've had a spouse cheat on you, you spend the rest of your life looking for it to happen again, expecting it. I'm not good for anyone. I'm incapable of trust. You deserve better than that."

"You don't get me at all, do you?" Mimi could no longer contain the six tears she counted dripping down her face. "I want the man I'm with to be jealous. I want him to feel so strongly about me that it devastates him to see me with someone else. I want that dedication, that devotion. Like my parents had. I want whoever I end up with to demand fidelity and to give it to me in return. As a matter of fact, I wouldn't settle for anything less."

"That's why I came up with this pretend marriage in the first place. I can't promise you any of that. I won't give you the authentic thing you crave and deserve. We've made a mistake I hope it's not too late to correct."

"Of course." Mimi brushed the few cold tears from her cheeks. With a gulp of an inhale, she willed herself to get out of his office without breaking down.

Jin should never know the depths to which his finality was killing her. She needed to make him think she was in agreement, that during the masquerade of married life they had done a little bit of experimenting, and gotten it out of their system. Now they'd go back to being the friends they always were.

She repeated, "Of course, Jin."

It would be as simple as flipping a switch.

Sure it would.

Nothing went smoothly when Mimi and Jin went back to the flat that night. They both shuffled around the apartment, tidying up and taking separate trips into the kitchen to forage for food. There was a bitter draft in the air, one that Jin remembered only too well from when his marriage to Helene fell apart. Or when his father was at his worst.

"I can make something. We could have eggs and toast," Mimi said, shutting a cupboard as Jin came into the kitchen for a glass of water.

"Ah, yes, Mimi's cheesy eggs," he snipped. While she wasn't that interested in the domestic arts, Mimi had been whipping up breakfast for dinner for as many years as he knew her. A menu that sounded as good as any, Jin thought, considering his lack of appetite. He just wanted to fill his empty stomach and go to sleep.

"Do you want them or don't you?" Her tone was impatient.

"That would be great," he clipped back.

Mimi set to work, going out of her way to not make eye contact while she did. Jin ducked quietly into the master suite. Hoping she wouldn't notice while she cooked, he gathered up all the clothing, electronic chargers, and various items of his that had made their way into the bedroom they'd begun to share. Tonight, and during all nights in the future, he would sleep in his boyhood bedroom as was the original arrangement. Which they shouldn't have deviated from.

The strain was palpable as they sat and ate their eggs. A memory flashed in Jin's mind.

"I remember a time eating these cheesy eggs," he blurted out, hoping a little reminder of their long history might leaven the mood. "You were probably eighteen. I was sitting at the table with that forest-green tablecloth that your mom liked. The one Aaron and I used to tease her about, saying that it was comfy cozy."

"My mom liked you a lot. Aaron and I were so tired of the blueberry muffins she'd bake every week once she discovered you enjoyed them."

The side of Jin's mouth ticked. "I remember two things about that day you made the cheesy eggs. One, yours were the best eggs I'd ever tasted. And two, when you served them up for me and Aaron, your eyes were bloodshot. I had the feeling you might have been crying. But I didn't think I should say anything so I didn't."

"You were dating Leslie."

Leslie Wang. He was surprised that Mimi even recalled her name.

"Were you crying that day?" he asked, holding a forkful of tonight's eggs in midair.

Mimi sat quietly as she seemed to be making a decision. One thing that was certainly different from that day so many years ago was Mimi herself. She was in college then, with cheeks that were easy to blush. He couldn't have pictured that girl becoming the brazen, sexy, accomplished woman sitting across from him.

Finally, she spoke in such a low register that he had to listen carefully to hear her.

"You know how I told you that I want to be with someone who would be jealous if he saw me with someone else?"

Doctor Freud would have a field day with Jin and Mimi. Jin grew up in an unhappy home with a father who was incapable of love. Where jealousy was used as a weapon. Mimi lived in a caring family where she regarded jealousy as a measure of devotion. They could hardly have been from further apart beginnings.

"It goes both ways, Jin. That day you're remembering. You were full of enthusiasm about your date with Leslie the night before. You'd gone to a basketball game."

"That's funny," he mused. "I don't even remember."

"You were asking me for advice on what to buy her for her birthday."

"I have no recollection of that. What did I get her?"

"You broke up before her birthday."

Jin let out a snort. "So you remember that detail, too."

"I remember everything. That's what I mean about it going in both directions. Just like I want someone to be jealous if they thought I was with someone else, I'm that way, too."

He put his fork down. Mimi drew her own fork in a circle around her plate. He could tell she wanted to say something but was having trouble getting started. "What is it?"

"You never knew how jealous I was over Leslie. And Helene."

It slowly dawned on him what she was telling him. That she valued jealousy as an emotion of someone in love. And that she felt jealousy about the women he'd been with. Therefore...

The words tumbled out of Mimi's mouth. "I'm in love with you, Jin. I always have been." She bit her lip afterward.

Thirteen years' worth of experiences dropped into his mind like a photo collage. Holding her when her mother died and then again after her father's death. Her making dinner for him after he broke up with Helene. The hundreds of times they'd worked closely together over a pattern or sewing machine. The thousands of movies, concerts, restaurants, every block in New York. Mimi in his life had become second nature to him, always there. And now, in an instant, all those memories took on a new meaning.

"You're what?"

Her lips trembled ever so slightly. "Did you really not know?"

Was there some cute kid sister of his best friend flirting over the years? Sure. A little teasing. Lots of cuddling. Traveling. Grieving. A road shared.

Had that all been a lie? He'd been thinking one thing while she was thinking something else entirely?

"You hid it well."

"Of course I did. I couldn't take a chance of you finding out."

"Why didn't you tell me?" He knew that confession would be hard for anyone, but keeping her feelings a secret must have been just as difficult. "Does Aaron know?"

"I never told him. But now I think he may have known all along."

"Does my mom know?"

"No. Of course not." Although if Aaron had figured it out, what was to say Bai hadn't also? Regardless, she continued. "You and Aaron were best friends. Our families cared about each other. I wasn't going to be the one to cause ripples. I planned to get over you. Then you married someone else so I knew there was no hope. Next I met Gunnar, but I couldn't have loved him even if I had wanted to. Because I never stopped loving you."

His brain raced down memory lane. "You were a bridesmaid at my wedding."

"You can imagine…"

"How awful that must have been for you."

"By the time you got divorced, I knew you wouldn't give love a second chance, and certainly not with me."

Oh, how her words were bouncing all over him inside. The way he'd come to feel about her had him confused. In this false marriage he'd found something very true. But he'd sworn to never love, and risk loss, again. A vow he was going to stick to.

"So now you know, Jin. And you were right when you said that Aaron catching us was an alarm sounding. I can't continue to make love and pretend all the wishes I've had for thirteen years are coming to fruition. It's not fair to me and it's not fair to you. We were naïve to think we could pull off this charade. I can't play anymore."

Mimi put her hand over her mouth as her eyes overflowed with tears. Jin wanted to take her into his arms and tell her everything was going to be okay. But it wasn't. He merely watched as she pushed away from the kitchen table, stood up and dashed into the master bedroom.

She returned a few minutes later with a small suitcase packed.

"Don't worry, neither the entire fashion industry nor your mom will find out that I'm leaving," she said with vitriol in her voice. "At least for tonight, though, I'm going to stay at Aaron's. I hope you understand."

She came back to the table and placed a quick, dry kiss onto his cheek. It felt like a slap.

CHAPTER TEN

"SCORES THREE FROM the line!" Aaron gloated as he shot a clean basket. Jin bent forward with his hands flat on his thighs as he took in a heaving breath. His best friend was doing a pretty good job of wearing him out on the basketball court.

"I'm coming back, Stewart." Jin exhaled with a growl. He'd texted Aaron a couple of hours ago to see if he was available to shoot some hoops. Jin hoped the exercise would help him blow off the uncomfortable steam that was percolating toward a boil inside of him. With a lunge of sheer will, Jin darted around Aaron to get close to the basket for a layup. "Not dead yet."

Yesterday, after the night spent alone in the apartment, Jin had called Aaron at work.

"Look, man, I messed up big time," he apologized to his friend. "It wasn't my intention to hurt Mimi. You know that."

"It sounds as if you've broken her heart."

That stung. The last thing Jin would want to do was cause Mimi pain. She'd been nothing but good to him, and he'd repaid her with a blistering rejection that sent her retreating. He knew that his cruelty was for her own well-being in the long run though. He'd never be a good husband, with the trust and faith she wanted and was entitled to. A grand romance was not in Jin's future.

Yet with this marriage charade his thoughts and emotions toward Mimi had grown and shifted in ways he wouldn't have expected.

For starters, he adored living with her. Her lovely face and affectionate smile being the first things he saw every morning were gifts so exquisite he thought surely they had been sent from the heavens. More divine still might have been to fall asleep at night holding her so very close to him, making him feel part of something actual and valid and healthy.

It all seemed natural, it all seemed right. So many little facets about what togetherness could bring were a pleasant surprise to him. They were sincere. And yet they weren't, because they were only temporary.

When he concocted this ruse, Jin hadn't actually considered what would happen after the year was over. He supposed that he assumed he and Mimi would go back to being close friends who marched through the trials and tribulations of their lives together. Professionally, he hoped she'd grow into the designer he always knew she could become. That LilyZ would be as solvent and prosperous as it was under his grandfather's tutelage.

Jin's own behavior of absurd jealousy when he saw Mimi with other men, and now with her confession of love for him, meant that those *what's next* decisions had to be made sooner rather than later.

Had he really not known that Mimi had been in love with him? Honestly, she'd concealed it well. Yes, she had a certain approving look that she'd always given him. One that made him feel good about himself. They complimented each other freely, held similar values, understood each other's sense of humor. Commiserated with the same point of view about hardships they'd endured. But none of her behavior was anything he perceived as strange given the circumstances. Now he wondered if there were clues that he'd missed all along.

Mimi told him that she hadn't confided in her brother about her secret love for him. "She said that she'd never talked to you about her…feelings…for me," Jin said, uncomfortably, to Aaron on the phone last night.

"True. Not a word in thirteen years. But I always knew."

"You what?"

"A brother can tell."

"And you didn't say anything to me? To her?"

"Was it really my business what my little sister had been thinking about you all this time? I could have been completely off base."

"You could have warned me before I married her."

Aaron grunted. "Fair enough. I started to but then…"

"Go on."

"I weighed the benefits against the risks, like any stockbroker would. I thought you could handle it."

Apparently, he couldn't.

He glanced over to the nearby stairs down to the subway station. Last time they'd shot hoops here, Jin had watched as Mimi ascended those stairs, bringing her unique brand of sunshine along with her. When he caught her eye, she'd flashed him a charming whole-hearted grin.

Overshooting a throw that Aaron was able to re-bound, Jin circled around his friend to try to get the ball back. He looked over to the subway stairs again. The huddled masses of New Yorkers shuffled up and down those steps, most in their dark woolen clothes of winter.

Scanning left to right and then back again, no matter how hard Jin searched he didn't see Mimi in the crowd.

Of course not. She wouldn't be coming to meet him. He and his second wife had split up.

Yet the Zhangs had a showing to pull off and every-thing depended on it.

After he'd showered and trekked the stairs down to the studio, he was relieved to see Mimi at work on a machine.

"Oh. Hi." She lifted her eyes when she saw him ap-proach.

"Did you come straight over from Aaron's? He and I were just playing basketball."

"I know, he told me."

She went back to her task.

Images whirled around in Jin's mind, as violently as a tornado.

His mother crying late at night.

One of his father's conquests making advances to-ward a twenty-one-year-old Jin at a party.

Mimi in the cabin they'd stayed at alone.

The delighted expression of a kid atop his father's shoulders that Jin had noticed at the Lunar New Year parade.

The shock of seeing Mimi in that cafe with Uri.

His wedding.

"Ah…" A feverish confusion escaped his lips with a whoosh that Mimi didn't hear over the hum of her sewing machine.

He studied the back of her head as she sewed. Her auburn hair was so lustrous. It had been like the finest thread in his hands those nights they'd made love, all five of his senses immersed in her as they were carried away in a splendid joining.

"Mimi," he said loud enough to get her attention and she turned to him.

"I'm very sorry about all of this."

She nodded slowly.

"Once we get through this showing, we won't have to spend so much time together. If you can stand to be married to me for the sake of our careers, I'll make it more bearable. I'll get you your own apartment. We'll find a way to keep it a secret. The time will pass quickly and then we can divorce."

Her eyes opened round as she continued to hold back from saying anything. He wanted to swoop down and cover her inviting mouth with his, and take her tightly into his arms and never let go, which were the opposite actions from the words he was speaking.

The thoughts that churned in him were insane. Were all his firm decisions, his survival tactics, being laid to rest? Did the unthinkable happen, had he become ready for what he thought he never would?

No.

Maybe.

No.

"We have to find a way back to our friendship," he all but pleaded. "I asked Aaron to forgive me for crossing the line. Can you?"

"You didn't coerce me into anything. I take responsibility for my own actions."

She turned back to her sewing and said nothing else, apparently finished with the conversation. Punishing him with her silence.

He'd hurt his friend. His *friend*. Always had been. Hopefully always would be. On top of that, something unplanned had grown large. Low in the pit of his stomach, Jin knew. What he felt was going to be difficult to deny. Impossible, in fact. His wall had been knocked down.

"It's seven thirty in the morning, where are you coming from?" Bai quizzed Mimi in front of the Zhangs' building as she approached.

"Oh. I…uh…went to get breakfast." Mimi covered even though it didn't sound convincing. It was unfortunate timing that Bai had arrived at the same minute as she did. She'd hoped to already be in the studio when Bai got there to help with the showing for the retailers today.

Bai gave her a slow gander that Mimi feared was recognition. Mimi was on the street early in the morning in one of her finest dresses with a coat over it. She'd dressed at Aaron's, where she was now living again, although they hoped to hide that from Bai.

Bai was a smart woman and Mimi worried she quickly put together the clues. "Breakfast?" Bai inquired, noting that Mimi's hands were empty.

"I ate it while I was walking."

Mimi punched in the key code outside of the building and let them in. They went up to the studio and she flicked on the overhead lights as they were the first to arrive.

"Where's Jin?" Bai questioned. Lending further strangeness to the situation since Mimi assumed he was upstairs in the apartment, but she wouldn't know for sure.

Stacks of party goods had been set up by the little office kitchen. "We're doing tea." Mimi jumped into the job at hand to get out of the awkwardness and avoid the question. Bai was going to be the liaison for the caterers. "We ordered all sorts of cakes from Happy Phoenix Bakery. Egg tarts, sesame balls, almond cookies, rice cakes with sweet stuffing."

"A tea party?"

"We decided to throw in a little theme since it's New Year's, and because of the Chinese influence on the blouses we're showing."

"That's good."

Mimi was glad they'd moved on from the breakfast issue.

"We picked out the hottest Mandarin pop music to play during the showing. The caterer is bringing lanterns to hang for decor. We hired a lion dancer. The retailers will have been dazzled all week by the big flashy shows so we figured we had to do something special."

"I'm proud of you for pulling all of this together so quickly. You know Shun would be proud of you, too," Bai said.

Mimi didn't think that Shun, who had a reputation for honesty, would have much approved of her and Jin's hijinks, as fundamentally honorable as they were.

The sound of Jin's footsteps preceded him as he came down from the apartment. "Morning," he mumbled and went straight to his office. She figured he had too much on his mind to put on a grand husband show for his mom's benefit. Today would be a whirlwind. They'd all somehow get through it.

Jin's quick escape didn't elude his mother's watchful eye.

"What's going on with you and Jin?"

As Mimi rolled a clothes rack out from where it had been left last night, the directness of Bai's question froze her in her tracks.

What could she say that wouldn't unravel the information Jin didn't want his mother to know? About Wei's will being an attempt to ruin Jin and Bai and the family's reputation. About the fake marriage pact that was now as thin as the thread Mimi plucked from one of the skirts on the rack. About how she and Jin had made love, had thought for a fleeting moment that the pretend could grow into the authentic. She surely couldn't tell Bai about the feelings she'd held for Jin since the first day she'd met him.

Although this was Mamabai, who Mimi had always gone to for counsel and comfort after her mother died.

Yet she couldn't tell Mamabai that Jin had shattered her heart when he told her that he could never love her. That would crush her anew, as Mimi knew how much Mamabai cared about her.

Nor would she explain that, unable to withstand the torture of living under the same roof as Jin, she'd gone back to Aaron's. How Jin told her that he'd rent her an apartment, and they'd keep their split under the radar and remain married for the designated year.

Last night, Mimi had tossed and turned restlessly on Aaron's sofa bed. There was so much to process. Her first major showing as a designer. Would the retailers like her designs or would they think her an amateur, thereby bringing shame to LilyZ and its legacy? Even if she succeeded, could she work with Jin day after day now that, finally, he knew what she'd been holding private for all these years?

She'd sobbed into her pillow, not wanting to wake her brother. After she had no more tears left, while reaching for a glass of water on the side table, her hand had wrapped around the thimble that Jin had given her in lieu of an engagement ring when he asked her to participate in their charade.

It had been Shun's, Jin told her. The white bone china was cold to the touch as she rolled it between her fingers. Studying that handpainted detailing of a junk boat, she thought about how much effort it took to create this one tiny item. Everything worth having took work...

Why couldn't Jin see that?

"Mimi." Bai brought her mind back to the studio. "Now come on, tell me what's happening between you and Jin."

"Maybe it wasn't so easy to go from friends to husband and wife." Mimi wanted to talk to Bai but there would still be parts of the story she needed to censor. She glanced over to Jin in his office, out of earshot of the conversation.

Bai seemed to be able to read Mimi. "Has Jin done something that's hurt you?"

"I think that after Helene, he has more barriers than he realized." Which, in reality, was an out-and-out lie because he'd told her from the start that he'd never love or trust a woman again. That wasn't something new that had occurred to him. He'd simply put his theory to the test and proved himself right.

"You've been in our life long enough to know that my marriage wasn't good," Bai said as Mimi took one of the blouses off the rack and began inspecting every inch of it. "Wei was a troubled man, and he didn't choose to overcome his obstacles. Or to create a partnership with me."

"But you stayed with him for decades before you finally left."

"I suppose I don't admit defeat easily. For me, that was a mistake. I don't want to see you make the opposite one and give up. Your parents didn't."

"What do you mean, Mamabai?" Mimi shifted her eyes to meet the older woman's.

"Your parents were madly in love until the day each died, weren't they? But not from the day they met."

"Do you know something I don't?"

"When your mom was in her last weeks, I sat at her bedside. We talked about a lot of things."

"I remember."

"She told me all about Benjamin and their road together."

"How they met when they were both supervisors at a summer camp."

"Then didn't see each other again until the following summer. And then not again until the summer after that even though they didn't live that far apart."

"My maternal grandfather was very protective."

"That's not what your mother told me."

"It wasn't?" Mimi shot Mamabai a questioning look. She knew something about her parents Mimi didn't.

"No. She told me the reason they didn't see each other was because your father didn't choose to. He wanted to date other girls and wasn't willing to give up his freedom."

"Huh?"

Mimi could hardly believe what she was hearing. Her sweet doting father, who looked at her mother like the sun rose and set in her eyes, didn't want to commit to her? The man who, in fact, couldn't even keep himself alive after his wife died, allowing his body to surrender to the hereafter in hope that he would be reunited with his love? Why had neither of her parents ever told her the truth about their courtship? Were they embarrassed?

"She loved him," Bai said with eyes boring into Mimi's, "so she waited. And he came around. Perfect and easy aren't either of those. Your mother isn't here to tell you this but I think she'd want me to say it. Don't give up on Jin."

"Thandy, have you met my wife and newly named designer Mimi Stewart?" Jin introduced Mimi to LilyZ's most profitable retailer. With Thandy Luard's well-curated shop on Fifth Avenue, Jin needed her onboard with this new collection.

Mimi shook Thandy's hand. The woman was all class with her short hairdo, tweed jacket and pearls. Now in her sixties, Thandy had been on the New York scene for decades, and had been carrying the label from back in the days when Shun was still trying to make a name for himself.

"It's a pleasure to finally meet you," Mimi said with a charming smile, "Jin has told me how much he values your input."

"I look forward to seeing what you've come up with."

Jin scolded the pulses tightening across his forehead and told them to be quiet. Yes, everything depended on this show. And yes, there was something even more important than LilyZ that needed to be resolved inside of him. He'd thought everything to death. It was time for action.

He greeted all the retailers as they arrived to the studio and took their seats. On cue, the lighting technician dimmed the overheads, and began to flash the red and gold beams that announced Mimi's theme of a modern take on traditional designs with Chinese influence. The catchy music combined contemporary beats with ancient Chinese instruments and melodies.

They'd decided not to do a catwalk given there were only a handful of pieces, so instead the models came in from all four corners of the space and walked around in groupings.

As Mimi had intended, the clothes were cut in two different sizes with models chosen accordingly, who came close enough to the guests as to let them really see the fabric and hang of the clothes. Jin could tell from the buzz in the room that the new designs were being received favorably. His heart swelled with pride for Mimi, who rose to this occasion like he knew she would. His wife was a remarkable woman whose name would someday be known in the fashion world and beyond.

After the showing, the caterers served the cakes with a variety of teas poured from antique Chinese pots. Jin made handshake agreements with the new retailers, who were complimentary and committed to carrying the pieces.

"You've done well, son." Bai slid up beside him during a quiet moment. They both surveyed the room, eyes landing on Mimi who was laughing with the two people she was standing beside.

"For the company, yes. For my new designer, yes. For my wife, not so much." Although that was about to change.

"I know. She told me."

Jin had come to a conclusion. And now that he had, it washed over and over him in waves like an ocean's tide touching the shore.

"Did she?" he asked, eyes still on his spectacular wife who slipped her hand in her jacket pocket and patted something there.

"What you grew up in wasn't normal, Jin. I always worried that because you didn't have the right example of a marriage as a child, you chose a woman who was like your father. I'm glad you didn't make the same mistake I did by staying with her."

"I know, Mom."

"But I don't want you to abandon love."

"I'm not. It just took me awhile to realize that mine was in front of me all along."

Bai pivoted her head toward Jin, beckoning him to make eye contact.

"Good, then." She nodded once. "We understand each other."

He planted a kiss on his mother's cheek.

Once the showing was finished and deals had been made, Jin was anxious to have time alone with Mimi. He found her tidying up the staging area where clothes were strewn about.

"Where's the pencil skirt?" Mimi asked herself aloud.

Jin picked it up from a table right behind her. "Funny how something can be clearly in view but you don't see it."

Mimi smirked. "I've noticed." He handed her the skirt, which she put onto a hanger and hooked on a rack.

"I can only imagine the torment I've caused you over the years," he said in earnest. "To tell you the truth, if I had known you had romantic feelings for me when we were younger, I don't know how I would have reacted. You were my best friend's kid sister. Even though we're only two years apart in age, that's how I saw you."

"There's nothing we can do about it now," she said while continuing to busy herself collecting her tools from the table. "I guess our destinies were predetermined."

Jin wrapped his hand around her upper arms to still her and get her to face him. "Yes, *our fates* are sealed."

This was it. This was his moment. With overflowing elation in his heart, he knelt down on one knee while taking Mimi's hand in his.

"I love you, Mimi. I've always loved you as a friend but I've come to see that I love you in that other way, too."

"You do?"

"I've fallen in love with you. And I want us to be together. Not just for a year but forever. Can you be patient with me? I have a lot to learn about healthy relationships. Will you show me the way?"

Her eyes pooled as she looked down at him on bent knee.

"Mimi Lynn Stewart, will you *stay* married to me?"

Jin would never forget the smile that swept across her radiant face. "Yes, Jin."

"I have to buy you a ring."

With her free hand, Mimi reached inside her jacket pocket to remove something that she handed to Jin. It was his grandfather's china thimble.

"I decided to keep it with me today for luck," she said. "The hand painting of the boat at sunset is so detailed and intricate. It reminds me of the beauty of determination and its rewards."

For the second time, Jin fit the thimble onto Mimi's fingertip.

Then he stood and took his wife in his arms, knowing he would continue to do so for the rest of their lives.

EPILOGUE

One year later...

MIMI HELD ON to the stair rail with her right hand as she made her way down the steps from the apartment to the studio. She'd been careful about that lately.

Her husband Jin was standing at one of the cutting tables, talking to a small group of new employees. Holding up a navy blue wraparound dress that Mimi had just given the go-ahead on, his pleasure with the garment was obvious and filled her with contentment and pride.

In a year's time, Jin and Mimi had begun to rebuild LilyZ into the exclusive and profitable label that Shun Zhang had dreamed of. The company was doing so well that they'd hired new management to meet the demand for distribution. Following Jin's business plan, they'd expanded from selling through twenty retail shops to thirty-five worldwide, moving toward his goal of fifty. Uncle Fu in Hong Kong was even moving into a larger manufacturing space to accommodate the production.

Aaron had saved enough money to buy an apartment near Wall Street. She was helping him choose furnishings. And Mamabai was well and happy, although not as happy as Mimi figured she was going to be when her daughter-in-law shared some important news with her.

But Jin needed to be the first to hear it.

She grabbed the sketch pad that she kept on the desk opposite Jin's, in what had now become their shared office.

After his meeting finished, he came to join her.

He greeted his wife with a sensuous kiss, as he always did.

"How is the best young designer in New York doing today?" he flattered her.

"Grateful to have a boss that respects her work so much," she said, flirting. The beaming smile she got in return filled her heart with joy. "Can I show you something?"

"Of course." He gestured toward her sketchbook, which she opened and laid out on his desk.

"What's going on here?" He pointed to some unusual pleating at the waist of a skirt she'd drawn.

"Room to grow."

"What do you mean?"

Mimi teased by not answering him, until he ventured a guess.

"We're going into maternity wear now?"

"Well, a woman should be able to look chic while being comfortable during every phase of her pregnancy, shouldn't she?"

"Sure."

"I know I, for one, intend to."

Mimi delighted as comprehension slowly made its way across her true love's face.

"You mean…?"

"Let's hope he or she likes clothes."

Jin swept Mimi into an embrace then placed one hand flat against her tummy. As he kissed her face over and over again, unable to conceal his excitement, he told her, "Just like LilyZ, our family will never go out of style."

* * * * *

COOKING UP
ROMANCE

LYNNE MARSHALL

For those who may be searching for relatives they never knew existed.

Chapter One

Lacy Winters pulled her bright pink food truck with the brand-spanking-new logo—Wrap Me Up and Take Me Home—onto the busy construction site at 10:45 a.m. Friday morning. Little River Valley wasn't exactly the business hub of the state of California, being that the small city voted way back to never allow unnecessary building or chain stores of any kind. That was part of the charm and draw for the residents. However, Mayor Aguirre had recently made a deal for added senior housing in the town, which was tucked fifteen miles inland between Ventura and Santa Barbara. The homes were sorely needed since many adults chose Little River Valley for their retirement, and the sprawling homes that dotted the hills lining the valley were too big and expensive for most fixed incomes.

Thanks to the mayor's foresight, one hundred new cottage-style units were being built, and that meant a good-sized construction crew would be employed. Which also presented a great opportunity for Lacy, because on that construction site there would be workers who needed to eat.

Before Lacy left home, she had posted on her social media page, the one with a photo of her standing in front of her foodmobile as the cover picture. Off on new adventure today. Wish me luck! #lookingforwork.

Her late father's list of best businesses from back in his food truck days had included Franks & Gardner Construction at number one. After her permits and licenses for running the small business were in order, and the truck was repainted—which cost a fortune but was so worth it because, well, it was pink and had a great advertising logo on both sides—she'd looked them up and found out about their new building site nearby.

She gulped a breath and drove the twenty-four-foot kitchen-on-wheels onto the dusty makeshift driveway, watching for nails or other damaging debris.

"Here goes," she whispered. Her heart fluttered from nerves as she headed toward the temporary on-site office trailer and parked.

The city had strict rules for trucks like hers. Rules about when, where and the need for general approval to set up shop. In other words, she couldn't park just any old place she chose. Except she had chosen this place, and she had seriously high hopes of getting the gig.

Lacy wouldn't want to get off on the wrong foot. No. Not little ol' redheaded maverick her. She cleared her throat and straightened the logo-laden apron, fully aware neon pink clashed with her hair. It was one small-style humiliation she'd have to swallow for the greater good— her new business! And since when did "style" and "Lacy" ever come up in the same sentence? But, back to her logo, branding was everything these days, and pink turned out to be her color. Who knew?

She took the few steps from the steering wheel to the newly overhauled kitchen area and flipped the switch for the awning over the service window. Showtime! She watched proudly as it quietly opened, wondering if this was how actors felt when the curtains rose. All she could do was smile through the itchy excitement. She'd done it. She'd taken the next step in her life. And, boy, did she need a "next step" after all she'd been through this past year. Her mouth went dry and she took a swig of water.

"May I ask what you're doing here?" The deep masculine voice out of the blue surprised her, and she jerked as bottled water splashed over her chin and dribbled down her front.

"Oh!" She wiped her chin with the back of her hand, acting casual, like she did this all the time—made cold calls at construction sites in hopes of drumming up new business. In her case, über-new business since, *if* she got this gig, it would be her first regular job as a food truck owner. Too bad her trembling fingers gave away her so-called nonchalant, just-show-up approach. "Um, yes." She leaned forward onto the service window, forced to look down at the man, who appeared too young to be the long-time big honcho. Probably just his on-site guy. "I was hoping to talk to Mr. Franks?"

"He's here in name only." The tall, striking, dark blond man with suspicious green eyes didn't let up watching her and was probably waiting for the full explanation.

That threw her. Franks wasn't the guy? So much for Dad's list. He'd only been gone a year, and yet the list was out-of-date. She cocked her head, trying to add things up. Daryl Franks was the name her father had put first, but she'd found Franks & Gardner in the town business directory. Now he was telling her Franks was a name only. Had the man retired or died? More important, if Franks was gone, was this vaguely familiar man—because who could forget a gorgeous face like that—the gatekeeper?

Flustered, she had to think fast.

"Uh, may I speak to Mr. Gardner then?" She said it an instant before her vision landed on an official name tag pinned to his minichecked green-and-tan shirt. Zackery Gardner, Construction Manager. "Oh, hello." She didn't give him the chance to point it out. He wore the fitted button-up shirt well, the long sleeves rolled up his forearms revealing a dusting of hair lightened to gold by a ray of sunshine peeking through the leaves.

"Hello." He waited. Patiently? Folding his arms, legs in wide stance.

It was her turn, and she had better make good her reasons for showing up unannounced.

"So, Mr. Gardner, I see you've started a huge project here and I wondered if you could use my services for your workers?"

He canted his head. "And your services are—" Uncrossing his arms, he studied her truck, then looked back at her. "Getting wrapped up and taken home?" he said each word slowly, as though reading her logo aloud. Had she detected a mocking tone?

Obviously, her cutesy title had fallen flat for him, or he was purposely playing it dense. *Dear Lord, please don't let him think this is a mobile massage parlor!* If he was teasing, that was mean, though perhaps deserved, for her having made a cold call. At first, she'd considered phoning before showing up. Then she'd talked herself out of that, thinking the huge truck would do a better job of convincing someone to give her a chance than a nervous voice over the phone. Her father had once told her, before she'd applied online for her first job, that it was harder for a potential boss to pass on an applicant while looking into their eyes. So, as tough as it'd been at the time, she'd taken her teenage self off to the smoothie store in town instead of simply submitting the application through the website. Yep, she'd gotten the job, which led to another job and another. And here she was today, making sure her baby blues didn't blink under the scrutiny of the site manager's sexy greens.

Holding tight to her pride, she chose to ignore Gardner's gibe about the name of her truck and take the higher road. She was looking for long-term work, after all. Not just the occasional wedding gigs that, thanks to the current trend in California of hiring food trucks instead of caterers, those outdoor marriages provided. A place like this, which clearly had a long way to go before completing the senior housing, could guarantee six months or more. That would be a great start. With references. But she was getting ahead of herself.

"I make hearty wraps to order, and assorted hand pies. May I show you the menu?" She reached for one, since she hadn't yet had time to post the big menu on the outside of the truck. She wouldn't do that—overstep her bounds—until she was hired. Though maybe she'd already overstepped those bounds by showing up uninvited. "Perhaps I can give you a sample?"

In all truth, she'd hoped she'd find Mr. Franks, like she'd planned, and he'd have a huge stomach hanging over his belt buckle, a man always eager to eat. She would've appealed to his appetite and secured the job with ease. So much for meditation and envisioning her future. Why did she even bother to listen to online self-help podcasts?

The Not-Mr. Franks, the well-built man who obviously watched what he ate, stepped toward the window, so she leaned over to give him the also-neon-pink-flyer-styled menu. Maybe she should have rethought the color before targeting construction jobs. Her fingers touched his at the handoff. Zip, a tingle ran up her arm. Well, that hadn't happened in a long time. *Odd*. Had he felt it, too?

He removed his hard hat while he perused her face. Hair that was longer than she'd expected swept across his forehead and covered half of his ears. Nice waves. Nice suntan. Nice smile lines. Wait, he was smiling at her.

She forced a tense, overwide smile. "See anything you like?"

His eyebrow shot up as his gaze held firm with hers. Oh, crud, she hadn't meant to say it like some old come-on line. Understandably, he could totally take it wrong, but she hadn't meant it *that* way! His steady stare with the one raised brow said otherwise and made her wonder what was going on in his mind. *Really, dude?* Her thoughts quickly slipped to insecurity. "Food-wise," she added hastily.

His green eyes twinkled playfully for an instant before he gave her a benevolent smile and glanced back at the menu. "What do you recommend?" Thank goodness, he hadn't taken the lowbrow tease route, because these days she wouldn't work for a man who did.

"If you allow me to fire up my grill, I'll make you the Chicken Done Right wrap. Oh, and I've got all the permits to operate and the health department certificate, if you'd like to see them." Being in construction, the man had to know all about the importance of pulling permits.

He thought, his lower lip pushed out the tiniest bit, and, darn, that was a sexy look, which she had no business noticing. "Chicken sounds good. And I can see your permits from here." They *were* posted in frames on the kitchen wall. All she'd needed to do was gesture to them, but no, she'd gone her usual route of explaining too much.

"How much time do you need?" He broke into her self-doubt and chronic overthinking.

"Since the grill needs to heat first, ten minutes?" Her index finger went up, thinking fast. "But if I was serving your guys, it'd only take five minutes." She tightened the elastic on her ponytail, glad she'd put a word in for herself and her short-order-cook abilities. "Because the grill would already have been heated up." There she went, repeating herself again, but only because she understood the importance of being redundant when necessary. Then, with his nod to go ahead, she turned on the grill and gave him another wide smile. "I pride myself in being fast."

Both of his brows shot up this time, accompanied by an amused expression. Yeah, she seemed to be on a roll. Thank goodness, she only had two feet to stick in her mouth. She blinked and took a tiny inhale, avoiding his tolerant gaze by getting busy.

Why did she keep feeding him old lines, and why were his reactions pointing in all the wrong directions? Because he'd started it by not getting her puns in the truck logo? Wrap *her* up and take *her* home? Or because of him, and the fact he was total construction-god material and everything about him spelled *S-E-X*, and...

No way was she in any mental or emotional state to think about such things. And yet he'd taken her there on a zip line. Not good.

Her hand flew to wipe a wisp of hair out of her eye, not having felt this nervous about cooking for someone in ages.

"I'll be back in ten," he said, ignoring her jitteriness

and thankfully not taking the usual route of many men. *You pride yourself in being fast? Well, then, I'd really like to try that out*. Duh and har-har-har.

Not him. Maybe all the hoopla from recent sexual-harassment scandals had all men—and it was about time—on their best behavior. Even at construction sites, leaving her looking like an old-school ditz. Which she definitely wasn't! She slid on the ponytail hairnet and put her bright pink toque in place. May as well complete the picture, because no way would she ever let one of her easily identifiable hairs land in her food.

Seriously, though, he didn't strike her as the type to not respect women. Just a hunch, but there was something kind about his demeanor beneath that hard hat. Something she recognized. Remembered?

Zackery.

An eerie chill tiptoed down her spine, suddenly transporting her back twenty years to when she used to accompany her dad to his work sites during summer vacations right here in Little River Valley. The first huge crush of her lifetime had been on a grown-up. Well, in reality, the guy was probably a teenager, but in her little-girl eyes, that was an adult. A handsome construction worker. She still remembered his name. Zack. Blond. Green eyes. Long wavy hair, back then, really long. Swoonworthy in a Thor kind of way. She and her immature heart had vowed to never forget him.

Except she had until just now.

A full body shiver nearly had her missing the sizzling grill with the marinated chicken concoction. It was him, had to be, except twenty years older and, in her opinion, sexier than ever. Because what had she known at eleven about sex appeal?

She'd had the most amazing and superinnocent daydreams about him then. Simply because he'd been nice enough to smile at her and tease her about her copper-red hair. *You look like a new penny. Maybe I should call you Penny instead of Lacy?* In her little-girl fantasies, he'd held her hand and told her how beautiful she was. They'd walked through meadows of wildflowers, and, as dreams go with little girls, he'd delivered her first kiss. Her idea of what a kiss would be like, anyway. A chaste kiss, because again, what had she known about any of that back then?

His mouth came to mind, while he'd read her menu with that lower lip man-style pout. She wouldn't mind trying out everything she'd learned about kissing with him since she'd grown up. She snorted and made a dry swallow. Whew, was the grill superhot or something?

Wait. In her rush, she'd forgotten to turn on the vent and open the back windows. After a quick push of the chicken around the grill, she slid open the extra windows and wiped the tiny sheen from her upper lip. Where had she left the water?

Finding the bottle, she took another drink and focused on making the best dang wrap she could. Her welfare depended on it since she'd recently quit her other job. While she was at it, she'd warm one of her apple hand pies from the batch made fresh last night. Wasn't that every man's favorite?

For the sake of the next phase of her career, she sure hoped so.

Ten minutes to the second later, Zack Gardner strolled from his office toward the bright food truck. The sight of it made him smile, but he kept it to himself. Wouldn't want to encourage her when he had zero intention of letting the redhead set up shop. That girlie rig was meant for kids' parties and Santa Barbara beach volleyball games, not construction sites. Any serious business person should know it, too.

A flash of her natural red hair while she cooked sent a memory whirling through his mind. The color was the kind so many women tried to match in salons, but usually fell flat. Hers was nothing short of stunning, and he'd only met one other person with that shade in his life. He'd gotten his first summer temporary job in construction when he'd been nineteen. He recalled that he couldn't believe how hard the job was and how ravenous he'd been, *all* the time. There'd been a long line of jobs and food trucks over the past twenty years, all blurry. But he remembered his first real job and first food truck just like it was yesterday because, well, everything was *the first* back then. The Winters Breakfast and Lunch truck. That was it. That guy hadn't needed a catchy name or flashy color. Winters's truck had been institution white with black lettering on the side. And didn't the middle-aged guy have to bring his kid with him during the summer? Just like Zack would have to do over spring break next week with his own ten-year-old daughter, Emma. His memories grew stronger. Back then, John Winters made the best cheeseburgers he'd ever tasted, and Winters's daughter had bright red hair just like her father. A copper penny came to mind. Could this woman be that kid?

He narrowed his eyes, studying the foodmobile. Erase the neon-pink paint job, and it looked about the same size and style as that other food truck. When she'd first pulled up and had caught his attention through the office window, he'd had a hunch the truck was vintage. Here in Little River Valley, people liked vintage stuff. On closer examination, it most definitely was an original, even for twenty years ago. He had to respect someone who valued history. It showed insight.

Getting nearer to the truck, with a delicious aroma perking up his nose and appetite, even though it was way too early to think about lunch, he made a snap decision. He'd keep all his memories to himself because, as he'd previously decided, he wasn't going to let her set up. The guys were perfectly happy bringing their lunch pails or piling into cars and driving into town on their break. Why get her hopes up, make her think they had some connection, by playing the reminiscing game?

Those bright blue eyes noticed him coming and another inviting smile creased her lips. *Don't even think about it. Women are bad news, especially ones that look like her.*

"I hope you're hungry," she said with an eager-to-please expression. An expression that came off far too sweet to ignore. How could she be bad news?

History, remember? As in *all* women.

Still he fought off a smile. He hadn't been hungry fifteen minutes ago, but now his stomach growled in anticipation. "Sure smells good."

She handed him a supersize paper plate with the enormous wrap nearly filling it. "Whoa, this thing's huge."

"I know how big construction workers' appetites can be."

Yeah, he did, too, but he no longer did the hard work, not for the past five years, anyway. He'd put in his time breaking his back with construction company after construction company, and eventually worked his way up to foreman. Now he was the owner-manager. Half of this wrap was going home to share. Just like her logo said, he'd wrap it up and take it home.

He bit into the wrap. Holy heavenly taste buds, she

knew how to season, and the chicken was melt-in-your-mouth tender and juicy. Filled with unexpected vegetables and bits of potato swimming in her special sauce, the mouthwatering spinach-green wrap was more a meal in a megasize tortilla than a substitute for a sandwich. She should've named the truck *Manwich—Sandwiches for men with manly appetites*. But Emma would love the wrap, too, and it was so much healthier than their usual fast food. Still, he didn't want to get Ms., uh, *her* hopes up. "What'd you say your name was?"

"Lacy Winters."

Dang it! Memories were strange things, popping up after lying dormant for years, and right now his recall worked at hyperspeed. "John Winters's girl?"

She nodded, a hint of surprise in her stare.

He knew it. How many people walked the earth with that color hair? *Penny!* "This is pretty good," he said, before he had a chance to remember he wasn't going to go there—reminisce—or give his consent for her to park on his construction site.

There went that extra bright smile again. It was hard to take his eyes off her, especially while mouthwatering flavors hit his tongue. He looked around for a place to sit and couldn't find one, so he left the plate on the food truck counter and, using both hands to hold the wrap, took several more bites.

"Can I get you another napkin?"

Sauce dribbled over his chin and onto his hands. "Thanks."

"Would you like a drink?" she said, after handing off the wad of napkins.

"Water's fine." Wouldn't want anything to compete with the delicious ingredients he was ingesting like a man who hadn't eaten in days. "What's this?"

She'd placed, next to his wrap, a much smaller plate holding a pastry with a light brown crust.

"That's half of one of my apple hand pies. I heated it for you."

Why wait until he was too full to want or be able to enjoy dessert? He grabbed it and took a bite. Warm melt-in-your-mouth piecrust hit his taste buds, the kind he only remembered from his mother's kitchen, until now. Cinnamon-seasoned, obviously fresh apples sweetened to perfection broke through as he chewed. "What's your background?" He couldn't help talking with his mouth full.

"I've been a cook at the Local Grown Restaurant here in town for the past three years. Before that, I was a short-order cook at Becky Sue's."

"That breakfast and lunch diner?"

She nodded, then continued. "My dad got me started in the food industry. This is actually his truck."

He knew it!

"I got it updated and overhauled after he died last year."

The man would probably roll over in his grave if he knew it was pink. "I'm sorry to hear that. You know, I remember your father. He had red hair like you, right?" The Winters food truck had shown up at a lot of construction sites he'd worked over the years, but not with her. Except for that first summer.

Her prideful closed-mouth smile and nod told him she loved her dad, and was both pleased and surprised Zack had remembered the man.

He finished off the hand pie and took a swig of water. "I'm fairly sure I remember you, too." With a happily full stomach, and in the presence of a pretty woman, he was suddenly in a chatty mood. "You were about this tall."

He leveled his hand waist high. "And skinny. Looked like you were *all* head with that wild red hair." He half grinned, proud of his recollection.

Well, so much for Lacy's little-girl daydreams. He'd thought she was "all head" and skinny as a rail? At least he remembered her. *Bet you didn't know you were my first imaginary kiss, did ya?* For some crazy reason, probably from still being raw for the last several years, after losing the two men she'd loved most, her dad being the latest, she'd let Zack hurt her feelings. Irrational thinking or not, calling her "all head" had stung, and Lacy did a lousy job of hiding her reaction.

She studied her feet, dejected, awash in insecurity. Why had she thought it was a good idea to wear a chef toque in a food truck? To him, she probably still looked like the puff pastry dough boy with a red wig.

"Hey, I'm sorry," he said, catching on, a sincere cast to his gaze. "You've certainly filled out since then."

It should be his turn to cringe. Filled out? *Now* who was saying awkward things? He was trying to fix the unintentional slight, but, still wincing from her childish response, she let him marinate in the iffy-at-best comment rather than immediately letting him off the hook.

His shoulders tensed, and his collar rose slightly up his neck as he must have realized how his statement could come off. "Did not mean to make you uncomfortable, Ms. Winters. Apologies." Even his cheeks looked a little peachier than earlier on the gorgeous olive-toned tan.

She nodded, appreciating his minor squirm. He was a man of few words, but he'd said the right ones just now. "Call me Lacy." May as well take advantage and move in while he was in a vulnerable position. "So, what do you say, can I park here during the week? Feed your guys?"

Amused by the obvious battle going on behind those

seriously green eyes, Lacy watched as he thought. Ate. And thought more. He glanced over his shoulder to the men on the site who'd stopped working to check out the pink foodmobile. If he'd let her, she'd sell a crateload of food to those men right now. She was ready for this. She knew how to cook, and she'd had a great role model in her father. Maybe she wasn't completely up to snuff on the finances and business side, but she'd work it out as she went along. She just needed a shot to prove she could deliver on her own. Because, on her own, as it turned out, was how it was going to be. Forever? She shrugged.

Her father had died suddenly—she hadn't had a chance to say goodbye. Taking over his truck was her homage to him. Plus, it promised to get her out of the four-walled kitchens she'd spent too many hours trapped inside, where stress, too often, drove the show. That wasn't what she wanted anymore—this was. Outdoors. Hungry guys. She could do with a little less noise, but why be picky?

She was ready to be her own boss, to take charge of her life. This overly bright truck was her ticket to renew her love of cooking and reclaim her independence. She wasn't looking to get rich, just to get by. She didn't want to put too much pressure on Zack Gardner or to come off as desperate, but she slipped a subtle *please, please, please* glance his way. No harm in sending subliminal messages, right?

He was obviously still fighting some internal battle, looking at the other half of his chicken wrap, checking out his work boots, gazing at her silly logo again, then into her hopeful stare. "Tell you what," he said. "I'll try you out three days next week, Monday, Wednesday, and Friday, and we'll see how it goes from there."

It wasn't a total yes, but it was a maybe, and *maybe*

was better than good enough today. Yes! She'd count it as a victory. Besides, she was bound to win over those hungry-looking men who'd quit sawing and hammering and were still watching the show over by her pink truck. After they'd had a taste of her hearty wraps, they'd be begging their boss to let her come back.

"That's a deal. May I leave my menus for your men, and heat up a few more hand pies for them to sample as a thank-you? I've got a pot of coffee ready to go, too." She'd thought ahead and set up for half of her hundred-cup coffee maker, just in case. "Just say the word."

She'd arrived not only hopeful but prepared for success, and now it'd paid off.

His somewhat flirtatious smile alarmed her. It set off a relay of tingles across her neck and shoulders, and strategically dipped below her collarbone, making her glad she wore a full apron over her thin top.

"Sounds like a good idea."

Putty in her hands! She'd been privileged to see his handsome and far-too-appealing smile again. And it did wonders for her mood.

"Thanks." And he was thanking her!

She tipped her head and grinned, unashamed how glad she was he'd given her a chance. It was all she asked. Then she got right to work heating a couple dozen assorted hand pies as the coffee brewed. While she did, she couldn't help but notice that Zack had picked up the rest of his wrap to take home. Oh, yeah, she'd sold him all right. Good food in person was always better than a phone call sales pitch. *Thanks, Dad.*

"See you Monday," he said. "We break for lunch at noon."

"I'll be here by eleven thirty!"

"Park under those trees." He pointed to a shady spot

across the way. "I'll rig something up for the men to sit on."

If that didn't sound promising for a permanent spot and job, what would?

Grinning, she watched him walk off toward his office, long strides, narrow hips, construction worker arms and shoulders. Once he was inside, after she'd let herself imprint that fine image in her mind—because, come on, no way was he ever going to be more than a nice fantasy in her life—she finished her preparations for the guys. With everything laid out on the counter and the coffee brewed, she honked her *Happy Days* theme horn, a horn she'd spent an entire day choosing from the usual and long list of food truck horns. She'd chosen that one because she knew it would make her dad grin. She couldn't help but notice Zack Gardner peering out his modular office window through the blinds at the sound. Then the guys came like zombies to feed at her truck, and she handed each of them a menu to take with them. "I'll be here next Monday. Be sure to bring your appetites."

Her cheeks were nearly cramping. She hadn't smiled this long or hard, or been this happy, since she'd landed her first job as a line cook right out of community college working up to short orders in record time. All without going to culinary school. How's that for beating the odds, Dad? He'd always been proud of her following in his chosen profession, chief cook and bottle washer.

Sunday afternoon Lacy showed up early for a wedding reception at the Santa Barbara Museum of Natural History. She parked, as instructed, out of sight of the outdoor wedding ceremony on the museum Mission Creek grounds. Four other trucks were there for the three-hour-reception gig. She'd been instructed to serve three different wraps—chicken, steak and vegetarian—and to skip the pies since another truck would be the main cake and dessert truck. *Whatever.* The job was paying a flat rate, which was fine with her. She'd make a good profit. With the next installment payment on her updated truck overhaul, plus the custom paint job due, she was happy just to be here. And in the day and age of monkey see, monkey do, who knew what other jobs it could lead to.

It was a lovely spring day, California style. The sun was out, temperatures in mid seventies, with only a hint of a breeze. The old and modest museum, designed in the Spanish Colonial Revival style, was located in the Mission Canyon area of Santa Barbara and had been recently renovated. It was beautifully redone, combining minimal architectural improvements to enhance the surrounding nature. Each complementing the other. Literally nestled in riparian oak woodland, the museum setting seemed idyllic for weddings.

Lacy glanced around at the young, hip and rich group arriving in the reception area. The ceremony must be over. A few women even wore hats, maybe influenced by the royal weddings in England over the last few years. Who knew the reason, but those hats dressed up the crowd. It made the occasion extraspecial, which caused Lacy to smile. The few spring pastel dresses mixed with the artsy black many guests chose to wear made for a nice contrast.

She'd thought hard before accepting her first wedding job last month, when she'd just finished revamping her father's food truck and had gotten all the required certifications. Weddings were a tough subject, even after all this time.

Five years ago, she'd been engaged to be married to the greatest guy on earth. She'd never believed she could feel so much love for someone other than her parents. Of course, her love for Greg had been on a totally different level, and she couldn't wait to be his wife. Ever the military gentleman, he'd gone old-school and, in her mother's rose garden, dropped to his knee to ask her to marry him. So thrilled and excited by his question, she'd fallen to her knees to be face-to-face with him when she'd said yes. They'd cried and laughed and hugged and kissed, and then, because she'd had the house to herself that day, they took it inside.

There'd been one problem though. He'd been called up for a six-month deployment to Afghanistan, so they'd have to wait at least that long before they could tie the knot. Going in, she'd known and accepted that this would be the life of a military girlfriend and future wife. What were a few months in a lifetime, they'd rationalized together to help make his leaving a little easier.

Two months after Greg had left, his parents called, sounding shaky and asking her to come to their house. Once there, they'd all been told together in person by an army major in their jurisdiction that Sergeant First Class Gregory Timberland had been killed by friendly fire. Lacy, though stunned, remembered thinking what a horrible job that major had, having to tell families the awful news. In his low and respectful voice with a slight tremble, the major had gone on to say that one of Greg's own guys had killed him in a horrific mistake. It was an accident, of course, but nevertheless, who had come up with such a terrible term for what had happened? Friendly fire had to be the world's worst oxymoron.

She couldn't imagine the horror the other military guy—the one who'd made the mistake— must have felt when he'd realized what he'd done. At the news, she'd melted into a sadness so deep she couldn't imagine ever seeing her way out.

The last time she and Greg had spoken over the internet had been two days before that earth-shattering news. Greg had been animated and full of life, and they'd made a few more plans for their wedding, laughed together, then said they loved each other. She'd loved him so much. Then he was gone. Along with all her dreams. The next few months had been a blur, and only after her father had insisted she get out of bed and stop acting like she'd died, too, did Lacy try to pick up her life without him. A task she couldn't imagine pulling off.

That had been five years ago, and losing Greg still hurt. The flowers also reminded that she'd let her mother's rose garden go to weeds after her father died. The place where Greg had proposed. Mom. Another person she'd loved and lost. Now guilt edged in along with the other sad memories. All because of today's beautiful wedding grounds. She'd been blindsided with Greg's memory and, worse yet, had let herself go there. Which led to thinking of losing her father and her mother. All the people she loved. Now she had to quickly wipe her eyes or run the risk of crying into the steak marinade. The memory was still too painful. But if she got the regular job at the senior housing building site, she wouldn't have to take these wedding gigs anymore. Wouldn't have to be reminded. So she'd do everything in her power to make sure she got that job.

Later, after the wedding and during the reception, a young woman, one of the hat wearers in pale blue head to foot, stood in the short line for a chicken wrap. She made a strange expression when Lacy handed the food to her, as if time had stopped for a moment when they looked at each other. After she took the wrap, the young woman started to step away, but quickly turned back. "Eva?" she said, sounding incredulous.

Lacy shook her head. "Uh, nope, I'm Lacy."

"Oh." The woman kept staring eerily at her. "Thanks."

"I hope you like it."

"I'm sure I will. Thanks." She looked up again. "You look exactly like Eva."

Absurd, right? *Yeah, all redheads look alike.* Heard that one a few thousand times before. Though under the circumstances, the wedding and all, plus the fact the young woman wore a really cool blue hat, Lacy wanted to be polite.

"Don't they say everyone has a doppelgänger?" A nervous laugh escaped Lacy's mouth as she said it, doing her best not to let on the young woman's observation had unsettled her.

"Wow. You laugh just like her, too." A dumbfounded expression accompanied the hat-wearer as she held the bag with the chicken wrap tight to her chest and walked backward, staring at Lacy the entire time until the crowd curtained her. Then the brunette's hand, holding a cell phone, rose over a couple of heads.

Lacy swore she'd just had her picture taken.

Chapter Two

Sunday night, Zack sat at the kitchen table and caught up on some paperwork while his ten-year-old daughter, Emma, heated canned soup in a pot and made her one and only specialty—grilled cheese sandwiches.

"Dad, can I cut up some carrots and add it to the soup? It'll make it more healthy."

"Hmm?" Concentrating on organizing business receipts, he'd only tuned in for the last couple words. "Healthier," he corrected. Their deal was, if she wanted to cook, which she wanted to do all the time lately, he had to be in the kitchen with her.

"Yes, that's what I'm saying." She let go a large and loud sigh, her current favorite thing to do whenever he corrected her or didn't pay enough attention, which he'd just done both.

"Sure." He laid down his pencil and pushed the pile of papers aside, because he had some making up to do and business could wait. Since his divorce, he'd made a promise to himself, on behalf of Emma, to be all he could be for his daughter. "I'll watch."

Another sigh, but she also smiled, a look he treasured. He stood nearby as she used the peeler and carefully cut small round pieces from the thin carrot, then tossed them into the heating chicken-and-rice soup. She smiled up at him again as she did, making his insides warm right up to his chin. How could his ex-wife turn her back on their daughter?

He squeezed her shoulder. "Good job," he said, which garnered another smile from her.

Emma had the cutest overbite in the world, and he dreaded the day some friend might tease her about it and she'd suddenly be all about getting braces or those new invisible things. The condition affected her two front teeth as if her tongue—or thumb as a baby—had pushed them that way. Mild at best, the teeth only stuck out a tiny bit. And yes, she had sucked her thumb back then. Self-soothing, the pediatrician had called it. Soon enough, when she and her friends started taking selfies and she could compare her smile with theirs, she'd probably catch on and become self-conscious about the small imperfection. Why did everyone need to have perfect teeth anyway? He loved her just the way she was.

"You gonna watch me grill the sandwiches?"

"Of course."

"I know how to be safe. When's the last time I got burned?" Occasionally she'd test out being a preteen, and without a woman's input he was often taken off guard.

"I can't remember." It was easy being benevolent with Emma. Come to think of it, he was the last person to get burned while scrambling eggs, but he didn't need to remind her.

"You can set the table." At ten she'd already learned to delegate—his kind way of avoiding calling his daughter bossy. He figured it was because Emma didn't have a mother figure, and his guilt over that helped him put up with a lot. Not that she was spoiled. He cleared his throat. "I'll let you know when I'm ready to start the sandwiches."

He did a double take. "Yes, ma'am." She looked like a natural standing on a footstool, fixing their dinner. When had she become so grown-up?

She'd had to suffer through his mediocre cooking since her mother left a year and a half ago. Mona was only so-so in the kitchen, too, so the poor kid didn't exactly have the best training. Lately, though, Emma had discovered the *Junior Chefs* series on TV and had been nagging him to let her take cooking lessons. At ten? How would he even go about finding a person to teach a child cooking? The kids on that show probably had parents who were culinary geniuses. Was cooking an inherited trait? If so, sweet Emma was doomed.

She may have inherited the brown hair and eyes from her mother, but their personalities were miles apart. For that he was deeply grateful. Where Emma was naturally bright and sunny, even if a little bossy, Mona had always been moody and hard to read. Maybe because she'd been more interested in flirting with doctors at the hospital in Ventura, where she'd worked, than keeping a home going and teaching her daughter how to grill herself a sandwich. Or better yet, making one for her. But he'd promised not to be resentful about the whole mess of their failed marriage, so he took a breath and tried to let it go.

Mona had cheated on him exactly once, that she'd admit to anyway. She said it was just her luck that she had gotten caught. Not by him. No. By the hospital, while making out in the ward supply closet with one of the orthopedic residents. Turned out they'd been doing more than that at various spots in the hospital for months. Which blew her one-off excuse right out of the water. For once, justice had been served, since both nurse *and* doctor lost their jobs.

When Zack filed for a divorce, Mona moved out. He'd assumed a custody battle would follow, but it never happened. He shook his head at the incredulous memory. How could she leave this beautiful child behind? Not even fight for her. He squeezed Emma's shoulder again after she flipped the sandwiches and gazed up proudly at him. "See? I know how to be careful."

"Well done."

They'd gotten off to a rocky start after Mona had left, Emma hurt and missing her mom, him angry and nearly devastated by Mona's lies. But they'd made it through their first Christmas, then Easter and both of their birthdays together, and they seemed to be getting the hang of this father-daughter thing. Just the two of them. His little girl deserved a happy normal life, and he was determined to give it to her.

Cooking lessons. Where did you send a kid for such things?

She made an exaggerated inhale. "Sure smells good. My mouth is watering." Her chocolate-colored eyes lit up. "Remember that delicious wrap you brought home for me Friday?"

How could he forget. It was the best meal he'd had all week. "Yeah, you wouldn't share it with me."

"Because you already had your half!"

True, but he could've easily eaten the rest without Emma ever knowing about it.

"Anyways," she said, "That would've gone great with this soup."

"So will the grilled cheese. You have a knack for pairing food."

Raising a ten-year-old daughter by himself often baffled him. He only wanted to do right by her, but he worried in the beginning he messed up more than he got things right. Their life together was leveling out now, the two of them had gotten closer, and he cared about this small human being more than he ever thought possible. The last thing he wanted to do was throw things out of kilter again.

He'd love to see Emma learn how to cook if that was what she really wanted, since his talents were in construction not the kitchen. Even his burgers left something to be desired, often dry and tasteless, in need of extra ketchup and mustard.

Because of that TV show, Emma had recently shown a huge interest in the subject of cooking. Wasn't it a practical life skill everyone should learn? Besides, he didn't want to raise the girl on fast food. She deserved better.

His mind went back to the redhead, Lacy, for about the dozenth time over the weekend, and it wasn't strictly over the fact she was a great cook. Mona had caused him to recoil from all things female, which made thinking about Lacy all the more aggravating. It'd been a long time since he'd even noticed a woman, but how could a guy not notice that amazing red hair and those eyes that looked like a piece of the sky itself? See, that's where he could get himself into trouble, and who needed the frustration at this stage in life. She was a great cook, too, from what he'd tasted so far. He'd slipped up and sort of hired her. Temporarily, he reminded himself. But it was probably a big mistake. What had he been thinking? Hopefully, his crew would like her wraps as much as he had.

"Starting tomorrow, when you have to come to work with me, we can share your choice of wrap three days a week." Easter and spring break had rolled back around, which meant no school. Last year it had cost a fortune to send her to day camp at the YMCA; this year he figured she was old enough to entertain herself and still get some extra dad time.

The bit about the wrap got Emma's complete attention, her big brown eyes watching him as if he held the key to life.

"The food truck that wrap came from is going to be parking at my construction site for lunch tomorrow, Wednesday and Friday."

"Really? Yay, I can't wait!" Emma ladled soup into bowls with such excitement that a lot wound up on the counter.

He grabbed a paper towel and mopped up the hot spillage. "You're gonna like her truck. It's pink."

"My favorite color!"

That truth hadn't gone unnoticed the day Lacy had driven up. He threw out the paper towel and got a sponge for the rest of the cleanup. "Don't forget to bring things to keep yourself busy tomorrow."

"Like my crocheting? And my *Bettina Ballerina* books?"

"If you like. Anything but watching movies. You're going to have to entertain yourself a lot while I work."

"Like I have to do around here?"

That stung, but it was true. "You're good at it, aren't you?"

She nodded, gave that adorable smile, and all he wanted to do was hug his little girl.

"Everything's ready, Dad," Emma said, pure pride in her high-toned voice.

"Wow, this looks great." The sandwiches were browned to perfection, then placed on small plates with a pickle spear each, and the soup was in wide bowls, steam rising from the warm broth. He carried the hot stuff to the table and let her handle the grilled cheese.

"It's called presentation."

She'd obviously learned that from the *Junior Chefs* show, because he simply threw food on the plates. His kid had already figured out how to arrange things to make them look inviting. The next thought hit with a ball of anxiety: he'd be in way over his head by the time she was a teenager.

"Someday, I want to be a cook for a big restaurant," she said, delivering her plates, then rushing to grab some paper napkins. "I just need to learn how."

"Shortcake, I don't doubt you'll be able to do anything you put your mind to." He sat. "Now let's eat. I'm so hungry I may need seconds."

Halfway through the meal he got an idea. "Maybe we can search online for some kid-friendly recipes that you can try right here at home. And I can help." Maybe he'd pick up a few cooking tips, too, as it would be right at his level.

Her already large eyes nearly doubled in size. "Could we?"

His eleven-year marriage may have hit the dumpster, but he'd struck pure gold with his daughter.

Lacy arrived home from the wedding job and got right to work cleaning the truck. A few minutes in, it occurred she hadn't updated her social media today. She accessed her page on her cell phone, and where it asked the question What's on your mind? she posted: Worked a wedding today at the Natural History Museum. So Pretty. Have a new job starting tomorrow. Can't wait. To encourage interaction, on a whim, she asked: Do you believe everyone has a double somewhere out there? Then she posted a couple pictures of the museum surroundings, and the backs of several of the hat wearers' heads because they looked so springlike and pretty. Before she signed off to get back to work, she'd already picked up a few likes but, so far, no comments.

She had a big day tomorrow and needed to set up for the Gardner construction-site job. Saturday she'd prepared and marinated the steak and chicken in twenty-gallon plastic containers, enough for both the wedding and the new job. Half of it was left in the industrial-sized refrigerator in the garage for tomorrow. She'd also made up the tuna and egg salads, chopped all the veggies, diced potatoes, and made sure she had enough assorted wraps, cheese, lettuce, tomatoes, pickles and olives for no less than a hundred sandwiches.

Excitement buzzed through her over the shot at being permanently employed, though the odd feeling since that hat lady had called her Eva still hovered. What if she did look exactly like someone else? There went the hair on her arms again.

She checked her social media for comments. There were many more likes; still, no one had chimed in on her pressing question.

A couple hours later, when all was set to go for tomorrow, the strange feeling still hadn't faded. Maybe it was because after her father passed, she'd become an official orphan. What if there was someone out there, another relative? Could there be? She'd been feeling so alone since her dad died, yet instead of reaching out to friends and out-of-the area relatives for comfort, she'd been keeping to herself. She was lonely, but somehow it was also safe. In fact, for the last year she'd been making a point of protecting herself, because, well, who else was going to? She was all she had.

Her mother had died in a car accident when Lacy had been ten, something she still hadn't gotten over. Her mom had left for her shift at the library one morning and got hit head-on by a cement truck barreling around a bend. Just like that. Gone. It had been a tough age to lose the most important person in a little girl's life. There simply was no replacing a mother. Her dad had done his best, but mostly he seemed baffled by the little female in his life, and Lacy had no way of knowing men were so different from women on the emotional scale, something that would have helped her understand his awkward reactions whenever she tried to tell him her deepest thoughts. After a while, she'd simply given up. Not that she didn't love him. Of course she did, but communicating was altogether different with her dad than with her friends. So she often longed for her mother and ached to talk to her. Unfortunately, twenty-one years later, her memories of her mom were dim except for one thing. She knew she'd been loved and even cherished. She'd felt it in her soul. Just like she knew without a doubt her father had loved her, too. She'd been wanted and loved by her parents and that should be enough for any person. Why wasn't it?

And then, when Greg had been killed during deployment five years ago, she didn't think she'd ever get over losing the love of her life. He'd been everything she'd longed for—compassionate, caring, tender and easy to love. He'd also been fearless and willing to sacrifice, and the adventurous part of him had sent him away…to never return. Lacy's hand rubbed circles around her chest remembering how her heart had been ripped in half the day she'd gotten the news.

Last year, her father had suffered a major heart attack while exerting himself loading a stack of twenty-gallon containers of homemade potato salad and coleslaw onto his food truck, and had died suddenly. A neighbor had found him in the garage, and Lacy had been grateful it hadn't been her. She'd fallen apart completely when the police officer had showed up at the restaurant's kitchen and notified her. The three most important people in her life had all been taken from her without warning. Now she was thirty-one and single, without parents, husband or siblings. A total orphan.

Her life experience so far had pounded home one major point—she lost the people she loved.

Sadness and longing wrapped around her until it was hard to breathe. She'd always thought of herself as a family person. She'd chosen not to move out of Little River Valley like most of her high school friends had done. Instead, she'd wanted to live close to her father and saw him several times a week. He was all she had, and she treated that bond with great care.

Since he'd died, she'd moved back into her childhood home because she'd inherited it. It felt so empty without him, which forced her to accept that she wasn't meant to be alone. Yet she'd made no effort to reach out to new people and instead had drawn inward even though she'd always hated being an only child. Truth was, she felt stuck, like running in a dream getting nowhere, longing for something out of her reach.

As far back as she could remember, she'd thought something had been missing. As though they'd been meant to be a bigger family. When she would ask her parents why she didn't have a sister or brother, they'd get all tongue-tied. Enough so that she'd learned to quit asking and, instead, worked on accepting that they'd simply run out of time. Yet there'd been a big hole in her heart, and she couldn't deny it, long before Mom had died. As if something else had been ripped away, leaving a huge gap in her life.

What was with the gloomy black cloud hovering low tonight?

Slipping into the dumps certainly wasn't how she wanted to end her day. Not on the eve of a new start! But her memories had been stirred at the wedding, and something deeper had gotten released. That person had called her *Eva* and told her she looked *exactly* like her. So strange. Truth was, when most kids created pretend pals, she'd had an imaginary sister named Jilly—even when Mom was alive, so Lacy couldn't rationalize that it was because of losing a parent. For as long as she could remember, she'd wished for a sister, as if without one she could never be whole. Jilly helped fill that void until Lacy knew the time had come to grow up and leave her secret sister behind.

Then years later, on a group date, she'd met Greg and soon after had never felt more complete in her life.

Spurred on by the day's events, old thoughts and new questions, she strode to the guest bedroom in the 1960s California ranch house, the room with the attic opening. Once there, after pulling down the door with a broomstick-length hook and unfolding the spring-operated ladder, she climbed up and switched on the dangling single lightbulb inside. Boxes and boxes of her parents' papers were stored up there. Hopefully, someone had taken the time to label some of them.

Unable to see well in the dim light, she chose willynilly two boxes filled with papers and manila folders, and dropped first one and then the other through the attic opening. They landed with loud, reverberating thuds on the floor, leaving a small dust cloud in their wake. The first box brought her small calico Daisy Mae out of hiding from another room, and the second box sent the cat lunging back for cover.

"Sorry, sweetie!"

A muted meow assured Lacy her little girl cat was okay. Probably ticked off, but okay.

After lifting the first box onto one of the twin beds, she rifled through it, finding ten years of federal and state tax forms. If she had the time one night, she'd shred them all. Lifting the second box, she remembered she needed to defrost the assortment of homemade hand pies she'd premade and kept stored in her deep freezer in the garage…the same one her father had used for food truck supplies for over twenty years.

She really didn't have time for this wild-goose chase. With all those pies to thaw tonight and bake in the morning, she'd have to get up early. She also needed to take inventory of her paper goods and plastic utensils tonight or she wouldn't be able to sleep a wink. Everything had to be perfect tomorrow, because a potential long-term job offer depended on it.

Remembering the smiles on the faces of the construction crew on Friday when she'd handed out the pies and cups of coffee helped push that dark, dreary cloud away. Why drag up those old memories when all they did was bring her down? From now on she'd concentrate on the bright side of things. The future. Maybe that would bring her luck. She could use it.

She'd look through the second box another night. Besides, she had some making up to do with Daisy Mae, not to mention getting her beauty sleep. She wanted to look good when she officially started the construction job, which, in a perfect world, would lead to more interaction with the handsome Zackery Gardner.

One last check of her social media, where there were over a hundred likes. There were also a few comments in reply to her question about believing in everyone having a double. Most said yes. One person said something that made a lot of sense: We might think someone looks exactly like someone else until they stand side by side, then we'd see the difference.

Yes! Exactly. So logical. The woman at the wedding just thought Lacy looked like someone, but all she needed to do was have them stand side by side to realize how different they were. One last person Lacy didn't know well said: I don't think anyone could look exactly like me unless they were my twin.

The candid comment made Lacy scoff. Right. Then the hair stood on her arms again.

The sun was shining and the temperature a pleasant seventy-five degrees when Lacy pulled onto the Gardner construction site Monday at 11:15 a.m. Zack had asked her to be there by noon, and she wanted plenty of time to set up and heat the grill. Following his instructions from Friday, she drove toward a small group of sycamore trees set away from his modular office and parked in the shade beneath them. The sound of a thousand woodpeckers wreaking havoc jumbled her thoughts. The crew was obviously hard at work framing the next batch of houses. She hoped that meant they'd be hungry.

Before she set the brake on her truck, a young girl shot out of the office missile-straight through the dirt toward her. Lacy climbed from the cab just in time to meet the little brown-haired cutie as she hit the truck steps.

"Are you the food lady?" Breathless, the child inhaled before she blurted the next phrase. "I love pink!"

Grinning, because what else was Lacy supposed to do under the adorable circumstances, she nodded. "I am, and I love pink, too."

"Pretty apron." Could those dark eyes look any brighter?

"Why thanks. I like your sparkly pink T-shirt, too."

"Thanks!"

"Emma, honey, leave Ms. Winters alone so she can get set up." Zack wasn't far behind, looking not only apologetic but impressive in a tan work shirt, the familiar snug jeans and work boots. He hadn't worn his hard hat, and she got a good view of his due-for-a-cut dark blonde hair. Also impressive. This was his daughter? Which probably meant he was married, too. Of course he'd be.

Poof went her secret fantasy of picking up where they'd left off when she was eleven. The absurd thought almost made her laugh outright.

"We were just introducing ourselves," Lacy said, trying not to give away her disappointment over him likely being married while also trying to sound upbeat, in case Emma was about to get in trouble for rushing the truck.

He held back a bit, letting Emma be. The girl fidgeted like a little bunny. "We don't want to interfere with your setup."

"I do have a few things to pull together, so…"

"Can I help?" Emma blurted.

Would it be a help or hindrance and throw her off schedule to find something for Emma to do? "Um, tell you what, give me half an hour to set up my kitchen, then I'll let you put out the napkins and plastic utensils."

"Okay!" Such enthusiasm.

Why was she here, anyway? Oh right, spring break,

but did that mean Zack's wife also worked? Probably. Two-income households were a sign of the times, especially in California.

"Great," Zack said, a pleasing glint in his impressive green eyes.

Was that glint from being a happily married man? She wasn't looking anyway; in fact, she'd been hiding out from all things "living" for the last year, focusing solely on getting her dad's truck redone and taking it on the road. Still, a tiny voice in the back of her head was really disappointed.

"We'll be back later."

Later. Oh, right, she had a job to do—impress the heck out of him! She hoped *later* meant he would also order lunch. Handing out free coffee and pie samples to his men on Friday was one thing—who didn't want free stuff? But bringing the customer back to order lunch, in this case fifty construction guys, give or take a dozen, was a wide bridge to cross. She hoped she'd made a good enough impression to coax at least half of them back.

The thought of having to earn her way into a job made her heart flutter, or maybe it was the extra sneak peek she'd taken of Zack's backside while he'd guided his delightful daughter by her shoulder back to the office. *Quit looking! You're not interested.*

Besides, he's married.

Scratch *flirting* off the day's agenda, *snort*, as if she would if she had the nerve in the first place. This man was boss material. She needed a job not a crush.

She couldn't very well stand around and gawk at a really fine male specimen—she had work to do. Before she reentered her truck, she opened the outside menu, which listed the complete rundown of wraps, at affordable prices considering their size and contents. All self-explanatory, too. Chicken Done Right, Put a Steak in It, Ham It Up, Eat Your Veggies, Name That Tuna, Eggs-xactly, and Down by the Sea, a daily seafood special, today's being a cold wrap of bay shrimp with her unique take on coleslaw. Plus, the day's assortment of hand pies—apple, peach, blueberry and puddin', today's flavor being chocolate. Who wouldn't want to try out her menu at least once?

With hope cinching up her insecurity, she stepped back into the food truck and got right to work heating the grill, opening the vents, setting out the marinated steak and chicken, and all the other accoutrements.

True to her word and exactly a half hour later, little Emma popped up on the doorstep. Like a puppy off a leash. "Are you ready for my help?"

"I sure am." As Lacy scrambled to grab the paper napkins and box of plastic utensils, it occurred to her she hadn't started the coffee. "Crud!"

"Are you okay?" Emma's wide eyes and mild shoulder-hunch indicated worry. Unnecessary worry.

"Oh, I'm fine, honey, I just remembered I have to get the coffee brewed before the guys show up. Oh, and if you want to stick around, I'll let you hand out the bottled water or canned sodas when they buy them."

"Okay! This is fun." Emma took the napkins and plastic forks and trotted outside to the pull-out counter. She rushed back in the instant she'd finished, her little pink-sneaker-clad foot tapping. "What else can I do?"

"Uh, well, how about putting the mustard, mayo and ketchup bottles out for me?"

"Okay!"

It certainly didn't take much to make the child excited. A flash of being around the same age and helping her dad during the summers led her back to the handsome first adult crush of her life, Zackery Gardner, who just happened to be Emma's dad. The married guy with a family. But really, what were the odds of crossing his path again? What a coincidence.

Everything went quiet. Silence fell over the truck like a thick blanket. What happened to the busy woodpeckers?

Lacy glanced at her watch. Noon. No need for a horn or whistle to mark that. Evidently, the construction crew knew instinctively and had stopped working. Her previously distracted stomach flutters immediately reported back for duty. Taking a deep breath, as if her future didn't depend on selling wraps to new customers in order to land a regular job, she hopped into place behind the counter and waited.

And waited.

Until the silence became painful.

Looking down the site, half of the men sat on the concrete slabs of the houses eating from lunch pails, and a dozen or two had hopped into cars and driven off for someone else's fast food, no doubt. They didn't even bother to look at her as they drove by. She hadn't won a single man over by handing out her desserts last Friday. She guessed she was not good enough to pay for. She'd never once used the word *crestfallen* in casual conversation, but it turned out to be the perfect word to best explain how she felt right then.

As her heart sank, dragging her self-esteem with it, Zack came out from the office leading a line of three other employees behind him. One woman, two men. Not counting Little Miss Enthusiasm. He stepped up to the window, a sympathetic smile creasing his mouth. "Lunch is on me," he said over his shoulder to the office staff, his left hand resting on the food truck counter. When all her concentration should've been on the noble act Zack had just performed, instead she couldn't help noticing there was no sign of a wedding ring.

The small group of employees looked over her menu and each made their order. No two alike. Next Zack gave her his—Put a Steak in It, no onions.

"May I have my own wrap, Dad?" Little Emma spoke up.

"Sure, Shortcake."

His sweet gesture of buying everyone lunch made Lacy's eyes go glassy, but instead of letting humiliation take over, she got right to work making the best dang batch of wraps she knew how. Being a hand talker, she'd learned over the years she couldn't talk and prepare food at the same time, so she went quiet. Otherwise, she'd never get anything made. Out of gratitude, when she was finished, she threw in a pie for each of them.

"Coffee's on me, if you'd like," she said, as she processed the last order and gave Zack his change. They all obviously appreciated her throwing in the free stuff, but seriously, she'd made a fifty-cup urn of coffee that was going down the drain anyway.

He winked, and she felt twelve again, nearly blushed, too. Which wasn't right because he was married, and that interchange had been *so* wrong. As she cleaned the workstation, her stomach twisted with defeat. She'd had such high hopes for this job, and after today's sorry showing, he probably wouldn't even invite her back for Wednesday.

Just about ready to give up, she noticed two construction guys moseying over toward her truck. Maybe they were curious after seeing their boss and the office crew get their lunch. They read over her menu and both ordered the steak wrap. If they really liked the food, maybe they'd come back and tell their work friends, too. If she was still there on Wednesday.

Then, as she made their wraps, a couple more guys made their way to her order window. "Ham It Up and Name That Tuna. Got it!"

All it took was someone leading the way. Thanks, Zack!

The female employee was the only one to take her lunch back to her desk. Everyone who stuck around to eat stood, since there wasn't any place to sit. Hadn't Zack said he'd set up something last Friday? Though standing, they all seemed to really enjoy their meals. At least there was that.

"This is the best tuna sandwich I ever had!" Emma said with her usual intensity.

"Let me have a bite," Zack said.

"No Dad, you have your own."

"I thought we shared stuff."

"Oh, okay."

He took a huge bite as Emma griped loudly. "Hey, leave some for me."

"It *is* delicious, but I can't believe you're going to finish it."

"Well, I might leave room for some puddin' pie."

"Then let's wrap this up and take it home," Zack said, extra loud, making a point to catch Lacy's gaze, like a proud kid while saying the title of her truck.

As down as she felt over the lack of customers, she couldn't help but smile.

But, hey, Zack had already broken his promise to set up places for people to sit. Everyone was forced to stand to eat the two-handed wraps, a messy business. He probably didn't expect her to come back, or he wanted to see how the turnout was first before he made the effort, so why bother now. Good call, too, after the day's paltry sales.

With only fifteen minutes remaining in the lunch hour break, and after selling only a dozen wraps, Lacy got an idea. She made a cell phone call to Zack, who'd gone back inside the office.

"Mr. Gardner, is it okay if I take some wrap samples to the guys out on the construction site?"

"I don't see why not," he said, after a second of silence. Construction had stopped. "Just watch out for nails and…"

"I will. Promise. Thanks!" She hustled to make two of each wrap on her menu, then cut them all into four pieces. With Emma sticking around like she was on the clock, Lacy grabbed two trays and, after covering them with a paper liner, put half of the sandwiches on each of the trays.

"Emma, can you carry one of these trays for me?"

"Okay!" Bright-eyes was on it.

Lacy grabbed a stack of flyer-styled menus, stuffed them in her apron pocket and headed out the door. Since the crowd hadn't come to her, she'd go to the crew.

With Emma grinning and playing the perfect hostess, offering samples to the men who worked for her father, and with Lacy playing backup, they passed out every single quarter-wrap. Who could possibly refuse? Better yet, the men seemed to like them. Really like them. So she got another idea.

"If you bring the flyer with you on Wednesday, and buy a wrap, I'll throw in a free coffee and hand pie of your choice."

A few of the men took the menus right off. As more of them ate the various wraps, another handful took flyers. The interested response was better than nothing.

Heading back to her truck to clean up and shut down,

some of the men who'd returned from eating off-site followed her.

"I'll take a flyer," one of them said, then another and another.

"I've still got coffee if you'd like a cup."

Half a dozen stuck around for that, and since they were hanging around, she gave them some of the leftover hand pies, of which there were many. The assorted pies clearly got their approval, and soon a few more guys wandered over. Who didn't want a free dessert?

It hadn't been a winning day, but at least she hadn't fallen completely on her face.

When she was all set to leave, she thought she should take a walk to the office, to see if Zack even wanted her coming back on Wednesday.

Hating the insecurity that was strung around her like Christmas tree lights after New Year's, she stepped inside, doing her best to hide her true mood. One of the guys Zack had bought lunch for looked up from his desk and smiled. "That was a great seafood wrap."

"Oh, thank you. Glad you liked it. I, uh, was hoping to talk to Mr. Gardner?"

The mobile office was small, and she could see Zack's modest room in the back corner. He knew she was there, and the guy in the front area didn't have a chance to reply before Zack gestured for her to come over.

Not wanting to appear timid, she mustered what was left of her confidence, holding her head high before she stepped inside. Thankfully, she'd remembered to take off her toque and remove the hair net.

"So what do you think?" Zack started.

"Wasn't a very good showing. I was hoping a lot more guys would try out the food."

"We've been here a month now, and they've gotten

used to their routines. I think you should give it another shot, that is if you think it's worth your effort. Come back on Wednesday and Friday, too—if you don't have a better place to park somewhere else?"

Sitting behind his desk, laptop open, looking so darn appealing and being about as considerate as a person could be, Zack said the words she'd hoped for. Come back. She fought the urge to rush to him and throw her arms around his neck. Pure fantasy, of course, since she'd never do that to a near stranger, no matter how wonderful they were. Especially if they might be married. And a potential work contract.

"I'll be here."

Emma showed up from another office. "I wish you could come tomorrow, too."

"You're such a sweetie." It was easy, and felt natural to draw the child close to her waist and deliver a single-armed hug. What she couldn't do to the father was safe to do to his kid. Emma seemed to really crave the attention, too. "You were a big help today."

"That's because I want to be a cook when I grow up."

"You do? That's great."

"So, we'll see you Wednesday, then?" Zack broke in. "Same time and place?"

She looked Zackery Gardner in the eyes, feeling a powerful surge of something run through her that had nothing to do with getting a second chance, and pretended to be cool as a seasoned cucumber in rice vinegar. Cool was necessary around such a man. Especially since he was a *family* man.

"You betcha."

Wednesday, when she pulled her rig onto the construction site, she couldn't help but notice someone had set out a bunch of overturned wooden crates. Had Zack done it for the men to sit on? If so, that was progress and a sign of good faith. She sure hoped she could fill those makeshift seats today.

Out the door ran Emma from the office and, following behind, Zack.

"Hi!" Emma said, looking as if she was bursting to tell Lacy something.

"Thought setting up some places for the men to sit might bring more guys over," Zack explained as he made the last few steps to her truck.

"I can sure use the help and it's certainly worth a try. Thank you."

"Probably should've done it for Monday, but I think you'll have a much better turnout today."

"I hope you're right."

"Dad gave them a *peck* talk and said they should try your lunches."

"Pep talk," Zack corrected.

"You did?" Warmth started at Lacy's neck and rose to her cheeks. He'd only do that if he wanted her to stick around.

He looked flustered and maybe a little irritated, thanks to Emma's honesty. "Well, I have a bit of an ulterior motive."

"Other than helping me sell food and keep this job?"

His appealing sun-tinged eyebrows tented, and his normally heavy lidded eyes narrowed the tiniest bit. "Well, yes."

"Will you teach me to cook?"

Instead of snapping at Emma for letting the cat out of the bag, like some parents would, Zack tossed Lacy a hopeful look. "Emma really wants to learn how to cook, and…"

Who needed to think about such a sweet offer? "I'd love to."

Emma clapped, then rushed to hug Lacy's waist tight, just like the other day.

"Of course, I can't exactly teach her how to cook here." She used her hands to motion around the construction site and toward her truck under the trees.

"Right," he said. "We were hoping you might be available Saturday afternoon?"

Saturday afternoon—wasn't that a family kind of day? Where was his wife, and why wasn't she teaching Emma to cook? Did he have one? A wife? No ring. Maybe for safety reasons, he left it off at work. But his daughter seemed starved for female attention. However, Saturday afternoon didn't exactly fall into dating time zone, and any dates Lacy had ever gone on had not so far included a child, a mystery wife or cooking lessons. Still, she looked forward to getting to know both of the Gardners better. "Would you like to drop her off at my house?"

Those sexy, sleepy-looking eyes studied her carefully. "Would you consider coming to ours?"

Chapter Three

Saturday afternoon, Lacy showed up at Zack's house at the appointed time, three o'clock, with a single tote bag of groceries in hand. It was obvious the man was in construction, having taken a typical Little River Valley home and remodeled it into something amazing. A large porch wrapped around the entire house, promising a huge back patio. He'd painted the structure a trendy gray and highlighted it with beige-and-stone-colored river rockposts. The double front cherrywood doors with added stained-glass sidelights covered nearly half of the front of the house and made quite an impression. Lacy stopped briefly in her tracks to take it all in. Wow. He knew what he was doing, and she'd hire him in a minute—if she could afford a renovation.

Emma must have been watching through the large add-on bay window, another feature Lacy loved, because the little girl opened the door before Lacy reached the top step.

"Hi!" Emma said, looking tiny in the travertine-tiled entry.

"Hey you. Are you guys ready for me?" Having admitted on the drive over to a boatload of nerves about seeing Zack Gardner off duty made Lacy try particularly hard for a cool and breezy greeting. She stepped through the threshold into a surprisingly modern looking step-down living room. The floor changed to hardwood or maybe an upscale laminate that looked like wood but could handle heavier traffic. Not that there'd be that much going on with a small family, but maybe the Gardners threw a lot of parties? That didn't ring true, still she wondered. There was recessed lighting, and the open floor concept led right to the kitchen. Nice. Homey. Surprisingly so.

Zack appeared from down the hall, a warm smile on his face. "Hi. Welcome."

He took her breath away just by showing up, immediately putting her on edge. "Thanks." She tried her best to keep a calm facade. "Your house is gorgeous."

"Glad you like it." Without asking he took her grocery sack and headed to the updated kitchen. The only thing more appealing about a seriously attractive man was a gentleman. Shoot. She was a goner.

Emma grabbed Lacy's hand and led her there. Grateful for the reminder why she was there in the first place, she squeezed the little girl's fingers.

"What are we cooking?"

"I thought we'd start with something everyone loves— spaghetti and meat sauce. The easy and tasty way. Do you like pasta?"

"I love it." With such enthusiasm, the child was bound to be a great student, and Lacy vowed to keep her focus on her, not her dad.

Except Zack dressed in casual khakis instead of jeans,

and a sage-green sport shirt that made his eyes even
more impressive. Hard to look away from. He unpacked
the bag, setting the contents on the wide neutral-toned
quartz countertop. Another nice upgrade. The man had
excellent taste. Though obviously remodeled, the kitchen
was a modest size but with enough space for the three of
them to easily move around. She needed to think practically, and who knew if he planned to stick around or not?

A small round oak table in the center of the kitchen
seemed out of place. Maybe it was a sentimental piece.
There was no doubt it was where the father-daughter duo
took their meals together. Breakfast crumbs were still in
evidence. Lacy put her purse on the table, then moved to
the stainless-steel sink with the stylish extrahigh arched
faucet to wash her hands. She could get used to a kitchen
like this. And Zack? Another story.

Focus, Lacy, focus.

"First things first, right Emma?" Handwashing 101.
Since her hands were busy, Lacy gestured with her head
for Emma to join her at the sink.

Emma stepped right up, taking the obvious hint. Holding back a bit, leaning on the counter on the other side
of the stove, Zack waited his turn.

So this *was* going to be a group lesson. Fine with her,
as long as she could get over her jitters. The more the
merrier, though his presence kept her body and mind
humming, which could prove to be very distracting. Her
year of going inward had left its mark, and now she suffered the consequence of cutting herself off from the
world. One good-looking guy, and she was a basket case.
That had to be it, right? Well, that and their history of
him being her first adult crush. Him and Brad Pitt, anyway. Hmm, so she did like dark blonds.

Where was she now? Spaghetti!

"The good thing about spaghetti is it's easy, and all you need is a salad and maybe some bread to make a big and satisfying meal." Lacy pointed out both the long, fresh loaf of bread and the bag of triple-washed organic greens. "Some people make the sauce completely from scratch, which calls for advanced training. So, to make things easier and to take less time, I'm using Italian crushed tomatoes and some regular tomato sauce—" she half covered her mouth with the back of her hand, her voice a whisper "—from cans."

Lacy let Emma hold and look closely at the cans so she'd remember what to buy in the future. Then she pulled out the jotted recipe on a filing card she'd put together earlier, printed especially for a ten-year-old to read, and handed it to Emma. Then, under Lacy's direction, Emma went right to work choosing the pots and utensils with which to cook.

Though busy teaching Emma how to dice an onion and a bell pepper, then how to use a crusher for garlic, Lacy was acutely aware of Zack. How could she not be? He may have stood back to give his daughter the run of things—after all it was his daughter's cooking lesson—but he never left the room. Lacy imagined many fathers would take off at the first opportunity. He'd been handed some golden free time if he wanted, but he chose to stick around. When he'd said they both might learn something, apparently he hadn't been kidding.

After the onion and pepper sautéed in olive oil for a while, they added the pressed garlic and she let Emma help her tear apart the ground beef and stir the pot with a long-handled slotted spoon.

"This smells sooo good?" Emma said, as though a question. "My tummy's growling."

Zack smiled. Lacy knew because she'd kept her acute

peripheral vision on alert. He stepped over to peek in the pot, then he winked at his daughter in approval. Even though the gesture wasn't meant for Lacy, it still caused a warm reaction, a bull's-eye in her heart.

The only thing more appealing than a gentleman? A good father who obviously loved his kid.

"What's your favorite kind of pasta?" Lacy asked Emma.

"I don't know."

"Later, while the sauce simmers, we'll talk about all the different kinds, but for today, I brought basic spaghetti, okay?"

"Okay!"

Lacy handed Emma a long wooden spoon. "This is to stir the pot with from time to time, after we add the tomatoes and sauce."

Emma took it, making note of how long it was—the better to stir in a tall pot with—and then playfully pretended to conduct an imaginary orchestra. It occurred to Lacy that playing in a kitchen was probably a necessary part of teaching a kid to cook, So, not caring what Dad thought, Lacy pretended to play a violin.

"Would you like something to drink?" Zack asked, hopefully not because the girls had made him uncomfortable with the silliness.

Maybe she should feel embarrassed, but the smile on Emma's face was worth it. And she was, after all, the reason Lacy was there.

"Sure," Lacy said. "Were we being too loud?" She mugged.

He gave a tolerant closed-mouth laugh, the kind that sounded like loud breathing. "Not at all. I just thought all that conducting and fiddle playing might make you both thirsty."

That was another thing to like about him, his willingness to let his kid be a kid, not expecting Emma to be perfectly behaved, though she was pretty much borderline perfect in Lacy's book.

"I've got iced tea, water, or I can make some coffee if you'd prefer."

"Iced tea sounds good. Thanks." She glanced up as she thanked him, and their eyes met and held for what she thought was longer than necessary, because any amount of time staring at Zack's eyes was too long. She'd already figured that out. That familiar little zing through her body that he always managed to evoke quickly followed.

Could there be more going on here than cooking lessons, and not just with her? Part of her wanted to run and stick her head in a pot; another part seriously hoped so. Though she wouldn't want to ruin Emma's shot at cooking lessons. Or her new food truck gig, since business had picked up on Wednesday, and by Friday just about everyone stuck around for her lunches. Zack had told her the job was hers if she wanted it. Of course, she did! She'd run home and bragged about it on social media, too.

File under: Life is full of surprises. Monday I'll be starting a new gig on—get this—a construction site! Plus, I get to teach a child to cook. I'm excited!

Next, she ran a quick poll: What's your stand on kids in the kitchen? Yes or No?

At last check she'd had fifty-six likes and the yeses outnumbered the nos three to one.

"Can I have a soda?" Emma broke in.

"How about a juice box?" Zack parried.

She made a face. "Naw, I'll just have water."

"Good choice!" he said.

It was also good to know Zack didn't spoil Emma, and she didn't get everything she wanted. Well, other than cooking lessons, but that was practical. She seemed well adjusted, probably because of his efforts.

"Want to know why at first the guys held off trying out your wraps?" Zack asked casually as he filled two glasses with ice, then poured cold brewed tea in one and refrigerator water in the other.

"I didn't serve hamburgers?"

"Nope." But that got another smile out of him. "Because they said your truck looked like it served ice cream, not good, solid food."

"Well, I can see how they might get that impression."

"I took a bit of razzing from them about the bright pink, and the name, too."

They laughed together, and somehow she relaxed a little and felt closer to him. It was probably a crazy observation, but laughing with someone had always felt intimate for Lacy and was a great way to break the ice with new relationships. Not that they had any kind of relationship going. Heavens, no, she was far too out of practice, and a man like him, well, the ladies probably lined up.

She took the proffered drink and nearly guzzled half of it while he handed the second plastic glass to Emma.

"Thirsty?" Zack teased.

She nodded self-consciously. Under his watchful eye Lacy felt like she was on the hot seat.

"What do we do next?" Emma asked, uninterested in the ice water.

Lacy had completely zoned out. Forgotten what she was there to do. Because, that was what happened when she looked into Zack Gardner's eyes.

"Um, what does the recipe say?" She took pride in covering for her lapse so well.

Emma dutifully read the note card, got the can opener out of the drawer and, with Lacy's assistance, after draining the excess grease from the cooked ground meat, they added the sauce and crushed Italian tomatoes to the pot.

"Now give it a good stir with that wooden spoon. We'll wait until it comes to a boil, then turn down the heat to let it simmer. Later we'll add some extra Italian seasoning." She'd brought an Italian seasoning blend to make things easier for Emma.

The child guarded the sauce like it might burn if she blinked. Watching Emma stir and smell the sauce over and over was sweet and touching.

Time passed quickly, Lacy drinking iced tea and chatting with daughter and father as they prepared the meal together with a strong sense of camaraderie. It felt great, and she wanted to hold the moment in her palm to protect it. *Remember, being around people is a good thing.*

Without being asked, Zack set the table as Emma and Lacy finished the lesson. Soon Emma had a really good idea what all the different pastas they'd discussed were good for, and Lacy made a promise to teach her how to make an easy version of lasagna down the line.

Next, they made the salad, adding a few extra vegetables to the baby greens to make a heartier dish. Emma's favorite part—Lacy knew because Emma had exclaimed it—was to cut a loaf of French bread in half lengthwise, drizzling it with olive oil and seasoning it with a little garlic powder, the Italian seasoning blend they'd used in the sauce. They topped it with shredded parmesan cheese in preparation for lightly broiling.

"When the bread is done and the pasta's cooked, we'll add a tablespoon of balsamic vinegar to the sauce and you can stir it one last time, then we'll serve dinner."

"I can't wait!" Emma said.

"Neither can I." Zack's deep voice from directly behind Lacy sent a chill over the back of her neck. She was grateful she'd left her hair down today, grateful he was unaware of her reaction.

Zack had forgotten how good it felt to eat a delicious home-cooked meal with a woman. A beautiful woman like Lacy. She'd won him over right off with that gorgeous red hair, but add in those pale blue eyes and the delicate cleft in her chin, not to mention those pretty lips, well, at the risk of seeming superficial, he was a goner. Though he certainly had reservations about their age difference, him hanging on to thirty-nine for dear life, and her barely thirty-one. Still, there was something unique between them. He clearly remembered her as a little girl, and she remembered him as a young hard hat dude. What were the odds of ever meeting again?

He glanced at his daughter to take his mind off Lacy, and saw how ecstatic she was to eat a meal she'd played a major part in. There was that, too. Lacy had a natural way with Emma, her involvement not put on or motivated by any ulterior motive. The two of them honestly liked each other. A huge plus. But what was not to like about Emma? Yeah, he was biased.

"Shortcake, this dinner looks spectacular. You did a great job." After watching his daughter preen over the compliment, he made sure to catch Lacy's glance and nod, letting her know how deeply he appreciated her being there. "Lacy, we can't thank you enough for spending your Saturday afternoon with us."

"It was my pleasure." He believed her, too.

He'd set a place for her at the table that barely accommodated three, but she seemed to be packing up, as if preparing to go home. "Aren't you sticking around to eat with us?"

"Oh, well, um, I wasn't sure since this is technically a cooking lesson for Emma."

He shook his head, surprised she hadn't planned to eat with them. "Please join us."

"Yeah, have dinner with us, Lacy. I want to show you how good I can cook!"

Lacy laughed lightly, and Zack thought it was the best sound he'd heard all day. "Well, in that case, I'd love to."

To emphasize that he had indeed planned on her staying for dinner, he opened a cupboard and pulled out a bottle.

"I've got the perfect chianti to go with the pasta." He smiled at Lacy, then slid a deadpan stare to Emma. "None for you, squirt. Pour yourself some milk."

Later, the meal was great, the company natural and way too easy on the eyes, making it hard not to stare at Lacy. She was so darn sweet to Emma, too. Why wasn't a great woman like her with someone? Too personal? Well, he couldn't let the sudden silence at the dinner table go on much longer or it would feel awkward.

He took another bite of the delicious spaghetti with meat sauce and thought. There was one question he could ask. "What made you want to own and operate a food truck just like your dad?"

"Well, beyond the obvious of seeing how much he'd always loved it, I guess in a way I'm doing it in homage to him."

"You mentioned he died?"

"Yes, last year. It was sudden, and it's been hard without him, since my mother..." Lacy glanced at Emma, as though thinking twice about what she was about to say. They hadn't talked about what had happened to Emma's mom, and Lacey wisely dropped that line of conversation, sensing it was also painful. He was thankful she had, too. "Anyway, he supported our family with his small business, and though we were far from rich, we had a good life." She nibbled on another bite of salad. "I like the independence of being my own boss and making my own hours, too." She put down her fork, receiving his full attention. "Having a food truck is like owning a tiny diner. It becomes a community affair. I hope to have regular customers, that when people see me coming they'll know I've got something good for them to eat and wait for me to park."

"You're refreshing." He couldn't help himself—she was. "You seem to know exactly what you want, and it's nice to know not everyone is only out to make a buck."

"Well, I wouldn't mind making it big, but it's not my goal." She laughed that cute jingly sound again. "I drive a big pink truck, not exactly a serious statement, is it?" He also liked how she used her hands when she talked and didn't take herself too seriously.

Emma had been busy eating her smaller serving of spaghetti and meat sauce and cleaning her plate with the garlic bread. "I want to drive a pink truck someday," Emma chimed in, and they all had another good laugh.

"Thanks a lot," he teased Lacy for her influence on his kid.

Laughter was a sound Zack hadn't heard much of in this kitchen over the past year and a half since Mona had left. And long before that, being honest.

When it came time for Lacy to leave later, he didn't want her to go. He wished she'd stick around and watch a movie with them, then, after Emma went to bed, he could have time with her to himself. There was so much more he wanted to know about her.

They'd entered a sticky situation, whether she realized it or not. He had the upper hand, too, since he was the one in charge of her setting up and selling food to his men. But he'd never use his position like that. All he wanted was for Lacy to succeed, no matter what their personal relationship turned out to be. He also wanted his daughter to have cooking lessons without breaking his budget. It was probably best to keep things strictly business. Definitely safer. Yet she made him wish for more. A first since Mona pretty much crushed his interest in the fairer sex. Because they could be deadly.

After Lacy and Emma said their goodbyes, Zack broached the unspoken topic. Their business deal. "What do I owe you for today's lesson?"

Her face scrunched up. Had he offended her? "There's no charge."

"But if I took Emma anywhere else for cooking lessons I'd have to pay. If nothing more, for your time."

Lacy dropped the are-you-kidding act and got serious. "It has been my pleasure getting to know Emma, here." Emma who'd wrapped her arms around Lacy's hips and hugged her close, like they were already old friends. That was great to see, but also set off a tiny alarm for Zack. "As well as you. I'm fortunate to have found the perfect spot to break in my new business. That's payment enough for me."

"Well, I'm at least reimbursing you for the groceries," he said, figuratively put his foot down.

"Fair enough."

Zack also liked that Lacy knew when to back down from a friendly debate. To be reasonable.

"What're we gonna cook next week?" Emma broke in, unaware of the money issue, her little head turned up, her eyes inquisitive and crinkling with excitement.

* * *

After another week on Zack's construction site, Lacy had picked up more customers every time she parked. By Friday she'd nearly run out of pies. A wonderful problem!

Lacy had needed to switch the next arranged cooking lesson from Saturday to Sunday since she'd gotten another invitation to work a wedding on Saturday. This time, it was an outdoor wedding at a private beach in Carpinteria that paid really well, and she didn't want to pass up the opportunity.

Sunday afternoon, during the second cooking lesson, Zack showed as much interest as Emma in learning how to bread and bake chicken tenders instead of deep-frying them. Lacy couldn't deny what a good man her very first crush had turned into, and how lucky Emma was to have him as a father. The next part—how overall appealing he was—she was still trying desperately to ignore and failing miserably.

The natural progression of joking around and getting to know each other in an easygoing manner had made Lacy long for things she'd given up on. Feelings and aspirations she'd shut down after losing Greg. *This. This was what I wanted for myself, my own family.* When that option had been ripped away, she'd given up on it. Zack and Emma were a reminder it was out there.

"Okay, Zack, your turn to smash the potatoes." She handed off the old-school potato masher, and as she did, his smiling eyes met with hers. That familiar warmth curled through her body, and when he winked—his playful show-off attitude meant for the "girls" in the room— her heart pinched.

She might be rusty, really, really rusty, at the art of flirting, and he didn't seem much better at it, but she could've sworn…

Truth was, it, whatever he'd just done, had been happening a lot with Zack Gardner, even at the work site. And every single time they did whatever it was they'd started doing, because she'd completely forgotten how that worked or felt, he'd caused a similar reaction. It all added up to a word she had nearly forgotten—along with flirting. A far more dangerous word. *Chemistry.*

Going way back to her eleven-year-old self and the first summer she'd spied Zackery Gardner, even then her brain had recognized what it was. She hadn't pinned a word on it back then because what did she know, but she understood that young construction guy made her heart squeeze and her mind go foggy. Of course, she didn't understand the word back then. But she certainly did now. And yes, he still made her heart squeeze and her mind go foggy, which terrified her.

The dinner of chicken tenders, smashed garlic potatoes, and fresh peas and carrots had been another success. Emma was thrilled to learn all the steps in the simple recipes. Lacy was confident that Emma, following the handwritten recipe card, could do everything herself the next time she tried, too. When they sat down for dinner, since they'd settled it last weekend and now it was a given that Lacy would join them, it felt like a good old-fashioned Sunday dinner at home. Something she'd lost and had yearned for ever since her father had passed. Truth was, it felt too good at the Gardner home, and it mixed her up.

After saying goodbye to Emma and Zack around eight o'clock, with that nostalgic sensation flitting around in her chest and banging up against her heart, she headed to her father's old Camry parked in the driveway. With a homesick smile on her face, she slipped inside and turned the key. Nothing.

Yes, the car was old and, yes, this was another way

she kept in touch with her father's memory. However tonight, it'd let her down. The car, that is. Not his memory. She tried again. Nothing.

Zack and Emma had already closed the door, no doubt heading to the kitchen to do the dishes together. Her underhanded method to ensure they had more father-daughter time. He could teach her that part of cooking. The cleanup!

She called for roadside assistance and hoped to avoid disrupting any more of their evening by staying put in the car and waiting. Scrolling through her cell phone, she got involved in social media, then reading emails, and discovered an offer for another wedding job next month. *Why not?* So she replied.

"Is there a problem?" Zack tapped on her window.

She jumped and squealed, then, seeing him standing there, sighed as the tension disintegrated. "I have a dead battery."

"Want me to try to jump it?"

"Thanks, but a truck should be here any time now."

"Why didn't you knock on the door, let me know?"

"Didn't want to bother you."

"You're not a bother, Lacy," he said, seeming genuinely bothered by her assumption.

She wasn't? Something about that phrase made her insides light up. Could what she'd been sensing around him be more than one-sided? And wouldn't that be a new kind of terrifying if it was?

He hung around while she secretly freaked, then she got out of the car and they waited together on the welcoming cushioned chairs of his front porch. He probably thought she was a nutjob.

"How old's the car?"

"Oh, it's got to be ten years, over a hundred thousand miles. It was my father's. I can't bring myself to part with it."

"I can understand that."

"Sure, a guy could, but my girlfriends all shake their heads over my ride." The friends she'd quit reaching out to since she'd dedicated herself to being a loner.

Her answer made him smile, and she was just about to get lost in his eyes when the tow truck arrived. She showed the guy the problem. The usual jumper magic didn't charge the battery, so the driver offered to tow the car to his gas station for further evaluation.

"I'll drive you home," Zack said.

The night had become too complicated with battling feelings and car problems, but still Lacy accepted his offer, even while blinking yellow caution lights popped into her mind.

"I just need to put Emma to bed and call our neighbor to keep an eye on her while I drive you."

"I'd hate to leave Emma alone."

"It'll be fine. Mrs. Worthington looks in on her all the time. And she's happy to bring her knitting over and sit for me. She's known her since she was a baby."

Lacy remembered doing her first babysitting job when she'd been twelve and being left briefly on her own when she'd been Emma's age, so she didn't argue. "If you're sure."

His hand reached for and held her forearm. "Trust me. I'm sure. It'll be all right. Plus, she's probably got her cell phone nearby if she needs anything."

His dead-on stare, with those heavy lids and penetrating eyes only looking greener in the tow truck headlights, left her no doubt. Okay. She nodded. "Thanks."

But he'd never held her arm before, never sent a flurry of sensations tingling across her skin, and she needed recovery time from the simple act of him placing his palm on her skin. More important, how could she keep him from noticing her reaction? One she hadn't experienced since she'd been with Greg.

"Well, at least it's a beautiful night to have to wait for a tow truck to hook up my car, right?" She hoped her unsteady voice didn't give anything away. Hoped the topic of weather would keep him preoccupied.

He gave a contented smile and leaned against the car. Could he have felt the same whatever-it-was she had? Probably not.

Not to be obvious about her shaken state, she joined him at the car, and they leaned back together nearly touching shoulders. Lacy narrowly escaped it, thinking she couldn't handle a second contact so soon after the first—the one she was still recovering from. They gazed up at the waxing moon, inhaling star jasmine from an overgrown nearby bush, trying to identify all the parts of the Orion constellation, but having to settle for his belt and left knee. It was too early and not the best time of year to find The Hunter.

"That one is called Rigel," he said, pointing to the bright star, nowhere near boasting, just repeating a fact.

"How do you know that?"

"I'm from Utah, you know, the third highest state. Lots of sky and stars to gaze at, and I did a lot of it growing up."

"And why'd you leave?"

"Not a lot of opportunity for work, and the pay couldn't match California."

If he hadn't come to California looking for a job, she never would've met the younger version of him when she'd been not much older than his daughter. And she definitely wouldn't be standing here with him tonight. Funny, how life worked out liked that.

Fifteen minutes later, after the roadside service towed her car away, Zack delivered her to her house. When she got out, he insisted on accompanying her to the door. Unsure of where things were going and totally aware of him being right behind her, she turned to thank him when she got there. His head canted, eyes concentrating, seeming to have some internal debate going on. It gave her chills. Again. What was that about?

She found and put her key in the door.

"I was wondering," he began, so she stopped and turned toward him. "Maybe next week, after Emma's cooking lesson, I could hire a babysitter and we could take in a movie or something?"

Out of the blue he'd popped a question that sent her mind spinning. Maybe he had felt that zip and zing earlier, too. Sure, she'd imagined flirting with him a little back at his house while they cooked together but had assumed it was mostly on her part. Though he had kept catching her doing it while they made the meal. Now he'd just asked her out. On a date. The flirting couldn't have been one-sided. And was no longer safe.

While wrapped up in her own internal debate about the significance of his asking her out, he scoped out the neighborhood, looking almost suspicious. What was he up to?

"I'd like that," she said finally, a surge of adrenaline accompanying the simple reply. Like it was a big deal, which it was.

His head shot back around. "You would? I was beginning to think you hadn't heard me."

Thanks to the onslaught of nerves, she laughed, perhaps a bit too hard. Had he expected her to turn him down? "Yes," she said, smiling far more than she probably should've. "I would…like to, that is…" Like being a teenager again, the moment seemed overly important. But being honest, that was how she felt. She would like to but was also anxious as all get-out about it.

His eyes immediately relaxed, and he looked happy. "We can talk more about that tomorrow."

Tomorrow, that was right. She'd be at his construction site, folding wraps and heating pies and wondering where he was and what he was doing. Oh, maybe this wasn't such a good idea. "Okay."

With her head reeling, she went back to the key left in the lock on her door, attempting to open it. She glanced self-consciously over her shoulder, wondering if she should invite him in or something, but he'd gone back to checking out her neighborhood, and he'd asked his neighbor to sit, which had to be an inconvenience for her, even though it was a better part of town.

"I know it's not as nice a street as yours, but I'm perfectly safe here." In case that was what he was thinking.

He'd gone serious, searching her face, studying her eyes with his amazing ones. "I'm sure you are." He stuck his tongue into the side of his cheek. "I was just wondering how nosy your neighbors were."

The odd explanation sent a puff of a laugh through her lips. "Why?"

Sincerity oozed from his expression. He smiled gently, then placed a hand on each shoulder, the move starting something thrumming along her spine. He gingerly steered her behind the overgrown red hibiscus bush. The bush, which had been there as long as Lacy could remember, blocked out the view of half of her tiny porch. "Because I was also wondering if I could kiss you goodnight."

The humming under her skin turned to a buzz and shot straight through her, right down to her toes. She needed to swallow, but without speaking or thinking, she lifted her chin to meet him halfway as his mouth made contact with hers.

It was happening, though she still couldn't believe it.

Softer-than-expected lips surprised and pressed lightly against hers. They were warm and gentle, not needy, but extending a subtle invitation. Instead of fighting her feelings, she let the kiss run over, through and around her, all the way to tickling the backs of her knees. If he hadn't kept such a firm hold of her shoulders, she might've moved her arms around his neck and pulled him closer. But she let him be in charge, since it was his idea, and she needed to figure out the meaning of this kiss!

It was clear the kiss wasn't meant to be sexy or pushy, just a sweet, getting-to-know-you gesture. Still, it set off a euphoric pop right in the center of her chest.

And boy did she like how Zack Gardner kissed.

Chemistry. They had it. She may have recognized the possibility years ago, but she *knew it* for a fact now.

Chapter Four

Zack drove home from Lacy's on a high, until he started realizing what he'd done. He'd kissed a woman for the first time since his divorce. It was a big deal and, honestly, he wasn't sure he was ready for it; yet, some other part of his brain had taken over and besides kissing her had asked her out. The reason he hadn't kissed anyone before now had a lot to do with being gun-shy. Mona had done a number on him, and until tonight he'd felt it was too soon to move on. It probably still was, but hey, he'd made his move, and it felt exhilarating.

He'd known Lacy for a couple of weeks, and from the very start he'd felt a connection with her. He wasn't looking for that, and he'd never expected her to be interested in him. It'd happened anyway. Sure, they'd gone back a long time, twenty years to be exact, but that quirky part about history wasn't the reason he'd made the move. It was this. He liked her. He'd been around her long enough to know that for a fact. He liked her personality, her never-say-die attitude, her crazy foodmobile, the way she treated his daughter, the bond she and his kid had already forged. Especially that. Emma needed a person like Lacy in her life as much as he did.

Did he? Yes! And wasn't it about time?

Mona may have decimated his confidence, but he wasn't completely ruined if he wanted to date again.

He hadn't liked much about any woman for a long time, so it was a bit unnerving to start now. And keeping it real, he also liked her looks. Superficial or not, he couldn't deny she made him a little crazy with that red hair and the way she wore an apron. The draw was dangerous, he knew—guys always got in trouble falling for looks—but he couldn't ignore it, either. The kiss had proved that. The thought of what turned him on about Lacy besides her appearance made him laugh over the absurdity—her food truck and spunky attitude—on the drive home. His tastes had sure changed since before he was married. And that was good, showed maturity. So he may as well face the fact that his attraction to Lacy boiled down to one thing—she made him feel good. He hadn't felt that way in ages.

He stopped laughing abruptly when his mind wandered back to the actual kiss. Yikes. For a first-time, "maybe we should, maybe we shouldn't" kiss, they'd knocked it out of the park. Together. That was the part that could get him in big trouble, too. It could also ruin the great start with Emma's cooking lessons. What the blazes had he been thinking?

That life could get normal again. About time, too. Scary as it was, he was a grown-up, and it was time to accept that life went on and maybe even got better.

Now he had a date lined up for Saturday night after Emma's next cooking lesson. Like a regular person. Would wonders ever cease? Thanks to Lacy showing up in his life, he'd gone from a guy stuck on automatic to a man with a social calendar...with exactly one date planned. He chortled at the absurdity. But hey, it was a start.

For tonight, that was enough. In fact, it was more than enough. Instead of overthinking every little thing, he'd enjoy the small risk he'd taken by asking her out, and the successful outcome. She'd said yes. Little steps.

Though there was nothing "little" about that kiss.

Lighthearted and smiling the rest of the way home, he decided to invite her to visit his Santa Barbara work-site on Tuesdays and Thursdays. If she was looking for a five-day gig, why not give it to her?

His brows nearly collided with the next thought. Was that unethical? Dating a woman who needed his business?

His foot went to the brake a little firmer than he'd meant as he slowed to pull into his driveway. He was jolted forward, and the smile he'd pasted on his face for most of the drive home slipped away. He didn't want to open a whole can of "human resources" worms. He just wanted to enjoy the company of a nice woman, on not only *their* first date, but *his first* since getting divorced. It was a big deal, no way around that.

But it was also just a date, he reminded himself. Just a date with a nice woman. Nothing epic or significant.

Right. The kiss came to mind again. Definitely epic.

Getting back on topic, dating wasn't a requirement for Lacy to continue working for him. No matter what happened, he planned to make that perfectly clear. That had *never* been his style. If things fizzled out between them, she'd still have a job.

The more disconcerting thought turned out to be, what if things *didn't* fizzle out?

Monday, 11:30 a.m. Lacy, as was her routine over the last couple of weeks, pulled onto the construction site blasting her silly *Happy Days* horn. The food was prepared and ready to become wraps, the pies were already baked to a light crusty brown, and she'd keep them warm under the heating lamp. All she had left to do was set up her cold drinks and make the huge urn of coffee.

One thing was different today, though. Last night she'd shared a kiss with Zack. She'd let it unravel her world a bit, had almost posted about it on her social media page like a dorky teenager, and had subsequently thought about that near perfect kiss until she'd fallen asleep. Not to mention doing a recap the instant she woke up this morning. Could she handle a social and business association with the man? Bigger question—was she capable of handling dating anyone yet? Regardless of being unsure and confused about Zack, today she'd worn mascara and lipstick and had combed her hair in an updo. With a fancy hair clip.

Gee, you think he might notice?

The goofy thought had her spurting a laugh at the absurdity as she parked. Construction briefly stopped, with all eyes on her in the big pink truck from guys she'd trained like Pavlov's dogs to drool upon her arrival. Hadn't taken long, either. *Three days a week, fellas, bring your appetites. Lunch is on*.

Life was good, had gotten exponentially better last

night, and for the first time since her father had passed away, she felt optimistic for the future.

No sooner had she parked, opened her serving window and put on her apron than she noticed Zack standing on the other side. A sight she'd longed for, even thrilled a little over. He wasn't wearing his usual hard hat, and his light denim shirt made his baby greens pop, but what stood out the most was the smile. The man wore a smile that framed straight teeth and drove deep groves on either side of his mouth. From that grin, he was most definitely glad to see her, and the feeling, good sir, was mutual.

"Hey," he said, taking her all in, at least from the waist up, since she was behind her truck counter. She liked that he hadn't tried to hide it, either.

"Good morning," she said, both hoping he'd notice her hair and feeling a little self-conscious, then chiding herself for being insecure. *Grow up.* You already know he likes you.

He glanced at his watch. "I guess it is still morning. Yeah. Well, good morning, then." Okay, so they were off to an awkward start. But there went that slow, try-to-take-your-eyes-off-me smile, and her knees knocked a little. "Before it gets crazy with lunch orders, I wanted to throw something out there."

More goodness? He'd greeted her with a smile just now, had kissed her like a prince last night, and asked her on a date. What could he possibly be tossing around now? "Sure. Shoot," she said as though she fielded off-the-cuff options all the time, while secretly going on alert.

"I've got a second construction site in Santa Barbara, building more senior living apartments there. Since you're tied up on Mondays, Wednesdays and Fridays here, I was wondering if you'd be willing to drive up there and feed my guys on Tuesdays and Thursdays, too?"

Five days a week? That had been her plan from the start. A full-time job. No more weekend weddings to make ends meet. A steady gig feeding hard hats, something she'd dreamed about since she was a kid. "I'd love to! Wow. Thanks!"

Instead of being glad along with her, he looked concerned, which confused her. He'd just given her a great opportunity—why the sudden change?

"I hope you don't think this is related to anything we did last night," he whispered as he leaned in.

That was the last thing she would've put together from the offer, but now that he'd mentioned it... "It's not, is it?" On her side, the only strings attached to that kiss had been a longing for more. Never in her life had it occurred to her to kiss her way into anything.

He shook his head briskly. "Not at all. Let's call it a coincidence."

She pointed the spatula she held at him. "I like how you think." She shrugged, palms up. "Everything about us seems to be one big coincidence."

With one brow raised, he'd gone thoughtful again. "I think you're onto something there." He took time to study her, evidently liking what he saw. "Suddenly I'm really liking coincidences."

She couldn't help the blush. He'd said such a sweet thing and now her cheeks were heating up. There was no hiding it—the man got reactions out of her, which both pleased and terrified her. She'd been hiding out for a long time, and she knew where to run if it got too tough for her, but right now she just wanted to be where she was. Outside. Interacting with people. With Zack. Progress, right? Still she would hold on to her safe zone, just in case.

"Look, I'll let you get set up. Wouldn't want to make the guys wait."

Yep, he'd noticed her full blush. "You'll have your usual?"

"Uh, think today I'll go with Name That Tuna."

"Albacore!" she teased, her pointer finger raised.

It took him a second to catch on to her nerdy joke, but then his shoulders popped along with his short laugh, sweetly tolerant of her effort at comedy. "Cute," he said, a hint of flirting in his eyes, giving her the impression the word *cute* was meant for her, not her dumb joke.

Holy heater, had someone left the burner on?

That was what she liked so much about him—their attraction was obviously mutual. How often did that happen in life? Until recently, she'd been convinced it could only happen once, and Greg, the love of her life, was gone.

Oh, man, this business between her and Zack could really go somewhere. Which both frightened and thrilled her. Fortunately, the apron covered the very physical reaction skittering across her chest.

Monday night, Daisy Mae found a new favorite place to lounge—on top of the second storage box from the attic that had sent the cat into hiding two weeks ago. It reminded Lacy she'd been so distracted with the new job and, more recently, with Zackery Gardner that she'd never opened it. Gazing at her cat elongated to the max across the cover and purring like an electric fan, she surmised now was not the time to check it out. Still, it got her thinking about something she'd put out of her mind since that wedding. The hat wearer who'd called her Eva.

Eva. Her doppelgänger?

Nah, to some people redheads often looked alike, since they couldn't get past the hair color to notice the faces.

In fact, if she ever saw this Eva person, she'd probably laugh, then be shocked and quite possibly dismayed at how dissimilar they looked. Just like that commenter on her social media page had said. She understood people were notorious for skimming over appearances, categorizing people into groups, deciding they looked alike for generalities—in her case red hair and blue eyes— not specifics. That had to be the thing with that person named Eva.

Don't give it another thought.

Still, the notion brought out of hiding a feeling she used to have all the time growing up—the old and intense longing to have a sister. Someone to share every little thing with, like her first kiss with Zack! Because she'd been shutting people out the last year, she couldn't think of a single friend she'd want to tell about that kiss. She'd had best friends all her life, shared with them like anyone else would, too, but secretly always longed for the best friendship of all— that with a sister. What could beat that?

Lacy glanced at Daisy Mae sprawled across the lid again. Who had time to look in a dusty old storage box, anyway, when she needed to prepare for tomorrow's new construction-site gig! Wiping her hands as if she'd actually shooed her cat away from and touched the dirty box, Lacy dropped the interest and redirected her energy toward tomorrow. Then she headed for the garage to get supplies from the refrigerator and freezer.

Tuesday morning, Lacy understood the drive would be longer than usual from Little River Valley to the coast of Santa Barbara, so she left early. Good thing, too, since her GPS didn't know the exact location of the new building site because it didn't really exist yet. She came to a stop at the end of the paved road. In the distance, above the street, she saw two stories of apartment framing along the ridge of a hill. The pristine cloudless sky was California blue and the ocean's teal tones sparkled in the distance under the nearly high noon sun. Zack had stepped it up a few notches here. Wow, some seniors were going to retire in style.

Five minutes later she'd navigated the winding dirt road to the site. The seniors may have a great view, but it would be a PIA to go grocery shopping and run errands from all the way up there. On the other hand, with these upscale dwellings, they'd probably have people who did that for them, anyway.

After scanning the area, she parked the truck under the shade of another ancient oak tree and prepared to set up, deciding to hold off on the foodmobile horn until she was completely ready. The place was isolated, and her truck was the only takeout nearby. The workers probably all brought lunch pails. Glancing around at the loud and hectic construction going on, she hoped Zack had told the guys about her coming today.

A short time before noon, Lacy had completed her preparations and decided to check out the single wide mobile office before metaphorically clanging a lunch bell with the silly horn. Even though the construction sign said Franks & Gardner, she wanted to make sure this was the spot. As she walked, she considered that this was probably something she should've done first, not after she'd set everything up, but, oh well.

When she was ten feet out, Zack stepped through the door with a wide grin pasted on his face, relieving her of any last-minute concerns. Right spot. Right man. Sure felt right.

"Your timing is perfect," he said with a broad smile.

"Good to know. It was quite a trek up that hillside."

He grimaced. "I should've warned you, sorry."

"That's fine." She clapped her hands while imagining running into his arms and laying a big kiss on him that would make the already beautiful day turn magical. An adult version of her little-girl fantasies about Zack. What had gotten into her! Him. Obviously. One little kiss. An upcoming date. She felt more alive than she had in ages. Would her silly expression give her away? Instead of going with her gut, because who did that sort of thing real life—certainly not her—she turned and headed toward the truck.

"Hey," he said, making her ticker pick up a beat or two without trying.

"Yes?"

"Thanks for coming." With the full sun making him squint hard, she couldn't tell if he'd just winked at her or not.

"Of course!" She squinted back, along with what felt like a jack-o'-lantern grin.

"The guys are gonna love the wraps."

How could she resist a man who believed in her?

Fifteen minutes later, the workers mobbed her food-mobile like she was the only game in town. Because she was. Still, she noticed many had put their lunch pails aside to order from her. A high compliment, and a far cry from the first time she'd shown up at his other construction site. Maybe word had traveled among the hard hats? If she didn't deliver the goods with hearty guy-sized wraps, she might find herself twiddling her thumbs on Thursday.

Forty-five minutes later, given the good groans and moans emanating from the lunchtime crowd, including two women who weren't office workers but part of the crew—which impressed her to no end—she figured everyone liked her food. Some had even ordered the day's deal: buy one, get half off the other. She'd thought up that one on the longer drive.

"I told you guys you'd love it." Zack's voice carried above the contented sounds of sloppy eating, as he approached her truck.

"Hi! Hungry?" she said, high on the great lunch turnout, yet noticing a distinct look in his eye that made her think about something other than food.

"Yes. How about my usual?"

The thought they'd known each other long enough for him to have a "usual" brought contentment she couldn't describe. "Chicken Done Right. You're on."

Jumping into making Zack's sandwich, she realized how fast with preparations she'd become since working the construction site in Little River Valley. There had to have been close to sixty people loitering around her truck, and she'd managed to serve them all within the lunch time frame. With fingers flying making Zack's Chicken Done Right, a huge shadow at the order window grabbed her full attention. A holdout, huh?

This construction guy had to be six-six with shoulders like a refrigerator. He'd removed his hard hat and surprised her with shoulder-length ink-black hair, pulled back and tied with a leather string. From his appearance, she guessed he was Native American.

"I'll take two Eat Your Veggies," he said, surprisingly soft-spoken.

A guy his size, a vegetarian? "Buy one, get one half-off. Sure." Her brows shot up. Though one of her healthiest wraps, it was the least ordered, and usually when it was, it was by the leaner types.

She quickly finished Zack's order and put it on the

counter for him to take without charge, then got right to work making the big guy's lunch.

"Thanks," Zack said as he grabbed and left, after talking briefly with the huge worker. "You still looking for extra work?"

"Yes," the big man said.

"I may have something for you. Come talk to me later."

"Yes, sir."

Zack being referred to as a "sir" drove the point home about his being a lot older than her, but apparently, her heart didn't give a hoot. Men his age were in the prime of their lives, she'd always thought. A few silver strands at the temples did remarkable things for men nearing and in their forties. But who had the luxury of standing around daydreaming about a man when she had mouths to feed!

She loved being busy, putting the wraps together, but she'd missed her chance for another gaze into Zack's beautiful eyes with this last-minute order, and the twinge of regret surprised her. Was she ready for these kinds of feelings again? Maybe things were moving along too quickly? Thinking about their date this weekend put a smile back on her face. Apparently, she could hide out only so long without missing walking among the living again. No doubt about it, Zack made her feel alive.

"I'd like one of your banana puddin' pies, too, please," the big man said.

"Of course. Would you like more of anything?" She pointed to the assorted vegetable choices for his sandwiches, and he nodded at bell pepper strips, shredded zucchini and sliced roasted cauliflower as she piled it on.

"More cheese, please?" he said, with that surprisingly soft voice.

"Cheddar or Jack?"

"Both?"

"Sure." Since no one was lined up behind him, he'd probably be the last for today, and there was no harm in being friendly. "What's your name?"

"Benjamin. They call me Ben."

"Would you like extra pickles, too, Ben?"

"Thank you. Yes."

So polite. Sweet in nature. Maybe it was true about gentle giants. Or perhaps it was a cultural thing. Seeing him closer, she was positive he was Native American, and being in this part of the state, she wondered if he might be a Chumash descendent. But now, three more guys had lined up for a second helping of who knew what, so she didn't take the time to ask.

"Here you go, Ben. I'm Lacy."

"Thank you, Lacy." He paid for and took his food and went to a tree stump in the broad sunlight to eat his vegetarian meal as she sold three more desserts and happily ran out of coffee for the first time ever.

By the end of her first day at the Santa Barbara site, she'd surprised herself with a new record of sandwiches sold, and, from the looks on the workers' faces, customer satisfaction abounded.

Before she left, she snapped a picture of the ocean off in the distance and posted it. I'm branching out. Now serving wraps in Santa Barbara two days a week (T.Th.) Life is good!

She grinned, taking one last look around the work site before closing down and heading for home.

Since meeting Zack Gardner, things were certainly looking up.

Chapter Five

Saturday, the night of Zack and Lacy's first date, Zack battled an onslaught of second thoughts. What made him think he was ready to date again? And how would Emma react to him taking over "her" friend, Lacy? This was territory they'd never explored together before, and though he thought he knew his daughter, he suddenly had no idea how she might react. If only he'd thought to talk to her about it.

It was too late now, because he'd gone ahead and made special plans and worked out all the kinks, except for one. Emma.

He and Lacy had agreed to have the late afternoon cooking lesson for Emma as usual. The only difference was that, since he wanted to take Lacy out for dinner and a movie, he'd arranged for Mrs. Worthington to come to share dinner and a movie with Emma, too.

For a guy who thought he was beginning to know how

to read his daughter, when he watched her now, he didn't have a clue what ran through her head. She seemed fine enough, interested in the lesson and, as always, happy to see Lacy, but who knew for sure? Tomorrow she might never want to talk to him again.

As if that wasn't confusing enough, earlier when Lacy had walked in, dressed more for a date than a cooking lesson, he'd had to deal with first date jitters mixed with thoughts of how soon could they be alone. As he always did when completely out of his depth, he gritted his teeth and pretended everything was under control.

So far, he'd made it through the cooking lesson and the babysitter showing up. Still, thanks to the added stress, he hoped for a chance to retouch his deodorant before he and Lacy left.

"Okay, Shortcake, since the lasagna is in the oven," he said, still having a hard time concentrating on food when Lacy looked so fantastic. "Now's a good time for us to go."

The moment she'd arrived in those black legging-style pants and the clingy gray patterned tunic with short cap sleeves and high waistband, as in right under her breasts, and a deep rounded neckline accentuating her breasts, his mind had taken a detour from cooking.

Lacy had worn a necklace, too, something he'd never seen her do before, and the blue and black beads of varying sizes rested on the creamy skin across her collarbone. Very distracting. He'd never wanted to be a necklace in his life, until now. She'd also pulled her hair back and to the side in a low ponytail and had wrapped a tendril of hair around the elastic. He didn't know why, but that intrigued him, made him wonder what he'd need to do to unravel that hair and let the rest out. And those were the kind of thoughts that set him reeling, because he hadn't let himself think that way since the separation and divorce. The long copper waves of hair over one shoulder teased mercilessly for him to touch them. He'd refrained for two reasons. She hadn't said he could, and they'd been cooking. With Emma.

Emma, who by the way, had seemed a little sad when he'd told her he was taking Lacy out for dinner. Emma really liked sharing the meal after cooking it, and tonight Mrs. Worthington was the lucky one.

"In forty-five minutes, when the timer goes off," Lacy said, bending to make eye contact with Emma as Mrs. Worthington looked on, "don't forget to use the oven mittens to take out the pan." She went out of her way to be thorough and help Emma understand the setup.

He liked that Lacy explained everything to Emma, not Mrs. Worthington. Since the cooking lessons were for his daughter's benefit, it only made sense Shortcake would be in charge of the baking, too.

"Okay. And the salad is already made," Emma said, catching on to the routine with a pleased smile. So far, so good. She hadn't slipped him a single "why are you betraying me?" glare.

"That's right. And you did a great job on that." Lacy squeezed Emma's birdlike shoulder. She obviously believed in the hands-on approach, something Zack found endearing because of the positive way it affected his daughter. The kid had rarely gotten such attention from her mom. "Then, while the lasagna sets, you can put your rolls on the oven rack to warm. Five minutes should be fine for both the lasagna to set and the rolls to warm."

Zack also got a kick out of her need to use her hands whenever talking. He wondered if she'd be able to carry on a conversation if they were tied behind her back. Yikes, that put a surprising image, one he wasn't ready to explore in front of his daughter and longtime neighbor. Or Lacy, for that matter. He had no idea where they stood on any level other than that she'd accepted his offer to go out. Still, he reacted to her in surprisingly strong ways.

"What's so funny?" Lacy asked.

Oh, right, he was amused by her overusing her hands to explain things, and that had led to that thought about hands being tied behind her back and… "Nothing. I'm just an observer, here." Close call.

Her index finger went up, signaling another thought. "Oh, and use the oven mittens when you take out the rolls, too." Fortunately, she was distracted giving instructions and didn't notice Zack had gotten a little hot under the collar in a good way. A good and long-forgotten sensation. Gah, he was already in trouble and they hadn't even stepped out the door.

Lacy looked Emma in the eyes as though calculating how much a ten-year-old could be counted on to follow the list of instructions. Knowing his kid, she was right in wondering about that.

"You want me to write it down?"

"I got it," Emma said, as though she'd just been told the secret to life. Oven mittens rule. Use them.

"I'll keep her on track," Mrs. Worthington spoke up.

"Great. Thanks."

Emma picked up the oven mittens, tried them on, turning her hands this way and that, then put them back near the oven. "It smells sooo good!"

"I know, I'm getting hungry," Lacy said, giving a huge encouraging smile.

"Then why aren't you eating with me?"

Uh. "Because we made plans to have dinner together at a restaurant, like I mentioned."

She'd conveniently forgotten, but didn't protest, just stood there considering his words.

Zack couldn't help but hug Emma for being such a good sport. Somehow, during years of a rocky marriage and while going through a nasty divorce, he'd managed to raise a great kid. "Okay, then, are we good to go?"

"Have fun, Dad." Was it his imagination, or was Emma growing up before his eyes?

He hadn't tested her with dating since her mom had left. He'd had no idea how taking a woman out would go over when he'd run the idea by her, but she'd acted without a single qualm about her father's new social calendar. Still he'd worried. Maybe she'd been secretly worried about him, too, wondering if he'd ever get a life again. So many of her school friends' parents were divorced and dating, so why wasn't he? Most likely, Emma approved because it was Lacy he was asking out, a person Emma knew and liked. Whatever the reason, relief washed over him, and when they finished hugging goodbye, Emma looked at him, her huge brown eyes filled with genuine joy. His heart squeezed tight enough to make the backs of his eyes prick. He cut that short, patting her narrow back. There was no way he would let Lacy see him tear up before their first date. What kind of message would that send?

"Now that we've got everything worked out, I'm going to use the bathroom really quick before we go," Lacy said, grabbing her purse and heading down the hall. She'd been coming to their house enough to know where it was.

A few minutes later, when Lacy reentered the living room, she stopped abruptly. She'd obviously tidied up her hair and freshened her lipstick. Maybe it was the sweet citrus scent that rushed into the room along with her, but something took his breath away. Now, on top of all the other thoughts rolling around in his head, the strongest was how much he looked forward to this date.

Since Emma and Mrs. Worthington had forty-five minutes to kill before dinner would be ready, they'd gotten down to their favorite activity together, and Lacy had noticed.

"I've always wanted to learn how to crochet and knit," she said, sounding both impressed and envious.

"I'll teach you," Emma said, obviously tickled.

"You will?" Lacy said, equally excited and noticeably sincere.

"Sure, since you're teaching me to cook, I can show you how to do this." She held her latest project up for Lacy's approval.

Lacy moved closer. "It's your favorite color, I see."

"Of course!"

"Is that sweater for one of your dolls?"

"Uh-huh. I'm growing out of playing with my dolls, so now I like to make clothes for them."

More proof his little one was maturing.

"I'm so impressed," Lacy said to Emma before glancing at Mrs. Worthington's huge afghan project, while the woman mindlessly clicked her knitting needles, adjusting her glasses as needed and occasionally sucking her teeth. "Did you teach her?"

"My mama did," Emma volunteered before Mrs. Worthington had a chance to answer.

Lacy glanced at Zack before she commented, as though getting his okay to pursue the topic. He gave a relaxed nod. "I always wanted my mom to teach me, but…"

Now her glance was sheepish, as though she hadn't meant to go there. "Well, Emma is a great teacher, aren't you, Shortcake?" He wanted to help Lacy out of whatever rut she'd inadvertently gotten herself into.

Emma, oblivious to Lacy stumbling on her sentence, nodded up and down, though her concentration was on the pink yarn and the silver crochet hook in her hands. An ancient look for such a child. "I'll show you next Saturday," she said from the couch, not missing a stitch.

"It's a date," Lacy said.

"And speaking of dates, are we ready?"

"Definitely," she said, gazing at him with a contented look that managed to rev him up. He seriously needed to get out more because so far he'd been overreacting to everything about Lacy.

After they said another round of good-nights, Zack led Lacy down the driveway to his garage. The one flaw in his plan was Lacy had driven over to his house for the cooking lesson and so he wouldn't get to walk her to her door later tonight. Why hadn't he thought of that before now?

He'd made reservations at a cozy café in Ventura, the restaurant a revamped classic 1930s California beach cottage. Both near the beach and close to the theater for their movie, he'd decided it would be the perfect spot. Not to mention the homey atmosphere and great gourmet food. He'd asked his administrative secretary for a recommendation, and when he checked Harold's Café out online, he knew it was the place to take Lacy.

He checked his watch, and they were early enough for a drive by the ocean before arriving for their seven-o'clock reservation. Spring was stretching out the days, but by the time they reached the coast, the sun was preparing to set, scattering tangerine and several shades of red hues along the horizon.

"I never get tired of this view," Lacy said with a sigh.

"No matter how intense things get, I can count on that ocean to talk me down," he added.

Zack gazed at Lacy, deep understanding about the Pacific Ocean and its cures arching between them. "You hungry?"

"Starving."

As they drove inland to Harold's Café, he filled her in on the story about a guy who'd come here as an immigrant over twenty years ago and worked his way up from washing dishes to running his own successful restaurant with a great reputation for sophisticated cuisine. She seemed as interested in the story as he'd been when he'd looked them up online. His main goal was wanting very much to impress Lacy.

Later, Lacy was a believer as they traded bites of her chicken piccata and his medallions of pork tenderloin. Zack had a glass of deep red wine, and Lacy chose a sauvignon blanc to go with her chicken. They sat in the section of the house toward the back of the small restaurant that obviously used to be a bedroom. Appropriate for where his mind had been going since first seeing her today. He'd count their dinner seating as another coincidence but would keep it to himself. The walls had been brought down to chair rail level and, along with several windows opening to a side yard, the small room felt intimate instead of tight. Just enough for four other tables for two.

He couldn't remember being this excited about getting to know a woman since he'd first met his ex-wife. But thoughts about Mona were the last path he wanted to go down tonight, not with bright eyes sitting across from him. The muted light of the café accentuated the dimple in her chin, and he found himself staring once too often.

"Sorry," he said when she'd caught him the last time. "I just think you look so pretty tonight. Can't help myself."

She blushed, as she always did when he paid her compliments, which he *really* liked. "You do know you're exceptional looking, right?"

Her eyes went wide. She blushed deeper. "I grew up getting called Raggedy Ann and Ronda McDonald-head."

He shook his in disbelief. "Kids are so stupid." He hoped Emma wasn't being called names and not telling him.

"Being a redhead isn't for sissies." She grinned as she put the last bite of the chicken in her mouth.

"I think of you as a woman who knows what she wants and how to get it. And I've got to admit, I like your unorthodox way of going about doing it, too."

"Are you referring to my pink food truck?"

"I might be." The lingering gaze they shared turned into one of the most intense moments Zack had experienced since he'd been a young bachelor. He might be pushing forty, but that youthful desire was still going strong, and it put a mischievous smile on his face. Flirting was fun at any age.

But she went serious. "May I ask you a question?"

He'd probably made her uncomfortable by watching her a little too intently. He was out of practice. "Sure. Shoot."

"What happened to Emma's mom?"

Speaking of shooting, he'd make this straight from his hip. "We're divorced. Nearly two years now."

She looked surprised. "You don't share custody?"

"Nope." He didn't want to spend their first date and a great dinner discussing how his ex-wife preferred to be completely single to having contact with her daughter. It was too painful. And infuriating. Nope. Not going to go there.

"I thought maybe she'd died, like my mother. I keep

almost mentioning it around Emma but stop myself. I worried it might upset her."

"I wondered what was going on with you earlier."

"That obvious?"

He shrugged it off. "If Emma is upset about Mona not being around, she doesn't tell me. How old were you when you lost your mother?"

"Emma's age, ten."

"Cancer?"

"No. Automobile accident. That's why my dad used to bring me to his work sites."

He nodded, realizing Lacy and Emma had a lot in common, losing their mothers so early in life. "Makes sense." He ate a bite of dinner roll and wondered something else. "Have you ever been married?"

She shook her head after taking a sip of her wine. "I was engaged, though."

"Fell through?" He found that hard to imagine.

Her fingers divided around the wineglass stem as she rubbed her thumb on the condensation on the glass base. "He was killed in Afghanistan."

His hand sped to hers and squeezed, and she lifted serious eyes in response. "That was five years ago."

"Still got to be tough," Zack said, holding Lacy's hand for several seconds. He shared the sad memory with her as best as he could. How awful it must be to lose someone she'd hoped to spend the rest of her life with. It occurred to him that not only did Emma and Lacy have things in common, but Zack and Lacy did, too. Mona had let him down in a horrible way with her cheating. The last thing he'd ever expected when he'd said "I do" was to get divorced.

"Will you be having dessert tonight?" The waiter brought mini menus, interrupting their moment.

Zack checked his watch. "Might be cutting it close."

She shook her head to the waiter. "Thanks, but not for me."

"I'll buy some candy at the movies, though," he said after the waiter had left.

"The chocolate-covered mints?" She looked hopeful, which made him grin.

"Whatever you want. Sure."

Later, after Zack and Lacy thoroughly enjoyed the latest superheroes movie with a cast of thousands, he held her hand as they walked back to the car. It felt right, walking with her, enjoying every minute. She gazed up and gave a reassuring smile, so he squeezed her hand. That was when an idea popped into his head.

The half-hour drive home was filled with easy conversation, mostly about the movie and the amazing special effects. Followed by a short discussion of who was their favorite superhero and why. She'd claimed Captain America and he questioned her choice when Tony Stark aka Iron Man was clearly the coolest of them all. He'd actually expected her to say Thor, for obvious reasons, but once again, she'd surprised him going for the clean-cut geek-ish disc thrower.

Before they reached his house, where her car waited, he turned down a street with a cul-de-sac, part of his great plan, then parked beneath a huge oak tree that had to be a century old. She looked at him expectantly.

"Mind if we sit here for a while?"

"Fine with me."

He especially liked how easygoing she was, as if her expectations were whatever played out. "I've had such a good time tonight, I guess I don't want it to be over just yet."

"Great dinner. Great movie."

"Great company," he added, which made her smile again. Then it occurred that he'd played things wrong. "I should've suggested we go have coffee and a real dessert, sorry." He reached for the start button on his car, but she stopped him.

"This is perfect. We've had enough to eat—well, I can only speak for myself since I ate almost the entire box of Junior Mints—and besides, who needs the noise of a coffee shop?"

His shoulders relaxed, and hands dropped to his lap. "It is peaceful here, isn't it."

"Very."

He rolled down the window and let in the cricket and frog serenade. "I used to come here to think during the divorce." Not that he wanted to bring that up again, but he was just being honest.

"Sounds like you need a change of memory for this place," she said, leaning closer, taking his face in her hands and looking briefly into his eyes. He knew what was coming but was still stunned by the intensity of his reaction, as if he'd mainlined espresso and his heart sprinted instead of beat. Then she kissed him and everything disappeared except for the sensation of her lips on his, and how it spread across his body. Her mouth was smooth, dewy, opened just enough for him to feel the inside rim of her lip, some kiss. Where his kiss last week had been tentative, tonight hers was intentional, and he was excited about where this might be going. Then the tip of her tongue supercharged those nerve endings he'd put on alert since she'd first walked into his house.

Craving more, and since she'd started it, he pulled her closer, a difficult task with the console between them. His hands wandered across her shoulders and around her back, loving how she felt, then as they kissed deeper.

Receptive and responsive, Lacy found his tongue, and soon the satisfying sounds of necking, heavy breathing and above-the-waist groping, which she did equally to him, replaced the silence. Sounds he'd missed. Really missed. Sounds and sensations he couldn't get enough of right now.

His fingers dug into her amazingly fresh smelling hair, something he'd wanted to do all night, as he kissed her again and again, marveling over the way her lips felt, how velvety the inside of her mouth was, tasting sweet like mint. The playful way she teased him with her tongue flat out rattled him, which only made him want more.

Things got complicated from there, in a fun way, and he was fairly certain if there'd been more room in the car—if that annoying console between them had magically disappeared—she might have wound up on his lap. She was as into it as he was, no doubt.

Without giving up on the kissing, he explored a twisted position or two, attempting to get closer to her. One caused a twinge between his shoulders, the other a kink in his neck. Then, while shifting his posture for a third time, he bumped his head on the ceiling of the sedan.

Reaching for the jolt of pain on his scalp, he accidentally elbowed her in the jaw. "Sorry!"

"That's okay."

"You all right?" Her hair was messed in a dozen different ways and his noggin throbbed.

"Fine—you?"

"Not really."

They laughed at the absurdity of the moment. Hot. Bothered. And bumped up. What else could they do? They'd tried their best and learned there were reasons teenagers moved to the back seat of a car to make out.

Old lesson, relearned. But he hadn't really planned for this to happen in the first place when he'd parked. She'd been the one who'd started it. Which only further proved how out of practice he was in the dating department.

Unfortunately, the head bump put a damper on that hot-to-sizzling moment. Damn.

Later, after driving back to his house, they parted ways sharing another toe-curling kiss in his driveway. Zack held the car door for Lacy, then reluctantly watched her drive off. Once she was out of sight, he took the path from the garage to the front door, unsteady on his feet, certain his hair was as wild and crazy as hers had ended up, grinning at the thought. Drunk with sensations.

Drunk on Lacy.

Chapter Six

Monday morning, Lacy updated her social media page: Had a great weekend and week. Love my new job. Then she added a picture she'd taken last Friday at the construction site from her view behind the counter, with all the guys sitting around gobbling up her food.

The rest of the week, Lacy and Zack passed secret flirty looks on the job and shared more than a few smoldering glances at both construction sites. So much so, she wondered if his crews noticed? He'd also called her every day of the week after Emma had gone to bed, just to check in, see how her night was going. He never gave heavy hints or made her feel awkward. Their conversations were friendly summations of their evenings. Just his way, he'd said, of keeping in touch. So considerate! So down-to-earth and sweet.

Which rattled her. It'd been five years since Greg had died, yet some buried part of her still wasn't sure about letting go. With Zack, she'd let her honest attraction take control, which was fun though scary. She'd totally come on to him in the car the other night, and if the dang car console hadn't been in the way, who knows where they might've wound up? Thankfully, being turned on by someone still wasn't equal to opening her heart, but if it was, losing those she loved would be front and center in her brain. Maybe she could keep this business of dating Zack in a safe place.

She thought about his dreamy eyes and wondered who she was kidding.

On Saturday, she arrived at his house in the early afternoon and barely made it to the porch.

"I've been waiting all morning!" Emma said with a smile and excited brown eyes as she opened the door.

Lacy hugged her hello. "You have?"

"I got you a present." Emma rushed to the couch and pulled something from a white plastic bag like it was already Christmas morning. "Your very own set of crochet hooks!"

"Wow, aren't they pretty." The hooks came in an assortment of sizes and bright metallic colors. "Thank you." The gift touched Lacy more than she was prepared for, and she took a second to gather herself. "I love them. Thank you."

Emma's wide eyes became bigger. "And I got you this beautiful yarn to learn with. Dad said I could." She handed her a skein in a shade of light green. "It's called pistachio. Dad said that's a nut, but I just like how it sounds. *Pistachio*," Emma exaggerated. "Isn't it pretty?"

Lacy oohed as she took the items and examined them. "I love this! What should my first project be?"

"To keep it easy at first, maybe a set of place mats?"

"That's a great idea, especially since we met because of cooking."

Emma appeared not to have thought of that angle until now, and when she did, she embraced the significance behind their first project. "Yeah, and you can pick a different color for each mat and…"

"Hold on there, Shortcake," Zack said, finally making an appearance, kicking up Lacy's heart rate as he did. "Your feet are barely touching the ground." He walked across the living room and gave his daughter a fatherly one-armed hug. "Wouldn't want you bumping your head on the ceiling or launching out the front window."

"Dad! I'm just excited because I get to teach Lacy something, for a change."

"And I can't wait to learn," Lacy said, matching the enthusiasm in Emma's voice.

"Okay, this is all too awesome for me," Zack said, saying "awesome" like a teenager would, yet trying to sound overwhelmed while grinning his way through.

"Dad!" It was the first time Lacy had heard frustration in Emma's voice for her father's teasing. He clearly got the message.

"Okay, I'm going to leave you two to yourselves and go do some manly work, like mowing the lawn."

Lacy thought briefly how nice it might be to watch Zack mow the lawn, especially if he took off his shirt, but Little Miss Eager Beaver tugged her back to the moment.

"And once you learn how to do this, I can teach you how to make granny squares and you can crochet them all together and make your very own afghan!"

"I can?" Something told Lacy that learning to crochet was about to rock her world.

Zack tried to stay out of Emma and Lacy's way the rest of the afternoon, choosing to do yard work rather than the needed paperwork in his office. But he couldn't help glancing into the living room whenever he came into the house for water or to use the bathroom. Seeing Emma so happy, she and Lacy head to head over the yarn and hooks, talking about who knew what, just hanging out, made his heart squeeze. He couldn't say he missed something he'd never actually experienced, because this wasn't the way Mona had mothered. When she'd taught Emma how to crochet it had seemed more like a "let's get this over with" task. He knew a good thing when he saw it, and Zack had yearned for this kind of motherly involvement for Emma since the day she'd been born. Lacy was special.

Damn, the heat must be affecting him, sweat getting into his eyes, because they stung. One thing he knew without a doubt—he'd always made sure his baby girl got all the attention she wanted from him. He flat out didn't believe he could spoil his kid with too much love. He also understood nothing could replace a mother's love, and the way Emma thrived under Lacy's attention clarified how much his girl had missed out on. He gulped down the tall glass of water and hightailed it back outside, not wanting to interrupt their moment.

One other thought occurred on his way out the back door—that he could mess up Emma and Lacy's new friendship by getting more involved with Lacy. It was obvious how attached Emma was to Lacy. Maybe his pursuing Lacy was selfish and it could be devastating for Emma if things didn't work out, but didn't he deserve a full life, too? Truth was, he liked how the house felt full again, and more like a family lived there than it had in years. And he was tired of living like a monk. Really sick of it.

One last troubling thought made his brow crinkle

when he hit the sunshine out back. They'd only just started dating, so it was way too early to think like that.

Later, while he showered, the "girls" made dinner. The mixed-up feelings swirling around inside kept him there twice as long while he tried to sort out what the heck was going on with his emotions. Why had seeing Emma with Lacy messed with his mood so much? Sad on one hand for family experiences never achieved, and happy on the other for today, Lacy with Emma, and every day since meeting Lacy.

He lathered, and more thoughts of Lacy and what she did to him invaded his mind. She'd felt so great the other night. Okay, that was one more reason he needed the extralong shower.

It was dangerous to let his daughter get attached to her. He smiled ironically under the shower stream. Who was he trying to kid? Or was he projecting fears reserved for himself onto his daughter? Seriously, who was Lacy and where did she fit in? Was she just a nice-for-now experience, or could she become permanent? After what Mona had done to his life, he wasn't anywhere near ready to go there with a woman again.

He flipped the temperature control to cold and shocked himself out of thinking altogether.

Dinner turned out to be another good meal made great by the company. "What's this?" he asked, taking his place at the table.

"A supereasy chicken casserole!" Emma blurted, as though an expert.

"I chose something nice and easy this week, because—"

"I made the biscuits," Emma broke in. "From… What's that word again?"

"Scratch."

"Yeah, they're not out of a can."

"Then please pass me another," Zack said, taking his place at the small kitchen table for two, now easily accommodating three. Lately, he missed it when Lacy didn't join them, which was every night of the workweek. Odd thought, but just one more he couldn't deny.

After Zack tried a bite of the casserole and a biscuit, it was easy to shower compliments on his daughter. "This is delicious." He meant it, and he was proud of his little shortcake for going after her dream and especially for being good at it. Thanks to Lacy.

In ten years, he hadn't seen his daughter look happier, and there went that pang in his chest again.

Mrs. Worthington arrived as planned after the meal, and Zack had to admit, though the day had been terrific, what he looked forward to now was adult time with Lacy. Just the two of them. Not about to make the same mistake twice, he'd follow Lacy home in his car.

"Be good," he said to Emma on his way out the door, mentally chuckling that he had no intention of doing the same.

Later at Lacy's, not wanting to rush things, he suggested an evening walk. She lived a couple houses away from his friend the mayor, Joe Aguirre, and a few blocks away from a corner park. After having seconds at dinner, he could use the exercise. When they started out, they held hands, but on the way back to her house, he put his arm around her shoulders, and hers went around his waist. He measured his steps to match hers and it felt right. Being with her. Walking under the stars, their hips connecting, just talking about small stuff. This was just as much what he'd been missing as having a woman beside him at night.

The nearness of her set off thrumming throughout his body. He felt alive and ready to take on the night with her by his side.

"Your daughter is a good little teacher."

"And you're a great influence on her."

"You think so?"

"Absolutely."

"That makes me happy."

"Good to know. Oh, and since that makes you so happy, how about helping a guy out tomorrow?"

She stopped. "With?"

"I've got a date with two little girls at the amusement park and I really could use some backup." Would she accept his plea for help?

"You realize she told me all about your big day tomorrow already, right?"

"Why am I not surprised? The kid's an open book."

"It's what we women do when we crochet together," she teased, then went more serious. "You sure you need my help?"

"Do I need to get on my knees?"

That made her laugh, as he knew it would, which proved they were already well into the dating game. "Then sure. Why not."

He put his arm around her as they started walking again, tucking her near, liking how she felt. "Thanks."

With little need to have a deep conversation, Zack felt close to Lacy. She was completely with him in the moment, this simple yet special time together. He had no doubt, and it felt great. They'd spent all afternoon together, like a family. But having her to himself, he'd easily shifted to thinking like a man with a woman. This one special woman.

She silently unlocked her door. He followed her inside,

and as she fiddled around in the kitchen, he studied her home. The house, evidently where she'd grown up, now belonged to her. It wasn't at all what he'd expected—a place caught in the past, left as she'd received it. Instead, it looked freshly painted and updated with comfortable furniture and a feminine touch. He liked what he saw, especially when she came into the room with a wine bottle and two glasses.

They shared some cab and after, when their kisses and twining bodies became too confined by her icy blue couch, they had the luxury of picking up and moving to her bedroom. She suggested it, and, though surprised, without a second thought he jumped at the chance. Holding his hand, glancing sexily over her shoulder at him—which did all kinds of exciting little things to his body and spirit—she led him down the hall to the door at the end.

Her room with cool gray walls, a queen-size platform bed in grained light wood with headboard and matching side tables, and a dark Indian influenced bedspread with pops of bright yellow here and orange there, again surprised him. Like unwrapping a present one layer at a time. He liked that about her, though he hadn't let himself get that far in his thinking—how she lived or what her decorating tastes were. And right now, it was the last thing on his mind, yet he still noticed, because he wanted to know all about Lacy.

The thought jolted him almost as much as the sight of her peeling her top up and over her head. Like any gentleman would, he tamped down the interfering thoughts and jumped in to help her undress.

A meow stopped him pre-bra removal, followed by something rubbing his leg.

"Who's this?"

"Daisy Mae. This is quite a compliment for her. She's usually a one-person cat."

"She planning on sticking around?" he said, hands itching to unlatch her bra.

Lacy laughed lightly. "I doubt it. Just ignore her."

And he did.

Then they were naked, and Daisy Mae cleared out. After having already explored most of each other back on the couch, he laid her down on the bed, pausing, taking her all in. A sight he would definitely refer to again and again—the first time he'd seen her like that. He soon joined her on the cool sheets, marveling over her body, the touch and the heat of her skin as she covered him. Eagerly they twisted and tangled in a whole new way, and he wasn't going to lie. He'd come on this date both hopeful and prepared for just this moment. When it came time, after they'd gotten to know each other up close and extremely personal, out of breath with desire, he leaned over the side of the bed and fished out the little foil packet from his pile of denim on her floor.

He made a point to capture her gaze before he opened it. She nodded her clear message of yes, she wanted him. As much as he wanted her? The way he felt right then, that was doubtful. Still, her obvious consent set off a chain of mini explosions across his body before they even touched each other again.

Lacy rested her head on Zack's muscular shoulder, snuggling close, still swept up in the afterglow. She'd missed this more than she knew. They'd forged a whole new universe. Heady and indescribable. Daring. Complete. Definitely that. She'd been stunned by how great they'd been together. As if they'd known each other before. It wasn't like she and Zack had rushed into anything, yet, considering his divorce and her situation, making love after knowing each other for less than a month seemed like a whirlwind affair.

She hoped it wouldn't be a one-night stand. How would they face each other at work if it was? Had she made a mistake jumping in bed with Zack? How could something feel right and wrong at once? Maybe she should back off some, but he'd already asked her to help him tomorrow with Emma and a friend at the fun park. It'd be rude to back out now, and it might give him the impression she hadn't liked making love with him. Which she definitely had. It was just the old nagging thoughts, caused by getting close to him, that had taken her by surprise.

"You okay?"

And he'd noticed. Time for quick thinking. "Um, yeah. Just got ahead of myself worrying about seeing you around Emma tomorrow."

"The only thing you need to worry about is how big my grin's gonna be."

She laughed lightly, glad he'd distracted her from the prior confusing thoughts. "I think Emma's already caught on."

"I've been that obvious?"

"We've been." She smiled at him and kissed him lightly on his nose.

After a brief distraction, where he seemed to be thinking about what she'd implied, he took his cue and kissed her gently on the mouth.

She hadn't let anyone near since Greg. She'd tried dating here and there, but could never get into it. For the last five years she'd been positive there would never be anyone else. That was a topic far from being dealt with, and since she was kissing another man, a topic for another time. Right now Zack deserved her full attention, and Greg had captured hers for the five long years she'd missed and yearned for him.

Was enjoying being in Zack's arms a message that it was time to pick up and move forward? That didn't mean she'd ever forget Greg, because she knew she never would. But right now, she was becoming so distracted.

Zack drew her closer and kissed her forehead, a tender way to end the earlier passion that had torn up the sheets and nearly burned through the mattress. What had gotten into them?

Them. This was no coincidence. Plain and simple.

Her mouth went dry considering what she'd just done. Her surprising desire had been matched completely by his—there was no doubt they'd wanted each other. This was long overdue in her life.

She inhaled deeply as she went over the last amazingly enthusiastic thirty minutes, and soon his mouth twitched in a knowing response. Thinking while kissing, he'd caught on.

Over the years, she'd learned through the tough times to break it up, to keep things light whenever possible. For survival's sake. And after letting thoughts of Greg highjack this new feeling, out of the blue she'd found a way to stop the heavy old memories from consuming her again.

"Well, I'd say we certainly broke the ice," she said, bringing her right smack back into their moment while daring to look at him. His hair was a poufy dark blond mess, and she could only imagine how hers looked.

He let go a laugh and she joined him. Thankfully, it released the last of the tension that had tiptoed back between them, even though only moments before they'd been serious as pure sin and all over each other.

"Yeah, there's just no way to act normal around you

at work," he said, once he'd settled down from laughing and had taken her hand in his.

"Guys pick up on that stuff, don't they?" She was by no means an authority on such things, but she had a solid hunch.

"No more than women," he said, as though an expert on all things "new relationship" and the effects on co-workers.

"Then I'm not going to make eye contact with any of your crew."

"Good idea. Neither will I." They'd gone back to talking at the ceiling, but now he slid his gaze toward her, and the instant she met it, they burst out laughing again. And it felt so good.

"You're right, I should be more worried about facing Emma tomorrow."

"Maybe she'll be too busy going gaga over the rides to notice."

"I hope you're right."

She did, too.

Were they being totally immature or simply comfortable with each other? She sat up, looked at him, naked, dusted with just enough blond hair over his chest and arms, looking godlike in her bed.

"This is how I'm going to serve your crew." With his full attention, she imitated how she'd hand off her sandwiches without looking at the customers. He laughed more. Then things went quiet. Joking around or silent, she still wanted him, and evidently the feeling was mutual. Again.

Soon his hands found their way into her hair, gently tugging her to him for another kiss, and another and…

She straddled him and the last edge of sheet that had yet to be pulled from the mattress was soon set free, along with Lacy's body. All because of the smooth and amazing touch of Zack Gardner.

He'd had to go home—of course he did. Lacy understood, but still the thought of curling up with him and sleeping had such merit. Mrs. Worthington was waiting, though, and Zack had already been far too long overdue to use the excuse they'd been to see a late movie. Well, that was his problem. She smiled devilishly, a problem she was positive he felt had been worth it. She certainly had.

Wow, they were compatible. Was there such a thing as overly compatible?

When he'd kissed her good-night, she'd felt desired and valued, and knew in her gut he wasn't using her. The man didn't have a "user" cell in his body. She'd seen proof of his authenticity with the way he cared for his daughter.

Had he been with anyone since his divorce? She would've expected as much with a man like him, but in the beginning, he'd seemed as much out of practice as her. Soon enough they'd both been on a supersonic learning curve. Wow. After initially having to do some housecleaning with old feelings, including guilt, she'd cut herself some slack and gone with the moment. Again, wow. Ready or not, she was glad to be on this new adventure with Zack, even though she still had conflicting feelings about whether it was a good idea. Sure, all the physical stuff was incredible, but would that be worth the cost if things got serious? Was she even capable of opening her heart again?

There she went, overthinking, trying to put a cloud above her head again. "Stop," she said aloud. "Let yourself enjoy something for a change."

Then she took a moment to relive the last touch of their lips at the front door, causing a warm vibration to tickle her insides and sing her to sleep.

Though Sunday was meant to be a PG kind of day, sex seemed to radiate off Lacy and Zack. His steamy looks behind the backs of Emma and her friend didn't help a bit. Fortunately, it was a sunny day, so she could blame her constant blushing under his scrutiny on the heat. Such a different kind of heat.

"Can we go on the roller coaster first?" Emma pleaded almost immediately upon their arrival through the home-town-styled gate in the huge open field.

"If that's what you both want."

"Want to, Meghan?"

"Sure."

Emma and Meghan, her tall lanky friend, had evidently planned to wear jeans and matching T-shirts the color of sunflowers. At least this made them easy to pick out in the crowd.

Maybe it was something about the carnival atmosphere—noisy crowds, the scent of kettle corn, fun in the air—that made Lacy feel like a kid again. Excited. Anticipating a good time. Until she glanced at Zack, standing in line to buy tickets for two ten-year-olds. He was the real draw, looking sexy and strong in jeans and a pale blue polo shirt with the out-of-shape collar. As her recent memory served her vividly, he was a male specimen whose picture was worthy of pinning to the inside of a school locker.

He made her feel young and vital again, and...

"After this ride will you go with me on the Ferris wheel?" Emma said, practically jumping up and down.

Full-on brakes ended Lacy's inner praise of Zack. Ferris wheel? No way! She'd cursed the invention of them since she'd been eight years old and had gotten stuck at the top with her mother, who'd been no help in calming her down. Turns out she'd inherited a fear of heights from her mom, and they'd both barely held it together for the full quarter hour they'd been stuck suspended high above the fair while the problem was fixed. Lacy had been positive they'd soon fall to their certain death, and her mother had done an extremely poor job of denying it. She hadn't set foot close to one since.

"Uh, maybe Meghan will go with you?" Lacy tried to weasel out.

"They have a rule that anyone under twelve has to be with an adult."

"Then your dad will do it, I'm sure."

"But they're two-seaters and he'll have to go with Meghan to be nice, and I was hoping you'd go with me, so we could all go together?"

Oh, my gosh, maybe twenty-three years was too long to hold on to irrational fear, but Lacy still wasn't feeling the love for that big round wheel with dangling seats. How had the ungainly ride ever passed a single safety test?

"Please, please, please?"

Biting a mental bullet, Lacy woman-upped. "Only for you." And to set a good example of how to overcome fears.

"Yay!" Emma jumped and clapped, her hair, pulled into a ponytail today, looking like a pom-pom.

"Did I miss something?" Zack showed up with a three-foot length of ride tickets.

"Lacy's going on the Ferris wheel with me when we all go after the roller coaster."

Zack glanced at Lacy and winked, and her headlights

came on, no apron. How would she make it through spending the day with him without making a spectacle of herself?

Hmm, did they still have the tunnel of love at these parks? Maybe they could sign on for the extended edition? Besides being outrageous, her thoughts made her laugh as they all walked to the roller coaster. Which helped her anxiety about the Ferris wheel some, but not nearly enough.

"What's so funny?" he said, taking her hand as they strolled behind the girls, who jogged toward the line for the ride as though in a race.

"I'm just having a good time." She squeezed his hand and, since the girls were otherwise occupied, he leaned in for a kiss, and she savored all two seconds of it. How great was this? Being at the local amusement park with her new guy and his kid.

Zack had to squeeze in with the girls for the roller coaster ride because of age restraints, and Lacy stood outside, sun pounding on her head, watching and laughing as they made the long and slow trip up and then, in anticipation of the big drop, went over the top. Zack, with his mouth open and clearly enjoying himself, wedged between two squealing girls with eyes like something on Snapchat, nearly made her heart leap out of her chest. He was a good man. No doubt. Good in more ways than one, for sure.

Immediately after exiting the ride Emma came running up to Lacy. "Will you go on the roller coaster with me?"

"Again?"

"I love it!"

"And Meghan?"

"She doesn't feel so good, so Dad's going to stay with her."

How could Lacy not say yes, when Zack was racking up hero points left and right. Maybe it was time to impress him? "Okay!"

Emma grabbed her hand and tugged her in the direction of the line. While they waited, a cotton candy vendor came strolling by.

"Is that not the best smell in the universe?" Lacy commented.

"Can we get some?"

Lacy dug into her purse and bought one to share, which they went through in record time in line, the fluffy pink sugar spindles melting in her mouth, traveling directly to the pleasure center of her brain. Like a lab rat, Lacy's hand kept going back to pull off more, stuffing it into her mouth, the sugary goodness causing her to *mmm mm* with each bite.

By the time they boarded the ride, the cotton candy was long gone. And whoa! Lacy had forgotten what it was like to have the bottom of her stomach drop out over and over again. Not a good combination with cotton candy in it. But Lacy powered through the ride, buoyed by the happy squeals of her seatmate. Together, they laughed and cried in a good way, screamed and hugged, and sooner than expected the ride was over. Thank goodness! As they walked off, Lacy sensed she and Emma had forged yet another bond in their new friendship. Even though Lacy had developed a case of indigestion, it was worth the reward.

Then, Emma reminded her of the promise to ride the Ferris wheel.

Gulp.

When the day at the amusement park had ended, and Lacy had faced her old fears and conquered them—the Ferris wheel wasn't bad at all, and it ran like clockwork—

Zack took them out to eat at the best pizza parlor in Little River Valley. After the hot dog and cotton candy she'd had earlier, Lacy couldn't remember eating more junk food in one day since she'd been a teenager. The carefree hours spent with Zack and Emma were a gift Lacy hadn't dared to dream about in years. It all felt so good. She had the good sense to roll with it, to enjoy every moment and to savor the new friendship with a little girl and her "he's too sexy for his old polo shirt" dad.

Her reward was another amazing lip-lock with Zack on her doorstep when he delivered her home. Emma had fallen asleep in the car after dropping Meghan off, so they didn't have an audience.

He held her face and kissed her long and deep, letting her know how much he wanted her and bringing back the sensation of riding that roller coaster all over again. Wow, she could get used to this. And her little-girl self had once had the good sense to recognize him as something special right off, all those years ago.

He was so much more than a coincidence. More like a meant-to-be.

She inhaled him as they kissed to their hearts' content. Soon they ran out of that contentment and grabbed and groped at each other, obviously ready for more.

He ended the hot and nearly torturing kisses, because there was nothing further they could do on her doorstep unless he backed her against the wall behind the hibiscus bush?

"I wish," he said, looking deeply into her eyes.

"Me too," she concurred breathily, reading his mind.

He let out a quick breath, pulling himself together. "Well, thanks for helping a guy out today." Not exactly all business, but definitely on track.

"I had a great time."

"Me, too," he said, sounding surprised by the admission and helping her feel it was partly because she'd been there. "See you tomorrow."

She stood dreamily on her porch, watching him stroll slowly back to his car with sleeping Shortcake in it. This had turned out to be the best weekend ever. Though she wasn't going to post that online. She'd keep all the greatness to herself.

Chapter Seven

After the wild ride of the weekend, especially today at the amusement park, Lacy should have been exhausted and fallen right to sleep. But her body still buzzed from being with Zack Saturday night and kissing him goodnight just now on the porch. And after spending the day with both Zack and Emma, her mind couldn't shut down. So first she relived all the sexy parts—which was the entire Saturday night, beginning when she and Zack were on her couch and ending up in her bed.

She also replayed the good time she'd had before their date, hanging out with Emma, learning to crochet at the age of thirty-one. Loving how the yarn felt and how her very first place mat, light green, pistachio "like the nut," was already shaping up. Then getting the cotton candy scared out of her on the roller coaster earlier today and facing old fears thanks to Emma's dare on the Ferris wheel. Her cheeks tightened as a sweet smile rolled out. Great memories.

There was one word that perfectly described the whole weekend experience. Family. And thinking of family, her parents first, her out-of-control thoughts extended to Greg and the family she'd hoped to have with him once he'd come home and they were married.

On her own version of a roller coaster with alternating waves of nostalgia and sadness, she mused that if she hadn't lost Greg, she might have a toddler waddling around the house right now. Not wanting to get melancholy, she pushed back. Don't go there, not after such a great evening with Zack. *Why am I trying to ruin it?*

Zack and Emma were alive and in her life now. They were the closest experience to a family she'd had in ages, and it felt great. She needed to focus on now, not the future she'd lost with Greg. He was never coming back, but he'd always occupy a part of her heart, being the first and only man she'd loved enough to want to marry. The old "if things could only have been different" argument fell flat now, because things *were* different. Zack and Emma were the here and now.

Holding on to the past to honor the man she had once loved might seem like a noble thing, but missing out on a future because of it suddenly made no sense at all.

She wiped at an escaping tear, needing to distract herself. All these ruminations about family had set her up to think about her mom and dad. The two people who'd made her and given her a home, who'd taught her what love felt like. There was still so much of them right here. Her arms tingled and the hairs lifted. Her father's spirit was far brighter than her mother's because he'd been around so much longer than her mom. Now the only thing she had left of them were memories. "I miss you guys," she whispered.

The sudden yearning for her parents reminded her

about the boxes she'd found a couple weeks ago. Now seemed like the perfect time to get in touch with all she had left of them.

With the excuse of a late-night nosh, as if she needed to eat a single thing more today, Lacy headed to the kitchen. She drank some water, then grabbed a string cheese and retraced her path as far as the small guest room, to the second storage box. Fortunately, this time, Daisy Mae was nowhere in sight, having fallen asleep on her bed.

With the rope of white cheese between her lips, like a cigar, she dropped to her knees. Using both hands, she opened the box and dug out a wad of papers, and then another. Deeper down were manila folders and legal-sized envelopes. She sat on the bedroom carpet, back against the wall, shuffling through the loose papers, which seemed like a bunch of gobbledygook. With her free hand, she fed herself, chomping on the cheese until it was nearly gone, her attention solely on the folders and large envelopes. Daisy Mae slipped into the room and rubbed her head on Lacy's shoulder. After the initial introduction, her poor kitty had been in hiding the entire time Zack had been in Lacy's room last night. That was a long time, and the cat had hardly made herself known this morning before Lacy got picked up for her day at the fair.

Lacy smiled again at the fresh thought of Zack, even though this time something whispered caution.

Daisy Mae had probably assumed their house had been invaded by big, gorgeous and oh-so-sexy men, and lain low. The thought of invasions and Zack's handsome face looking down at her as their eyes connected and held during their lovemaking last night drew a smile that started deep in her belly, then took its time stretching across her face. This time, the steamy memory wrung a shiver out of her.

Out of pity for her confused cat, she gave Daisy Mae the rest of the string cheese. Finicky as ever, the cat sniffed and hesitated before grabbing the goody and taking off without so much as a *meow*.

Before she got off course, all dreamy about Zack again, she shuffled through more papers.

Something told Lacy to hold off on checking out the clasped envelope, so she thumbed through a couple of folders first.

After wading through piles of old home and car insurance policies, and pink slips for cars—some going so far back she didn't even remember them—she found the folder with her parents' marriage license. Then, her mother's certificate of death. A ball of emotion thumped deep in her chest. She stared at the paper that officially checked her mother off the roster of living souls, and, still raw from the night of unexplainable passion and vulnerability with Zack, plus the day of feeling part of his family, her chin quivered. Her eyes pricked. *Mom.*

After the amazing weekend she'd had, this was not the thing to do and was sure to bring her down. Still, as if it needed to punish her for having such a good time, that envelope called out to her. She examined the front, and then she turned it over to the side with the clasp, where she saw, written in fading pencil, *Lacy*. Which jolted her. On a deep breath she opened it, expecting to see her certificate of live birth and first footprints, maybe a picture or two; instead found a second document, which confused her. It was called an ABC final order amendment for her birth certificate with her parents' names listed. ABC—amended birth certificate. Had something been changed?

She rushed to her cell phone on her bedside table and

searched the term, discovering the form was required to make changes to the birth certificate. Which would become official once filled out and returned. Had something been spelled wrong on her original birth certificate? Or the date or time of her birth recorded incorrectly? Was the change something insignificant or *very* significant?

Filled with questions, she ran back to the guest room, suspiciously out of breath for rushing such a short distance, her heart thumping behind her ribs. Looking closer at her birth certificate, the final form was dated a month after her actual birth. Something had to have been amended, but what? And why had it taken so long? She dug deeper into the box, finding another manila envelope. With jittery hands, she undid the clasp, dreading what she might find. Still she opened it, because there was no way she could stop now.

Inside was something called a pre-birth judgment granting full parental rights to her mom and dad. Then behind that, another form, a declaration of parentage with only her mother's name and signature. A chill covered her shoulders and chest.

Why?

When she was a teenager she'd asked why her middle name was Taylor. Who had chosen it? What was the significance? Her parents had seemed uncomfortable discussing it, but she, being fourteen, had imagined some romantic reason for choosing the name and pressed on. Her mother finally told her it was an old family name. Being her usual determined self, she checked the family tree, or what there was of it. In the documents her family kept in an old ledger passed down from her father's family, nowhere did anyone have the name Taylor. Not on her dad's side, anyway. Maybe her Mom's? But there was no record kept on that side as far as Lacy knew. She'd run into a dead end back then, but she was thirty-one now, and she didn't have her mother around anymore to ask, nor her father. Why had she never asked him again? Her mother had been an only child, like her. Her father's only living brother was out of state and last she'd heard, Uncle Nathan was in early Alzheimer's.

There was one old friend of her dad who might know something about her birth, but he'd moved to Arizona. Did she even have his phone number?

She stood and stared into the bedroom dresser mirror. She looked just like her father. Had his strikingly red hair. His nose. But it was hard to find a feature from her mother, who had curly near-black hair, mahogany-colored eyes and olive-toned skin, and these papers seemed to explain why. Was Elaine Winters not her real mother?

Her pulse crawled up her throat. Dread and anxiety gripped her, when she thought of her life as one huge secret. She worked at but couldn't quite catch her breath as her vision dimmed on the periphery. Plopping onto the carpet, Lacy's buns hit with a thud. Pulling her knees close to her chest, hungry for air, she inhaled deeply, held it then blew it out, trying desperately to clear her head, to keep it together. All the while one word forced its way through her mind until it was on the tip of her tongue.

Adopted.

There wasn't anything horrible about being adopted— unless it was kept a secret. Why hadn't they ever told her? Were her parents hiding something more? Something they felt so strongly about they both kept the secret to their graves. Her Spidey sense erupted, not because she was in danger, but perhaps in danger of discovering something she might not want to know. She held her knees tighter to her, tucking them under her chin until her knuckles went white clutching her arms. She rocked gently side to side to release some tension while attempting to regulate the shallow breaths that accompanied a single crazy thought.

Could this be the reason she'd often felt as though she'd been ripped away from *something* or *someone*, as if a part of her soul had been torn off?

"Adopted," she whispered, as though trying it on for size.

Lacy woke up sobbing, crying from deep in her gut as if a stranglehold around her middle squeezed the tears out of her.

The dream had been so vivid. Maybe it was because she'd fallen asleep thinking of her mother. Or until last night, the woman she'd always thought of as her mother. Or maybe the sad dream was because a sense of betrayal had tiptoed into her thoughts just before she'd fallen asleep. Whatever the reason, at some point early in the morning Lacy had a nightmare. It hadn't happened immediately. No, the bad dream had waited its turn until after a long patch of restless sleep. As she lay vulnerable, paralyzed and helpless to fight back, the vision stealthily made its way in just before she slipped into REM.

She fell to her knees and spread her arms over the cold coffin, thinking how smooth it felt, kissing the grain of the wood, then sobbing her goodbyes. Forced to be final, she fought back, thinking if only she held tighter Greg might come back. Or was it her mother. Or her father?

It was all of them.

Gutted, she was alone without anyone she loved.

Soon, all that was left was cold and complete emptiness as her eyes slowly fluttered open. She was on her stomach, still distraught, her arms stretched across the bed as they had been over the coffin moments before. She must have kicked off the covers and the early-morning chill left her shivering. She checked. It was 4:07 a.m.

Lacy rolled to her back, thinking of all the people she'd lost. Adding them up in the different stages of her life. Her mother at ten. Greg at twenty-six. Most recently, her father when she was thirty. Then the disturbing thought reappeared.

I lose what I love.

With her entire body aching, she warned, *don't go there again. Don't set yourself up for more pain.*

What was going on? She sat up, rubbed her eyes and, filled with dread, walked to the bathroom.

You lose what you love. Don't set yourself up for more pain.

But she already had. Because, as of last night, she'd officially fallen for Zack Gardner.

Butterflies swarmed her chest. How had she let such a careless thing happen?

Monday at Zack's construction site felt like an ill-fitting shoe. Lacy tried her best to pretend nothing had changed since she'd seen him last, since they'd made love and had a wonderful day at the amusement park, but she failed. Turned out she was no good at faking friendly. Not that she was grumpy or anything, but pulling a smile out of her apron pocket when she was worried sick proved to be more challenging than she'd ever imagined. Before today, she'd never had to try with Zack, he'd just naturally brought the glee out of her. But since that dream, a dim light was cast over him, and a great guy like Zack didn't look nearly as appealing after she'd kissed that coffin. Or found out she didn't really know who she was. Adopted?

It was all too much, but she had a job to do, so she'd focus on that.

He had to have noticed her mood shift, too. He tilted his head and studied her while he waited for and collected his lunch wrap from her truck.

"You feel up to coming over this Wednesday night?" he said when no crew member was near.

"Wednesday?" Was she up for that? Being with him again, the setup for loss and disaster? And pain. She couldn't let on about the crazy path her brain had taken since she'd last been in his arms. Her dream. "Sure, why?"

"Emma won't be home Saturday—she's spending the day and night at Meghan's house. A birthday party. So I thought you could give the next lesson on Wednesday." He waited, probably expecting a knowing glance or a glint of serious interest on her part about Saturday belonging to just the two of them. Was that what he had subliminally offered? Another night with him? A week ago that would have been the answer to her dreams. Now, thanks to a real dream, she wasn't sure she could handle being with Zack again.

So right then, the best response she could give for spending more time alone with Zack was a forced tenting of her brows. "Wednesday's good."

He took his wrap, that questioning head tilt in place, and said, "See you then."

Tuesday at the Santa Barbara construction site, Lacy showed up, opened the food truck and awning and was well into fitting the filled containers into their slots on the stainless-steel serving counter when there was a crash somewhere out there on the building site. On any other day, she would have thought little about the sound because she was used to loud noises since working construction jobs. But this one was different, and was followed by men yelling and rushing around. This time, something was seriously wrong.

She stopped to watch, but the ruckus was out by the farthest house frame, so she stepped from her truck, squinting to see better. Still no visual. Then she migrated toward the area, but only as far as Zack's office. He burst through the door, not seeing her, and ran toward his men, phone in hand.

"Call 911," one of his crew called out.

Zack stopped only long enough to punch in the numbers as he sprinted toward the commotion, phone by his ear.

Lacy stayed out of the way, though adrenaline pumped through her veins as she got closer and strained to catch what the men talked about.

"Fell from the ladder," one man said.

"Is he conscious?" Zack asked.

"You okay, man?" another asked.

Lacy couldn't stop herself. She trotted closer toward the group, chastising herself for doing the equivalent of slowing down at an accident on the freeway. But she'd gotten to know these men serving them lunch every day, and some had even talked about their families with her. She worried for whoever had been injured, and part of her needed to know things would be all right.

"Ben, what happened?" Zack asked.

Ben! Lacy made it to the gathered crowd and edged along the back of the group until she could see around them. Ben sat upright holding his arm, and there was blood all over him. Her stomach turned, and she averted her eyes. She'd never been able to handle the sight of blood.

"Ben." Zack sounded amazingly calm under the circumstances. "What happened?"

"Sliced my finger, lost my balance. Fell. I think my arm's broken."

"Dude," someone else close to him said. "Your finger's missing."

"Find his finger!" Zack said, as though an everyday order. "We can keep it on ice and maybe they can reattach it."

Oh, gawd, Lacy had heard all she could take. She headed back toward her truck, hands jittery, worried about Ben's condition, her stomach tight and queasy. She grabbed a bottle of water, sat under the awning of her truck and waited for the wave to subside. A light sweat had popped out above her lip. In the distance an ambulance siren grew closer. She hoped they could find the construction site better than she had her first day. And she also hoped by now they'd found Ben's finger!

Wait, Zack had said to keep it on ice. She ran back inside her truck to the ice maker and grabbed an extralarge drink cup, filling it with ice cubes just in case they found Ben's finger. The thought of what might go inside the ice-filled cup caused her to sit again, long enough to take a few calming breaths. She'd never seen an amputated appendage and never wanted to. But right now she needed to think about Ben and his needs, not her aversion to all things gory.

Sure enough, Zack soon sent a guy to collect some ice.

"Did they find his finger?"

"Yeah."

Good! Lacy handed off the full cup to the guy who always bought the Ham It Up wrap, saving a few precious moments—thanks to her thinking ahead—and receiving a look as if she were a mind reader.

Queasy or not, she'd kept her presence of mind and done the right thing.

Thirty minutes later, the emergency medical services team had put Ben inside the rescue vehicle and prepared to leave. They'd asked for more ice and filled a large specimen bag for his finger transport. She caught a glimpse of Ben on the gurney. It was good to see him alert and responsive, though stoic as always. But with his arm misshapen from being broken and his hand apparently missing a finger, who could blame him for not being chatty. The poor man! Lacy stayed out of the way, but sent him good thoughts, though worried about his welfare and the extent of his injuries. She was also concerned about his wife. This was not at all the kind of news the spouse of a construction worker ever wanted to hear.

Lacy thought of the alternative—the kind of news no woman ever wanted to receive after an accident—the kind she'd once gotten—and welled up. This could have been so much worse. What was wrong with her, wearing her feelings on her sleeve and acting unpredictable? She was usually the cheer-up girl, not the overly dramatic.

Maybe that was what discovering at thirty-one that she'd been adopted did to a person. It'd thrown her off balance, made her question her identity. Or maybe the cause of her raw emotions was that dark, haunting dream, and big Ben's accident was the trigger.

Just after the ambulance left, as Lacy tried to get her mixed-up thoughts in order, Zack showed up, setting off another crazy cocktail of reactions. Concern. Anxiety. More worry. Love. Fear. *Wait, love?*

Lacy jumped to her feet doing her best not to let on what a vulnerable mess she'd turned into. "Is Ben going to be okay? Are you?"

"Yeah, he should be okay. We're all shaken, but please stick around and serve lunch. The guys need a break."

Of course, Zack would put his men first, and the request only made sense.

"For sure," she said, glad to have a purpose on the day that had been turned on its ear.

Zack stood, arms folded, serious. "Listen, I need a favor."

"Of course!" No need to think. She'd do anything to help him.

"I'm going to the hospital to make sure Ben's okay and that his insurance is in order, and to be there for him until his wife comes. But I usually take off early on Tuesdays to pick Emma up after school."

"I can pick her up. No worries."

His knit brows immediately relaxed. "Thanks. Don't know when I'll get home."

"Don't worry about a thing. I'll make her tag along with me on my errands and I'll see to it she gets fed. You do what you've got to do. Don't give us a second thought." All she wanted to do was hug him and ease his responsibility in this one small way.

He cupped her arm and squeezed. "Thanks." Relief was obvious in his tense eyes, though he looked paler than usual. Why wouldn't he? He'd just gone through an emergency. "Don't know what I'd do without you."

"Let me make a sandwich to take with you. You need to eat, too."

"Not hungry. But thanks."

As Zack strode to his car, Lacy wondered how often something like this occurred in his world. He'd handled the ordeal valiantly, willingly taking on the burden, decisive, unflappable and, being the owner of the company, without regret. The way any truly good man would.

From what she could tell, the last thing on his mind was a lawsuit, because only Ben's welfare mattered.

When she fed the guys, making sure they all knew lunch was on the house today, she looked at each of them in a new light. Any day they showed up for work a freak accident could happen to any of them. Even when utilizing the safest techniques, which she knew Ben did because he was that kind of man, it was simply the risk of the trade.

As the men filtered through collecting their wraps, she watched for any others with missing fingers. Gross, but true. Fortunately, all ten digits were present and accounted for with this group. For some reason, that eased her mind.

She happily fed the crew coffee and dessert, too. They were her Santa Barbara crew, and she was glad to be of assistance. As she watched them chow down, there was new respect in her heart for all of them. Especially Ben.

And, most of all, for Zack.

Chapter Eight

"I hope you don't mind shopping with me," Lacy said to Emma Tuesday afternoon as they approached the warehouse-sized grocery store in nearby Ventura.

She'd picked up the surprised and delighted Emma at school in Little River Valley, as promised, and handed her a bottle of water and one of her French apple hand pies. As the child gobbled up the goody, Lacy explained why she'd come, that Zack was at the hospital.

"Is Daddy okay?" Those were her first words, which made sense to Lacy since it was just the two of them, her and her father. Against the world, as it were. And she should've explained more.

"Yes. One of your dad's employees was injured and he's making sure the man's getting the best care. So he's fine, just gonna be late."

Once inside the big-box store she grabbed a cart.

"If you'd like, you can stand here." Lacy gestured.

She'd seen other people let their kids stand on the small vehicle-sized carts before, feet on the under tray and hands on the push handle. Now, with temptations on every aisle to drag the girl's attention away, Lacy saw how it saved time to add kids to the cart rather than let them roam free.

"Okay!" Emma was apparently thrilled by the unexpected field trip and everything it entailed. Her dark hair was pulled back into a ponytail today, and she wore navy blue track pants with a bright pink T-shirt, looking cute as always and ready for anything. Lacy noticed Emma only had two styles for her hair, down or in a ponytail, and she figured it was because she didn't have a mom around to try special things. Maybe sometime she'd try French braids on Emma or the double fishtail thing she could never do on herself.

As Lacy pushed, she loaded the cart with bags of onions and other vegetables, meat, chicken and ham in twenty-pound increments, three-foot-high stacks of wraps, which the child had clearly never seen. Emma watched, her feet and hands solidly in place, totally fascinated.

"Wow, that's a lot of food!"

"I know. I literally serve a small army." Lacy smiled, enjoying the company and how easily Emma was impressed.

Throughout the other chores of the afternoon, involving multiple stops, Emma didn't complain once. After arriving home, as Lacy finished unloading everything she'd purchased, placing the items into the refrigerators and storage shelves in the garage, she showed her little friend around her house.

"I like it here," Emma said, at the end of the tour.

"I'm so glad." Surprisingly, it meant a lot to Lacy that

Emma liked her home and felt comfortable with her. "Oh, and this is Daisy Mae." Who'd come out of hiding for the clear purpose of snooping. *New voice? Must check out.*

"You have a cat?" Virtually everything in life excited Little Miss Sunshine.

"Sure do," Lacy said through her smile.

"I keep asking dad for a pet, but he says no."

"Maybe we can work on getting him to change his mind." This risk could get Lacy in big trouble since she hadn't discussed it with Zack first, not to mention the fact she'd insinuated herself into his life more than she had the right to at this stage.

Emma clapped, then threw her arms around Lacy's waist and hugged tight. "Thank you, thank you, thank you!"

Lacy couldn't help responding to the hug and loved how holding the delighted child felt, how her hair smelled fresh and her little neck looked clean beneath the ponytail. Would now be a good time to offer to experiment with her hair?

Time stopped for two long seconds until a deep chill reminded her how dangerous getting involved and caring could be. It took her aback, and she let go of the girl quickly, pretending to have a sudden need to straighten a doodad on the nearby shelf. Emma noticed.

"I don't want Dad to get ticked off at you, though," said Emma, who was intuitive on top of every other sweet quality she possessed.

"Well, all we can do is bring up the subject, and the rest will be up to you and your dad."

"I think he'd listen to you."

"You think?"

"I know." She said with such certainty Lacy was inclined to believe her.

Did Lacy have some influence over Zack already, and did he really care what she thought? Well, he certainly did in the bedroom, that she knew for sure. Her cheeks went warm and she needed to change the subject. Why did the man have such power over her reactions?

"Want to see my bedroom?" Gah! Not nearly enough of a subject change!

"Yes!" As predicted, Emma was thrilled to see Lacy's room, even though it was without a single drop of girlish pink in it.

"Aww," Emma said. "I like your stuffed cat."

The tattered and worn stuffed cat was something Lacy had never been able to part with. Her mother had given it to her, and even now when she made her bed, it was the finishing touch after all the decorative throw pillows.

"I've had that since before I was your age." She opted to leave off the part about who had given it to her since moms could be a touchy subject with Emma.

"Wow!"

Oh, to see the world through a child's eyes again. Lacy smiled and led Emma gently out of her room.

"Is this your bathroom?" Emma asked on the way out, as though she'd never seen one before.

Later that evening, at Zack's house, after making a quick and easy dinner, Lacy and Emma passed the time waiting for him to get home by crocheting. Of course, that was only after Emma had done her homework. No way would Lacy mess up on that, because Zack was one conscientious father.

She couldn't help enjoying herself around Zack's kid. Emma was only ten, still oblivious to the hormones that would soon invade her prepubescent body, and she had a naturally sweet disposition. For now, anyway. Zack was a lucky guy where kids were concerned.

As they crocheted side by side in contented silence, besides enjoying the added bonding while working on a project with someone she liked, Lacy heard a faint whistle. A quiet but noticeable nose whistle—like a distant squeaky squeeze ball emitting one pattern on inhale, another on exhale—made itself known with each breath Emma took.

"Are you stuffed up, kiddo?"

"I have allergies sometimes." Emma gave the infamous allergic salute, using her palm and wiping upward from the tip of her nose.

"I hope it's not to cats." What if she'd set off an allergy attack by introducing Emma to Daisy Mae? The horrible thought went right to her chest and squeezed. Because she cared. About Little Miss Sunshine.

"I don't think so."

An odd sensation came over Lacy, an urge to nurture, and she spoke before she understood what the force was. "Ever use mentholated rub?"

"What's that?"

"Stuff you can smooth on your chest and under your nose. It has eucalyptus oil in it that helps open your nostrils so you can breathe better."

"No. I just breathe through my mouth at night."

Why did that response kick Lacy in the heart? Like everything else she'd learned about Emma, the girl adjusted to the imposition without a complaint. The tiny nose whistle and the thought of little Emma out to the world sleeping with her mouth agape touched Lacy deeper than she knew was safe. The kid was precious, not a griper. And she seemed extremely well adjusted for someone who'd been through her parents' divorce at a young and impressionable age. Lacy was struck with an overwhelming need to mother her. Simply couldn't help herself.

"You know what? I'm going to bring you some the next time I come over."

Emma scooted closer to Lacy, a big smile on her face, then she rested her head on Lacy's shoulder. "I wish you were my mommy."

Lacy froze. Things had gone too far. Had she inadvertently fed into this? How was she supposed to reply to that! Besides wanting to run for the hills, which every cell in her body was telling her to do, she was at a total loss on how to respond.

A key was shoved into the front door, immediately drawing Emma's attention and saving Lacy from formulating a logical, coherent response. Thank heavens. Because she was baffled and completely ill at case. She'd taken that fledgling mothering instinct too far and it had backfired. The child wished she'd be her mommy.

And I lose the people I love. Don't go there.

"Daddy!" Emma rushed toward the door as he pushed through, and Lacy was relieved by the separation.

"Hi, Shortcake." He looked tired. Wrung-out, to be exact. Probably hadn't had a bite to eat since breakfast. Yet he was clearly happy to see his kid, because he was a good, good man. Lacy had half a mind to rush toward him and give him a hug, too. Instead, she tentatively put down her yarn and stood, giving Zack time to say hello to his daughter after the very long day.

"Lacy made me the best grilled cheese sandwich ever!"

"She did?" He hugged his daughter close and glanced across the living room with a grateful nod.

"Have you eaten?" was all Lacy could think to say.

He exhaled. "Haven't had a chance."

"Let me make you something." Lacy started for the kitchen.

"That's not necessary. I can't thank you enough for stepping in today as it is. You don't have to make me dinner, too."

Something told her to back down on the meal and let the man take care of himself. "How's Ben doing?"

Zack tipped his head. "The break was clean, it was his radius, and all he needed was to have the doctor set the bone with a cast. I'm later than I thought because his wife doesn't drive, so I picked her up and it took a long time for Ben to be released. Then I took them home," he said while kicking off his work boots and flopping onto the closest overstuffed chair. "I'll have one of the guys drive his car back tomorrow." He rubbed his left eye. "Unfortunately, the finger couldn't be reattached. It's his index finger, left hand."

"Eww." Emma made her presence known.

"Hey, Shortcake, you should go get ready for bed. I'll be right in."

"Okay." Without being told, Emma came to Lacy, hugged her again and, lifting her face, pursed her lips.

A kiss? Lacy's heart squeezed tight, causing her to squeak her response. "Night, honey." She pressed her cheek to the child's lips, and tender, happy images of sunflowers and moonbeams invaded her mind. Not good. She could fall so hard for this child if she wasn't careful. Not to mention already falling for the dad.

And her overbearing life survey said, *Watch out!*

Emma rushed off for her room to Lacy's relief, until she glanced at Zack and saw his admiration. Their gazes met and melded. Far more than gratefulness filled his stare, and tingles started at the crown of her head and trickled down her neck like tiny raindrops, then over her shoulders, eventually pooling behind her knees.

The man needed to wear a sign. Dangerous. Keep AWAY. Simply irresistible.

"So Ben will need to help out in the office for a while." Zack must have sensed her discomfort and carried on with specifics. "He's a newlywed, needs the money, and he refused to sign up for disability." Zack also refused to set her free from his smoldering stare, even while discussing work.

"Do you have work for him?" Though she found it hard to think, she managed to come up with one good enough question.

He scratched the back of his neck. "I'll think of something."

Zack Gardner was not only handsome, but decent, noble, and caring *and* fair and...

Lacy needed to leave. Now! "I should go," she whispered, only because her voice was unable to engage while under his intense scrutiny. "Give you a chance to relax. Put your daughter to bed."

She gathered her purse and started for the door. Zack stood, came to her, put his hands on her upper arms, leaned in and kissed her. A long, dreamy kiss that put all wrong thoughts in her head about a man she could love, a home and a family. A sweet kiss that turned scary, fast.

"I gotta go," she said, breaking free.

"See you tomorrow," he said, sure as the sun would rise.

"Don't forget that mentho whatever!" Emma's high-pitched voice was the last she heard, leaving Lacy to wonder if she'd also witnessed their kiss? Things were getting so complicated. No matter how Lacy claimed she didn't want to get involved, because she *couldn't*, Emma's shout out made Lacy smile. Yeah, she'd come back for more tender torture. What else was she supposed to do?

Wednesday, after a couple of the crew had retrieved the car, Zack asked Ben to come to the Little River Valley site. The stubborn man refused to take even one day off. Zack had thought of a way to utilize Ben's knowledge and expertise. In fact, last week he'd already decided to use Ben, with his respectful and nonintimidating way, in the new capacity. The accident only pushed things up. He'd send Ben out to do this week's home visits to assess and give estimates. No time like the present to test him out. The plan had been, if Ben did well, he could pick up those extra hours he'd been asking for by working weekends making house calls for potential clients' home improvement jobs. But since he couldn't work the crew line due to his injury, Zack had decided to start him out in the new capacity today.

Usually, when one of his guys was injured, they had no qualms about going on disability, but maybe because Ben was an independent type, or maybe it had something to do with being Native American and not wanting to be beholden to the US government. There were a dozen other possibilities, but the bottom line was that he'd refused. Zack worried losing the index finger might interfere with Ben's ability to work on fine detail, but he'd go out of his way to help him out with rehab. That is, if he could get Ben to agree.

He pushed back in the chair behind his office desk, put his hands behind his head and gave himself permission to think about something nicer than running a company. Lacy came to mind immediately. He smiled thinking how much he'd liked seeing her there with Emma last night. How coming home to a woman had once been one of the great pleasures of his days, especially after having a child. Until it *wasn't* with Mona, when more often than not, she wasn't around when he got home, and Emma had been left with Mrs. Worthington.

He shook his head to put the bad memories aside, not wanting them to spill over onto Lacy. Instead he gave himself permission to think how much more than kissing Lacy goodbye he'd wanted to do last night. Even though tired and hungry, the sight of her had shot him full of energy. The ensuing smile was slow but soon consumed his face.

She was different than Mona—he knew it. She had to be. Because he'd never again put himself through what he'd experienced with his ex.

Wednesday evening Lacy showed up early, before Zack was home, fetching Emma from next door with her after-school guardian, Mrs. Worthington. Being alone with Emma again drove another point home about Lacy's changing outlook. *I'm getting as attached to her as she is to me. It's already too late to avoid being hurt if things don't work out with Zack. Too late for both of us. All three?*

Her stomach sank as she put the ingredients for a healthy chicken piccata on the counter with Emma eagerly looking on.

"So I thought using half zucchini noodles, or zoodles as we call them, instead of all pasta would be a good compromise on sneaking in veggies. What do you think?"

"Great, maybe I won't even know I'm eating that green stuff," Emma said as enthusiastically as ever, even when she didn't like something. Which always put a smile on Lacy's face and tugged at her heart. The same heart that'd had enough aching for a lifetime.

"Lacy? Next time you shop at a regular store, can I go with you?" Emma said. After closely observing everything Lacy had unpacked, Emma had asked how each item would be used in their dish. Lacy had explained in simple terms the answer to each of her questions, until this one. To be honest, the question made her stumble. Shopping struck Lacy as something families did together. Not like the other day when Emma had tagged along at the big-box store for food truck necessities. This was different and so much closer to home.

Grocery shopping was meant for families. Like Zack and Emma.

But Lacy could see the purpose of learning to shop along with cooking lessons. She'd think of it like that— not as a family outing, but a necessary function of learning to cook. "That would be fun, too. I'll even let you write out the list when we talk about what we want to cook and what we'll need to shop for."

Emma's eyes brightened. "That's what I want to learn next. How to shop. Dad doesn't like to, and sometimes he just grabs stuff, and nothing matches up. Or he forgets stuff."

"We all do sometimes." Lacy could easily imagine Zack at the supermarket going through the motions of stocking the pantry back home. Her heart twanged in a good way, again, causing another mental caution flag to raise. *I'm falling for him and I'm not sure I can handle it.* She did her best to ignore it so Emma wouldn't catch on to her mood shift and badger her with more questions.

Later, with Zack arriving home while Lacy and Emma fixed dinner, things seemed far too domestic. And too close to a buried dream she'd once entertained—getting married, raising a family. Since having that nightmare, along with the addition of looking through the new *I lose what I love* lens, Zack's arrival seemed almost cruel in how good it felt. His subtle, possessive touches to her arm and lower back were hard enough to take as they moved around the kitchen preparing the meal and setting the table. But the romantic light glide of his knuckles along her cheek when she announced dinner was ready, while he serenely smiled at her, nearly had her running out the front door as if her hair had been set on fire. Obviously, that wasn't the reaction he'd expected.

His very presence did magical stuff to her body, moved her in ways she'd given up hoping for. Truth was, she'd stopped wanting those things that scared her because, well, her track record didn't bode well for the future.

After the dinner cleanup, Emma helped Lacy learn some basic knit one purl two stitches while Zack puttered around in the garage. So domestic. Too domestic?

"Will you put me to bed tonight?" Emma asked Lacy when Zack came back inside breaking the news about the time. Uh-oh.

"Is there some kind of routine I need to know?" Lacy asked Zack, hoping he wouldn't mind her taking his job.

"Oh, she'll fill you in on that part." His eyes looked deeply content. It was clear that she wasn't stepping on his territory, because he seemed happy to share the duty. But they were all three tiptoeing into new and possibly sacred territory. The point hadn't gone unnoticed by all three of them, from the respectful mood in the family room.

Emma giggled. "Come on!"

Lacy followed her little friend down to an overwhelmingly pink accented bedroom, seeing firsthand that Zack could indeed be an overindulgent father. The juxtaposition with the strong contractor made her smile.

"This is my bed, isn't it pretty?"

The off-white finished wood frame was perfect for a little princess. "Did your mom decorate the room for you?" Lacy knew it was a touchy subject, but curiosity had won out.

"Nope. Dad did, I think last year," Emma said as she undressed to her panties, dropped her clothes on the floor and left them where they fell, then rummaged through her dresser—the same off-white finish as the bed and as tall as Emma—for her pajamas. The child was completely uninhibited around Lacy.

Zack had taken great care with this room and, like all things Zack and Emma, it touched Lacy in the most tender part of her heart. Before she let emotions take over, she acted. "Oh, hey, now would be a good time to put on that mentholated rub." She'd brought the jar along when Emma invited her to tuck her in.

Emma put her legs through the pj's bottoms, then sat on the bed. "Okay."

Then Emma allowed Lacy to put the rub on her narrow chest. "We'll wait until after you brush your teeth for the next part," she said when done.

Emma put her pj's top on and went to the bathroom to do her routine. Lacy deduced she was old enough to wash her face and brush her teeth herself. While waiting, Lacy picked up the forgotten clothes on the floor, then pulled back the covers. Surprise! The sheets were a neon-pink pattern against a white background. Lacy shook her head and smiled. Zack.

Back in a flash with her hair wild and loose, Emma jumped onto her bed. Then Lacy put an index-finger's worth of the wonder balm under Emma's upturned and whistling nose, like an invisible mustache.

"Thanks," Emma said, making a funny face. "It smells weird."

"I know, but it should help you breathe better."

As always, Emma was more than happy to take any advice Lacy dished out.

"You know what my mother used to do when I was around your age?"

Lacy shook her head, some of the wild dark brown hair sticking to her gooey mustache.

"She used to brush my hair before I went to bed," Lacy said, removing the few long strands from under Emma's nose. "Would you like me to do that?"

Her head nodded, eyes bright. "My brush is in the bathroom."

Lacy quickly retrieved the brush, full of long hairs, and manually pulled them out as she walked back to the bed. "If you want, I can wash this brush before I leave tonight so it will be fresh for you tomorrow?"

"Okay."

Emma sat perfectly still as Lacy gently brushed her hair, careful not to tug any knots. The silence said it all. It was a good idea. Another popped into her head.

"Maybe sometime you'd let me try French braiding or fishtail braiding your hair?"

As expected, Emma's shoulders shot up in an excited way. "That'd be so cool!"

"Okay, then. It's a plan." A couple minutes later, with Emma's hair looking beautifully smooth, Lacy put the brush in her lap to take with her.

"I'm gonna pray," Emma announced.

"Okay." She sure hadn't seen that coming.

Emma steepled her fingers and squinted her eyes tight. "Thank you for my dad, for taking care of me. Please keep him safe."

Amen, Lacy thought.

"And thank you for Lacy. She's helping me learn to cook, and I really like her. Please make her happy."

Did the kid sense her emotional battle?

"Amen."

"That was a lovely prayer. Thank you for including me."

"I always do."

"You do?"

Emma nodded, then leaned back and put her head on the pillow. "Since you started giving me cooking lessons."

"Well, I'm honored. Thanks." Lacy had the urge to lean over and kiss her but fought it. "Good night, Emma," she said, instead.

After turning out the light, just when she was about to close the door, Emma piped up. "You can call me Shortcake if you want."

Lacy chuckled. "I think that's your dad's special name for you. Maybe he should be the only one to use it?"

Emma sighed. "I think I can breathe better." Her busy brain already on to a new subject.

"That's great." She shut the door, brush in hand, and went straight for the kitchen.

Putting Emma to bed had been far too alluring and domestic. Definitely out of her comfort zone. Saying goodnight to her little friend reminded her how much she loved being in the Gardner home, how she could see herself there on a regular basis. Again, cautious shivers warned her not to go there in thoughts or wishes. Probably not in her future. And it wasn't safe. For her or them.

The garage door, which was connected to part of the kitchen, was askew, and she heard Zack working on something. After removing the built-up hair from the brush, she washed it with dish soap and laid it on the

mat on the counter to dry. She took a glass from the cupboard, filled it with ice, then tea from the refrigerator,
and headed to the garage.

"Thought you might like something to drink?"

He stopped sanding his project. "Thanks."

She carried it to him. "What's this?"

"A black walnut wall hanger for beside your front door.
I'm going to put your address here—" he pointed to the
front panel "—and you can put a small plant or two in
this pocket area. Should look good at your house."

"I love it! Thank you." She put his iced tea on the
counter, and if his hands weren't busy with tools and
sandpaper, she would've hugged him.

For some odd reason, she was glad she couldn't. "Well,
I'm going to let you work on that while I try to make
heads or tails out of my latest dinner mat."

He smiled his reply and her heart overflowed with
good feelings.

And later with Zack in the living room, Lacy was
helpless under his all-out assaulting charm, with hungry kisses and mutual groping on the couch. After living
alone for so long, how could she not want the attention?
Then, when the make-out session heated up to the boil-
ing point, he surprised her.

"Sorry to cut this short, but I don't feel right having
you stay over, or us making love with Emma in the house.
It might confuse her," he said.

It hadn't yet occurred to Lacy, while she was wrapped
up in her own confusion, how Emma might or might not
feel about her father moving on with another woman.
She was so busy thinking of the reasons she should steer
clear of Zack and all he offered, she'd conveniently forgotten how Emma's feelings might factor in. Yet Emma
had told her she wished she was her mother and had let

Lacy brush her hair tonight. They'd even made plans for a hair-braiding session. Maybe having her father get involved with a new woman would be hard to understand, though. Maybe Emma thought only of Lacy as a friend, not a mother figure. Yet, she'd been the one to say it earlier tonight. "I would never want to make her feel uncomfortable."

As the heat in his gaze cooled, he gave a lopsided grin. "But Emma's spending the night at her best friend's house Saturday. Remember? Let me take you out for dinner and a movie and bring you back here, so we can pick up where we're leaving off tonight."

Her mantra, *You lose what you love*, tried to edge its way in, but with her body in charge, and Zack having done a great job of warming her up, she selfishly pushed it aside. This guy had everything she wanted; she was tired of pushing people away and being lonely, and he was asking her out again. No way would she refuse.

Only a fool would do that. Or maybe the foolish part was taking a step deeper into Zack and Emma's lives.

Zack's spell wore off Lacy a bit on Thursday at the Santa Barbara construction site, when he wasn't around, and by Friday, though she saw him multiple times at the Little River Valley site and even served him lunch, Lacy didn't know what to do about their date.

You lose what you love. Her annoying mantra repeated over and over in her head, seeming to get louder every time she saw him.

Stop it! She wanted to yell at the negative thoughts. *Quit messing up my life.* She was sick of being alone. All she had to do to avoid pain was to not fall in love with him, to just enjoy the moment. How hard was that?

Evidently, a lot harder than she'd imagined.

There Zack was, in front of her food truck grinning at her, and he hadn't changed an iota. He stood looking handsome as ever, hard hat in tow, all manly and commanding. Her body certainly remembered him, reacting as it always did with random sparks and tingles in his presence. But she was unable to fight a parallel reaction. Her cautious mind was turning into an iron maiden, threatening certain torture if she pursued him further. *This is your warning. My final warning?*

Then Ben, with his arm in a cast, approached Lacy's truck, drawing Zack's attention away, allowing her to breathe and regain her composure. Ben usually worked the Santa Barbara site, but since the accident he'd been working wherever his boss was. Zack pulled Ben aside to talk. As Lacy watched from across the yard, the men spoke quietly for a minute or two.

After the conversation ended, Zack retreated to the office and Ben gave Lacy a funny glance when she took his order. The expression reminded her of the same kind of look the woman wearing that blue hat at the recent wedding had given.

Chapter Nine

Zack had the house to himself on Saturday and couldn't wait to see Lacy again. He'd been thinking about being with her since last weekend, and especially since Wednesday night when they'd gotten worked up but with no place to go. It was his rule about not having Lacy stay over—since she was the first and only woman he'd been with after the divorce—so he couldn't complain.

He dressed for his date in anticipation of time spent with the one who had his full attention. Wearing his nicest pants, a slim-cut buttoned shirt and his least scuffed shoes, he made a mental note to buy a new pair soon, or at least get these professionally polished. Sliding behind the wheel of his car, he marveled over how quickly he'd gotten in over his head, already wanting more with her. For the first time since his divorce, he saw a future that not only involved his daughter, but a full-grown woman. Lacy.

When he knocked on her door and she answered,

something seemed off about her. Sure, she appeared to be happy to see him, and they kissed hello, but part of him sensed she was putting on an act. Not good. What had changed since Wednesday and why? Had it been because he'd cut things short the other night? Had he inadvertently insulted her in some way? Not wanting to throw a wrench into their date right off, he'd keep his thoughts and worries to himself for now.

They had a perfectly nice dinner at another trendy restaurant, of which Little River Valley had many, but throughout he got the distinct impression she was holding back. Seeming not quite herself.

When it came time to leave for the planned movie, Zack glanced across Main Street to two doors down, then made a snap decision. They needed to have some fun.

"Want to blow off the movie and go there?"

She glanced in the direction he pointed, at the flashing neon sign, and her eyes went wide. "Are you serious?"

"I'm serious as that dessert we just devoured, but the real question is can you handle it?" He'd known Lacy long enough to figure she'd rise to a dare.

Finally a spark of the old Lacy, the woman who'd been MIA tonight, showed up. "Is that a challenge?"

That was what he loved about her. "Definitely." What the hell was he doing? He was a horrible singer and would surely make a fool out of himself! Still, for the sake of fun, which they severely needed, he took her hand. They crossed the street heading for the local karaoke bar, which, given the sound on the street, was already in full swing.

It was dark inside and too loud to talk, so they found a table and ordered a couple of beers. It was a mostly middle-aged crowd, and the choice of songs proved it. But that was what you got on a Saturday night in Little

River Valley, since teens and young adults tended to migrate to Ventura or Santa Barbara for the bigger nightlife. Zack scrolled through the songs on tap.

The host started out the next set with "Purple Rain," the Prince classic, and everyone chimed in. From what Zack could hear, Lacy wasn't half-bad. Then one after another, bad and good singers, since they had an all-singers-welcomed policy, made their way to the microphone. Some sang their hearts out while others laughed all the way through; some were terrific and others horrible. In other words, a typical night in karaoke land. Which gave Zack the nerve, but only after downing his entire beer.

"Want to go up there?"

Lacy tensed noticeably, her body contracting inward. "Uh, maybe after this?" She lifted the half-full mug of beer.

"Okay." Since it was his idea to come and he'd accepted her challenge back on the street, he'd do the decent thing. "I'll go first."

She did a double take, watching him like he'd just turned into an alien from the planet of Are You Kidding? In full bravado, because what else did he have as a mediocre-at-best singer, he made his way to the stage. Utilizing his stock overconfident face, the kind he used to make as a kid in answer to any dare—and still used when making a high bid on a job—he sought out Lacy's gaze. She was laughing. Good. She needed to lighten up tonight. If he had to make a fool of himself to get her to do it, he'd be glad to take the hit. Besides, Lacy was the only person in the room he knew. He hoped so, anyway. The place was a dark and typical bar, so who knew for sure.

He stopped the screen at "Private Eyes," a Hall & Oates classic from the early 80s that was still evidently a hit here in karaoke land. He started singing the well-known song, feeling far less confident than he portrayed. But by the time the chorus came around, he sang in full voice. It helped that half the group in the lounge sang along.

The second time the chorus came around, he looked straight at Lacy, who appeared to be either horrified or rapt, he wasn't sure thanks to the poor lighting. He kept singing anyway and switched up the words just a bit. "I *need to know.*" The whole point of the song was a guy trying to figure out if a woman was letting him in or cutting him loose. Zack could totally relate with Lacy. He needed to know. When it circled back to the bridge, he got bold and used the old two finger point to the eyes, then turned it toward Lacy to be conspicuous. *I'm watching you.*

He knew he was not a great singer, but evidently he was good enough not to get booed off the stage. Amped up from taking the risk and not falling flat on his face— and maybe the mild applause had a little to do with it— he waved Lacy up. At first, she hesitated, but being a good sport, she soon stood, quickly downing the last of her beer and made her way to the stage.

He chose something that had been around forever and that everyone on the planet should know, just in case she wasn't a follower of current popular songs.

"Come on," he said as she drew closer. "We can do this one together."

She glanced at the screen, studied it for two seconds as her eyes widened, then gave a nod. And they were good to go singing Elton John's famous duet with Kiki Dee.

"Don't go breaking my heart," Zack led off.

Lacy followed, enthusiastically swearing she couldn't even if she really tried. Not bad for a karaoke novice.

Soon they were both into the easy song, and most of

the crowd was singing along with them, which made their occasional goofs easy to cover. The most important thing was Lacy was smiling and giving her all. She seemed to be having a great time, too. That was the girl he'd missed lately.

As they left the stage when the song was over, one guy, obviously under the influence, couldn't hold his tongue. "You guys sucked." He cupped hands around his mouth. "Boo."

The candid comment cracked them up and they laughed all the way back to their table.

"Did he think we didn't know that?" she said, still laughing.

"I don't know, *Kiki*, you sounded pretty good. Mind if I call you that?"

"I kind of like the ring of it," she teased back. "But, uh, yes! I do mind."

They sat in time to hear "Love Shack" sung by another so-so singer, a stocky woman with wild greying hair, in a bright Hawaiian shirt, looking like a leftover flower child. But the song was so much fun, the entire room chimed in, especially at the refrain. Who said the over- and well-over-forty crowd didn't know how to rock out?

Coming here tonight was the smartest decision Zack had made since hiring Lacy and asking her out. As time went on, and more beer was served, the mood and music shifted. The DJ started playing Michael Bublé songs. There was a small dance floor off to the side, and Zack offered his hand, then led Lacy out to dance. She came willingly, and it felt great to hold her in his arms, and when the refrain came around again, he sang it with conviction, especially the *I love you* part. And she sure looked great just the way she was, too.

Her gaze met his and the familiar internal thrumming

started. She sent the best, though subtle, messages with those baby blues, and he gobbled this one up. *Kiss me* was his interpretation, so he did. Long enough for the music to end and the lights to come up before he stopped.

Once they'd returned to his house, Lacy had climbed back into protective mode. What was going on?

Had he come on too strong? Dumb choice of song to dance to. He knew it! Was she having second thoughts about getting more involved with him? With him *and* his daughter? Maybe it was the package deal that bothered her. Though nothing had changed on that front, and it had never seemed to bother her before tonight. It was probably just him. Maybe the same thing Mona had gotten tired of. Him.

There had been one solid takeaway from his marriage breakup, though. Where he'd settled for the lack of communication with Mona, he swore it'd never happen again.

"Is everything all right?" he asked finally, while they sat on his couch and shared some wine. A guy could only guess unless he asked.

"Yes." Not the least bit convincing.

He put his arm around her and pulled her close. "I don't believe you," he said, over her hair, not looking into her face, giving her the opportunity to tell him what was up without being stared at. The way guys liked to talk about their problems.

"I've been preoccupied with some leftover business with my father's estate. And my mother."

"You mentioned she died when you were ten?"

"Yes, and the paperwork from my father involves her, too."

"Do you need a lawyer? I know a great one who happens to be our mayor."

"You know Joe Aguirre?"

"Long, long time. He helped with my divorce, too."

"Hmm. Well, that's nice to know, but I don't need a lawyer, I don't think. Yet." She seemed tentative at best.

His hand skimmed her back and he longed to pull her closer but, sensing she'd resist, he held back. "You want to talk about it?"

She glanced up, placed her cool hand on his cheek. "Not really." Then, proving him wrong about resisting, she kissed him, and they dropped the subject like a superbad idea. Soon, as always, they both got lost in all things physical between Zack and Lacy.

Both with and without clothes.

In no time at all, he introduced her to his California king-size bed with the new and fresh sheets, the same bed that had felt too big for one person for the last couple of years. There, she seemed to forget all the worries that had her withdrawing from him during dinner and after karaoke. Just like hitting the singing bar, changing the scenery, moving to his room, turned out to be a great idea.

Holding her, making love to her, feeling her come apart at his touch, made him surer than ever he'd found the right person. Something he'd never expected to happen after his divorce.

He didn't want to scare her off by coming on too strong too soon with words she might not be ready to hear—like the mistake he'd made dancing with her to "The Way You Look Tonight"—so instead he did everything in his power to blow her mind another way. Not telling but showing her how he felt. In bed.

Hours later, sated, bodies entwined, minds sufficiently blown, they'd dozed together until Lacy pulled away from Zack. He lifted his head as she disengaged and sat on the edge of his bed, then looked back at him. Moonlight through the gaping bedroom curtains dappled her expression, making it hard to read.

"I think I better leave."

He sat bolt upright. This wasn't part of the plan. He'd even bought eggs, fresh vanilla nut coffee and English muffins to make her breakfast. "Why? Everything okay?"

"Everything's great. I'm just not ready to spend the night."

"With me?" His chest muscles tensed with her silence.

"I guess. Not yet, anyway."

"We've done everything else, why not sleep with me?"

Last Wednesday, he had been the one who'd hesitated, now it was her turn. He reached out and pulled her close. "Have I done something wrong? Is there something you'd like me to do? All you have to do is tell me."

She shook her head. "You're wonderful, Zack. I'm lucky to be with you. And I'm totally confused."

"Let's talk about it, then."

"I'm not ready."

"Is anyone ever?" He'd just had the same battle the other day.

"Will you bear with me a little longer?" She'd shut down and there was nothing he could do to convince her otherwise, except let her deal with it in her own way.

"Of course." Did he have a choice?

She leaned forward and kissed him. "Thank you." Her expression was sincere, and he didn't doubt her need for space and time, though the ache in his chest tightened. Why did life always have to be complicated?

She used the bathroom and came back to his bedroom to dress. He'd thrown on his boxer briefs and jeans and sat on the bed waiting, his stomach twisting. The last thing he wanted was for her to leave without explaining what was going on, but she seemed content to silently put on her clothes with an audience. Him. And he gave her his full, though solemn, attention.

When she was at the point of slipping into her shoes he couldn't stop himself. "Next Saturday? Emma? Cooking lesson?"

With worn-down shoulders she gave a defeated smile. "Can we make it Wednesday, again?"

A safe night. He'd been honest about her not staying over last Wednesday. Obviously, she hadn't forgotten. The only thing going for it was the fact it was only four days away instead of seven.

Even with the sudden confusion between them, the words *I love you* fought to get out. But he clamped his mouth shut. No way did he want to seem needy. Would saying those words come off as desperate or, worse yet, manipulative, even though it was the honest-to-God way he felt? The last thing he wanted was to add to her confusion or doubt if admitting they loved each other was the sudden hang-up. If she wanted to be with him, he expected her to be sure about it. He threw on his shirt. No, now was not the time for his heartfelt declarations. Now was a time of watching and waiting. Hoping for the best. Not pressuring.

Not at all how he'd imagined the night would end. And driving her home and walking her to the door was the hardest thing he'd had to do since meeting her and letting her in little by little. But good things, like loving Lacy, were worth waiting for, and she deserved the time she needed to work through whatever caused her to hesitate.

Still, he was of the impression women liked to talk about their feelings. Mona used to insist she did until she stopped communicating altogether. Evidently not Lacy, and her stoic silence on the drive home surprised him.

He pinched the bridge of his nose to ward off the

throbbing pain that had moved from his chest and started like a jackhammer behind his forehead and temples.

Not at all how he'd expected this night to end.

Lacy let herself in the door with thoughts spinning and emotions grappling. Her heart pounded. She wasn't ready for this, falling for Zack. For the sad yet simple reason she didn't want to lose him. Watching him sing his heart out to her at the karaoke bar proved the point. He wasn't kidding when he'd sang along with Michael Bublé on the Sinatra Classic, "The Way You Look Tonight."

He was the chance for a real "rest of her life."

Mournful memories had become all tangled up with the natural feelings of love. All the fun flirting with the guy she'd crushed hard on as a young girl had turned to kisses and foreplay and something far more serious. Giving herself completely to him in bed. She'd done it willingly, and loved every minute—no regrets there. But her heart was a different story. Apparently, it still needed to be guarded.

And she couldn't forget the other part. Bonding with Emma. Was this what she wanted, a ready-made family, a second chance for one, at least, or would Lacy be Zack and Emma's worst nightmare?

What a mess she was. Because of that damn rotten dream dredging up all the pain and sorrow she'd kept buried for so many years. Reminding her that just when she thinks her life is perfect, things change. The thought of opening her heart to love again terrorized her. When had she become such a coward!

Her pulse sped through her chest, a sense of panic accompanying it. Then a more practical thought occurred—this carelessness could also cost her her job. Maybe she should take that last-minute fill-in wedding gig she'd been offered this coming Saturday. At least then she'd have a good reason for skipping out on him that night.

From one week to the next, everything wonderful had been turned on its head because of her history with the people she loved. She was alone in the world and had to look after herself.

She couldn't slip up and start caring too much for Zack.

Monday, Zack had obviously taken her hint, and sent his assistant, Mike, to fetch lunch. Even as disappointment trickled from her head to toes over not seeing him, she was grateful for the break. Having to see him and deal with her battling emotions while making his staff lunch would be too much. She could mess up, get their orders wrong, then everyone would know something was up. She finally caught sight of him—which caused a full-body reaction not unlike getting run over by a steam-roller—and waved with a shaky hand as she drove off for the day after the lunch service.

He waved back, but through the rearview mirror she saw he was solemn, with no trace of a smile. And because of that, it was a wonder she hadn't run off the road.

What must the man think?

Tuesday, at the Santa Barbara construction site, Ben was back there for some reason, but certainly not working with the building crew. He approached after letting all the others order and pick up their meals, since they were on the clock and he evidently wasn't.

Seeing the inquisitive look on his face reminded her that was how he'd watched her last time. What was up with that? His unwavering stare was downright eerie.

"Do you have a sister?" he asked, out of the blue after giving his order for the usual two vegetarian wraps.

"I wish." She stopped scooping braised tofu into the large spinach wrap. "I used to pretend I had one. How about you, sisters? Brothers? Both?"

"I have many siblings, but that's not why I asked."

She should've known the man didn't make light conversation.

She was stretching and folding the round wrap like a huge burrito but stopped mid-tuck. She glanced up and saw new uncertainty in his gaze. Which made her wonder where he was going with the line of questioning.

"Mr. Gardner asked me to do an estimate on a bathroom remodel in Santa Barbara last week, and I just came from delivering the bid. The woman at the house has red hair, just like yours, but shorter, and her eyes were blue, like yours, and, well—"

As if ice water trickled down her spine she shivered over what she sensed he was going to say next.

"—she looked exactly like you."

How long could she go on making excuses about how redheads often looked alike and imply that everyone else was getting it wrong? That something about copper-red hair made the person's features blur, and people interpreted that as looking the same. Furthermore, Ben couldn't possibly know for sure whether they looked alike or not unless they stood side by side. Even though copper-red hair and blue eyes was the rarest percentage of redheads, if that was truly what the woman had, thanks to hair dye and contacts, it didn't mean she was Lacy's double. Far from it.

A person had a higher chance of being struck by lightning than being born with her combination of hair and eyes. But what if the woman was left-handed, too? Suddenly, Lacy was invaded by uneasy feelings.

"Her name is Evangelina."

Evangelina. The name hit her like a burst of adrenaline.

Eva for short? Wasn't that what the woman at the wedding had called her? What were the odds? Now goose bumps accompanied the chill down her back along with the fight-or-flight response. A real-live doppelgänger?

"Are you sure she looked *exactly* like me? Maybe just similar?"

"I could've sworn it was you the first time. Almost asked if she was Lacy. And I've seen her twice now."

Uncanny.

The dead-serious look on Ben's face nearly made Lacy drop the wrap. She clutched it tighter. He didn't strike her as the kind of guy inclined to exaggerate *anything*. That was probably why Zack sent him out to make estimates and give quotes since the accident. But how was she supposed to respond to what he'd just said?

"Has Zack met her?"

"No. Only talked to her on the phone."

For some crazy reason, that relieved her. Also, she needed proof this woman was her spitting image. "Then next time take a picture."

She tried to make light of it, for Ben's benefit, rather than let on how earth-shattering his statements were. Ben paid for the wraps with his one good hand, then carried them away and without further comment strolled off to singlehandedly eat his lunch. She hoped she hadn't insulted him, but how was she supposed to react? The mere thought of what he'd implied sent shivers down to her bones.

Later, as she cleaned up the food truck preparing to drive home, her hands still trembled as she thought through what he'd implied. So, what if a woman looked just like her?

Would it automatically mean they were related, or was

it just a fluke of nature, the kind that popped up in the big wide world from time to time. Surely people looked alike without being…sisters.

Or could her living, breathing double have anything to do with that change in her birth certificate? It had occurred a month after she'd been born and made her mother the legal adoptive parent. Her *mother*. Not her *birth mother*? If the one person she'd known for ten years as Mom wasn't actually related, then who was her real mother? And who was this person out there making people think it was her?

Lacy's head started to spin with wild thoughts. Maybe she should have one of those DNA tests that were so popular these days. What would she do with the results if she discovered that she did indeed have a sister? The container of mixed egg salad she held slipped through her fingers and splattered onto the truck floor.

She dropped to her knees to clean up, but her thoughts wouldn't stop coming.

Dad, I need you to answer these questions.

With the dearth of living relatives, all she could do was hope the answers were somewhere in the remaining manila envelopes from the attic.

Zack wouldn't describe Wednesday at the Gardner house as strained, but it sure wasn't like things used to be when lovely Lacy came over to give Emma cooking lessons. Still, he kept his mouth shut and his thoughts to himself, because he couldn't very well have a frank talk with Lacy about their personal relationship with Emma right there.

He planned to do that later, after he put Emma to bed. He'd make sure there was no pressure, just an open invitation to fill him in on what was going on inside Lacy's mind, and to see if there were any updates since Saturday night.

Zack's favorite cook had taken an abrupt step back and it felt awful. She hadn't even bothered to offer a reason yet, other than some concerns about papers she'd found at home. Just as his thoughts and actions had started heating up she'd pulled back. He didn't want to make a federal case out of it, but under the circumstances, he *could* refer to his cheating wife and let that general lack of trust in women be reinforced. Mona had gotten tired of him and looked around for something more exciting. Could he be that kind of fool twice?

He didn't want to go that route of thinking. Not with Lacy. She was different. He swore she was.

Earlier, Emma had asked Lacy if she'd come over on Saturday, too, but Lacy had bowed out with the excuse that she had to work a wedding in Santa Barbara. Zack thought she'd given up those gigs since working his sites five days a week. He could tell Emma was sad about their standing Saturday lesson being canceled for the second time, which, of course, upset him. Was it time to protect his daughter first, put the relationship second?

Instead, he went out of his way to stand up for both of his favorite girls. "Shortcake, last week you had plans with Meghan, well, this week, Lacy has to work. Sometimes things just work out that way. There's always next time, right?" He cautiously glanced at Lacy, wondering about a next time, and she gave an unconvincing nod, which made his stomach sour a bit, regardless how great the food looked and smelled.

Zack hated looking at Lacy with suspicious eyes, yet he couldn't help but notice her having conversations with Ben at the Santa Barbara site last week. And those conversations seemed intense.

He was also aware of her frequent texting tonight while cooking, which may or may not have had anything to do with the other thing, but his mind was spinning into new territory. She'd never carried on a separate text conversation at his house before. And Lacy acted secretive when she answered those texts.

Without trying, while Emma and Lacy put a casserole together, and before Lacy had dropped news about working a wedding on Saturday, he saw her phone light up on the counter. It was lying faceup. It wasn't like she was hiding it, and he couldn't help noticing the name that flashed. Ben Greywater. His employee. And his heart had dropped to his gut.

Zack tried to brush it off as none of his business, but Lacy had changed so drastically toward him this week. She refused to talk about it, and something had to have prompted that change. Later, after he put Emma to bed, he would ask her again what was bothering her. That promise got him through a strained dinner. He was worried that even Emma had noticed. Not good. The kid had been through enough already.

Later, after Emma and Lacy said goodbye, and he'd gone into his daughter's room to say good-night and tuck her in, when he'd come out, Lacy was gone. Without even saying goodbye to him.

So wrong, and completely unlike her.

Frustrated, he immediately called her, but she didn't answer. It was probably a good thing because right that minute he'd wanted to give her a piece of his mind.

Seriously? Was this how she handled relationships? He'd had enough of sketchy women, and he really didn't want to add Lacy to the list.

After he'd cooled off a bit, he thought more. Instead of sitting on the verge of telling her he had feelings for her, he needed to be more cautious now. But this taking off without saying goodbye was unacceptable and made him angry. Part of what he'd liked about Lacy from the start was she didn't play games. Who had time for that? So her slipping off, avoiding saying goodbye to him, was wrong, and she needed to be told. He never planned to be taken advantage of again.

Being a dad, he couldn't very well drop everything, run off and confront Lacy. If he valued what they had, he didn't want to completely blow it by forcing her to explain why she'd suddenly gotten cold feet—if that was what was going on. Who knew, since she wouldn't talk to him about it.

He paced, and thought, growing only more confused.

He needed to tread lightly and spontaneously; racing after Lacy was not the way to go. Even if that was exactly what he wanted to do, and even if he could. There was someone else to consider—Emma. Whether he liked it or not, there were three hearts wrapped up in this new, and currently malfunctioning, relationship.

The problem was, it was too late. The damage had already been done with Mona's infidelity, and Lacy waffling only reinforced that old insecurity. Lacy refused to admit anything was wrong, yet she was acting like the entire landscape of the earth between them had changed. It completely baffled him, and feeling baffled made him defensive. She was acting squirrelly and had something going on with Ben, too. He wasn't going to jump to an irrational conclusion without confronting her first, but he needed some truth.

He called again. No luck. If only she'd answer her phone!

By changing her mind so quickly about him without explanation, Lacy had found his weakest spot.

Trust for women. Or the lack thereof. Ben was as solid as they came, but something odd was going on between Lacy and him. There had to be a logical explanation. If only she'd talk to him.

Her not answering her phone only added to it. "Lacy? Why not pick up? I'm worried about you. Call me so we can talk." The message probably sounded desperate, but damn, she'd pushed this to the limit.

Instead of Lacy calling back, all he got was a text from her.

I got home okay. Just need some time to think.

And how long would that be? The thinking. Because by his calculation it had been an entire week so far. Was this what he'd heard his guys talk at work about as ghosting? Suddenly being dropped by a woman without explanation. Left with unanswered texts and nothing else?

After the crazy night she'd put him through, he needed time to think, too! And ticked off about her putting him through all this drama, he didn't bother to reply to her text.

Chapter Ten

Evangelina DeLongpre liked to take her baby for a walk in his stroller to the Starbucks on Coast Village Road in Montecito on Sunday afternoons. The barista there knew her drink and immediately started to prepare it as Eva found a table outside and got situated. When her Grande Nonfat Latte was ready, she picked up Noah and headed back inside.

"Eva?" a voice from the rear of the coffee house called out.

She turned. "Hey, Suzanne."

Her acquaintance approached, one of the other long-term baristas, an over-sixty type who made up for what social security lacked by working in a coffee house. "Were you at the Natural History Museum wedding last night?"

Eva shook her head. She hadn't been to a wedding for ages, and she'd spent her Saturday night like all the rest since adopting her son, alone watching Hallmark movies on TV.

"I could have sworn I saw you."

"Not me." She picked up her drink and, with Noah on her hip, headed for the door to sit outside in the sun where the parked baby stroller reserved a table.

Suzanne beat her to the door and pushed it open. "Well, there's someone out there who looks exactly like you, then."

"I seriously doubt that," Eva insisted as she avoided the barista's conspiring stare and passed through the door, heading for the table. As though she lived a double life and had finally been found out. She'd been accused of looking like any number of redheads over the years, so this was nothing new.

"Wait!" Suzanne followed her, digging into her purse, then pulled out her cell phone. She thumbed through a series of pictures until she found the one she was looking for. "Check this out."

There was a long-distance shot of a bright pink food truck called Wrap Me Up and Take Me Home, and behind the serving window was a redheaded woman. Eva squinted and looked closer, then used her fingers to enlarge the picture to better see the woman's face. Suzanne hadn't been kidding. There was a strong resemblance, but the magnified picture was extremely pixilated and blurred the features. Still, seeing a near look-alike, instead of the usual "in the ballpark" person, jangled her nerves enough for her to question the wisdom of adding espresso to the mix. After placing her drink on the table, she studied the picture again and fought the raw reaction—*this really does look like me*—forcing composure.

"If you want to convince me that I've got a double

walking around out there," she said, taking the deny-and-lie route, "you'll have to do better than this."

Suzanne straightened her thin spine and narrowed her eyes. "I'm going to take that as a personal challenge," she said, pocketing her phone in the green Starbuck's apron and heading back inside.

Zack was still completely baffled by Lacy's sudden change of heart. She'd run off after the cooking lesson without saying goodbye last Wednesday, had sent exactly one text, and hadn't returned his subsequent phone calls with offers to talk things through for days. He assumed this was indeed a ghosting breakup. But why?

Because he'd looked into her eyes and sung along with Michael Bublé on a romantic song. Telling her in a round-about way that he loved her.

He'd been at the Little River Valley site on Thursday, instead of in Santa Barbara, and Friday he'd had a morning meeting with investors that ran until after lunch, so he'd missed her again. Part of him was grateful he hadn't had to face her on the job.

That Saturday he'd kept busy running Emma around town collecting items for a school project—a diorama of her favorite book, *A Wrinkle in Time.* By Saturday night, it took total willpower to keep from calling Lacy again. Who needed the humiliation? He didn't want to come off pathetic, though he also needed to get to the bottom of what had mysteriously happened between them, especially since everything had seemed to be going so great.

Sunday morning, he did yard work while Emma worked on her project, and after his shower, in the late afternoon his cell rang.

"Hi!" he said, surprised yet cautious when he saw Lacy's name pop up on the call screen. "What's going on?"

"Sorry I left the other night, and that I haven't called before now, but I got a message that kind of threw me that night, and there are other things going on."

Other things? Was that enough to go incommunicado for days and days?

"From who?" Concern swirled through his thoughts, though he was still angry at her for going AWOL on him without explanation.

"What?"

"Who was the message from?" Didn't he have a right to know if his employee had told her something that had made her take off without saying goodbye?

"*Who* isn't important, but the message is what rattled me, and I should've said good-night Wednesday. I'm sorry. I needed to get home and look into stuff. Then that all led to other things."

Could she sound more vague?

"Want to come over and talk about it? We could all have dinner together." Yes, it was a sneaky tactic luring her over with the promise of Sunday dinner, family style, with Emma, because that was where his self-esteem had slipped over the last several days. Using his daughter as bait. Sad and sorry.

"I'm sorry, Zack. I'm not ready to talk. Please try to understand."

What was going on, and why was Lacy being so evasive? He measured his voice, but it was getting harder and harder to do, because a deeply wronged feeling was taking hold in his thoughts. "If you say so. I'll try," he said, short and clipped.

"Thank you," she whispered, before saying goodbye and clicking off.

At least she'd called, so maybe this wasn't a case of ghosting. But what the hell? After tucking the phone in his hip pocket, old suspicions came flooding back. He'd seen Lacy talking to Ben, and there was that text last Wednesday from him. Now, apparently, she didn't want anything to do with him, and was quite possibly letting him down easy with "stuff going on" and "I'm not ready to talk." Worse yet, "please try to understand." Well, she needed to understand something, too.

Why did it seem that when he let a woman under his skin—in Lacy's case, into his heart—she couldn't be depended on? Did he have a knack for picking the wrong kind of woman?

He threw together a makeshift dinner for himself and Emma, with a couple cans of this and that, then added boiled potato and called it a stew. It was probably a good thing Lacy hadn't accepted his invitation. But during dinner, the worst possible thoughts invaded his mind. Was history repeating itself? Doubt had rushed in and blurred the fact that Lacy was completely different from his ex-wife. Yet there was the blaring assumption taking center stage. *She's probably interested in Ben.*

"What's wrong Dad?"

"Nothing, Shortcake." He couldn't have sounded phonier. Here he was panning Lacy for keeping tight-lipped about what was bothering her and doing the exact thing with his daughter. But she was a kid and didn't deserve the angst. He hadn't been the only one to suffer when his wife cheated. Emma had felt betrayed, too, but, being not quite eight, she was too young to express it in words. As she stumbled through the tough days of her mommy and daddy separating, and her mother moving out, she'd started wetting her bed again. For a sweet little girl who loved to give hugs, she'd withdrawn, started biting her nails and knuckles, often drawing blood, and she'd had more than her share of tummy aches. He never wanted to put his Shortcake through anything like that again.

Fact was, Emma adored Lacy. That was obvious. So why was Lacy doing this to both of them?

His chest squeezed at what it might do to his daughter if Lacy quit coming around and he didn't have a believable reason to give. The kid could get a complex. Probably because Emma had gone through the divorce along with her parents, she had a truth-o-meter that could always read when a person lied. So he avoided bringing up the subject of Lacy with Emma.

After dinner, he let Emma watch a popular kid's movie so he could have more time to think.

He paced, trying to keep it together where Lacy was concerned, knowing that where he was going in his mistrustful head was nuts. He needed to find a balance, yet he was unable to stop the growing doubt. He walked to the kitchen and filled a tall glass with water, forced himself to drink every drop to help clear his mind.

He kept busy, puttering with his car in the garage. Eventually, Emma said she was going to bed.

"I've got to be at school early tomorrow," she said. "The diorama project is due in the classroom before we line up outside."

Tomorrow was Monday. Lacy would be at the construction site. Or would she? The thought rattled him.

"What time?"

"Seven thirty."

Would he be able to face Lacy if he didn't talk to her tonight? Not the way he was feeling now.

"What's wrong, Daddy?"

He shook his head as if that would clear out the mess of emotions. "Nothing, Shortcake. I'll see you in the morning."

"Are you worried about Lacy?"

The kid had great intuition and he couldn't lie to his daughter. "Yes."

Emma knew only how to tell the truth, and on this touchy subject she'd zeroed in on the problem. "I am too," she said, barely audible.

She hugged him, and he kissed the crown of her head, wanting to hold her there and protect her for all time. He avoided wishing her sweet dreams like he always did, because she'd call him on it. Truth was, his night was doomed unless he got to the bottom of Lacy's mysterious retreat.

Instead of letting emotions take over, he thought things through. There had to be a logical answer because he knew Lacy. He had to trust his gut on that, not old and rotten experiences. Besides, Ben was a newlywed. Zack had been at his wedding, had seen how crazy about each other Ben and his bride were. He'd seen how out of her head with worry she'd been at the hospital the day Ben broke his arm and lost his finger, too. Zack also knew from interacting with Lacy that she was nothing like his ex. If Lacy and Ben were keeping in touch about something, both being straightforward types, there was a logical reason behind it.

Yet the not knowing was driving him nuts.

He thought he must have worn a path into the travertine tile in the entryway as he thought things over, trying to force calm and logic to take over his out-of-control emotions. He failed miserably.

Admit the truth. Lacy is the woman I'm ready to tell I love. Hell, I sang it to her. If she's hiding something, it's not another man. There's more to this than I can possibly know.

Why won't she share it with me? Did she not trust him enough?

He called her again. She didn't answer. Sick of it, he vowed to get to the bottom of this matter tonight. He made another call.

Mrs. Worthington arrived on his doorstep within five minutes, which had given him enough time to put on his shoes and grab his car keys.

He'd made a big decision. He wasn't going to sit back and wonder what was going on, letting doubt and unwarranted assumptions take over. He also wasn't going to let Lacy slip away. He cared about her too much.

Lacy deserved a chance to explain what was going on. And he deserved the right to hear that explanation. He wouldn't jump to any negative conclusions, not until he looked into her eyes and she told him what was really going on.

Lacy sat in the guest bedroom surrounded by papers. The second brown box had, underneath ten years' worth of tax returns, a sealed manila envelope that said "Taylor." Her middle name. The hair on her arms stood up. Someone with the name of Taylor had something major to do with her birth, and that Taylor person was probably the reason her mother had to "adopt" Lacy and why those changes were made on her birth certificate.

Lacy distinctly remembered her father flushing red and stammering that time she'd confronted him about her middle name as a teenager. Or had her mother said it? *It's an old family name.*

Whose family name? That should have been her comeback. Now there was no one to ask.

She opened the envelope and removed a single document called a Consent to Terminate Parental Rights.

She may as well have been hit by lightning from the jolt those words caused. She blinked, making sure she'd read the title correctly, and blinked again when her eyes went watery. Through blurred vision she skimmed the paragraphs that followed to the very bottom, where a single signature terminated one person's parental birth rights and legally handed them over to her parents. That signature was hard to read, but the first name looked close enough to *Jessica*. The last name began with a *T*, but that was all she could make out.

It was true.

The urgent knock on the door threw her out of her thoughts and into a tailspin. Her first reaction was to ignore it, because she wasn't sure she could move, but her body seemed to have a mind of its own. She jumped to her feet and, surprised by her speed, ran to the front door. She couldn't go through this alone. It was too earth-shattering.

When she reached the door, she immediately swung it open. Zack!

And she couldn't have been happier to see anyone in her life. No way could she make sense of what she'd just discovered on her own. She needed a second pair of eyes, eyes that weren't controlled by emotion, to read and make heads or tails out of the legal document.

"Zack!" she said, turning into a pool of emotion at seeing the most stable man she knew. If he hadn't caught her, she would've collapsed onto the floor.

"Honey, are you sick? What's wrong?" he said, helping her to the couch and gently placing her there.

"It's been crazy," she said. "I'm so sorry. I…"

"Just take a moment, pull yourself together. But I need to know if you're sick or need medical attention." The concern in his gaze—like she'd seen the day Ben got injured—comforted her. And that was what she needed more than anything right now. Comfort.

"I'm not physically sick, just shocked."

"Let me get you a glass of water. Wait here."

"I don't think I could move if I had to," she said, feeling light enough to float or seriously light-headed, she wasn't sure which. The one thing she knew for a fact was she was grateful Zack was here.

He brought the water and waited for her to drink as much as she needed. "Take your time. I'm not going anywhere. You've had me worried."

"I'm sorry," she said between swallows, "Haven't been myself." Deciding to leave the first part of the story out—the part about being afraid to let herself fall completely for this wonderful man and what a coward she'd been by avoiding him. But the second part needed to be said aloud; otherwise, it might seem too far-fetched to be true. "Found some old papers from the attic, and one thing led to another and—" she paused to take another sip "—I might have a twin sister!"

"What?"

"I know, crazy right? Ben was the one to tell me he'd seen my double in Santa Barbara. Did he say anything to you about it?"

"Not me."

Revived by the water, she was ready to let it all out. "Well, he wasn't the first person to mention they'd seen someone who was the spittin' image of me, and of course, I blew it off." She glanced at Zack and his undivided attention. "Because, come on, many redheads look somewhat alike, right?"

"I've never seen anyone who looked like you before. Believe me, I'd remember."

See, this was what she loved about Zack. She took

time to smile at him for making such a sweet comment. "When Ben said one of your potential customers, named Evangeline DeLongpre, looked exactly like me, well, to be honest, it freaked me out."

"Wow, that's amazing."

"That's what all those back-and-forth texts were about at your house last Wednesday night. My mind was so boggled I couldn't talk about it."

"I'm not exactly sure what I'm supposed to say other than that it's a relief, because I admit to thinking the worst. But I'm happy for you."

"The worst?"

"I thought you'd lost interest in me."

"Zack!" She cuffed him. She'd been pulling back from him for self-preservation; the last thing she'd want was to run off to another relationship. But how could he know that when she'd quit talking to him? "I'm so sorry I made you doubt me. I've been so mixed up."

"So it's not a good thing?"

"Having a twin? I don't know what to think."

"Why don't you start at the beginning?"

"Okay, you asked for it. I've been going through my father's papers trying to find the truth, but I've only found enough to confuse me. I'm pretty sure my mother wasn't my birth mother. And just now, I discovered a paper that essentially proves it."

"So this is why you've been avoiding me? Us?"

"Please don't think I'm awful, or crazy, but all my life I've felt something was missing, that I wasn't complete. I had the deepest need for a sister, like somehow I knew one was out there. And lately a couple of people kept swearing they'd seen my double. Then I find these old papers. And now I discover I'd been adopted, but only by my mother. If I'm adopted, why couldn't it be possible there's a sibling out there? Because, why didn't my dad have to adopt me, and why do I look so much like him, and if he's my real father, and there's this sibling out there, why didn't my mom adopt both of us? See? There are so many questions and I'm so confused. What if this person Ben met is an actual sibling! I can't explain how bizarre this feels."

"Mind-boggling."

"I know! But now the paperwork points in that direction."

"Like I said, I know a good lawyer." He tugged her to his chest and smoothed her hair.

She could only imagine what kind of wild woman she must look like, but it didn't seem to matter with Zack. "The thing is, I'm torn about digging deeper or letting it lie."

"That's a decision only you can make." He kissed her hair, and she felt safe and home, and worried that it could all be ripped away from one second to the next.

"Is it wrong for me to wonder what's going to happen with us?" he asked.

That came out of nowhere, and, boy, it was the last thing she was ready to deal with. She needed time to formulate her response.

"I feel like you've been dodging me," he said, beating her to the next topic.

Her mood fell. Did she expect him not to notice? "I've been working to solve the mystery left by my father and mother." She lifted her face to his, found him cautiously watching her. He deserved to know. "It's something I've got to do, right now. On my own. If I have a possible sister out there, I might have a birth mother, too. Which is the craziest thought, since I lost Mom so early. I might not be an orphan after all. I might have a sister and a mother out there, who knows?"

She could tell by his not responding, that she needed to do more to convince him. "I've been going back and forth about letting things alone or following this lead and finding out the truth. Just since talking to you, I realize this is my one shot and I think I've got to focus everything on it." She purposely left out the cowardly part about being scared to death about falling in love with him, too. That she was too afraid to listen to her heart, and this seemed like perfect timing to put some padding between them until she was ready to take a chance on loving someone again.

"What if this possible family doesn't want to be found?"

That stopped her like an arctic draft. She hadn't given a single thought to that possibility. "It will only matter if I track her down. Ben sent me a picture the other day. It's someone you'll be doing work for."

He pulled in his chin. "Really? Then we can handle it from that angle."

"I don't think that's a good idea."

"You're saying you don't want me to help you?"

"I think this is something I need to explore by myself."

"I see."

"It's not that I don't appreciate your offer, Zack, I just don't want to steamroll over someone's privacy and in the process fall flat on my face."

"But the paperwork you have may not have anything to do with this woman. Maybe you guys just happen to look alike."

"Yes, to all of that. But the thing is, because of this weird feeling I've had all my life about missing a part of myself, about not wanting but *needing* a sister to be close to, I have to find out."

Lacy stared at Zack, searched his stern face for a hint of understanding, but from the great guy she'd come to know as warm and caring, he'd suddenly turned into a master poker player. She took an uneven breath and quietly held it.

"Then I guess I'll have to wait and see about us," he said finally. He'd hesitated and looked suspicious about her need to pursue her possible adoption and the birth mother who'd given her to her parents just when they'd started to fall in love.

"You can understand my reasons for stepping back from us for now, can't you?"

Zack's hands slipped from her and he stood, obviously ready to leave—why stay when she'd essentially asked him to leave? Her pulse stumbled along, waiting, hoping with all her might she hadn't blown the best relationship she'd had since Greg. Praying he'd understand.

"I want you to be happy, Lacy. Whatever does that for you, I'm glad."

"Thank you." Her heart dropped to her stomach with guilt. She didn't deserve such a wonderful guy, maybe now he'd catch on.

"I just wish you'd let me be involved somehow."

What could she say? She'd explained why she had to follow this and that it seemed like something she should do on her own. It only mattered to her, right? No one else in the world could understand that feeling she'd carried all her life. She couldn't deny the convenient excuse it gave her to deal with her fear of falling in love with Zack, too. What better reason to avoid him than hunting for a long-lost relative or relatives?

Zack started to leave, but when he got to the door,

he turned back. "Before I go, there are some things you should know."

She stood watching, thinking her heart was going to come apart from the pounding pulse.

"I haven't been interested in anyone since my divorce. I looked forward to seeing you every day at the construction site. And when we started cooking lessons for Emma, I liked you even more. I know we could've taken things slower to see where it led, but I'm glad we went for it. I haven't felt as sure about making love in years. Because of you." He gave her a moment to let the last part sink in. "So I want to thank you for that right now, in case I don't get the chance after tonight."

"Zack, it's not like we're breaking up." How could she explain that she wanted something with him she feared would be ripped away? That she'd found the perfect excuse with the adoption issue to avoid facing that truth and having to deal with him and what they might turn into.

"No? 'Cause it sure feels like it."

She shook her head, confused and aching, unable to speak, her eyes filling.

"We're great together, you can't deny that."

"I'm not."

He kept the distance and she leaned against the couch for support, positive her knees might buckle at any second.

"No matter what else you're looking for, I want you to know I'm here for you, right now, right here. That since my wife cheated, I got cynical about ever being in a relationship with someone again. Wondering if I'd ever be able to trust again. Until you. So, if you're serious about me, bear with me and my mistrust, and what it requires."

She watched and waited. Whatever he was leading up

to was going to be big, and concern twisted into fear at the possibility of losing him.

"If you say we're not breaking up, and you are being honest with me, then you have to take the next step. Admit we're a couple. I just swallowed my pride, came over here ready to find out the worst. Fortunately, it's not another man you're all wrapped up in. But my coming here was a pretty damn big deal."

It was important. And she was so grateful he cared that much about her. If only things were different.

"I am being honest about needing to do this. And I can't tell you how much it means to me that you care enough to come here and face me. There's no one else. I promise. But I'm an orphan and I need a family. So, though it's not another man, it might be an entire family I never knew I had."

He glanced at his shoes and let out a short breath. "Well, at least it's not another man."

Lacy laughed with Zack, but only briefly, and it didn't relieve any of the anxiety building inside. He looked tired and sincere, and she was flabbergasted that he'd been honestly blunt with her. Her hands came to her mouth as her lower lip started to quiver.

"Surprisingly," he said, "it still hurts."

"I'm sorry." She wasn't sure she could stand another second.

"I feel rejected. I can take that for myself, but I don't want Emma to feel rejected, too."

"I'm not rejecting you or Emma."

"No? Seems to me you're pretty busy looking for one family, when another is standing right in front of you."

His aim had been straight and the pain swift. She fell apart, and probably because he felt responsible, he steadied her. "I'm sorry," he said. "That was over the line. Too much right now. Forgive me."

After several moments of her whimpering on his chest, trying to pull it together, with his hand smoothing her hair and her back, she forced out a single sentence.

"I'm just asking for some time to work things out."

He sighed, his shoulders straightening, as though to give him strength. "Fair enough." He let her go and walked back to the door. "Don't feel like you have to work at the sites while you're doing this soul-searching, okay?" She'd never heard him sound resigned before, which was just one more thing to shake her. She couldn't forget how important he was to her in all this. He'd gone as far as suggesting he and Emma could be a family to her. Oh, what a mess her life had been turned into. Still, she was grateful to him for seeking her out, making sure she was okay, showing he cared, even while being stern.

"Thank you. You really are amazing." Her heart filled with a rush of love she couldn't take right then. She held her ground rather than run to his arms as she wanted to do.

His sun-tinged brows lifted, letting her know how little sense he could make of everything she'd said and was doing. Yet, this was the best she could offer for now.

"Before I leave, I'm making it crystal clear. If you want us *to be*, it's up to you. All you have to do is call. But *you* have to take that step, because I've taken mine—" he shrugged "—and it didn't work out the way I'd hoped."

With fingers clutching the back of a chair, she forced a response. "Your coming here has meant the world to me, Zack." She needed him to know that.

"And still I leave alone." He paused over the irony, and the gut-wrenching effect dug deep.

Why not just run to him now? She'd never find another man like him as long as she lived. Yet her feet didn't budge, and her fingers were nearly soldered to the material on the chair from holding so tight.

"Having a wife cheat messes a guy up. I need to know you want me as much as I want you. And I can't lose sight of Emma and her feelings for one second."

"I know. I get it." Her hands moved up to her cheeks, where a second wave of tears continued to slide down.

It was obvious he wanted to come to her, ease her pain, but as her feet were a moment before, his cross-trainers seemed cemented to the tile. "And I hope I haven't made a huge mistake laying it all out here tonight, when you're obviously reeling from everything else going on in your life. But I feel strong about it." He pointed to his chest, then at her, and repeated himself. "You and I can't get overlooked. And maybe I piled on to your problems by coming here, but I had to do it, Lacy. Had to make you know how fast I let you get to me."

She understood completely, because the same had happened to her. She wished everything could be different, just the two of them and Emma, but those papers had changed her entire life.

She stood her ground. He stood at the door.

Without a kiss or a goodbye, he left, and with a full body shudder, Lacy understood exactly how much was at stake letting him go. Still, she couldn't move.

Chapter Eleven

Monday morning at work, after staring at the ceiling all night trying to make sense of Lacy's need to pull back from him, Zack went right to Ben.

"Take over the office and check up on the guys for me, will you?" He grabbed the prepared job bid from his inbox. All the form needed was a signature. "I'll take care of this." With new purpose, he headed for the door. "Call me if you have any problems."

He caught the questioning glance Ben gave him, which, coming from Ben, was a big reaction. Yeah, Zack was taking this into his own hands. If there was a woman out there who looked like Lacy, he wanted to see her firsthand.

His hands were unsteady as he started the car, and a swarm of something fluttery gathered in his gut. The things he did for love. He'd be the one to get Evangelina DeLongpre's signature, not Ben. If there was any chance this woman was related to Lacy, he owed her whatever information he could provide. It was also a selfish gesture, because one of the things he'd figured out last night in his sleeplessness was that her questionable birth circumstances were a major part of what kept them apart. If he could help solve the mystery, he might have a chance at winning her love.

During the thirty-minute drive to Santa Barbara, he took time to think through his motives. He loved Lacy and wanted her, and this quirky look-alike angle needed to be faced and dealt with. That was the practical side. He had it in his power to open the door, so he would. *Why not?* And he would do it for the woman he intended to share his life with. *If she'll let me!* All the rest would be up to Lacy, but at least he could open the door on this one part.

He stopped at the entry gate of what most people would consider a modern dream home though, given the view from his car, it was a bit too boxy for his taste. Built on a coveted hillside with huge wraparound windows overlooking the Pacific Ocean out there in the distance, it spelled opulence. The extent of his nerves over making this delivery continued to surprise him.

"Must have done something right," he said out loud, comparing Lacy's modest family home with this minimansion. In Santa Barbara, no less, which automatically doubled a home's worth. Location, location, location. They could rule out her being a public figure, since everyone would've noticed the resemblance a lot sooner. He wondered how someone the same age as Lacy could afford a place like this. For all he knew, she was a tech wiz. *If* she was the same age as Lacy. And if they actually looked alike. More questions to get answered, more reasons justifying him coming today.

With his interest piqued and his heart pumping, he pushed the visitor button and waited. After a good half minute, it seemed like nobody was home. Another surprise was the level of disappointment he felt, that he'd failed in his simple plan to get a firsthand look at Lacy's so-called double.

"Yes? Who is it?"

The voice made the hair on his arms stand. It sounded just like Lacy's. It also threw him for a moment, "Oh, hi," he said after a short pause. "It's Zack Gardner, of Franks & Gardner Construction. I have the final papers for your bathroom remodel and all we need is your signature to move forward."

"I see, well, you've caught me at a bad time." He heard baby babble in the background. Ben hadn't mentioned she was a mother. "Can you leave them for me in the mailbox and I'll bring them by your office later this week?"

Gooseflesh raced over his entire body. Though the phrasing was completely different, he could swear he was talking to Lacy! He searched for his voice. "Sure. Just drop it off at our office at your convenience. Or, if you'd prefer, you can mail it in." He wanted to kick himself for suggesting that. How was he going to see her if she mailed it? "Though it would be quicker if you brought it by the main office. Then we could set up a date to begin your project ASAP."

"Thanks so much for understanding. I'm in the middle of bathing my son before I put him down for his morning nap. I'd hate to ask you to come all the way back later."

She was considerate like Lacy, too.

"Not a problem. I'm a dad—I understand routines." The object was to keep her talking, but right now, he seemed to be the long-winded one. Not her. "I should have called first." He'd been so hyped up about solving what stood between him and Lacy that he hadn't thought the caper through.

"Well thank you, I appreciate it."

It almost sounded like she'd been educated in Europe. "You're welcome. Looking forward to working with you." And seeing you!

Disappointed, Zack left the papers in the slit of the locked mailbox and put his car in Reverse. Being more intrigued than ever about the "sound-alike" redhead, who supposedly looked exactly like the woman he loved, he headed back to work.

Over the last few days, Lacy felt just as horrible not seeing Zack as when she'd started falling for him. Nothing relieved her anxiety. Living on jangled nerves and coffee for the last forty-eight hours, Lacy came to her senses. She could lose a good man if she didn't reach out to him. He'd made that perfectly clear. If she kept being a coward, like a self-fulfilling prophecy, she'd be sure to be alone the rest of her life. Was that what she wanted?

It was foolish to think of herself as cursed. Childish, even—and she was a thirty-one-year-old woman.

Listless yet restless, with nothing to do but feel sorry for herself, she hated the situation she'd put herself in. Unable to move forward on the investigation or Zack. She was in an emotional rut. A funk, as her dad used to say. She preferred that term to having to admit she was borderline depressed.

She hadn't even scheduled any more wedding gigs after the last. What a mess.

She picked up her crocheting project for distraction and flopped onto the couch. Maybe it would help get her mind off the adoption business and the mysterious look-alike. *And* Zack. The simple pistachio-colored place mat reminded her it wasn't just Zack she could lose. Emma, too. The sweet child whose mother had left her. Had the mentholated rub helped her whistling nose? Lacy fought the sorry notion that by staying away she was merely adding to Emma's losses.

If a heart could twist into a knot and tie itself to a rib cage, Lacy's had. It was the only way she could describe the constant pain. And the only way to relieve that pain was to pace. Which she did for what seemed like hours. Walking. Thinking. Worrying. Wishing she'd done everything differently.

To the point of never meeting Zack? No way. He'd added so much to her life.

Lacy and Emma had a lot in common, too. They'd discovered it when Lacy had started teaching Emma how to cook, and then Emma had innocently blurted, "Dad says you lost your mom, too, but when you were ten."

Lacy had been quick to explain that losing a mother to death was more permanent than from a divorce. But the concept hadn't seemed to compute with Emma, probably because her mom was MIA. Then Lacy thought it through and understood—if a person never came around, they may as well be dead. That's what a child might conclude. Why didn't Mona want to be in Emma's life? How had that affected Zack, too? The thought bothered Lacy to no end, and she wished Emma was near so she could hug her. Zack, too.

Mona had obviously chosen another life over the one she'd had with Zack and Emma. Lacy's already aching heart pinched, causing her to gasp. Of course he wouldn't automatically trust her and her need for some space. Wasn't she doing the same thing? Choosing to replace them with her search for a sister who may or may not exist? Ben had a picture. She needed to see it, not hide out in her house. And she couldn't avoid Zack and Emma any more.

The sudden queasiness over facing the truth forced her to take several deep breaths.

When Emma had started teaching Lacy how to crochet, Lacy had mentioned it was something she'd always meant to ask her mother to teach her. But she'd never gotten the chance.

"I used to hate crocheting after Mommy left, because she taught me how, but now I like it again," Emma had said.

That last afternoon they'd spent together, Emma had confessed she'd wished Lacy could be her mother. That had been part of what caused Lacy to run. Brushing Emma's hair had also rattled Lacy, the fact that she was growing closer and closer to the child. Zack, of course, was the main reason for her pulling back, because getting in too deep with him was scary enough. *She lost what she loved.* But then when Emma made her wish out loud, the picture of a happy family became complete. Was that dream possible?

The battle continued from losing her mom so early, then Greg, and most recently, her father. It made her want all the more to find a blood family again. If one even existed. To belong to something. If they did exist, it might help balance the void she'd carried around all her life, and help her heal. Then, for once and for all she could pursue that happily-ever-after dream Zack hinted at. Yes, having it all was possible.

With her knees knocking over the thought, Lacy knew she wasn't ready.

The question remained, would she ever be?

Falling in love with Zack had started in motion the derailing of her guarded heart, and two nights ago he'd so much as admitted he loved her, too. His confession had felt like a train wreck at the time. More than she could bear. Now, with distance between them, frozen in place over trying to find a long-lost relative, along with two days of loneliness, soul-searching and some clearing of her mind, his words were hard to believe. Had he really said I love you while they were dancing, or had she imagined it? And since he'd said those words, the biggest question was, why had she let him go?

Not ready, remember, stupid? Besides, he'd *sung* them not said them.

The tired excuse bugged her. Why was she so needy? A coward? Dad would be so disappointed.

More pacing ensued, with the addition of nail and cuticle biting. When she drew blood, she assumed she deserved it.

Lacy forced herself to sit again and pick up the crocheting, hoping her bloody fingernails wouldn't stain the yarn. She'd never been more tired in her life. Tired of letting negative emotions run roughshod over her. Tired of being afraid of what life was supposed to be about. But didn't she have some control over allowing that little girl to lose another person, a person Emma saw as a mommy figure? And what about Zack, who'd been walked out on?

Are you that cruel?

The idea of hurting a completely innocent party finally rubbed the *stupid* from her eyes. She dropped the crochet hook and yarn.

I love Zack, with all my heart, and there's no point in denying it. Her love for him wasn't going away. It was too late to stop it. He—*and* Emma—were the family she hadn't even known she'd been longing for until they'd fallen into her life. They'd unknowingly become part of that lifelong nebulous but constant feeling of missing something or someone, and never knowing who. Under the missing person's category, she'd had plenty of people to choose from. Of course, she missed them all, but that was a completely different kind of feeling. It was grieving. Buried under her losses was something that had been there long before anyone had died. It was that sense she'd been ripped away from something or someone, as if a part of her soul was torn and in need of repair. How could she explain that to anyone? It couldn't be normal.

Zack was right in front of her, asking her to take the next step. To be a whole person. With a normal life. With him. Was it possible?

She was sick of being alone, and yet she'd sent him away insisting it was for his own good. As if she was protecting *him*, not herself. How crazy was that? Maybe she needed a shrink. Or maybe it was time to quit letting all those old and negative feelings hold her hostage? To stop letting that old sense of being incomplete ruin the rest of her life.

She had a choice to make. Stick with the old not-working-at-all plan or quit writing her personal self-fulfilling prophecy—one of the few words she'd retained from Psychology 101—which guaranteed her winding up alone, the last place she wanted to be from now on.

Break free. Do something. Move it, sister!

She rushed to the bathroom, washed her face and brushed her teeth, threw on her jeans and, sniffing her armpits first, put on a shirt. Instead of calling, because it was late, she hopped in her car and drove to Zack's house.

She knew he'd be home, and though it took all the courage she could muster, she was finally ready to tell him exactly how she felt. Even if she passed out in the process.

Because it was late, she knocked rather than rang the

bell, which might wake Emma. Her heart pounded behind her ribs and her mouth was dry, but she stood tall, determined to be honest and open with the man she…loved. Trembling, she silently prayed it wasn't already too late.

He must have heard her car in the driveway, because he opened the door almost immediately.

The saying about a sight for sore eyes couldn't have been more accurate. He looked as wrung out as she felt. Hair uncombed, dark smudges under his eyes, with weekend stubbles hanging on through Monday and Tuesday shadowing his cheeks. He was barefoot and probably hadn't showered yet. Still, he was the most glorious human she'd ever seen.

"Lacy," he said on a breath.

"Zack." The word squeaked out.

He held the door handle and watched her cautiously. Her pulse doubled. "May I come in?"

He stepped aside and swung the door wider. "Of course."

She'd made him wary of her, and the idea pierced her heart. He'd been through this before with a fickle wife, and Lacy had added to his mistrust. But now was the time to make it up to him.

Taking this step was the biggest risk of her adult life— becoming engaged in her early twenties hadn't come close to this sensation—and she made the move because of one word. *Love.* She couldn't hide from it any longer.

Zack was the one she loved.

She stopped in the middle of the entryway and swung around to face him. "I'll get right to my point, because I've wasted enough of your time denying the truth. Plus, you gave me the impression it was my turn to take the next step when you left Sunday night."

The tension around his eyes subsided. "That I did."

"I'm way beyond falling for you, Zack Gardner—I'm completely in love with you. I'm just sorry it took me so long to see it and admit it." Letting the truth out relieved her more than she ever would have imagined. "Please forgive me."

"For telling me you love me?" He stayed where he was, as if moving might change the moment.

"For making you wait so long to hear it." She rushed to him and fell into his open arms. They wrapped tight around her, and she knew she was home.

"You're worth the wait, Lacy."

Zack delivered an intense kiss, heavy with emotion and lighter on technique, but it was the greatest kiss Lacy had ever experienced. After the initial relief of them both coming clean with their feelings, their kisses became frantic and were soon overtaken with passion and need. Like always and from the start. His hands dug into her back and she nearly tore his T-shirt with her ragged nails. But so much more was going on. Her skin lit up and heat curled throughout her body. And there was only one surefire way to prove to Zack how much she loved him.

She tore her mouth from his. "Does that rule still apply about my staying over when Emma's home?"

"Hell, no, not tonight," he growled, lifting her as if knowing she was incapable of walking, carrying her to his bedroom, with her feeling like a princess the entire brief journey. When they arrived, he used the heel of his bare foot to shut the door behind them, then took her to his bed where they landed together on his mattress. They made haste in stripping off their clothes, searching each other's body for comfort, firing up their passion, and were soon grounded in truth. Through making love and connecting in the most intimate of all ways, they recovered everything they'd lost when Lacy had forgotten what was most important. The night he'd come for her and she'd let him leave. Alone.

Love. No other word came close to describing what they'd found again.

Much later, they still clung to each other until dawn peeked through the curtains and they finally went to sleep.

"Dad?" Emma said through the door. "Are you gonna drive me to school?" The door creaked open, letting in a cone of hall light and mortifying Lacy.

Zack sat bolt upright. "Shortcake? What time is it?"

Though Lacy's first response was to do the same, to sit up, she forced herself to lie perfectly still, hoping beyond hope the sheet and covers might disguise her body. But how could she hide her hair? Still, she held her breath, not moving, praying for a miracle.

"It's almost time to leave," Emma said, as her voice ventured closer to the bed. "Are you sick?"

"No, hon, just lost track of time." He scraped fingers through his hair in desperation, and Lacy reflected her own panic in his tone.

What should she do now? She scrunched her eyes tight, as if that could make her invisible.

"Lacy?"

Busted! She gulped, trying to cover her face with the sheet. "Uh, hi, Emma."

"Are you girlfriend and boyfriend now?"

"Emma, can you give me a chance to shower, please?" Zack stopped that line of questioning as quickly as it popped up.

"Okay, but are you guys gonna get married? Lacy!" she said, as though thinking of the most amazing idea in the world. "Are you going to be my mom now?"

Lacy wanted to curl into a ball and hide her face underneath the pillow. Shouldn't Zack be taking the lead on this? Yet, he seemed as flabbergasted as she felt.

"Hey, Emmy, let me take a shower and we'll talk about all this later, okay?" Zack said, firm, commanding, without shouting. Emma didn't seem to get the message.

As best as Lacy could tell, Emma had stayed put at the foot of her father's bed, probably shocked into motionlessness. Something Lacy could easily relate to. Or, was she simply an incredibly nosy ten-year-old?

Lacy's cheeks heated and her toes curled. There was no way she could face Emma that morning, not after all the things she and Zack had done to each other last night.

"Okay?" Zack pressed harder. "Skedaddle."

"Okay," Emma said, retreating to the door but not leaving. "Are you gonna have breakfast here, Lacy?"

"Uh. Probably not." Her response was muffled from her face still being buried in the pillow. It might take a week before she'd be able to face the child without turning a deep shade of crimson.

"Aw, shoot."

"Close the door, Shortcake." Zack made the firm and obvious order a warning. "Now."

The door finally shut. "Okay," came the muted reply on the other side.

Zack poked Lacy in the ribs. "Are you aware you've got a full moon going on?" he whispered.

Lacy gasped, checking out the short sheet situation over her backside, finally realizing there was indeed a draft over her rear end. All of it! But glancing back into Zack's playful gaze, with his bed hair resembling a mad scientist, she wound up giggling, and he snickered along with her.

"What's so funny?" Emma asked through the door,

having obviously hung around instead of giving her dad privacy.

Which only made Lacy and Zack burst into full-out laughter, the kind with tears and side aches, and nearly as tension relieving as all the great sex they'd had last night. But which, of course, couldn't really be compared with that sex. At all.

Chapter Twelve

Sometimes the only way to get Noah to take a nap was to go for a drive. Wednesday morning was one of those naptimes. Her baby just wouldn't settle down. But Eva had a purpose for the drive today. She needed to deliver the signed agreement for the bathroom upgrades she'd requested, and the main office for Gardner & Associates was located in Little River Valley, a forty-minute drive one way. The trip, with the double purpose, sounded like a good plan to her.

She put Noah in his car seat. He suffered through the usual complaints of being pinned in until he was strapped, snapped, and able to see the kiddie mirror on the back seat. Then he cooed and got excited about the little face staring back at him. Within minutes, he'd drifted off to sleep and soon enough Eva was on the 101 Freeway heading south with the tourquise blue ocean sparkling in the midmorning sun on her right. Thanks to lighter than usual traffic, she turned inland ahead of schedule. Knowing Noah fared better with a full hour nap, she took a detour through town on the main street to kill time.

Along with the unique department store named LRV after the town, where they sold only goods made locally, there were several trendy eateries, along with one greasy spoon café and a couple of teahouses. Oh, and she couldn't forget the three wine-tasting rooms, with and without appetizers for the price of the samples. Somewhere nearby there had to be a grocery store but that was probably banned from the main street. The town's well-known motto was No Chain Stores Allowed! Everyone knew it and respected them for it, inconvenience and all.

There was no way she could avoid the fact an election campaign was in full swing with signs lining both sides of the boulevard. On one side of the street she saw Re-elect Joe Aguirre for Mayor! On the other, Stop Mayor Aguirre from Ruining Our Town, Vote for Luella Barnstable! She shook her head, tired to death of election shenanigans, and drove on. Even in small towns these days, the candidates seemed to go for the jugular. What had ever happened to friendly debates, may the best man win and all of that?

When she reached the end of the small boulevard, there was an upscale spa nestled among a grove of citrus trees, which seemed to be calling out her name. Just Breathe offered full spa treatments and much, much more, according to the subtle upscale storefront sign in proper cursive. Oh, for the days when she could do exactly what she'd wanted and when she'd wanted. She chastised herself for sounding old. Age had nothing to do with the change in her lifestyle, but becoming an adoptive mother certainly had.

As if reading her thoughts, Noah squirmed and woke

up. "Hey, Pudge!" she said, her nickname for Noah, because, well, he was all folds! Think what she might about a spa day, there was no way she'd trade in motherhood for the unattached life again. "We're almost there."

The GPS led her to the Gardner office. She parked directly in front, head in. All she intended to do was drop off the papers and leave. The temperature was in the low seventies—plus she had a full view of her boy in the car—so she got out and rushed to the door, leaving him undisturbed. Her real reason for making this trip was to find that pink food truck and finally see for herself. She'd checked online and found Wrap Me Up and Take Me Home's page, though there hadn't been any recent posts.

The front office door was locked, and just as she was about to slide the signed papers through the mail slot, where who knew how long they'd stay before being noticed, she saw the handwritten note. *At local senior housing construction site today.* An address was given and a phone number. She added both to her phone.

Eva slipped back into the car, deciding to skip the call and see Zack Gardner in person, which she had yet to do. There was something about looking a person in the eye, before returning a contract, that all the polite phone calls in the world couldn't replace. If she was going to give him free rein with her too-small and outdated bathroom, she wanted to try out her Spidey sense on him first, because trust was a big deal to her, and he had to pass the test.

Afterward, she'd go off in search of Lacy Winters's pink foodmobile. Maybe she'd buy some lunch, too.

Zack couldn't stop grinning all morning at work. Having left a gorgeous redhead in his bed could do that to a guy. Of course, then he'd been faced with Emma's unending questions about his personal love life on the entire drive to school. He'd put his foot down and pulled the "that's none of your business" reply several times. However, he had assured his daughter that he and Lacy loved each other, and they'd see where things went from there. That seemed to shut her up.

Briefly.

Thank goodness they lived near her elementary school.

"Listen up, folks," Zack said over the loudspeaker in his mobile office. "Lacy will be back serving lunch today, at the usual time." More than a few guys whistled and whooped in the yard afterward. They'd missed her lunches, and he could hear them all the way up front. He'd used the excuse of her being sick when she hadn't shown up on Monday here in Little River Valley and at the Santa Barbara site yesterday, where more than a few disappointed and hungry guys had to change their lunch plans.

After a weekend of hell, and two of the dreariest weekdays since he'd served divorce papers to his ex, he could finally count his blessings. As of Tuesday night, around ten o'clock, Lacy had come to her senses. Obviously sooner, but that was when she'd arrived at his house to tell him. Thank the stars in heaven and right on up the chain of command to the top, she had. Though he was as nervous as he imagined she was about their going for it all, love *and* including marriage. He'd take his time breaking the news to his skittish lover because of how much foot dragging she'd done with just dating. Hell, he'd had to get over a crane-sized confidence deficit to admit he loved her, so he'd cut her some slack. It was a big step for both of them to take. He knew she was the one. Had known early on, which had sent shivers through his insecurities since he'd planned after the divorce to stay single until Emma was on her own. That's how long it seemed it would take to get over the damage Mona had inflicted on him by cheating. So much for plans.

Looked like they both had changes in store for them, and Zack had all the confidence in the world he and Lacy could handle it. Together.

Ha! As if he could micromanage his life plan. He'd been told since a boy back in Utah that God had a sense of humor. This time, the big joke was on Zack. He thought back to the sidesplitting session with Lacy in bed that morning, after being caught by Emma, and nearly blurted another laugh. It was just one more thing they did naturally together—laugh—and was further proof they were compatible.

The huge, looming form of Ben filled his office door, stomping out his grin. "There's someone here to see you."

Mental-fantasy break over, time to get back to work.

Lacy had been beyond discombobulated all morning since waking up at Zack's house with Emma wandering into the bedroom. She'd purposely hid out in his room until they'd both left for school and work. Then, during a shower in his fabulously large doorless Italian-tiled stall, complete with jets coming from every angle, she'd had more than a few fantasies about him being in there with her. "In time, my sweet, in time," she'd cackled naughtily, while toweling off. Afterward she dressed and headed home.

What an amazing night. Her emotions had been off the chart when she'd shown up at his house, but laying her true feelings on the line was the smartest decision she'd ever made. The only question being, why hadn't she done it sooner? Regardless, Zack had been receptive. Then fireworks started and the rest, as they say, was breaking news at eleven, X-rated stuff.

Since being with Zack all night, happily distracted from the huge change in her personal relationship status—which she had no intention of sharing on her social media page—she'd been scrambling to pull everything together in the food truck. She had mouths to feed!

She knew what her Little River Valley construction guys liked, and loaded up with extra steak and chicken in preparation for those wraps. Then, after one more run-through of her standard daily checklist, she hopped behind the wheel and headed to the site. There was definitely an advantage to living ten minutes away from your job.

Zack stood in preparation to meet Evangelina De-Longpre. Then, when she replaced Ben in his doorway, he suddenly had the need to sit back down. He froze, eyes wide, mouth probably open, he wasn't sure. So shocked he didn't know if he was sitting or standing. His ears rang from his pulse sprinting through his temples. For the first time in his life he couldn't believe what he was seeing.

She was the image of Lacy, but with styled, shorter hair with bangs. Plus, she had a baby on her hip. Other than that, it could have been Lacy. No doubt.

"Have I caught you at a bad time, Mr. Gardner? You seem a bit distracted."

"Uh, no. It's just. Well, it's uncanny."

She looked confused. In the distance the familiar *Happy Days* horn blared. Zack's heart nearly exploded at the sound. He needed to swallow so he could speak, but his mouth had gone bone-dry. He reached for the bottled water he kept on his desk and took a swig, managing to choke and dribble simultaneously, nearly sending water out his nose. After wiping his mouth with the back of his hand, aware that Eva's opinion of him was probably going from worried to frightened to let's call the whole remodeling thing off, he found his voice. There was only one way to handle this.

"Our lunch truck is here. Can I get you something?"

She seemed unsure, as though wondering why in the world they should stop everything and take a lunch break.

"We have a great local chef who makes the best wraps in town."

She glanced out the window to where the large pink truck had pulled into the site, then seemed to stiffen and hold her breath. "Is that truck, by any chance, called Wrap Me Up and Take Me home?" Her voice had changed to a tentative tone. Exactly like *Lacy* speaking in a tentative tone.

Now, from the quick flash in her eyes, she was the one to look off balance and possibly terrified.

An odd sense of peace settled over him. "So, you know already."

Color seemed to disappear from the creamy-complexioned woman, and it was apparent her baby had gotten too heavy to hold.

"Do you need to sit? I can take your baby."

The shock had shifted from Zack to Eva almost as if she'd had a premonition something earth-shattering was about to happen. Having just gone through the experience of seeing her, he understood and wanted to help any way he could. Then he wondered how she could possibly know her double was out there in that pink truck. Had Ben told her?

He reached for his stash of bottled water. "Here. Take a sip." He waited while she drank with a noticeably wobbly hand. She had to know about Lacy already. What else could explain this behavior? "How did you find out about her?"

"Someone had seen her at a wedding and showed me her social media page with the pink truck. I haven't seen her in person yet. Not even sure if she really looks like me, since her picture was from a distance."

"Oh, I can guarantee you look like her all right." He couldn't stop staring.

Eva's head bobbed up, concern and something else written on her face. Curiosity? Fear? Hope?

Zack wasn't sure which, and he could only imagine how Lacy and Eva would soon feel, finally seeing each other. He walked over and peeked through the mobile office window blinds beside his desk, seeing a small crowd gathered around the lunch truck. "We should probably give Lacy a chance to feed the guys before we knock her off her feet. And you look like you could use some time to recover, too."

Who was he kidding? So did he!

Eva agreed, seemed even grateful for the chance to recover her composure, but Zack only grew more nervous.

Lacy had parked in her usual spot under the huge oak tree, always grateful there were no plans to cut it down for the senior housing project. She'd seen the plans—Zack had shared them—and when the building was finished, there would be two memorial benches in place under this canopy of branches and leaves. The thought always made her smile.

She'd switched on the prepared coffeemaker and pulled containers from the refrigerator. Busy like a bee, she'd run through her routine preparations. Once everything had been in order, she'd flipped the switch to open her serving window and extend the truck awning. The guys knew her menu by heart. No need to post it.

The crew had already lined up, and she barely had a

chance to catch her breath over the next several minutes as, one after another, the guys gave their orders. It felt great to be back serving them! The best part was that time sped by.

Forty-five minutes later, she sold the last hand pie to one of her regulars, a young Latina construction worker, and then she turned. There was Zack standing beside one of the trees, which startled her. "You scared me! Want your usual?"

He looked rattled, as though another one of his guys had had an accident.

"You okay?"

He nodded in slow motion, making her worry that something awful had happened since that morning and he was on the verge of giving her the details. He hadn't changed his mind about them already, had he? Her heart fluttered.

"So, Chicken Done Right?" She forced herself to concentrate.

"Uh, for me, yes, but there'll be another order." He'd found his unsteady voice.

"Taking something home for Emma?" she said as she busily put his wrap together.

"No. Getting something for one of my new clients."

A fussy baby's vocalizations grabbed Lacy's attention, though not in view. "New client got a hungry kid to feed, too?" she said, head down, working efficiently.

Zack didn't answer. Because of his silence, Lacy glanced up, then froze. Something was up, and the fine hair on the back of her neck was suggesting she take notice.

He nodded, then gestured for someone out of her line of vision to step forward. "Maybe you should place your own order."

Chapter Thirteen

Lacy's doppelgänger stepped in front of the truck's order window. Surely this was a hologram or a trick or some ridiculous mistake. Yet the woman was real and standing right in front of her. Like a mirror. Shock invaded the blood pulsing through her veins, then headed south to her stomach and, nearly swooning from the effect, Lacy almost passed out. She dropped Zack's wrap, then gripped the counter for support. With her knees threatening to buckle, and her heart rate zip-lining every which way, she held tight to the stainless steel, staring at the woman and blinking, because this wasn't her imagination.

She was a living, breathing double.

"I'll have a Put a Steak in It, please," the woman said, as though it was the hardest thing she'd ever had to say.

Her own voice might have spoken the words, and a stunned Lacy shook her head. Had she heard right, what was going on? After a second blink, as her eyes adjusted to the sight, she saw herself. Standing right there in front of her. A far more polished version of herself. A woman who was clearly as shaken as Lacy.

This was real. This was happening, and there could only be one explanation.

"What am I doing standing here!" Lacy said, finally gathering her thoughts, finding her voice. Commanding her body to obey, she rushed to the side door and down the stairs. She stopped dead in front of her mirror image, afraid to make contact. "I've been told you were out there, but I just laughed it off."

"My name is Evangelina DeLongpre," the woman said, extending her hand, clearly as dumbfounded as Lacy.

"Lacy Winters." Lacy half expected to be touching herself when she took the hand and shook. Instead, she found a hand much softer than hers. Now solidly connected, ruling out all possibility of a hallucination, they studied each other closely. Lacy's amazement reflected perfectly in Eva's cornflower-blue eyes.

Unreal. Yet there she was. *So this is how I look to other people.*

"I'm adopted," Eva said, causing Lacy's heart to flutter uncontrollably. "And my birthday is…"

"November fourth?" Lacy finished the sentence. "I've just found out I'm adopted, too."

Spontaneous tears spilled between them. Lacy couldn't take another second of being apart from someone she'd been longing for her entire life. She grabbed the person born on the same day as her, who was adopted, like her, though not quite ready to call her *sister*, and hugged for dear life.

"You're thirty-one?" Lacy asked, just to make certain this wasn't all a hoax. Eva nodded, her ear moving up and down Lacy's cheek. This was happening.

It wasn't like hugging herself, but more like an extension of herself, the sensation comforting and soothing and somehow familiar. Unreal. The word *esoteric* came out of the blue and planted itself in her head. Had she learned that in Psych 101, too?

Eva smelled like gardenia and orange blossom and Lacy inhaled deeply. "Black Orpheum?" she asked, about a product she could never afford but loved to sample every chance in department stores.

Eva nodded again, the same motion, with her ear on Lacy's cheek. "My favorite."

Lacy pulled back so she could see her double, flabbergasted. "You're like a rich version of me."

Eva laughed lightly and Lacy joined her.

"Oh, my gosh, we even laugh alike!" Eva said. The perfectly coiffed and put-together woman seemed awestruck.

"I've got news for you guys—you're both hand talkers, too," Zack said from the sidelines, holding the little fella and looking natural as ever.

"We are?" they said in unison, the inflection on the end exactly the same.

They laughed again. Lacy fought the urge to say *jinx* and offer her pinkie, and soon more tears filled her eyes, the good kind. As the tears rolled out in an emotional mess, for the best and most fantastical reason in the world, Lacy shook her head and studied Eva.

There couldn't be another explanation. At long last, she'd found her twin sister. Well, actually, Eva had been the one to find her. With the help of Zack, she'd found someone who could never be taken away from her again.

It was hard to settle down that night, and Lacy was grateful she'd let Zack talk her into spending the night with him. He didn't have to try hard at all! They had nothing to hide since Emma had already found them out that morning. On his bed, she rolled into his invitingly strong arm and stretched hers across his chest. Nothing short of a perfect fit.

"This was one incredible day," she said with a sigh.

"I prefer to think of it as an amazing twenty-four hours," Zack said, kissing her temple.

Lacy was utterly drained from the lollapalooza of a day and unable to follow his meaning, her world having nearly stopped at one o'clock this afternoon, when Eva had appeared. She raised her head, questions in her gaze.

Zack lifted his free left arm and checked his watch. "Yeah, see, it's ten o'clock. Last night you knocked on my door right about now." He gave a sexy, knowing partial smile, loaded with double and triple entendres.

"Oh, yeah." How could she forget? Well, for one thing, she'd spent two hours that afternoon talking with a sister she'd never known she'd had, just to name one good reason. They would've talked all night if it hadn't been for Noah needing to get back to his routine. "My heart nearly popped out of my chest, it was beating so hard when I came over last night."

"And I'm so glad you did."

She put her head on his chest, a smile hidden beneath her wild mane. Mindlessly he ran fingers through her hair and they settled into perfect peace. Long overdue. This was good. So good.

"Of course, Emma drilled me this morning on the drive to school, and I told her I loved you."

Her head bobbed up. "Have you told *me* that?"

Now his smile was for real, not some mischievous hint like the moment before. "Officially? Hmm, not in so many words, but…" He went up on his elbow. "Didn't I sing it to you that Saturday night at the bar? And I'm pretty sure I showed you how I felt last night."

"Yeah, and I could say the same thing about showing not telling." She wouldn't let go of his gaze, which turned into a staring contest. A sexy, smoldering staring contest.

He put his free hand on her cheek and she snuggled against it. "I love you, Lacy."

She sighed, feeling for the first time in her life that everything was falling perfectly into place. Her eyes blinked closed, savoring the sound and the special moment, until he flicked his finger on her cheek and her eyes flung open. "Ouch! What was that for?"

"I just said I loved you."

"And?"

"A man likes to hear those words, too."

She pushed herself forward, close enough to be within striking range of his mouth. Then she kissed him. Long, slow, tender, and filled with every bit of the love in her heart. When she'd finished, her dream-filled eyes captured his warm green gaze. "I love you," she whispered. "More than you could ever know."

Silent but loaded messages about what was going to happen next arced between them. Zack pulled Lacy on top of his body. "Never thought I'd feel this way again."

"Me, either."

"I'm so glad you drove that big pink thing on my property that day."

"I knew it would be life changing." Even predicted it on her social media page.

"Understatement of the century."

They laughed lightly together, as they often did, Lacy enjoying the feel of Zack's bouncing diaphragm beneath her belly. She breathed in long and slow, savoring another moment she wanted to keep tucked in her heart for a lifetime.

"So, I asked Emma if it would be okay," Zack said.

"If what would be okay?"

"If I asked you to marry me."

Lacy popped up in a cobra pose. "What?"

"Oh, yeah, we're a package deal, Emma and I, and if she didn't want you as a stepmother... Sorry babe, but you wouldn't be here right now." He did his best to sound like a cold, heartless guy, and fell far, far short.

"That's harsh." It was easy to play along when it came to good guy Zack Gardner.

"But true. I would've been hanging out at the karaoke bar, looking for the next catch, if Emma didn't approve." There was that devilish smile again.

Lacy cuffed him. He pretended to flinch.

"You know I love her, too," Lacy admitted easily, her heart seeming to expand by the moment.

"And she loves you. That's apparent. And she's told me about sixteen times already."

Lacy chuckled softly before focusing on something he'd said earlier. "So, we've gotten a little off topic. Can you run that first part by me again?"

He pretended not to catch her drift. "You mean the part about being a family?"

"Uh, just before that."

He lifted his chin as though a lightbulb had just gone off above his head. "Ooh! *That* part." His arms went tight around her middle, and he rolled until they faced each other side by side on the mattress. He waited patiently for Lacy's eyes to drift toward his. His were serious and filled with sincerity. "Will you marry me?"

Even though only moments before she'd had a preview of what was on his mind, hearing the words, she became overcome with emotions, as if that hadn't already happened big-time today, and was unable to answer.

"It doesn't have to be right away," he continued. "I know you just found your sister and a whole new world has suddenly opened up, but, sometime in the near future, I intend for us to get married."

Tiny pins and needles started behind her lids, quickly followed by blurring and moisture, oh, so much moisture. She grinned through her tears, shaking her head. Could the day be more monumental? She'd finally broken free from her irrational fear of the caring-and-losing connection. Because today she'd found... She'd found her sister! And Zack. Finally. Her heart was open to love and to love fully, and it felt amazing.

"I'd love to marry you, Zack. I can't wait to be your wife and part of a family again."

"Then I want to put a rock on your finger by next weekend."

All the day's wonderful feelings converged, and suddenly Lacy was filled with energy. And those were pretty much the last words spoken between Zack and Lacy for a long, long time. Not counting moans, panting, short sexy instructions and naughty little outbursts. Then sometime after midnight, tight in each other's arms, they shared another joint declaration of "I love you." Putting the monumental day to rest on a perfect note.

Later, after a couple hours of sleep, in the wee morning, Lacy woke to use the bathroom. As she did, she wondered if Eva had someone like Zack? Already goofily grinning with her eyes closed while using the toilet, she smiled wider, guessing this was how it would be from now on—always wondering how her sister, *her twin*, was, if she was okay or what she was doing at any given moment. Even now, on the night she'd been proposed to by the best man on earth, Eva was in her thoughts. Because Lacy wanted to and couldn't wait to share the great news with her.

On the chance Eva might be awake, Lacy texted her. I just got engaged!

Lacy was headed back to bed when her phone lit up. I approve! So happy for you. Talk tomorrow.

Lacy grinned as she got back in bed. Yes, they'd talk tomorrow and tomorrow and the day after that and…

One week later…

"Have you ever felt like a part of you was missing?" Lacy asked, at the end of her and Eva's daily after-dinner phone conversation.

"Every single day," Eva was quick to reply.

It was wonderful having someone who knew exactly how she felt. "Oh, you know what I keep forgetting to ask you? What's your middle name?" There was so much they needed to find out about each other yet.

"Taylor."

What? Hadn't Lacy had enough jolts for the week? For an entire life? Her twin sister had the same middle name as her! How weird was that? "That's my middle name, too."

"That's crazy."

"I know, but what isn't crazy about us?"

Eva had gone quiet, and just before Lacy was going to jump in, Eva said, "Just one more thing we'll have to get to the bottom of."

"Agreed. Add it to the list," Lacy said, determined to find out what their adoption story was.

It was a whole week later, and the astounding moment of meeting Eva had yet to wear off. As though that wasn't enough, being newly in love with Zack, getting engaged, and having him beside her every step of the way through this crazy adventure was shocking in a completely different way. A meant-to-be and forever way, which got better and sweeter every moment she and Zack spent together.

She studied the addition to her left hand, a beautiful engagement ring, and her heart overflowed with love all over again. She shared everything with Zack and, where some men might become jealous by the time she invested in her twin, he was thrilled she'd found a long-lost sister.

Lacy and Eva had been communicating nonstop since meeting at the food truck. If they couldn't meet in person, they would text or call. Eva even "liked" Lacy's social media page and commented there when Lacy posted a picture of the two of them. Their story had caused a huge buzz with thousands of likes.

They'd made so many plans, as though trying to catch up for lost times, but realizing they could never make up for thirty-one years still broke their hearts. Along with stored-up anger. They didn't have to explain the feelings to each other because they knew exactly how it felt.

They'd been separated at birth and adopted into different families, raised completely opposite. Eva was rich, Lacy just trying to get by. Yet they'd recognized their sisterhood as easily as the way they looked.

They'd been created from a single cell, carried the same DNA, and had shared a womb and an amniotic sac for nine months. On some genetic level, to this day they remembered that. Remembered each other. Together from the start. And there was no separating them now.

* * * * *

MILLS & BOON

Coming next month

HER TWIN BABY SECRET
Therese Beharrie

He laughed. Gave in to the urge to tuck her hair behind her ear as he'd seen her do earlier.

She exhaled. 'What are you doing, Benjamin?'

He dropped his hand, looked at her face. 'I don't know.'

'You do know.'

'No, I don't.' He smiled. Almost as soon as he did, it vanished. 'Except for right now. Right now, I'm contemplating how to get you to kiss me again. I'd say it's an appropriate response to how incredible you look.' He shook his head. 'I was staring earlier because I didn't have anything to say. You're so beautiful. And this dress is…and your hair, your face…' He shook his head again. Offered her a wry, possibly apologetic smile. 'I'm sorry. I think the last couple days have officially caught up with me.'

Her expression was unreadable, but she said, 'It's been a rough couple of days.'

'Yeah.'

'Because of me.' She paused. 'I'm sorry.'

'You don't have to apologise. You already have, at least.'

'Right.' She leaned back against her door, which he realised only now she hadn't moved away from. 'This hasn't been easy for me either.'

'I know.'

'A large part of it is because you get on my nerves. A lot,' she added when he frowned.

'That seems uncalled for considering I just gave you a bunch of compliments.'

'You want acknowledgement for that?'

'A thank you would nice,' he muttered.

'You're right.'

'Sorry—could you say that again?' He patted his pocket, looking for his phone. 'I want to record it for posterity.'

'This, for example, is extremely annoying. But at the same time, I can't stop thinking about the kiss we had the other day.'

He stilled.

'Which gets on my nerves, too. An interesting conundrum. Am I annoyed because I'm attracted to you? Am I annoyed because you annoy me but I'm still attracted to you?' She exhaled. It sounded frustrated. 'I don't have answers, but I keep asking these questions. Then, of course, you do something decent, like pretend to be my boyfriend even though you have no reason or incentive to. You stand up for me in front of my brother, which I found disturbingly hot. In the same breath, you act stupidly, and tell your mother—your *mother*—that I'm your girlfriend. Which, tonight, we have to rectify.'

She shook her head.

'Honestly, Benjamin, these last few days have been the most frustratingly complicated of my life, and I'm an entrepreneur with a crappy family. And I'm *pregnant,* about to become a single mother. Complicated is the air I breathe. But you make things...' She trailed off with a little laugh. 'And still, I want to kiss you, too.'

Continue reading
HER TWIN BABY SECRET
Therese Beharrie

Available next month
www.millsandboon.co.uk

COMING SOON!

JOIN US ON SOCIAL MEDIA!

Stay up to date with our latest releases, author news and gossip, special offers and discounts, and all the behind-the-scenes action from Mills & Boon...

 millsandboon

 millsandboonuk

f millsandboon

It might just be true love...

MILLS & BOON

THE HEART OF ROMANCE

A ROMANCE FOR EVERY KIND OF READER

MODERN

Prepare to be swept off your feet by sophisticated, sexy and seductive heroes, in some of the world's most glamourous and romantic locations, where power and passion collide.
8 stories per month.

HISTORICAL

Escape with historical heroes from time gone by. Whether your passion is for wicked Regency Rakes, muscled Vikings or rugged Highlanders, awaken the romance of the past.
6 stories per month.

MEDICAL

Set your pulse racing with dedicated, delectable doctors in the high-pressure world of medicine, where emotions run high and passion, comfort and love are the best medicine.
6 stories per month.

True Love

Celebrate true love with tender stories of heartfelt romance, from the rush of falling in love to the joy a new baby can bring, and a focus on the emotional heart of a relationship.
8 stories per month.

Desire

Indulge in secrets and scandal, intense drama and plenty of sizzling hot action with powerful and passionate heroes who have it all: wealth, status, good looks…everything but the right woman.
6 stories per month.

HEROES

Experience all the excitement of a gripping thriller, with an intense romance at its heart. Resourceful, true-to-life women and strong, fearless men face danger and desire - a killer combination!
8 stories per month.

DARE

Sensual love stories featuring smart, sassy heroines you'd want as a best friend, and compelling intense heroes who are worthy of them.
4 stories per month.

To see which titles are coming soon, please visit

millsandboon.co.uk/nextmonth

MILLS & BOON
HEROES
At Your Service

Experience all the excitement of a gripping thriller, with an intense romance at its heart. Resourceful, true-to-life women and strong, fearless men face danger and desire - a killer combination!

MILLS & BOON
Desire

Indulge in secrets and scandal, intense drama and plenty of sizzling hot action with powerful and passionate heroes who have it all: wealth, status, good looks… everything but the right woman.

LET'S TALK

Romance

For exclusive extracts, competitions and special offers, find us online: